Chapter 1

It was not the best kind of night for a sexual rendezvous. The intermittent downpours of torrential rain were whipped along the deserted pavement, over the roundabout and hurled out across the sea, headlong into the black night. The sea broke over the wall in an attempt to drown an irritating newspaper stand that chattered uncontrollably in the gusting wind outside the Bay Café. The whole scene was wild with energy and dark but for the small amber pools of ineffective streetlight. Only a taxi stirred slowly from a parking space to leave a trail of spray and red taillights down the sea front in the direction of the castle headland. Not the kind of night to be on foot, not all the way out here, not unless you were very motivated.

"Come on Fay," muttered Grant impatiently as he drummed his fingers on the steering wheel. "I've driven fifty miles in this. Fifteen minutes early, exactly as agreed and if you don't show, I'm gonna go bloody ape shit!" Grant checked his watch, "8.00pm exactly, so much for 'synchronising our watches' then!" He turned on the blower to curb the condensation that crept up the windscreen, Grant's breath whistled through his teeth. With a shake of the head he tried to contain his frustration and enlisted both feet to add a new dimension to the rhythm. Could he compete with the rain as it pounded down on the car roof, you bet!

What was that? Grant stopped drumming, and strained his eyes through the windscreen, blurred by rain. He flicked the wipers on faster. Yes, there she was, down by the café, a slender figure dressed in black. A thigh length raincoat tied tight at the waist, long black leggings ended short above her bare ankles and shiny black stiletto heels. No hat or umbrella could work in that weather and so her long dark hair flailed at the mercy of the wind.

"See, I knew she'd look great in that!" his erection grew faster.

"Bloody hell!" his hands shook too. He was so excited but how to find the right gear.

"Bloody hell, come on, she'll be soaked to the skin," he cursed.

Try and slow it down, he thought, more haste less!! Mirror, indicate, and manoeuvre. Put it in gear, bit of gas, take the hand break off and away we......

GORRRRR.........ANGGGG! The air horn deafened him, well above the squeal of tyres and the spit of air brakes. A blaze of headlights filled the car.

"I can't see a bloody thing you dickhead," he yelled at the top of his voice. "Where the hell did he come from?" More air breaks, more revved up diesel engine somewhere very close to his right.

GORRRRR.........ANGGGG!

"Yes I can hear you," he raged, "they probably heard you in China! But what does GORRRRR.........ANGGGG mean exactly?"

He wound down the window to be confronted by the nearside front light of a large vehicle that towered over him. The engine was on tick over but the sound of a footstep on loose gravel just to his right made up his mind.

"I'm getting out of here!" shouted Grant and he booted the accelerator. In a flurry of wheel spinning, gravel and spray, he pulled out into the road and headed toward Fay. His brain worked overtime. I think we'll have to forgo the kerbside banter tonight Fay. If King Kong back there decides to take chase, things could get a bit awkward.

"Damn, it was all going so well," he slapped the steering wheel.

Just before the café, he switched on the main beam lights and braked to a halt. He leant across the front seat and wound the passenger window down. As the rain lashed in his face, he shouted into the dark.

"Come on, get in the car. We'll have to rethink things."

Grant stared through the open window, but could see nothing except rain swirl in the darkness.

"Fay, come on, I know you've gone to a lot of trouble, but there's a problem. Get in!"

He sat up a bit and looked through the windscreen that had finally cleared but there was still no sign of Fay.

"Where the hell is she!" he asked, "Oh shit!"

He swung open the driver's door in a panic, released his seat belt, leant out of the door and hung his head down below the sill to look under the car. Nothing there! He sat back in his seat with a big sigh. "Oh bloody hell, for one minute, I thought I'd run over her," he chuckled.

He looked in the mirrors, over his shoulder, through the rear window and then in disbelief, he asked the empty car, "where the hell is she?"

There was nothing for it, he'd have to brave the elements and get out of the car. Even in the few seconds it took to get round and open the tailgate, he got drenched. While he struggled with a cagoule, Grant scoured the scene for a glimpse of Fay. This took role play a bit far but at least King Kong had left. So if he could find her, maybe now they might just get things back on track after all. With that he slammed the tailgate shut, locked the car and walked round to where he'd last seen Fay and stepped onto the pavement. He looked across the road and scanned the scene, from high up to the right, where he'd been parked and then down and to the left by the sea wall. Even down the front and towards castle point, all the roads were bounded by smooth sloping grass. There was no one in sight. For that matter there was nothing big enough to hide behind either. The sea wall, periodically drenched in spray was a non-starter as well. Now that just left his side with the café.

Grant turned and walked across the flags to the café door and tried the handle. It wouldn't budge but something very sharp on the edge of the window grill caught him across the knuckles.

"Shit, that's all I need!"

Grant realised the overgrown bushes to his left that grew almost down to the curb were overrun with a Russian Vine. Where it had spread its searching tendrils up the tiled bay roof of the shop window, an archway had formed. Although it was dark in there, he could clearly pick out the pathway that emerged some twenty yards further up the road and continued over the brow of the hill.

Grant stepped forward under the archway.

"Fay," he called softly, "are you in there?"

After a few steps more, the flags came to an end and a gravel track crunched under foot.

He turned slowly and tried to make sense of the dark. It all reminded him vividly of his first sexual encounter with the girl next door in their den, built at the bottom of his garden. He was twelve and she was older by two years. She had breasts and proudly showed them to him. It was exciting even then, though she hadn't reacted at all to his touch. He'd got his first erection and now he'd got another one, only this time it was much bigger and he knew just what to do with it.

"Fay, are you in here. I'm sorry I didn't get down sooner but I had a run in with a manic lorry driver up the road, he blocked me in."

Now his night vision had improved, he began to make out branches, a wheelie bin and a blue recycling tub, full of newspapers.

"Oh, bloody hell Fay, you made me jump. Look, I'm really sorry…Fay? … Oh, you idiot!"

There in the dark was a life size female mannequin, dressed in a swimming costume, to advertise Ambre Solaire.

To the right he could just make out the shape of, yes it was a hatch back …and it looked like Fay's car. Yes, there was the real Churchill nodding dog on the parcel shelf.

"Oh Yes!" His mimic was perfect and he expected to hear Fay giggle. She always did but there was nothing, only the wind now that the rain had ceased. With eyes strained in the gloom, he tried to make out anything else in the car that might confirm... yes, there it was, one of Fay's earrings, the ones he bought her on holiday last year.

"Well at least I know she's here ...but where has she got to?" he muttered quizzically.

"Fay ...Fay, where are you?"

Grant strode out purposefully along the path and into the open again. He stepped back into the road, walked around the bushes and back to the car and half expected to see her leant on it with that smug little face. But no, there was still no sign of her. In fact there was no sign of anybody. It was 8.25pm and his knuckles were still bleeding. He wrapped them in a tissue from the car and got his mobile from the jacket laid on the back seat. As he waited for it to go through all that welcome screen stuff, he caught sight of a white car approach slowly down the hill. Damn, it was a police car. He'd just have to stay calm and maybe they'd drive by. He quickly accessed Fay's number and it began to ring as the police car pulled up alongside. The window wound down.

"Everything alright Sir?" enquired a polite but almost indifferent voice from within.

The voice mail kicked in.

"Just a second," Grant, bent down low enough to see the policeman within.

"Hello Fay, can you ring me back when you get this message?" asked Grant, as he tried to sound calm but cheerful and then he flipped his phone shut.

"You got a spot of engine trouble sir, with all this rain?"

"No the car's just fine... I'm having a bit of trouble locating my girlfriend." Not bad, thought Grant, for the spur of the moment anyway.

"How's that?" enquired the policewoman from the driver's seat.

"She rang to say she'd arrived, I was a bit late but when I got here, there was no sign of her," you're getting better at this, but don't over do it.

"How long have you been waiting?"

Grant looked at his watch, God it's 8.35pm. "About thirty-five minutes," he replied.

Well, we're going along the front and into town, we'll keep an eye out for her. Can you describe her?" asked the policewoman.

"Yes, she's tall and slim, quite good looking, with shoulder length dark hair."

"What was she wearing?"

Oh shit, now what. If he told the truth they'd put two and two together, oh bloody hell what a mess.

"A black raincoat and trousers I think."

"But then you haven't seen her, have you."

Was that a question? It almost sounded like a question. Maybe he should forget the fiction and just tell all and have done with it.

"It's… it's what she most commonly wears."

"Right."

"Is she in the habit of going off like this when you're late, you know, getting a bit of pay back?"

"No" ……he paused, "well actually just once before in London."

"What happened?"

"She was watching the whole thing from the café across the road," he answered, spreading out both hands before him, "kept me waiting about forty minutes. Finally, she sent a waiter out with a coffee and he told me that the woman in the window sent her compliments."

"Well she's got style, your girlfriend. Maybe you need to be more attentive," said the policeman.

The cheeky sod! Grant decided not to respond. He preferred to busy himself and look down the road for any sign of Fay but just then, the rain started to hammer down once more. "That's all I need."

"We'll be back this way in about half an hour, if she's not turned up…" Their voices trailed off as Grant ran for cover under the archway. Stood there watching the hissing, beating rain, he tried to think of what to do next. She couldn't have gone anywhere else but round there because there's nowhere else to hide. He made his way back to her car and tried the door but it was locked. With his hand on the bonnet he felt a little warmth still left in it. So Fay couldn't have been there that long when he'd seen her. Now his night vision had returned it became clear that the car was actually parked at the head of what looked like a cart track, with brambles and small trees to either side. He stumbled over the uneven ground and decided that it would be a lot easier to just get the torch from the car. He was right, the ground was pot holed and the torch picked out tree roots, small piles of carelessly discarded building materials and garden debris. He ducked under a low branch and reached some narrow stone steps which were difficult to climb among the dead leaves in the wet. Finally he emerged through a gap in a wall onto a deserted road. This must drop down to the main road, he surmised. A distant streetlight picked out the edge of the pavement that ended some yards ahead but the road continued past him and came to an abrupt end, just to his right, amidst overgrown brambles. The area around Grant had obviously silted up over time but even in this light, he could make out clearly pronounced tyre tracks in the mud, wide like those of a lorry. The rain and slurry from the hillside spilled over them and around his feet. Soon the tracks would be washed away and Grant realised that they must have been made earlier that evening, during the lull in the rain.

Shit! It's 9.15pm, where the hell could she be? He admitted, for the first time, he had become a bit concerned. He tried Fay's number again as he lent over the wall to look back along the track. He hadn't quite got the phone to his ear when what sounded like music, floated up from down there in the dark and he spotted a little flash of blue light. The voice mail kicked in and he hung up, the music stopped and the blue light went out. Surely it can't be! He ran best he could down the steps and rang Fay's number again. There it was, somewhere in front of him. He ducked low under a branch and the music became much louder. With the torch switched off he stood still and tried to guide his eyes though the dark to the source of the music. There! "Ouch! Shit!" he'd walked into another branch and it stung like hell. "Bloody voice mail!" He hung up irritably and dialled again. Finally there it was, the silver and black mobile. He picked it up, opened the lid and the 'End Call' displayed on his phone. This was Fay's but what was it doing here? Now he was worried. Of course there could be a perfectly logical explanation but what exactly would that be?

He stumbled back to his car but this time he was pleased to see the police. A short stocky policeman examined the offside wing of Grant's car, while a policewoman, with dyed blonde hair who looked barely older than a schoolgirl, talked on her radio.

"You had an accident this evening?" asked the policeman.

"I don't think so," replied Grant as he walked round to look.

"Well it's not much, but whatever it was, it was red."

Yes, sure enough there was a bit of a crease in the wing, just in front of the side mirror, Bloody King Kong!

"I take it there's been no sign of her then?" asked the blonde schoolgirl.

"No, but I found her car and her mobile over there," replied Grant and pointed through the arch.

"Well you've been busy! Could I have your name please sir?"

"Grant Reid."

"And your address?"

Grant watched the policeman walk behind her and disappear through under the arch, his torch in hand as he replied, "Flat 14 Karis Court, Lemont Avenue, Leeds."

"And your girlfriend's name?"

"Fay Crosswell …16 Melton Street, York."

"Does she live there alone?"

"No, it's owned by her friend, Leslie."

"How long have you known each other?"

"About two years but we've only been going out since just before we went on holiday, in June last year."

"And you arranged to meet her here, outside the Bay Café at 8.00pm?"

"Yes that's right."

"Bit of a lonely place to meet, were you planning to stay the weekend?" asked the policeman as he returned from his exploration.

"No." This was going to get difficult. He couldn't make up his mind how much to tell them. He didn't mind so much if they worked it out for themselves but he decided only to give simple answers. Why tell them things they didn't need to know?

"Is that her phone?"

"Yes," he handed it over.

"How did you come to find it in the dark?"

"I saw it flashing and I heard the musical ring tone. Did you go up the steps at the end and onto the road …and the lorry tracks, did you see?"

"Yes," he walked towards their car as he talked into his shoulder radio mouthpiece.

"What was she wearing?" asked the schoolgirl.

"Black leggings and a short black raincoat."

"As you've both got mobiles, why didn't you rearrange to meet somewhere else …..warm and dry?"

"I don't know, it didn't occur to me I suppose!"

"Didn't occur to her either."

"No." That was the whole point, we wanted somewhere private. Shit, this wasn't easy! "Shouldn't you be putting out a missing person call or something, it's been nearly two hours."

"We've sent somebody round to her house, to see if she's there."

"Oh…that was quick," replied Grant in a tone of surprise tinged with uncertainty.

"I've not heard anything yet," she said reassuringly.

The minutes passed painfully slowly but try as he may, he could think of no logical reason why Fay would want to prolong matters now the police were involved. What's more, his bladder was about to explode and that's always a bit of a distraction.

"I've got to go for a pee," he announced, heading toward the arch.

"You can't go in there again," protested police girl.

"But I can't wait any longer!"

"Go over there, behind the lamppost across the road, I promise I won't look!" she smiled.

There wasn't time to argue. Oh what a relief! As the pressure on his bladder began to subside, Grant looked back up the street to where he'd parked earlier. Oh God, that's better. Now he wondered, could King Kong have got parked up there on the road, then down those steps to the café and grabbed Fay, all in the time it took him to drive four hundred yards. It was a bit of a tall order …no, not enough time. All the same, it was a bit of a coincidence nevertheless.

"So you haven't seen your girlfriend tonight," asked the police girl as he returned.

She's a bit hail and hearty this one, thought Grant, quite pretty though, but a bit short on memory for a police person! "No, I told you, I was late and she wasn't here!"

"Did you see anybody else around?"

"Ah,… yes, there was a taxi. It pulled out from over there."

"Did you see which one?"

"I think it said Triple A on the light, it was difficult to see."

"Anyone else?"

"Yes there was a big red lorry up there," yes, mustn't forget King Kong, he scratched my by bloody car!

"Right, there's nobody at your girlfriend's flat."

From behind him, a man's voice called out, "Now then!" Grant turned to see that another police car had pulled up at the curb and both the young policemen within, tried to make eye contact with police girl. Well, they obviously fancy her, thought Grant with a wry smile on his face.

"We're just going back to the station," announced the nearest one, "we'll get a bite to eat on the way. Do you want anything?"

"No, looks like his girlfriend's gone… I might be here a while."

"I don't suppose I could go and get something to eat, all this talk of food …I've not eaten since lunchtime. I'm starving!" Grant tried not to sound too wimpy.

"Hm…. I don't suppose you'd like to take him along would you, only …." she replied as she raised an eye brow towards the policemen in the car.

"Well, yes we could …if you think that's best?"

"Yes, I do, that would be a great help," she replied.

He'd never been in a police car before but Grant hadn't cared much for the curious looks he got from the passers by, as they waited for policeman Brian to return from the chip shop.

"We're not eating them in the car Brian, it'll make the place stink!"

"It's a police car! .. not a bloody limo Dave, chill out!" mocked Brian.

"Yes that's right, he's here with us … Ok," replied Dave into his mouthpiece.

"Cosey wants a word," Dave nodded in Grant's direction.

"They're not gonna let us take them in there!"

"Well, we'll drop him off first, take the car round to the compound and eat them there then!"

"You can't bring those in here feller," said the duty officer.

"I'm starving," pleaded Grant.

"That's as maybe, but you still can't bring them in here!"

"Great!" and with that he handed his fish supper over to Brian.

"Now, if you'd come this way, DCI Cosey won't keep you long," said the duty officer over his shoulder. He led Grant down a narrow corridor with partially glazed panels to both sides and ushered him into Interview Room 3. Grant sat on the chair, with his back to the door and stared at the blank wall over an empty wooden desk, trying to collect his thoughts. Why had they brought him here? Maybe they've found Fay. Oh God, if she was okay! He stood up and ran his fingers through his hair. Why would they bring him here? Why not take him back to the Café? This is bizarre, the whole thing's become like a bloody nightmare! He turned to pace the room only to find his way barred by a man with mousey hair, in his late forties.

"Mr Reid? I'm DCI Cosey. Take a seat will you, this won't take long," said Cosey in a very matter of fact, even tone. He settled behind the desk and rested on his elbows to examine his hands. Grant sat there patiently and became more nervous by the second as he tried to read the man behind the bland expression. Cosey had a good head of mousey coloured hair though a bit windswept in contrast to his well cut jacket and crisp white shirt. The straight knitted tie seemed an odd choice and it hung loosened a little below the open collar button. It must have been a long day as he looked ready to go home.

"Have you found Fay?"

"No, I'm sorry we haven't," replied Cosey.

Oh what a relief… he wanted her to be found, but not like that!

"When did you last see Fay, Mr Reid?" Their first eye contact caught him off guard. Cosey fixed him with clear blue eyes that seemed capable of reading his soul.

"Sunday evening."

"The taxi driver says, he saw somebody that looked like your girl friend, at the café about 8.05pm."

"Right, so she did make it then," interrupted Grant, trying to sound surprised, in line with his original story but ...there was something wrong about this taxi statement!

"He also said that, he saw a car like yours arrive and park up the hill, about 7.45pm."

"How can that be?" Grant was confused. There was something definitely wrong here! How could the taxi ...

"Is it possible you are mistaken about the time you arrived?"

"No, we'd checked our watches before to make sure they were in time, synchronised I mean."

"And this is because you are in the habit of arriving late," smiled Cosey.

"What...Oh, the café incident, Yes," replied Grant. He struggled to keep up with the questions as he tried to reconcile the taxi driver's evidence with his own recollection. "She wanted me to be there early, so she wasn't standing around on her own," his brain worked frantically.

"What was she wearing on her feet?"

"High heels I think."

"So she was wearing a short black raincoat, black leggings and high heel shoes."

"Yes, .. well I mean I think so, I didn't actually see her," Oh shit! This had all become too bloody complicated.

"Not exactly the best outfit for a night like tonight. I mean she'd have been soaked to the skin in no time."

"I suppose not."

"So despite the inclement weather, you drove fifty miles to meet up with your girl friend, not at a nice comfy hotel, of which Moverley has many, and left her standing there, getting soaked to the skin, at a pretty isolated spot and dressed like a hooker."

"No, that's not how it was!"

"Well, let me tell you how it is Mr Reid," snarled Cosey as he pushed the chair out from behind him dramatically and stood up. Grant sat bolt upright in his chair. Cosey looked at him for a moment and then added in a calm and even tone, "your girlfriend's gone missing under suspicious circumstances and I don't think I've got all the facts yet. So I'm going ask you, if you'd be so kind, as to hang around here?" smiled Cosey. "As information comes in, maybe something will jog your memory and your cooperation, in the event that something untoward has happened …it could dramatically improve her chances of survival. Wouldn't you agree?"

"Yes by all means," smiled Grant uneasily. Deep down, he was grateful of the opportunity to clear the air, get things back on an even keel, not to mention he could help them to find Fay.

Cosey frowned, made an abrupt exit and closed the door firmly behind him.

"Shit!" hissed Grant under his breath. Now what the hell would he do?

Chapter 2

DCI Levi Cosey's bohemian fashion sense was the consequence of an untidy wardrobe. He absent-mindedly dressed each day in the thing which first caught his eye but always he topped it off with a khaki parka jacket, a relic of his misspent youth as a mod. Nevertheless he still checked his look in the tall mirror by the front door before he set out each morning. Back then he'd been a snappy dresser. Well polished hook and eye lace up shoes, checked hipster trousers, a lamb's wool pastel colour tank top and a button down pastel shirt to match. In his youth, the original parka boasted fur around the hood, sewn in by the loving hands of his first real girlfriend, Natalie. His hair had been short and spiky on top held in place by loads of men's hair spray but how that stuff had made his head itch!

The car started first time so Cosey settled back in the seat and allowed the nostalgia to flood over him as he drove towards the station on autopilot. He'd tried to lose his virginity with Natalie so many times. He pictured her firm breasts in that white angora jumper she wore. Yes, she always came up with some lame excuse, just when he thought his luck was in. They parted company about the same time he trashed the scooter, a Lambretta, with chromed side cheeks and a high back rest to match. Two tall aerials trailed dramatically from the back and sported the Shell tiger tails while the front fairing was mounted with six matching pairs of mirrors, set at all angles, to give the widest possible rear view, which Cosey rarely used. Down the High Street he'd raced one evening, more intent on his own stunning visual appearance, reflected in the long windows of an empty shop, only to run into a parked dumper truck. Fortunately, thrown clear he'd landed on his back, right on top of a huge pile of sand but the scooter was a write off. They don't make them like that anymore, he smiled. These retro scooters, the drivers just don't have the same sense of style. Back then the scooter was the chariot of an awakening youth culture…

"You bloody idiot," he bellowed at a cyclist who crossed his path with only inches to spare. "Why don't you watch where you're going?"

Awakened suddenly from autopilot he felt disorientated. Up ahead the familiar blue sign of the police station beckoned and he turned into the car park, glad to have arrived in one piece.

The journey to his office on the first floor was less eventful. He stepped through the open door, to be greeted by DI Kalum Benning who smiled and offered him a rather grubby looking bone china mug of tea.

"Any news on the missing person case this morning?" asked Cosey and groaned with barely a pause, "there's tea leaves floating on the top Kalum!"

"Sorry, tea bag broke. Still it's warm and wet," added Kalum.

"And that makes a difference does it?"

"There's no news, do you want me to make you another one?"

Cosey moved on and ignored the question as he strained the tea through his clenched teeth to add emphasis to his

He was still smiling blankly at the wall when the door opened and having deposited a flurry of paperwork on the desk, a dark haired young man in a suit, sat down on the chair behind the desk opposite.

"Good morning I'm DI Benning. Have you had something to eat and drink?" The question was aimed at Grant but he'd looked at the policeman for a confirming nod.

"Yes thanks. Is there any news of Fay?"

"And what news would that be?"

"Has she turned up?"

"No I'm afraid she hasn't and that, Mr Reid, leaves you in a rather awkward position right now!"

"Yes, I…"

"Well I'm not sure you do, quite honestly! Fay has been missing for…," he checked his watch, "best part of fourteen hours. For all we know, she could be at the mercy of some villain or laying in a ditch somewhere. Frankly, Mr Reid, looking at these notes," he flicked over the pages, "your explanation …story, shall we say, evolved as the night wore on. In fact, not to put too fine a point on it, I'd say you've been playing cat and mouse with us!" he added with a frown. "I hope your overnight stint in our comfortable little hostel has helped clear your thoughts. Whatever you had planned last night, it's in everybody's best interest if we could get to the truth now Mr Reid."

Grant stared at the palm of his hands in silence. He now felt quite stupid. With more time to think he'd realised they couldn't link what happened to his personal problem and he'd rather keep it like that. Their little clandestine meeting was Fay's idea, he'd just gone along with it. He hadn't even chosen the location. In fact, he hadn't told anybody about it so, unless this is one hell of a stupid practical joke, any information about it would have had to come from Fay anyway. Well, there's always Leslie he supposed, and her therapist would know. Why did she have to ring him with the details anyway?

"Mr Reid?"

"Right…Well, yes …. I felt embarrassed, I thought Fay was playing another trick on me, like the one in London," he gestured at the open file and Kalum looked down at the notes.

"Ah, she sent you a coffee."

"Yes, but as time went on I got worried and I didn't know how to back track without making it look as though I was up to no good, that I'd planned the whole thing."

"What do you mean by that?"

"Fay wanted to have a date where I picked her up as though she was, you know, like she was … on the game."

"Right…hence the tight leggings and the high heels," Kalum seemed keen to sustain the momentum.

"Yes exactly, I was to drive down and pick her up…. And then …. We were…"

"You were?"

"Well that was down to me…That was my task. I had to decide where to go and what we'd…"

"Right I'm beginning to get the picture," he consulted the notes once again and asked. "Why did you choose the Bay Café?"

"Well I didn't, Fay chose it, I assumed because there'd be fewer people around. She was insistent that I got there early to keep watch in case there were any unsavoury characters about."

"And, were there?"

"No, well ….There was a taxi that left just after I got there and parked up."

"What time was that?"

"Just a bit before 7.45pm."

"Are you sure?"

"Yes! We'd synchronized watches and everything!"

"Who's we?"

"Fay and I did, on Friday morning. I rang to make sure everything was set and that she'd not changed her mind."

"How did she sound?"

"Fine, she said she was sorry things had got out of hand and that she was looking forward to our evening."

"And was the taxi driver an unsavoury character?"

"Sorry? ..Oh, no, well I don't know, he drove off. I never actually saw who was driving. Now, there was this lorry though. Well, I had parked up at the top of the road so I could see the café and then I saw Fay. I was just …"

"So you saw her?"

"Yes, but only briefly because this great big lorry…."

"What time was that?"

"It was just turned 8.00pm. Anyway, this lorry came from nowhere and tried to block me in. He was blowing his horn, you know one of those bloody fog horn things, but I couldn't be bothered with him, so I put my foot down and got out of there. When I got down to the Café there was no sign of her."

"What happened to the lorry?"

"I don't know, when I looked up the road a few minutes later, it had gone, but I found some big tyre tracks up on that back road…."

"Yes there's …." Kalum tapped his finger on the notes.

"What colour was the lorry?"

"I'm fairly sure it was red, but those orange streetlights…."

"Yes, quite."

"Look I'm sorry, I was embarrassed and once you start…"

"Yes, once you start telling lies, nobody believes a word you say!"

"Yes, well…."

Kalum sat back in his seat and put his pen down on the notes.

"Your girlfriend is still missing but at the moment, there is no evidence that points to any wrong doing. I hope she turns up! Not that you'll be off the hook then even because you've wasted police time."

"I'm sorry!"

"For the time being I think you should go and we'll let you know if anything transpires," said Kalum as he nodded at the policeman who opened the door. "Have you left anything downstairs?"

"Oh, no," replied Grant with a weary shake of his head.

From this favoured window seat Cosey had always enjoyed the grandstand view. He liked the contrast between the dusty timeless dilapidation of Kimberley Street that wandered indifferently across the hectic and often noisy passage of life that plied the main road. Diagonally across the junction the launderette was busy. Two fat ladies folded sheets, duvets and towels, then forced them roughly into pale blue laundry bags. To the left Kimberley Street passed under the railway viaduct and fizzled out into a labyrinth of lockups and dead ends, abandoned cars and old stained mattresses. The Whinsper Empire settled there between the launderette and the viaduct about the same time the Plaza Cinema and the remaining buildings on the other side of the street were turned into self-storage units. Where did people keep things before self-storage he wondered? On this side of the main road the opposite corner was occupied by a vast hoarding that extolled the ice cold virtues of the latest Mitsubishi four wheel drive monster. Doesn't look very green to me! But now that's what he liked to see. With a smile he shifted his gaze on to the right and a small shop with peeling paintwork. Rakesh and another younger man he didn't recognise worked on a makeshift bench behind the grimy window and dismantled starter motors and alternators. Not that Cosey was into car maintenance but the rather badly painted sign above the door read, Starter Motors & Alternators Fitted While U Wait. People are actually doing some real work for a change he smiled, not all that virtual stuff on the internet. What a brilliantly descriptive title for 'almost but not quite work.' Why should he feel obliged to admire somebody that got paid for almost working? Surely there's got to be a day of reckoning when all those little bits of 'not quite' add up to a lot. The whole thing just grinds to a halt because finally the world stocks of all those vital components, the ones they should have made but didn't because they were 'not quite working' at the time, have run out. Then somebody will have to get off their arse and do some actual work!

He felt his feet suddenly slip forward and realised that he'd become a bit animated by his thoughts. He wondered if he'd been thinking out loud but a quick glance round the café reassured him that the other diners were too engrossed in their own thoughts to have noticed anyway. This end of Kimberley Street came to a dead end against a disused railway viaduct next to Rakesh's shop and sported two rather run down lockup garages in the archways. Sandwiched between the café and the viaduct, hemmed in by a rusty and dilapidated fence were the remains of Frank's Independent Coaches. Shame about Frank, thought Cosy. He loved the movies and used to go to the Plaza on the way home from work on a Wednesday night. It was on one 'Oldies Night' that Cosey, who pounded the beat in those days, found him, laid face down, on the manhole cover, all alone. He'd had a heart attack and died intestate. So the powers that be had left his unit just as it was all these years. Now the fence had rotted, and between the closely parked vehicles all plants known to man had flourished. Some of the buses still had windows but they were almost blacked out by the grime. The only paying passengers these days sought more carnal delights between the thighs of the local Tomcats.

With that thought in mind he gave the clientele the casual once over between the last mouthfuls of what was an excellent breakfast. He raised his empty mug to coax the waitress in the trainers from her daydream and she promptly bustled over with a top up.

"Sorry love, I was miles away. Was that alright for you?"

"Yes it was, in the words of Frank, truly memorable!" With a satisfied grin he handed her a tenner.

"Frank?" she looked puzzled.

"Probably before your time," he gestured toward the coaches.

"Oh, right. Blimey, that's a long time before my time!" she smiled, "I'll get your change."

He got up from his seat and followed her a few paces to the counter.

"You looking up some old friends then?"

"Not exactly," he grimaced and rearranged his parka on the walk to the door and let himself out onto the street.

He should have used the pelican crossing straight away but old habits die-hard. The little green man flashed approval as Cosey made his way across the road and towards the corrugated fencing that haphazardly enclosed the Whinspers. Even after all this time nobody had tried to improve upon Vick's poor attempt at over painting the graffiti and the words *THE FATTIES* were still quite legible. A short way along the fence, two large corrugated iron gates into a make shift car park were perched precariously open. Just inside on the left stood a tall rather new looking larch lap booth. The door was propped open by a very large, seated and grimy individual. His long thin black hair was tucked back behind his ears as he read from the middle of the newspaper as if oblivious to the world. But Cosey knew of old that appearances were very misleading with that one.

"Long time since you bin 'ere Mr Copsey," he said with a leer.

"Is Vick around?" Cosey ignored the deliberate mistake.

"No Vick isn't around, he's in the office," smirked Lionel Whinsper.

"Same old, same old Lionel," muttered Cosey as he crunched his way over the gravel towards a glazed door in the end of a metal container.

The Whinsper Empire was like an iceberg thought Cosey, because once past the tacky double glazed entrance, the cramped little foyer and grubby counter, there lay a warren of portable cabins on two floors, linked by corridors and metal stairways. Like a small shanty town, it hugged the inside corner of a huge dilapidated old galvanized shed and overlooked the vehicle repair and breakdown side of the operation. Stood in the corridor outside Vick's office Cosey took in the view to the sound of the local radio station and the whine of compressed air tools. In the workshop below several cars were parked haphazardly with their bonnets raised. Briefly a pair of greasy rigger boots and oily tracksuit legs stuck out from under the car to the right and twitched in time with the music and the clatter of a spanner. Then from beneath, the rest of Terry Hughes slid into view. He sorted through some sockets in an open red tool box, spun a ratchet spanner in his hand and returned to the car. His head and shoulders disappeared beneath the raised bonnet and the vehicle gently rocked as Terry applied some pressure to the hidden nut.

Cosey liked workshops, his father had been quite a mechanic and if things had turned out differently, well he might have become one himself. He remembered with a smile, how his Dad would pick him up when he came home from work and give him a hug. He would rub his bristly chin on Cosey's cheek. It made him wriggle and giggle amidst a strong smell of oil on his father's woolly pullover. Those rainy Sunday afternoons when they'd have the bonnet up on a car in the garage, his mother would come through with mugs of tea for 'you men' and then she'd pop a warm piece of freshly made oat cookie in their mouths.

The spit of air breaks abruptly brought him down to earth as a large red breakdown truck settled alongside a long container near the far wall. A young lad in his twenties walked across towards Terry, a pale blue work slip in his out stretched hand.

"You're really lucky, we don't usually keep these windscreens in but they cocked up an order for somebody else and we still had it in stock!"

Terry signed for it and the lad was off in a white van that waited at the entrance with the engine running.

The sound of Vick's phone call had subsided so Cosey let himself into his office. Vick was sat at his desk amidst the remnants of his dinner, old invoices, a glossy girlie magazine and some very dog eared files scattered on the desk before him. His fat hand clicked the mouse and the desktop screen erupted on his monitor but not before Cosey glimpsed the naked bottom of a woman.

"You'll go blind" said Cosey in a matter of fact, almost bored tone of voice.

"Now then Detective Chief Inspector Cosey, what can I do for one of Britain's finest?" oiled Vick.

"Triple 'A' Taxis is one of your little enterprises isn't it?"

"Yes, you had a complaint?"

"One of your taxis was in the vicinity of the Bay Café, Moverley on Friday night."

"Yes, one of your lot rang up on Friday night about that. What's the problem?"

"I'd like to talk to the driver."

"I'm not sure who was driving, let me check." He clicked his mouse through a series of windows, "Yes it was my brother Ron, we were short of drivers and he took a fare near there as a favour."

"Good old Ron! Is he about?"

"Hang on I'll see," and he dialled an internal number, "Ron, I've got DCI Cosey here, he wants to ask you about your taxi driving on Friday night." Vick replaced the hand set and added, "He's coming through."

"So how's business?"

"Keeping busy, you know."

It was like pulling teeth. Any crook knows that the best way to incriminate yourself was to talk too much and Vick had silence off to an art. Cosey looked around the room for anything that might occupy his mind and fill the silence. An assortment of differing filing cabinets took up one corner. A modern PC with the monitor stood on two old Yellow Pages directories looked rather out of place, wedged in between box files on another desk. Above it on the wall hung one of those old yellowing, black and white holiday photos in a frame.

"Is this you lot?" Cosey didn't wait for an answer, "it is, isn't it, that's your old man."

"Yeah, that was his boat. He was always going to take us out in it but I don't think he knew how to, so he'd make some excuse. You know like the tide isn't high enough or the wind's in the wrong direction," replied Vick brightly.

Blimey Vick, thought Cosey, but it didn't last, by the time he'd reached the end of his last sentence Vick's tone was lifeless and flat again. So Cosey stared at the faces and tried to pick up on the mood of the day. He came to the conclusion that the boys must have been herded up from their seaside fun, against their will and thrust into position because none of them looked at the camera. The adults had more sense of occasion and stood there with proud respectable smiles. Vick's father, Brian was a scrap dealer plain and simple, a little muscular man with a reputation as the local 'big hitter.' Bald head, sleeves rolled up, small moustache and he smoked a pipe. To be fair he hadn't gone looking for trouble but he wouldn't back down either. So if some feller, the bigger ones more often than not, were to turn up with some suspect lead or copper wire he'd more than likely lay them out if they tried to be a bit clever. Other than that he was as righteous as you'd expect your average scrap dealer to be. Cosey had only met him once at Frank's funeral and he hadn't lasted much longer himself. Now Bridgett Whinsper was quite a different matter. She was the large, florid looking Irish gypsy woman in the middle with a bad attitude, lots of freckles and a bushy ginger hair style. Her vast collection of floral and spotted dresses was legendary in the neighbourhood, all pretty much in the same style, wide at the hem and gathered under her huge bust. You could recognise her from a long way off as she shuffled down the street to the bus stop. Perspiration glistered on her face and she wheezed all the way. She ruled the household with the flat of her hand and kept the family together after Brian died. Vick was the middle brother and like most middle children he got overlooked by the others. He spent a lot of time on his own or just trailed around behind Ron. Lionel was the youngest and to be generous he gave the impression of being a little bit simple but Cosey knew he had a mean and sadistic streak. One lunch time, the previous owner of the launderette had dragged him away from a very nice steak and kidney dinner at the Café because she'd heard an animal screaming. When he got to the Whinsper's, Lionel had strung up a cat from the crane by its back leg having doused it in petrol; he'd ignited it, just as Cosey arrived at the gate. Lionel was spirited away for psychiatric help and released into the community after about five years, but that hadn't washed with Cosey, he just felt that Lionel was a bad one, end of story. Ron was always smaller than the rest even in those days. He'd become the brains behind the family business and having completely cleared the site of scrap, he'd gone on to invest the money in a couple of taxi cabs which Vick looked after. For himself he'd bought some garage equipment and started up a repair and recovery business. Between them they cleared the lower end of the yard for a parking lot that Lionel watched over, having become too large to really get about much. In recent years Vick, who must have some sort of glandular problem, had almost doubled his size.

"How many cars do you have now?"

"Usually have about ten on the go, mainly contract work."

"How come Ron had to take the fare?"

but …I know it's silly…" she caught a tear as it ran down her face. "It's not going to make … I'm so worried, I had to do something!"

"Well, I'm glad you did!" he said in a reassuring and appreciative tone as he pointed to a chair and nodded to Kalum.

"Would you like some tea?" enquired Kalum who knew that look of old.

"Coffee would be nice, thank you."

"I'll have the usual," added Cosey.

"Right," said Kalum and then they were alone.

"Do you share the flat with Fay?"

"Yes, we've been friends for years. When she split up with her last boyfriend about four years ago I'd just bought the flat. She came to share it with me, I was finding it hard financially and so it's worked out well. We have our separate lives but it's reassuring to know that you have a friend close at hand if you need one. We were both an only child and it's like we'd found the sister we always wanted."

"I know," he said with more true empathy than she could imagine. Cosey had also been an only child and he knew the feeling that welled up inside you, it was almost like grief. "How long had she been seeing Grant?"

"Um, I'd say for the best part of two years. I don't think it became what you'd call serious until they were on holiday together last year. Things had obviously changed between them when they got back."

"How did they meet?"

"In a wine bar Fay was out for a drink with people from work and there was this speed dating thing going on in one of the back rooms. On the way back from the loo she tried to get a peek at what was going on and as I understand it, Grant had a similar idea and they just got chatting. It started from there."

"To your knowledge have things been okay between them?"

"Well …well this …well you see this …"

Cosey could see the tears well up and choke her words.

"Just take it slowly, I've got plenty of time," he said in a quiet and understanding tone.

"Oh…well you see that's the reason I had to come," she sighed and dabbed her eyes. "She's fallen in love with him and although there's this problem, she's frightened that if she ends it, she'll never find anybody else."

"Problem?"

"Yes, she thought it was her but it turns out the specialist thinks it's more likely to be him."

"I'm sorry I don't quite follow," said Cosey as he tried hard to keep his curiosity at bay.

"You see the problem is I feel like I'm betraying a confidence saying anything to anybody at all but if…. but if…" her emotions got the better of her again. "But if ….something terrible has happened …oh, I will feel like I've abandoned her at a time when she needed someone more than ever!"

"Believe me, I know just what you mean," he spoke quietly and then in answer to the questioning look in her tearful eyes, "I do. If Fay were to turn up tomorrow, a picture of health and happiness then all would be forgotten but if,

God forbid, anything's happened to her then maybe you've got something to say that can make all the difference."

"It's about their sex life."

"Right" he said blandly.

"It's the way he is with her. I mean he doesn't do anything weird, he's not beaten her up or anything, although she said he'd been a bit rough, no, I mean over zealous."

"Ok"

"After the event he became suddenly distant, didn't want affection, didn't show any affection, in fact he would often take himself off to another room. Once she found him sitting on the bathroom floor crying for God sake!"

"How odd!"

"Well, she began to think it was something to do with her. She began looking at books, you know the sort of thing, 'Guides to Better Sex' and so on, but things just went from bad to worse. Well I felt so helpless, I'm no expert, in fact I'm not that bothered about it to be honest, too messy, and all that.....

"Yes, well."

"Oh I'm sorry. I didn't mean to.."

"It's Ok, just … carry on."

"Oh, well…Eventually she mentioned it to her doctor because she was getting depressed about it. He suggested counselling but the waiting list was more than six months, so he referred her to a clinic run by this Hungarian specialist. Well, one of the things I admire about Fay is that she's got a lot of get up and go."

"Right"

"So she went to see the specialist. On her first appointment he got her to fill in a questionnaire about sex. He said her responses were within the normal range but then he asked her to fill in one about Grant."

"Oh, yes"

"Yes, and that's the problem."

"What is?"

"He said that Grant displayed some symptoms of sexual addiction."

"Ooh, I see," at last, thought Cosey

"Well apparently, if there's a kind of imbalance between what they both like, yeah, or need then the therapist tries to help them narrow the gap and find a kind of middle ground. But… if one of them has an addiction to sex, they really need to work with them, otherwise the gap only gets wider. Do you know what I mean?"

"Yes I think I do. Did she discuss this with Grant?"

"Yes! They had a real set to about it. In fact …up until last week there'd been a real atmosphere between them, I thought it was over really."

"What happened last week?"

"Fay told me that the specialist had suggested something that might help narrow the gap and maybe Grant would be more receptive to the idea of visiting a specialist himself."

"I see."

"She didn't go into the details, but I know Grant rang her at work to arrange this weekend and that was all part of it."

"Right, I see that makes things quite a lot clearer. Is that everything?"

"Erm"

"Is it?"

"No, there's something else."

"Ok."

"One night, while things were bad between them, Fay got really upset. Grant had come round and he was just being really ...miserable and petty. She grabbed her coat and ran out, so I followed her, leaving him in the flat alone. Well, I'd been logged on with some stuff for work. When we got back they went into Fay's room and although their voices were raised from time to time, things gradually calmed down. So I went back to my laptop. Well, Grant had been using it, yeah, and he'd lost the website I was using, so I opened the history to backtrack and opened this live chat room by mistake. The page was divided into different screens each with a partially clad woman on a live webcam. When I checked the history, there were just loads and loads of these sites. I mean, we'd only been gone about maybe twenty minutes!"

"Right, I see what you mean," Grant's got hidden depths, hasn't he? thought Cosey.

"I mean if he's got an addiction and she didn't live up to his expectations, well maybe things got out of hand and then you don't know...what might..."

"Yours is the one in the patterned mug," announced Kalum cheerily, as he put the coffee down on the desk.

Nice one Kalum. That gave him a moment to think of what to say to her now, thought Cosey. Laughing boy's been a bit cagey all along and now he knew why, but there's no evidence of any wrongdoing. Being embarrassed about your sex life is hardly a crime. So we're back to the ten minutes each way before the police car arrived. Did he have anything to do with her disappearance or ... umm.

"That's very kind of you... No, I don't take sugar, thank you."

"Right then Miss...." Cosey paused.

"Turner, Leslie Turner."

"I'm glad you came in to see me. The information has been very helpful. If there's no sign of Fay tomorrow I'll probably send over DI Benning here to have a look over her things, if that's alright with you?"

"Yes, that's fine, I'll give you my mobile so we can arrange a time."

"Thank you that's a good idea."

"I do feel so much better having done something."

"I'm sure you do, you're a good friend Miss Turner, and remember what I said."

"Thank you." Cosey nodded in reply, "........and thank you for the coffee," she beamed at Kalum.

"It's a pleasure," smiled Kalum, and with that he escorted her up the corridor.

Chapter 6

With glazing along the east wall, Hector Katychmar's office was always pleasantly cooler in the afternoon, and the mixture of marble and dark wood wall panelling to three sides provided a restful but quite sombre atmosphere. A neutral plain coloured thick pile carpet covered the floor and an eclectic mixture of antique, chrome and glass furniture were arranged in a number of sociable groups. Hector's desk commanded a large area at one end of the room and apart from the usual stationery items, it sported a communications workstation and to the other side of the leather bound blotter, an audio visual control panel. From his high backed leather executive chair he could monitor and interact with everything that went on in the clinic.

The day had already been eventful and his last patient was just about to become involved in one of his role play adventures. This thoroughly unorthodox strategy had proved to be very successful as it forced a patient to discover for themselves, the root cause of their problem. Hector hurried back into the room after a much needed pit stop and activated the DVD recorder to catch the whole event on film.

Marion was an attractive older woman who had fantasies about younger men. She preferred the fantasies to real sex with Mike, husband number two, who was ten years her junior. They met five years ago whilst on a cruise with her first husband in the West Indies. Intoxicated by his good looks, she had met him in all manner of places on the ship for furtive and uninhibited sex. At the end of the cruise she left her husband and settled down with Mike who was an insurance salesman.

Hector pressed another button on the AVC panel and from behind a sliding panel in the wall a bank of six large monitors were revealed. Monitor 1, showed a view of the lift waiting area, Monitor 2, was focused on a close up of the storeroom door to the left of the lift and three other monitors showed the darkened interior of the storeroom from different perspectives. Marion rearranged her jacket collar and checked her makeup reflected in the stainless steel lift panel unaware that the storeroom door had opened slightly. A handsome young man in a white steward's jacket stood there one foot over the threshold. He smiled in her direction.

"Excuse me!" hailed the young man.

It was only just above a whisper but Marion obviously thought she heard a voice and turned.

"Oh, you made me jump!" she giggled with surprise and pleasure.

"Do you think you could help me? It's my first day and they've sent me to get some cleaning things but I don't know what to take."

"Well then, … I suppose that all depends on what it is you're trying to clean," she smiled and approached the door to look beyond him into the storeroom. "There's not a lot of light in there even if you know what you're looking for…."

She grazed her bust against his chest as she squeezed past him in the doorway. "Not much room is there!" she giggled, walked along the shelves and turned the odd thing towards the light to read the label. "Are you sure you're in the right store, this all looks more like stationery?"

"Well, I think it goes further round at the side."

She followed the direction of his outstretched hand and turned the corner to find a table in front of some shelves laden with boxes of paper towels, cans and bottles of...

"Yes you're right I think we've struck oil!"

She stood up from reading some of the labels and came face to face with him just as he turned the corner. For possibly ten seconds neither of them made a sound. They just stared at each other. Her gaze moved from one of his eyes to the other and back again, then she looked up at his dark curly black hair and reached out and touched it gently. "Do you think I'm attractive?" she asked softly.

"Yes," he whispered.

"You remind me of someone, he had hair like yours. That's the trouble with experience," she added with a tone of sad frustration, "it always reminds you of someone else, nothing's new anymore." She stared passed him blankly for a moment, then looked back into his eyes and the softness returned to her voice but it was tinged with sadness. "Tell me, do you find me attractive or am I just attractive for my age?"

"You're attractive ...whatever!" he replied brightly.

She looked from eye to eye again and then ran her hand behind his head and pulled him closer and placed a wet kiss over his lips.

"Take off your jacket and see if you can lock the door."

When he returned from his mission she had slipped her jacket off and was resting against the edge of the table with her hands placed palm down on the surface either side.

"Take off your trousers," she gestured with a little upward head movement. With her head tipped to one side she watched him kick off his shoes, unzip the fly and step out of his trousers as they fell to the floor.

"My, how you've grown!" she giggled.

He made a move toward her but she put out her hand, "grab some of that toilet roll and don't you dare mess up my clothes!" she commanded.

He put the toilet roll on the table, slipped off his boxers and laid her back onto the table. Then he lifted her up from the waist and slid her skirt up above her thighs. She helped him to pull the hem past her buttocks and then ran her fingers up his arms, through his hair and pulled his face close to hers.

"Help yourself, …I'm ready just help you…r ooh!"

Hector found his patient's intimate repartee both informative and erotic but personally he found the physical act of intercourse quite uninteresting. Certainly he wondered why pornographic films dwelt so much on this part. He often found people's comments during the act far more interesting as they were clues to all manner of other issues. Although it was all on DVD Hector still made scribbled freehand bullet point notes of his thoughts for the debriefing to follow. Marion's first orgasm happened quite quickly and her comments were few, mainly about the sensations

he noticed a tall slim oriental woman in a red dress with her back to him stood just outside on the pavement. She checked her mobile, she was obviously waiting for somebody and if he didn't hurry he would to be late as well.

Chapter 7

Whatever other traits Grant may have, tardiness was not one of them. In fact he always liked to get to an appointment about ten minutes early to acquaint himself with the new surroundings and get a feel for the place. The clinic reception was more akin to a hotel than any clinical environment he'd ever visited. On the first visit he'd actually gone back outside and checked the sign just to be sure he hadn't misread it. The modern soft leather armchairs contrasted with exposed steel and brickwork to create the strong retro feel associated with modern waterside developments. Uncharacteristically the floors were carpeted but the sounds still seemed to float upwards and disappear like whispers into the vaulted ceiling. The reception desk was discreetly sectioned off and the receptionist was always pleased to see you.

"Hello Mr Reid, how has your day been so far?" asked a shapely young woman, with a cleavage he found distracting. Well it's not exactly a cleavage, thought Grant, not in the accepted sense. There was no push up bra merely the hint of a well formed figure in well tailored clothes and that understated look drew his attention to the darkness, down there, behind that top button of her blouse. In fact, if later in the day somebody were to ask him what the receptionist looked like, he would have to describe her as such. Even the colour of her hair hadn't registered with him.

"Er …it's probably going to get more interesting now I'm here," he smiled as he took the little electronic beeper. When it was time for his appointment it would vibrate and the room number would appear on the screen in red.

Over in the main reception area he had time to take in the scene. It was just nice to have a bit of time to himself. What with Fay's disappearance and this bloody 'Pro Food' promotion, he needed time to relax. He took a deep breath and wondered where to start. Around the walls were pictures of differing sizes. Some were photographic and some were paintings or collages. There were also 3D exhibits and others involved multimedia displays where you had to don headphones and black goggles. Grant's favourite picture was of a woman in a red dress and he always left her until last. There was a sexual theme to all the exhibits, sometimes so subtle that you might miss it on your first visit. Other exhibits employed crude imagery reminiscent of the graffiti he'd seen in those smelly damp toilets by the sea. Although there were photos of men and women to suit all sexual persuasions he preferred the high quality photos of a single woman. Sometimes a slender dark haired woman would take his fancy, in a dark suit with a crisp white shirt, dark stockings and black shiny shoes. He'd pause for a moment and try to visualise what she'd be like up close in the flesh. Then later he'd see a blonde in a skimpy white angora cardigan fastened with just one button, otherwise naked but for the white knitted leg warmers. He'd look hard at her thighs, trying to recall the feel of the very soft, warm skin you find just there, just before you'd reach her fanny. He often allowed himself to fantasise about the women in the photos. Sometimes they evoked memories of a woman he'd known and he'd get distracted in the attempt to remember her name. He never felt at all self conscious because he'd quickly come to the conclusion that most of the people did exactly the same thing as they waited for their turn to come. He had ten minutes to kill so where should he start today?

Katychmar was a bit of an oddball in Grant's estimation. Whilst he would look you right in the eye when he asked a question or make an observation, he never really looked at you when you were talking. At first he thought Katychmar hadn't really listened but Grant came to realise that it was a way he used to concentrate on what you were saying. Thank God his eyes hadn't rolled about as well! On his first visit Grant had been asked to go round and study the exhibits, fill in the questionnaire, seal it in an envelope and hand it to the receptionist. Maybe five minutes later he'd been summoned by the electronic beeper to Room 8. As he'd entered the room a smartly dressed man sat in an upright chair to his right had asked him to sit down and face a screen. The lights went down and pictures of things he'd seen earlier were displayed on the screen one by one until there were maybe six or seven in total.

"My name is Hector Katychmar," The man seemed very relaxed with one leg crossed over the other and a very shiny black shoe seemed to point straight at Grant. "You've come to see me because there are things about your own sexual feelings and relationships you want to discuss?"

"Yes, I guess so," Grant had replied. He'd felt it was the right thing to say.

"These pictures are of the things you spent most time looking at down stairs. The last one of the woman in red is the one you looked at for the longest time."

"I thought she looked relaxed and above her surroundings, kind of untouchable. But then I noticed her eyes, they're looking straight at you and I couldn't make out what she was thinking. At first I thought they were smiling, but then I thought she was angry or frightened maybe."

"And how did that make you feel?"

"I felt like I was intruding. In all these other pictures," he gestured, "the women all seem comfortable or unaware that the photo has been taken but she has an attitude about her and I just can't make it out. It's familiar even but I just can't place it."

"The questionnaire you filled in, did you answer it honestly?"

"Yes, I didn't see the point in lying!"

"No, quite. Have you ever discussed any of the things listed with anybody before?"

"No, they seem too personal really, although you know blokes like to brag don't they so in that context I suppose I should say yes to some of them."

"Which would they be then?"

"Well, guys share girlie mags in the office and lend each other videos don't they and even go to lap dancing bars when they've had a few…"

"But you said too personal?"

"Yes …well …well I've got loads of mags, I mean loads and I download stuff off the internet. Sometimes I get so involved with it that it's daylight and I only get a couple of hours sleep before I have to go to work. Even at work I sometimes log on to a chat line."

"What about the lap dancing?"

"No, it's personal, I wouldn't want people watching."

"So you'd be happy if she was at your place and you were alone?"

"Too right!" he answered enthusiastically but then he felt a bit embarrassed and added sheepishly, "you know what I mean."

"Look let's get one thing clear from the start. Don't apologise to me for speaking your mind, I'm not sitting here in judgement, I'm trying to get to know your addiction so if it wants to speak out, let it!"

"I don't like that word 'addiction' it makes me feel weak and unclean."

"What made you seek help in the first place?"

"I've found it hard to find a girlfriend whose appetite for sex matches mine. I mean I've never used a prostitute but I've had more than one girl fiend tell me that's how I made them feel. They say I just don't seem to be interested enough in anything else. You know, I buy them a meal so that I can get in their knickers!"

"And was that true?"

"I began to think that maybe it was, particularly when my last girlfriend came out with it!"

"Why is she a cut above the rest?"

"Well yes I suppose she is. It's difficult to say really, we just got on so well. I mean, we went on a holiday to Greece and she wanted it all the time and that suited me down to the ground, it was fantastic."

"What went wrong?"

"We got back from holiday and it was like somebody had tripped a switch. At first I thought it was because she didn't want her flatmate to hear but then she was just the same at my flat. She said I wasn't affectionate enough, even on holiday, which I couldn't believe! She felt rejected after sex because I seemed very distant and sometimes I used to leave her and sit on my own."

"Why did you do that?"

"Well I…. well I always have I suppose"

"When you sit alone, how do you feel?"

"Like I want to be alone."

"Any feeling of anger or regret?"

"I feel sad sometimes."

"How sad?"

"Well quite sad …well actually sometimes very sad, I feel like I'm drowning in sadness."

"Is that when you decided you needed help?"

"She came in to me and I was crying once. She started going mad, said it wasn't normal and I needed help. Next day I was on a chat line when somebody walked into my office unexpectedly and I felt quite ashamed that they might have seen what I was doing. So when they'd gone, instead of going back on the site, I typed in sex therapy and I came across a questionnaire. A lot like the one I filled in earlier. It said that if I answered yes to more than four of the questions I probably needed help. I think I knew the outcome before I'd finished the questionnaire. So I followed their advice and contacted the doctor but the waiting list was very long. I thought Fay and I could make a go of things so I decided to go private and my doctor referred me to you."

"And I'm glad he did, I think we've already made progress. I like your honesty Grant, it's the only way forward, but you need to realise that we're dealing with very strong basic emotions and you're going to find it tough at times. Well, I think that's enough for our first session. Now, if you'd like to make an appointment at reception I'll see you again next week!"

He'd left feeling a million dollars but by that evening he was back on the internet and the overwhelming sadness had returned. It was as though it waited out of reach, somewhere in the shadows stalking him, just waiting for a moment of weakness on which to pounce. Now, three months down the road he had cut back on the videos and magazines but the sadness seemed to have become all the more pressing. His relationship with Fay had gone from bad to worse and he'd been at the point of calling it a day when she announced that she'd gone to a sex therapist and suggested the little rendezvous in Moverley. But what had happened last Friday night, surely she couldn't have planned it like that! What had happened to her? His head whirred again with questions, theories and doubts. He felt the sadness return and awoke from his thoughts to put on the headphones and black goggles and sought refuge in one of the multimedia displays. The woman was already down to her skimpy underwear. She slid down the bed on her knees towards him and reached out a hand. Grant instinctively stepped back a little to avoid her clutch at his genitals. No he wasn't in the mood for that today and he returned the equipment to its perch. He was almost there, the lady in the red dress only feet away. A new life size upright figure in bronze distracted him and he paused to take it in. She was naked but for the high heels and her knees pushed painfully wide by a horizontal chrome bar with a round plastic cue ball at each end. Her wrists were tied tight in front of her at waist height and a similar chrome bar was thrust behind her back and over the crux of each arm to force the elbows way back. Over the eyes of her bronze head was tied a black leather blindfold. It was a striking image and the lines of her body were superb. Grant circled three times but no matter how hard he tried he couldn't tune himself in to that kind of dehumanisation. His real instinct would have been to remove the constraints and cherish that beautiful body. "What a waste!" he muttered and shook his head before moving on.

The punk ballerina in fishnet tights was another new exhibit and he dwelt there a while to see if it sparked any reaction. No maybe next time! Finally it was time to look at his favourite lady in the red dress and he glanced at his watch. At least two minutes if Katychmar's not early. Now there she was, unchanged, still untouchable. Was she angry? No, not today, today they were friends. Was she frightened? Maybe he was intruding? Maybe it wasn't that he was intruding on her but on her thoughts. Maybe that's why she looked vulnerable!

A movement to his right brought him out of his thoughts only to be transfixed, unable to breathe. There, only eight feet away from him, stood a dark haired woman in a red dress looking at something behind the panel. He looked back at the picture, ran a trembling hand over his mouth and then looked back at her. He couldn't believe his eyes, only the face was different but everything else, well! His heart pounded in his chest, everything seemed detached and he daren't move in case she vanished.

Chapter 8

She felt sad at the deception but her family in Bangkok still thought that Lumaii worked in an office. At the end of each of her mother's letters there was always a grateful reference to the regular sums of money she'd sent them. England had seemed like it would be a place of opportunity but she arrived to discover that office work was office work the world over and was boring wherever you were. She missed the vibrancy of Bangkok and in truth she liked the attention of the bad boys in her neighbourhood. She liked to tease them.

"One of these days I won't be here to save you Lumaii!" warned her mother as she stomped ahead of her into their apartment, having confronted a boy with wide eyes. "Pimp!" she'd railed.

The poor boy had followed her up five flights of stairs to the front door, intoxicated by her long legs.

"This pimp," she'd continued, "thinks you're going to have sex with him on my sofa. I'll cut his dick off if he shows his face again!"

A wide smile broke out on Lumaii's face, as the scene still seemed funny even after all that time. It was just a symptom of the restlessness that awakening sexuality had brought into her adolescent life. Her curiosity had grown and got the better of her. She'd succumbed to it and tried something just a little bit risky to test the reaction amongst the boys.   In her early days at Business College she got a bit of a reputation as a tease and she prided herself on the amount of erotic pleasure she could elicit from the chase without being caught for the final act.

When she arrived in England she only seemed to attract the attention of older men, like her boss who always came on to her but it wasn't the same.   One day when he asked her to work late and the rest of the staff had left, he made his move.   She managed to fight him off and locked herself in the toilet.   From outside the door he hurled a mixture of abuse and apologies at her.

"You'll never have me!" she'd screamed.

"Why's that?" he'd bellowed.

"You just don't have enough money and your dick's too small!" It was the first thing that came into her head.

There was a pause, she heard him pace the floor and mutter.   Then he'd slid ten twenty pound notes under the door.   "Will that do for starters?"

"No!" she'd barked but a smile broke out across her face and she felt excited.

After a further pause, another five twenties slid under the door.   "It's all I've got. Think of it as a bonus!"

Lumaii was not a virgin, she'd eventually had quite an active sex life at college.   Sali, the boy that her mother chased away, had in fact had sex with her on her mother's sofa several times.   On one occasion they'd sat there under a duvet and watched a blue movie, munched popcorn and laughed at all the poorly contrived plots and bad acting.

That night at the office once again her heart beat fast as she stood behind the wood grained, plastic veneer door. A real life drama unfolded to the creak of plumbing. She'd made a life changing decision.

"What about your dick?"

"Er...It's not small, it's not small at all!"

"Show me"

"What?"

"Sh..ow m..e!"

She heard his zip unfasten and she unlocked the door silently. With her foot against the bottom edge of the door, in case he'd tried to force his way in, she'd opened the door a crack, just enough to get a peek. No, it's not small, she'd shut the door and slipped the lock again.

"Go up to your office and sit behind the desk like normal and I'll come to you," she'd shouted.

After a short while she'd heard him walk across the floor upstairs and realised that his office was probably more or less overhead.

He'd turned all the main office lights off so now the only illumination came from his desk lamp. She had walked softly into his office and stood just inside the door to wait for him to look up from the papers which he surely couldn't have been reading. When he did look at her he'd smiled a bit nervously and said, "I'm sorry about all that. I really didn't mean to frighten you but you are so lovely looking, I couldn't help myself!"

Lumaii stepped forward alongside the desk and reached out her arm and opened a hand to allow her white panties to fall on his desk. He swallowed hard and eased the shirt round his neck. She walked round beside him and sat gently on the desk, slid across in front of him and raised one knee briefly to clear his legs. She put a foot on each arm of his chair and very slowly slid her skirt back to her waist. His eyes became wide and his mouth opened as she lay back slightly.

"What would you like to do to me first?" she'd asked softly.

He hadn't needed much encouragement to bury his head between her legs and start to lick her.

The sense of detachment came as a surprise. She had gazed around the room at the neatly organised shelves and his coat hung on the coat stand. Periodically she had made a little upward movement of her groin accompanied by a little moan before she re-examined the ceiling. There were cobwebs she'd never noticed before and came to the conclusion that the cleaner needed the sack.

After a while he stood up between her legs and lent forward to take his weight on one arm. Then he reached down to line himself up and he slid his large penis inside her. He'd been quite gentle but she'd still put her hands on his hips to hold him back in case he got too carried away. The desk creaked rhythmically, she had put an arm round his neck and whispered in his ear, "Come on baby, give it to me real tender."

"Oh, you are the best….Oh, Oh, ….aagh, ….aagh"

That was quick! She thought. He slid back off her and dried himself with a tissue from the box on his desk.

"I'll have a few of those if you don't mind," she'd gestured with an outstretched hand and waggled her fingers.

"By all means, be my guest."

She got off the desk, pulled her panties on and rearranged her clothing.

"That was fantastic," he'd said with a big triumphant smile. "That was just something… something else!"

She'd walked to the doorway and turned to announce. "I'm not going to work here anymore."

"But, but when will I see you again?"

She'd looked at him, examined his big eyes and asked, "Do you want to see me again…. Can you afford to see me again?"

"Well….Erm… Give me your number and I'll ring you."

"No, I've got your number I'll ring you," and, with that, she'd turned, surveyed her desk, decided there was nothing she want to keep and walked out the door.

Now she was in big demand and could ask almost what she wanted. Hector had been a good client. He'd never been keen on any real sexual contact, in fact the only physical contact they had consisted of a handshake or a brief peck on the cheek. Sometimes when he'd worked late she might massage his neck. Very occasionally he'd ask her to do a slow seductive striptease for him while they both savoured a bottle of his favourite wine. Her main work for him was to perform sexual favours for his clients. Sometimes they could take a week or so if she had to accompany them on a holiday or business trip. They would lavish her with presents and treat her with respect. Other clients represented quite a different demographic and she wondered what service they could possibly provide that a man of his professional status would need.

Today she was to perform in a lift with one of his patients and for the occasion she'd bought a lovely red dress with her sister Sumlea that morning. As she got out of the taxi and walked the few steps to the clinic entrance, she savoured the feel of the material as it slid sensuously over her otherwise naked body. The lift was going to get pretty warm and steamy so she paused for a moment to enjoy the cool air on her skin and waited for Hector's phone call.

The clinic was on a corner in a busy commercial area of town and in every direction there were office buildings of one style or another. Diagonally across the street the entrance to the office block was flanked by a small newspaper shop to one side and a sandwich bar to the other. Further down to her right Lumaii noticed a Sushi Bar had opened up and two men were engaged in a heated confab, probably about the van parked on double yellow lines opposite. She spent a bit of time people watching and tried to guess from their appearance and body language whether anybody that headed in her direction would in fact go into the clinic. So far only one, the other nine had passed by probably so wrapped up in their own lives that they'd never really noticed the clinic let alone ventured in. Two people had come out. The last was an attractive middle aged woman who headed for the car park with her jacket clutched tight round her. Lumaii turned back to look straight across the street and surmised that the tissue in the woman's hand meant that she'd been crying. Her gaze settled on a small courtyard nestled between the buildings where the gravel walkways were edged with small box trees fashioned into balls amongst deep purple ground covering plants. Further behind some railings she could make out a tall stone fountain that bubbled above broad leafed Hostas backed by taller bamboo plants that swayed in the breeze. A man sat on one of the benches and ate something in a white paper bag as he browsed a magazine.

The mobile in her hand began to vibrate and Lumaii knew it was time to work. Before the ring tone had become anything more than a murmur she had answered it.

"Good afternoon Lumaii are you well?"

"Yes thank you Hector, just taking in the fresh air," and she put her head back to let one last blast of cool air blow through her hair.

"My patient is called Grant Reid and he is the dark haired young man stood about halfway across the back wall exhibition looking at a photograph of a woman wearing a red dress."

Lumaii turned, looked through the glazed entrance and picked him out quite easily.

"I see him." She surveyed the rest of the foyer, looked back at the door and touched her hair as if checking in the reflection because he'd just looked round in her direction.

"I hope the lift isn't going to be too stuffy for you this afternoon. I don't know what significance the red dress has for him but hopefully we shall soon find out. As usual I'll be monitoring what happens and at the first sign of any problem, I'll have two of the male nurses in there quick as a flash!"

"Okay Hector." She collapsed her phone and slid it into her bag, pushed through the entrance door and into the foyer. She walked at a leisurely pace and approached the back wall exhibition and stood for a moment to look at a photo of a punk ballerina. It really was an excellent picture.

The dancer with black and red flecked Mohican hair stood on points and wore a short black lace tutu with fishnet tights. It made her smile. She moved to her left and stood in front of a picture of a well endowed, topless man wearing only light coloured jodhpurs and riding boots. The picture hung on a short partition wall on the other side of which Grant stood still bemused by the lady in the red dress. She angled her position slightly and was able to step back into Grant's view and still appear to look at the man in the jodhpurs. After a few seconds she shifted her weight and took another short step to the side as if to get a better view. She had no need to look at him she could feel his gaze. She looked down towards his feet and then stepped forward and out of Grant's view. For a second he seemed undecided what to do but then followed her at a distance. She returned to the ballerina, it still made her smile. Grant stood a short way off and made out as if he were looking at a small sculpture on a tall white plinth. Without a doubt he was checking her out and it was time to make her move. She turned slowly in Grant's direction and walked slowly towards him and checked something in her bag. Grant's eyes followed her and as she stopped just short of a collision with him she gave a slight smile in his direction. She watched his eyes drift from hers, to her lips and then to her cleavage. Lumaii continued past him still at a leisurely pace but when about ten feet away she half turned towards him as if to speak but then continued as before.

In the reflection of the glass doors to the lift lobby area Lumaii saw Grant stop and take out the electronic beeper from his pocket and curse. He then pocketed it and continued towards the lifts. She slipped between the closing lobby doors and stood alone to watch the red numbers above the lift count down. Grant arrived just as the lift doors opened to an electronic chime and followed her into the small empty lift. She pressed the button for the fourth floor and the doors closed with a clunk.

Lumaii heard his breathing and could sense he was trying to keep it under control. Every now and then he'd take a peek at her. First her shoulders and down across her chest and the next time, down her back over her buttocks and then down her legs. She looked at him, their eyes met and they exchanged smiles.

"Are you going to the fourth as well?" she asked.

"Yes, yes that's right," he smiled and nodded nervously.

She looked up at the numbers to check them off. Four, five, ping the lift shuddered to a stop and Lumaii put out both hands to steady herself. She never liked this bit, it always made her jump. Once in Bangkok she had really been stuck in a lift twenty storeys up for over an hour and she knew how quickly people could start to panic, so she didn't want to over react and put Grant into a tail spin. After all, he was under a psychiatrist and sex addict or not, who knows how he would react.

"What the hell was that," Grant asked nervously.

The lights flickered and went out to leave only a pale glow from the emergency light.

"I don't know!" she replied with just a hint of anxiety.

"Are you okay?"

"I think so ….what do you think happened?"

"We seem to have gone past the floor I think, I heard the chime go long before we stopped."

"What do we do now?"

"Well, I think we'll try this for starters," Grant pressed the red emergency button.

"I didn't hear anything"

"No, nor did I," and he pressed it again twice.

"Well I suppose we just have to stay still and wait," remarked Lumaii with an ironic smile. Come on Grant she thought, don't you start to loose your bottle now. "I'm supposed to be at a barbeque later this afternoon," she added in an attempt to lighten the moment.

"Oh…Well, there's still time. It's not as if were in an unoccupied building, somebody's bound to notice there's a problem with one of the lifts, sooner rather than later I hope," he pressed the red button again.

This time something happened, there was a loud clang from outside. It was impossible to tell whether it was above or below but there it was again.

"That made me jump," said Lumaii with relief on her face, she had begun to wonder if he was going to lose it.

"Me too! The lift hasn't moved at all so I guess it's not bad news."

Then another sound, quite a way off but it distinctly sounded like a power tool followed by a metallic scraping sound.

"Yes!" said Grant with obvious relief, "there's definitely somebody out there." he looked at Lumaii, who responded with a confirming nod.

"Are you OK in there?" asked a man's voice. It was still difficult to tell the direction but they both looked upwards.

"Yes!" they replied in unison.

"What's happened?" asked Lumaii.

"Help is on its way, the lift has gone up too far and so we can't get you out through the escape hatch in the roof. We'll have to wait for the lift engineers to come from Manchester and they should be able to wind you down."

"Should be able to, that's not very reassuring!" Grant sounded anxious but then he smiled briefly.

Yes, Lumaii thought, realised that you've being a bit wimpy have you?

"We've locked off the winch so there's no chance of the lift moving, I'm afraid you're just going to have to be patient."

"Okay, thank you," Grant, exhaled through his teeth with a slow hiss.

"Well, that's a relief … My name's Lumaii," she smiled and held out her hand.

"Oh, yes and my name's Grant," he chuckled but this time he looked into her eyes.

Lumaii looked back into his for a moment, they were dark brown and despite his smile the expression in them was sad and tired.

"What brings you to the clinic today Grant, are you a doctor?"

"No, I'm a patient of Mr Katychmar"

"Oh so am I…I was on the way to pick up a prescription."

"I'd got an appointment with him. I seem to have been here quite a lot recently."

"I was the same until he prescribed this medication and touch wood it seems to be working. Actually you're the first patient I've spoken to."

"Yes me too, we all seem to walk around a bit like zombies."

"Yes," she giggled.

"We're all focused on our own problems and oblivious to everybody else."

"What do you make of the exhibition, it's quite unusual?"

"You can say that again …but I find it helps me focus on why I've come…I mean when you go to the doctors about something like…you know."

Lumaii nodded and leant back against the metal wall. With her hands behind her back she listened and watched his eyes closely. His gaze flitted from just over her shoulder and back to her eyes. She pushed her shoulders back flat against the wall and arched her back a little as she took in a larger breath of air. His gaze shifted to her cleavage and then over her shoulder and back to her eyes. She gave just the slightest of smiles, barely a movement really but she knew it would be enough.

"…..there are all these people with colds and walking sticks and kids…." Grant obviously found her distracting but tried to maintain the flow. "…and when you get in there you feel a bit of a fraud because you've no visible symptoms and it's hard to focus."

"It's getting warm in here," she leant forward off the wall to walk round to his side of the lift. She turned, slipped her hand behind her ear, lifted the hair up off her neck and held it on top of her head for a while. She watched Grant's reflection in the metal panel. He stared at her shoulders and across her chest. She turned her head and through the little window made by her raised arm she looked at him.

"It could be worse I suppose," he said softly.

"Yes it could," she smiled and rested her chin against her bicep. "You could have been an ugly sweaty Paedophile."

"Ha," he laughed, "no I'm not"

"Ugly and sweaty you mean?"

"No, I'm not a Paedophile!"

"So you like women?"

"Yes," he replied quietly with a nod.

She looked up as if to see if anybody was watching and then back at him and whispered as she looked at his lips, "and do you like naked women?"

"Yes"

"Have you got pictures of them at home?"

"Yes"

"Are they naughty?" She leant against his hip and began to turn slowly towards him. He watched her lips and she dropped her arm to rest her hand on his shoulder.

"Some …are very naughty," his voice was barely above a whisper.

She slid her hand down his arm and squeezed his hand as the strap of her dress fell off her shoulder.

"Are they like me?" and she leant herself against him gently. She could feel his erection grow quickly and placed a wet kiss on his lips as she pressed her groin hard against his penis.

He reacted instantly, ran both hands between her arms and down her back to grip her buttocks. He landed a profusion of kisses on her neck, reached down and pulled up her dress. He ran the palm of his hand up her thigh, over her naked bottom slid it between her buttocks and plunged his fingers into her virgina.

"Oh!" she tried to make it sound passionate but in truth, despite the lubrication she'd applied earlier, it was uncomfortable and certainly a bit sudden.

He backed her against the wall and whilst his fingers still wriggled inside her, he tried to undo his belt. Lumaii lent a hand.

"Thanks," he muttered through the kisses and heavy breathing.

His penis was entangled in the boxers somewhere and after a struggle she took a firm grip and simply yanked it hard out into the open. She reached down into her bag and with well practiced fingers, tore the wrapper and unrolled a condom down his penis. She lent back against the wall, opened her legs, lifted her dress and reached down to guide him. He pushed her hand aside and crashed against her with his body and proceeded clumsily to force his own way in.

His first attempt caught her too far to the left, inside the top of her leg and the second and third slid and bounced off. The fourth attempt hit the target but it stung a bit, maybe the clumsy sod has pulled some of my pubes in as well she thought. She managed to shift her weight and lift one leg to ease the discomfort. Grant was well away, nothing loving here though, it was all about him as he continued to pound away and lift her feet off the ground. I hope you've got an eyeful Hector and I hope it makes a difference. She'd caught Hector watching his big screens on one of her visits a while back. Initially his observations seemed clinical but gradually his comments became more salacious and it was the only time that he ever asked her to perform for him. They shared a bottle of wine and he'd asked her to take items of clothing off until she was naked all but her panties and shoes. Then he'd asked her to wander around his office and strike erotic poses over the furniture. When she finally sprawled over his desk, she'd reached down to stroke the bulge in his trousers but his mood changed suddenly. He'd obviously liked watching, so Hector hope you've enjoyed this. Maybe she'd end up in his collection!

"Oh," she moaned again, it was getting uncomfortable her skin had stuck to the metal and with every thrust it felt like a burn.

"Oh God," he shouted.

Thank God she thought.

"Oh God....Oh God. Ummmm Yes!"

"Oh...Oh... yes, oh yes," she whimpered, put her hand on the back of his sweaty neck and kissed him on the lips. "Oh," she huffed, "that was just....She couldn't wait to take the pressure off her back.

Grant stepped away but he didn't let her go. Instead, he dragged her away from the wall, spun her round and forced her onto her knees. This time he lunged at her from behind and hit the target first time.

"Oh!" she cried. It was no act. That had hurt and every time he plunged into her a metallic bang signified that Lumaii's head had made contact with the wall.

give in much to their ridicule. It all came to a head when under pressure from the boys he'd strung up a cat and set fire to it. The only glimmer of hope in an otherwise dark and troubled existence was his unlikely friendship with Zoe, the daughter of the local launderette proprietor. Lionel had been making good progress for some time and as he'd often talked about Zoe, Hector decided to let her visit him on a number of occasions. He'd monitored their meetings on CTV. The meetings had always been a bit lively but good humoured. They'd dance and sing at the tops of their voices to their favourite CD's. During her last visit Hector had received a phone call from another patient. He'd turned the volume down on the monitor to hear better what the patient was saying. He'd only taken his eyes off the monitor for a minute or so but suddenly caught sight of Lionel as he held Zoe off the ground by her throat and choked her whilst he sang to the music. Hector had run like a mad man but he was too late. Lionel was still singing and dancing round but he trailed Zoe's lifeless body around by the arm as though she were a rag doll.

The memory made him feel sick and now he could hear Lumaii's voice scream from the other side of the lift doors.

"My God why's it taking so long!" he yelled.

The doors opened slowly but the two nurses forced their way in. Lumaii tumbled out onto the floor and Hector tried to console her.

"Don't touch me, don't you dare touch me you fucking idiot!" she stumbled to her feet, "what were you waiting for, you could see he was hurting me," she brushed off Hector's attempts to console her, slid along the wall and sobbed her way towards the ladies toilet.

Grant had collapsed into the corner and sat with his trousers down below his knees, hands pressed hard against his head, tears ran down his face. "It's what you do, you've just got to take it," he whimpered. The nurses helped him to his feet and in hushed tones encouraged him to dress properly. He was still in a trance when they helped him out of the lift and followed Hector into his office.

They escorted him to a chair and waited for him to settle himself. After a few seconds Hector gave the nod and they took their leave, closed the door behind them and the room fell silent. Hector sat motionless for while, observed Grant and waited for the opportune moment to begin. There it was, Grant tried to focus on him.

"How did you feel?" asked Hector in a hushed and sympathetic voice.

"Oh," Grant rocked his head from side to side, "so, so."

His eyes looked blankly at him.

"Do you remember the lift?"

"Yes," his voice was vague and wistful, but he was obviously trying to focus on something. "It was like I was somewhere else."

"Did you recognise the place?"

"Yeah …it was my mother's bedroom, she was crying …and he was hitting her. I was shouting for him to stop," Grant's voice began to break up as he struggled unsuccessfully to hold back the tears, "but they can't hear me. He keeps shouting at her, why are you crying," he swung out a hand, "this is what you do, so take it …Go away, hide!"

His eyes were full of tears, wide and staring but he wasn't looking at the room now, he was like somebody sleepwalking, in a nightmare reacting to vivid images and sounds only he could see.

He drew his legs up, wrapped his arms round them, sat and rocked quietly for a while.

"Yes," Hector's voice was soft, full of compassion. "Then what?"

"I went back. She was sitting on the bed crying. She told me off!" he gestured like an appeal to the room for understanding.

"I told you not to come in here!" he mimicked his mother's voice. Then he switched to a childlike voice. "But you were crying!"

"Yes, but that's what I do, and now I must go out again."

"But I don't like to hear you crying."

"It's life, get used to it!"

"Get used to it!" he repeated angrily in his own voice.

Grant sat there with his feet on the floor and arms outstretched, tears ran down his cheeks.

"What's happening?" asked, Hector.

"She's standing up, drying between her legs with a towel and she's pulling her red dress down and retouching her makeup." Grant's finger traced the path of the lipstick. "She's straightening the bed covers, and checking the room, pulling on her jacket." Grant pulled his knees up to his chin and with arms wrapped round tight he rocked and hummed tunelessly.

Hector sat there motionlessly and just watched him. From time to time Grant looked up and took in a little of his surroundings, then rocked again and resumed his humming. Calm descended on him gradually. At first he just touched his chair then ran his fingers slowly through his hair. Finally he wiped his eyes and he looked round the room to get his bearings, the tension just seemed to drain from his face and he seemed relaxed. He looked at Hector and smiled, "Hi."

"Hello Grant. ...You've had quite an exhausting experience."

Grant smiled, his knuckles went white as he tightened his grip on the chair.

"Grant, I want you to just sit there for a moment and breathe."

Grant started to rock again, this time more strongly and his breathing became laboured.

"Come on Grant you must breathe,...you must breathe!"

"I can't breathe... I've got to get..." Grant wheezed and stared round the room like a scared rabbit. He sprang to his feet and raced for the door, swung it open and dashed through into the corridor. He ran down the stairs, two, three sometimes four, even a whole flight in one go. He looked desperate to get out. Hector trailed behind as Grant hit the crash bar at ground level and charge through a fire door onto the street. He ran into the open and came to rest against a railing in a small ornamental garden across the street where he collapsed over a railing. Water pattered down a large stone to his right and bamboo rustled gently in a slight breeze. Hector's footsteps echoed on the pavement and around the courtyard. In the distance a car door slammed, an engine revved up and then a car pulled away from the kerb. Grant took hold of the railings with both hands and pushed himself upright his breathing became more relaxed. He wiped his eyes and cheeks with his fingers and ran his hands through his hair. He took a tissue from his pocket and wiped it across the back of his neck and under his chin, then folded it in half to blow his nose.

Hector approached wearily and gasped, "She's right about your fitness level!" Hector took a few moments to recover but then he spoke in a quiet, calm and even voice.

"You've reached a turning point Grant. It's been a very big step for you and you're probably going to feel a bit rough for a while. Don't worry, that's normal. I want you to go home, relax, have a bath, make yourself a bite to eat and watch some TV or a video. Nothing too challenging just moving pictures to relax by. You've done well, really well!... I'll check my diary and I'll send you a follow up appointment for three or four days from now. In the meantime if you need to talk, this is my card, there's an emergency mobile number on there, just ring. It'll be okay." With that Hector left Grant to gather his thoughts. He felt pretty exhausted himself, he walked slowly back to the clinic and soaked up the sunshine and refreshingly cool breeze.

"What the hell do you think you're doing Hector, I'm not a slab of meat to be tenderized like that!" Lumaii sat at his desk. She'd waited and she was livid. She threw one of his pens over her shoulder and across the room, she strode right up in front of him with her eyes blazing.

"Why did you let it go on so long, you must have realised that he was hurting me?" She pointed a sharp finger at him.

"I had to wait for him! Everything that happened was like a reincarnation of the very thing that caused his problem, I had no choice but to let it go the distance!" barked Hector.

"Well they can go the distance with somebody else next time Hector, I've had enough. I'm not doing these sessions of yours again!" She opened a panel door and retrieved a coat she'd left on a previous visit. She thrust her arms into the sleeves, pulled the collar up at the neck and checked her look in the mirror.

"Now Lumaii, I'll make it up to you."

"No you won't!" she screeched and slammed the door shut. "It's enough. That's enough! He completely lost it in there. He could have stuck a knife in me or anything!" she grabbed her bag.

"But Lumaii listen!"

"No, that's it Hector. Enough!" and she swung the office door open so hard that it crashed into a chair and shuddered to a close behind her.

Hector sat down heavily in his chair and angrily pushed the blotter away from him. From the bottom desk drawer he pulled out a brandy bottle and poured himself a small one in a plain glass beaker.

"For medicinal purposes, this has been one hell of a bloody day!" he toasted the empty room.

Now he'd have to phone Ron. Hector, wished he could sever ties with the villain but he had his uses. This recent thing with Fay...now...He wasn't sure. Grant had turned the corner and it seemed such a shame to lay Fay's demise on him. Maybe he could find a more deserving victim. If only

them badly right from the start? Of course he's nice. The greasy little worm will do anything to get you in his stable!" Her mother's emotions so overwhelmed her that her voice shrank to a hoarse whisper and through tears of pride and anguish she'd pleaded with Sumlea.

"You have done well at the business school and I am so proud of you. Go to England and make something of yourself. It's not forever! But... promise me, you will come back and see me whenever you can. I couldn't bear it if I thought I'd never see you again."

A teardrop fell amid the coffee grounds and Sumlea grabbed a serviette from the glass in the middle of the table. She dabbed below her mascara while she scanned the café for any sign of Lumaii's friends.

Tami had always been very tender, he'd never made any advances, always treated her with respect. But her heart was in her mouth when he put his hand on her waist or simply just glanced the small of her back. He'd given her a small mobile phone charm, a little gold Buddha at their farewell, "I will always be there for you Sumlea, so if you need me, just call." She stroked the charm as it lay on the table and then checked to see if there was a text from him.

She had secretly longed to visit Lumaii but resented the way things had come about. She'd whiled away the weeks before she left Bangkok with daydreams of what England would be like. But now, although she was very happy to be reunited with her sister, England had turned out to be a bit of an anticlimax so far.

Since her arrival on Friday afternoon she had spent much of her time alone in Lumaii's flat, high up above the bay where there were no smells or sounds of life. Today had started really well though, the best by far. Sumlea had got up early to prepare a small surprise breakfast and they had sat and laughed until they were nearly sick about the ridiculous things Lumaii's first boyfriend had done to try and seduce her. Then a trip to town to buy a very expensive dress Lumaii had seen. She wanted to impress an important client.

"Let's hope he doesn't trip over his tongue," giggled Sumlea as they admired the posh carrier and the very small gift wrapped lipstick that sat between them on the taxi ride down to the Crossroads Café.

"I'm going to have to leave you with Zoe and Tina," remarked Lumaii casually, as she watched the landscape change on their journey down town, her mood seemed detached with overtones of sadness.

This café seemed a strange hub around which the lives of Lumaii and her friends revolved. To Sumlea it seemed to be a place where older settled types gravitated when they'd given up the struggle to make something of their lives. Her sister's friends hadn't materialised before Lumaii had to leave. Now the quiet murmur and clatter from the kitchen was overwhelmed by the crashing entrance of three student types still not recovered from a joke of monumental proportions. It was an unwelcome intrusion. They had noisily collapsed into chairs around a window seat and barely managed to avoid eviction by the waitress, much to the contempt of the other customers.

Sumlea turned her gaze to look across the café and out of the other window but she soon became aware that somebody rather smelly stood a little too close for comfort. She turned in curiosity to behold a very grubby and stained T shirt riding up over an enormous hairy belly that billowed over a pair of equally grimy tracksuit bottoms tucked into blackened oily rigger boots. The T shirt hung loosely from the rounded shoulders but was tight on the biceps and the wearer had significant 'man breasts.' He seemed to have no neck. It was more of a continuation of the jaw with stubble. The complete picture of sartorial neglect was punctuated by a small silver stud just underneath his lower lip. With expressionless eyes he gave her that once-over look.

"You are not Lumaii," he said in the voice of somebody with a chronic respiratory condition like a loud whisper.

"No, she go' on business. I think she will come back later, but I do not know time," she replied but tried not to give too much away. Lumaii hadn't explained what she did but Sumlea understood about good customer relations and so her voice was upbeat and she smiled politely.

"She should be with Vick, she's late now and he don't like people being late, he don't like it at all!" he became more agitated. "What time will she be back?" he shifted the weight from one foot to the other and back again.

"I don't know," repeated Sumlea politely, "what is it she does?"

"I can't say," he looked away awkwardly, "But he ain't gonna like this, he's gonna get real mad, he'll make out it's all my fault!"

"Well if typing or filing maybe I can help, I train in Bangkok like Lumaii." She tried not to sound too keen even though she was bored. She didn't want to undermine Lumaii's business but the messenger looked very seedy.

"I don't know about that, I'll have to check with Vick, he don't like strangers at the yard," and with that he turned and headed for the door as he pulled a mobile from his back pocket.

Sumlea watched him pace up and down outside the café window as he talked on the phone. She really hoped that it would end there or better still Lumaii would return. She checked her look in a small mirror from her bag and applied some of the new bright pink lipstick Lumaii had bought for her earlier. Yes, that looks better she thought and tossed the mirror in her bag. He was back and stood right in front of her now, she fiddled nervously with the lipstick under the table.

"Vick says you can come over and help until Lumaii gets back."

"Oh, I see," she felt unsure, she had no idea were Vick worked or what he did and wished that she'd not offered to help at all. Zoe and Tina could turn up any minute and they'd have coffee and a chat about girlie stuff and that would be much better than to go off with this scruffy individual to work for some bad tempered customer that Lumaii had probably tried to get rid of!

"Now then Terry, don't see you in here much these days," said the waitress brightly as she squeezed between him and the next table.

"Vick doesn't let me out much anymore," he smiled and turned back to reassure Sumlea, "don't worry about me, I'm just a mechanic. Vick Whinsper's got a nice office and a coffee machine and a new computer...over there," he pointed passed the launderette towards the open galvanized gates.

Sumlea turned to look in the direction of his gesture and slipped the lipstick into her skirt pocket.

Her first impression of The Whinsper's Empire deteriorated still further as she followed Terry through the gateway and over the gravel car park to the container with the white double-glazed patio door entrance. She hadn't liked the way the fat man sat at the gate, leered at her and muttered under his breath. Once inside they walked behind a high counter and down a corridor with small offices to the right. One was open with paperwork untidily strewn across a desk and the screen saver danced lazily across the monitor. Behind another door she heard a man's muffled voice offer some sort of instructions. To the left they reached a glazed section before the door. She could see a large workshop with a number of parked cars. Terry pointed to the raised bonnet of the black one and said. "That's where I work when I'm not being a gofer." Terry knocked and gestured Sumlea through the open door. "I'll get back to work," he said and left.

"Well now, you're the friend of Lumaii's that's going to help us out are you?" said a balding man from behind a large desk against the opposite wall. Despite its size, the desk, laiden with piles of dog eared manila folders, dirty coffee mugs and paper clutter, did not hide the enormity of the man. She could see now why somebody once wrote "The Fatties" on the fence. The overall impression of the office was one of grubby, imminent collapse. Even the girlie calendar was out of date and hung precariously on a bent paper clip.

"Yes, my name is Sumlea," she replied with a pleasant smile.

"Well, I'm Vick," he paused to study her for a moment. "A lot of oriental names have meanings. What does Somli mean?"

"Sumlea," she said slowly to help his pronunciation. "It means flower."

"Well, Sumlea," she smiled her approval of his effort. "I have some urgent letters I need you to type," he gestured towards the computer on the desk in the corner. "Are you OK with Word?"

"Yes, that will be no problem," she stepped up to the desk and took the folders from his outstretched hand.

"If you go to 'My Documents' you'll find a folder called 'Letters'. Use one of them as a template," he shouted to her across the room.

She settled to type the first letter and wished that she'd chosen a more modest outfit for the day. She had a good, slim figure with a small bust but her skirt was too short for this typing chair and despite her attempts to pull it down to a more respectable length the skirt was determined to ride up high on her thighs.

The letters were very similar in style to the template she'd chosen so within about fifteen minutes they were finished in draft. She spun round enthusiastically on her chair to face Vick and enquired, "Would you like to check them over?"

Chapter 11

It was all so natural but Sumlea had dropped her guard and walked round the desk to read the letter. As she lent forward to get a better view, Vick wrapped an arm round her thighs and his large hand laid a vice like grip on her knee. His shoulder pushed in the small of her back and she fell forwards with her hands on the desk. She supported herself on one hand and tried to turn and push him away but she was out of balance and he was too strong. She crashed down on the table. She struggled to straighten herself but he wrapped his leg around her legs like a snake. When briefly he released the pressure of his shoulder she managed to straighten herself and push her fingernails into his cheeks. But now with both hands free he swivelled her round with ease and slammed her down hard on her back. He wrapped his other leg round her thighs and pulled her diagonally across the desk in front of him where he pinned her down with one hand round her throat. For twenty seconds or so she struggled violently and tried desperately to release his grip but as the oxygen ran out she gradually became still and silent.

Vick felt in control and paused ready to enjoy the moment. He released the grip on her neck slightly and leant back to admire her lean thighs while he used his free hand to slide her skirt slowly up to her waist.

"Oh my what a lovely body you have Sumlea. What lovely pink panties you wear."

She groaned quietly as consciousness returned and he pulled the waistband towards him so he could see her dark pubic hair.

"What a lovely little pussy you have!" and he grinned and giggled like a schoolboy.

"I've got someone I'd like you to meet Sumlea," he smiled. "Would you like to meet my friend, would you Sumlea? .... Ha...Yes of course you would."

He tightened his grip on her throat again making her wince and pulled her up almost to a sitting position. Weak and dazed from the bang on the head she could put up little resistance. He slid his hand under her armpit and across her back. He grabbed the elbow of her other arm, turned her round and pulled her towards him along the table. He wheeled his chair back a little from the table and with his free hand, unzipped his trousers and delved inside. With a great effort he managed to pull out his very small penis.

His erection was only sixty millimetres long despite all the remedies he'd tried over the years and still it had a bright red tip. At school the other boys had teased him mercilessly about his 'lipstick' dick. One day he'd caught one of them and beat him so savagely that the boy had never returned to the school. Vick was excluded indefinitely. Sat on a low wall in the long grass one day near his home he'd been masturbating to pass the lonely hours of the day but when he'd finished Leanne Brewer, another excluded pupil, was stood a short distance from him watching. Rumour was that her mother was on the game and that Leanne would give blowjobs for a fiver. They formed a strange bond, both outcasts, both lonely. They'd meet up for company a few times during the week but Saturday was the day that Vick got his pocket money and with a fiver burning a hole in his pocket he'd meet up with Leanne for his oral delight. Her mother died from bowel cancer and so she had left town to live with an aunty but today Vick was happy, with a new playmate. He pulled her head down towards his penis but Sumlea began to struggle anew. Vick slapped her once and bellowed, "You know what's good for you girl, you give my friend some love or I'll crush you like an ant!" and he slapped her again and again. He squeezed her cheeks together, forced her mouth open and down over his penis. She gave a gurgled scream and cried out so much he couldn't close her mouth. He grabbed one of her arms and twisted it halfway up her back but she screamed even louder and he still couldn't get her to close her mouth on his penis. His erection began to subside with the commotion and his sexual frustration looked set to turn to anger.

He grabbed her by the hair and pushed her to her feet, "Dry your eyes and straighten your clothes!" he bellowed.

She could barely stand with her head twisted to one side in his grip and struggled to pull her skirt down. She tried to stem the tears with shaking fingers, wiped her hands on her top and brushed hair from her cheeks.

"And do something with your face!" he barked.

She felt for the lipstick in her skirt pocket.

"What's that?" he shouted.

"It lipstick, see it's lipstick." She pulled the top off with her teeth. "You like lipstick? Yes, you like lipstick?"

"Lipstick!" he yelled, and propelled her through the air and into a filing cabinet. From its perch behind his desk, Vick brought the window pole down across her nose with a sickening crack. A fragment of bone ricocheted off the ceiling and blood poured down her face. He lunged at her again this time in a stabbing movement that caught her in the middle of the chest with a crack and she hit the floor. He lunged again and again. Her legs flailed about to try to ward off the blows but he caught her once between them which made her squeal in agony. With every lunge he pushed her further away from him until finally he over-balanced and fell on his stomach onto the floor. This brief lull in Vick's attack gave Sumlea the opportunity to claw her way towards the door. Vick lay there and flapped like a beached walrus. His breathing laboured, his eyes bulged with exertion and whilst her progress was painfully slow, Vick got nowhere. He could only lie there and watch her struggle to her knees. Then she crashed headlong into the door and spilled out into the corridor. He watched her gasping for breath and then suddenly she was gone as the door swung closed behind her.

Chapter 12

In the corridor Sumlea found a door handle and pulled herself painfully to her feet. She clutched her arms tight around her ribs, stumbled forwards and gradually gained momentum. At the counter she rested for a moment as blood dripped on her bare arms. Everything looked blurred but she had to keep going, she had to get away. Her hands clutched along the edge of the counter as she pulled herself along to the far side. After another brief pause for breath she let out a cry and launched herself the remaining short distance to the door. Mercifully it slid open under her weight and she collapsed to her knees on the gravel outside.

It was now twilight and the ugly fat man at the gate had gone. Her feet scuffed along and sent showers of gravel in all directions as she tumbled through the gate. The air was cool and it helped revive her but she began to shiver uncontrollably. Her face was numb and the sharp pains that stabbed in her chest and groin made her feel sick. Progress down Kimberly Street was dream like and she gasped at her reflection in the launderette window. The sight of the great gouge in her nose and her top streaked with blood brought fresh tears to her eyes. The main road was thankfully free from traffic. She kept her feet going, going towards the lighted doorway and the sound of the Indian music that came from within. Rakesh had obviously never seen anything like it and as Sumlea stumbled into his open doorway he stood there motionless and mouthed silent words of shock. Sumlea collapsed on the floor with a thud.

Chapter13

Tina's voice was heavily spiced with frustration and relief, "Lumaii, where the bloody hell have you been girl! I've been ringing you for nearly two hours."

"I can't talk now Tina, Sumlea's been taken to hospital, she's had an accident and I've just arrived at the A&E," she waved a tenner at the taxi driver.

"Oh God, I was frightened that something might happen to her," Tina broke down into tears. "I'm sorry Lumaii, I didn't mean to be late but when I heard she'd gone off with Terry …"

"Gone off with Terry? Why would she go off with Ter…"

"There's your change," interrupted the taxi driver.

"Vick was mad with you because you'd missed your appointment."

"Oh shit! Fuck, oh shit!" Lumaii stuck two fingers up at the taxi driver and strode towards the entrance.

"She went over to do some typing for you."

"Typing?"

"I thought you were going to tell her?"

"I couldn't, this morning, I…it just wasn't the right time. She was so happy," the words stuck in her throat as tears filled her eyes. "Look Tina I've got to go!" she said hurriedly and pocketed her phone.

The lights in A&E departments make everybody look ill thought Lumaii. She pushed through the double doors and dried her eyes as she neared the unmanned desk. The red letters travelled across the display screen and spelt out the news 'WAITING TIME IS APPROX.... 1.HOUR.' A tired parent sat and gazed into space while his over indulged progeny tumbled, crashed about and dragged chairs into bizarre configurations in the otherwise deserted waiting room. A cold drink machine in the corner buzzed into life and then a rather indifferent voice addressed her from across the desk.

"Can I help you?" enquired a short, freckled and ginger haired nurse.

"I've come to…. my sister has been brought here in an ambulance."

"What's her name?"

"Sumlea."

"Just a moment," she replied and headed off down a short corridor out of sight.

Damn you Tina why can't you stick to the arrangements just once! Lumaii, stamped her foot and turned to pace the floor. Something had felt strange when the taxi pulled up outside the Crossroads Café. Tina's lights were out and while Lumaii stood there by the taxi and looked up and down the street, there was not a soul about. Only a breeze lifted a lonely page from a newspaper and dragged it along the pavement until it stuck in Frank's fence. Over the engine sound of the taxi she could hear Indian music from

dried blood on her clavicle, I'd say she's been very lucky to have survived a very brutal sexual assault."

"Oh Sumlea, oh no…oh no," she cried.

"I'm afraid she was unconscious when she arrived, so these are just clinical assumptions and we'd have…"

"She's come round!" called the nurse from the open door.

"Oh. Oh," cried Sumlea as Lumaii ran behind the doctor to the bedside.

The nurse put out a reassuring hand but Sumlea stretched out past her and clutched Lumaii's hand tight.

Sumlea's eyes bulged in an effort to speak through split and swollen lips.

Lumaii lent close to her face to hear her say, "bick, …bick"

And as she straightened slowly she saw Sumlea nodding, "bick..bick" and she slipped back into unconsciousness.

"I'm afraid you'll have to let us …" the doctor's words tailed off as he turned to find that Lumaii had gone.

The corridor had become much busier now but the sounds and voices seemed far away. Everybody else seemed to move too slowly and she crashed open the Ladies toilet door. Stood with the rim of the wash basin clutched tight in her hands Lumaii looked up into the mirror. She breathed heavily and her eyes were wide and cold. Her mascara had run and her hair was down on one side. She needed a plan, and searched the reflection for inspiration. If she waited too long he'd know she'd found out and she'd have missed her chance, she'd never be able to get near him again. She tore off some toilet tissue and set about repairing her appearance. "It's amazing what a bit of lippy and mascara can do!" She addressed the mirror but there was no humour in her voice as she fought back the tears. She turned both ways to see if her dress was creased at the back. Worth every penny! And she slipped on her coat and picked up her small handbag. She faced the door and took a large breath of air, turned the handle and stepped into the corridor again. Focussed on her thoughts and what was to come she felt a great calmness wash over her as the cool evening air kissed her cheeks.

Kimberley Street was deserted now that her taxi had left. Rakesh had shut up shop and her heels echoed emptily as she passed the galvanized fence. The gates were still open and a shaft of light from the office reception raised her hopes that Vick was still there. The door slid quietly open and as she passed the counter she noticed some small damp patches dotted on the floor and along the corridor. Somebody had been cleaning up, she could smell the cleaning fluid. A small light was on in the workshop but no one was in sight. There was movement behind the door, she could see the shadows and hear anxious voices.

"Stop fussing will you, I'll be alright," said Vick irritably.

"I've just got one or two things to sort out, give me a bell when you're ready to go," replied a voice she didn't recognise.

"Ok thanks Ron," and a door somewhere in the office closed.

She waited two full minutes and listened for Vick to settle himself. At this time of night he'd probably log onto one of his porn webcam sites so she wanted to give him time to get in the mood. For this to work, for her to avenge her sister, Lumaii would have to focus every tissue in her body and detach herself completely from her actions. One overplayed gesture or any hint of over eagerness and Vick would know. Big as he was, like the animal he was, he had an instinct for danger and she would be dangerously close. Her survival depended upon her complete calm. Lumaii clenched her fists tight as she took one last deep breath. She turned the handle quietly, stepped into the room and dropped her bag on a box by the door. She'd walked almost up to the front of his desk before Vick looked away from his monitor and greeted her coolly.

"You're late!" he barked, "nearly four fucking hours late!"

"I'm sorry Vick," she said quietly with a bit of a pout and turned her back to him. She slipped her coat off at her shoulders and stood there motionlessly as it slipped slowly to the floor.

"I've come here specially to make it up to you."

She turned half way round so that he could see her in profile and lent back slightly on her hip to make the most of the way the cut of the dress exaggerated her bust.

"I can't make it up to you properly if I think you're still mad with me Vick."

She walked slowly round the desk towards him and touched the back of her hair with her finger tips. She reached his chair, sat on the edge of his desk and toyed with the strap of her dress.

"You made me very angry Lumaii …..I do bad things when I'm angry." He had the voice of a man but his tone and facial expressions were those of a child who'd just been found out. He wanted sympathy and forgiveness.

"It looks like I'm going to need some space here to make this one up Vick, push your chair back a bit."

Still weak from his exertions earlier he struggled to get enough purchase with his toes to move the chair back but in short bursts, gradually he managed to move it to where his knees were clear of the desk. He looked quite exhausted. Lumaii placed her right foot between his legs and rested the toe of her high heeled shoe on the edge of the seat. She then brought her other leg alongside but rested it lower, against the inside of his thigh. He put his hand on her ankle and caressed her shin gently. Lumaii began very slowly to pull the skirt of her dress back towards her and Vick sat there mesmerised as the hem slid up her long slender thighs. She watched him intently waiting for that special moment when a man first sees the thing that turns him on the most. Lumaii had a real gift for timing and she went through all the moves like a highly trained ballet dancer. Poise and balance, gesture and expression were carefully choreographed to convey her sexual arousal due to the presence of her client. Vick would feel that she couldn't suppress desire for him and that her body had ripened in anticipation of every erotic pleasure he could imagine.

There it was, right on cue Vick's eyes stared wide, his pupils went very dark and he stopped breathing. "Oh Vick I love to do this for you," she sighed.

"Oh,.." He croaked, as if struggling for air, "I love you doing it too."

She slid her dress back almost to her waist exposing her dark pubic hair to his gaze and moved her foot from between his legs and rested it on his knee. As she opened her legs a little wider she lent back with her elbows on the desk and stared straight at him with warm sultry eyes and her raised leg swayed slightly. "Do you like my pussy Vick?" she whispered.

"Oh yes Lumaii...yes, it's the very best," he gasped.

She threw her head backwards and rocked it from side to side several times. Then she raised her head again, dropped one of her shoulders slightly and rested her head against her raised shoulder. "I need to see your friend Vick," she whispered from under her tousled hair, "I need to see him right now."

Vick fingers trembled as he struggled with his fly zipper and pulled out into the light his little erect penis.

"I need to see it properly Vick!"

With one hand Vick tried to hold back the folds of his flabby belly whilst the other strained to make the fly opening wider.

She slithered off the desk and twisted her skirt behind her and sank slowly to the floor on her knees. Lumaii ran her open hands along the inside of his thighs, reached out to pull his foreskin down and gently took the bright red end of his penis in her mouth. Vick watched as her head and shoulders moved rhythmically and he made involuntary moans and shudders as Lumaii worked her magic. She paused briefly to look up at him and smiled. "Is it good Vick?" she asked, sitting back on her haunches as if to admire his manhood. But now she caught sight of something which sent a chill right through her body and made her kneel up. There, below the drawers of Vick's desk, stood an old dusty fan heater which she'd seen on previous visits. Impaled in the grill was the bright pink lipstick she'd bought Sumlea earlier.

To this point Lumaii had kept it together, she was on automatic pilot and she knew exactly what Vick liked and how to sweet talk him. But the sight of the lipstick was a cruel reminder, she hadn't foreseen this, she couldn't possibly have known, the evil bastard! The tears welled up inside her and she lent forward, cupped her hand to her mouth, trying to contain the emotions before they broke through her defences.

"Oh , it's the best my little Lumaii," moaned Vick, "are you okay?"

"Yes, yes it's just a hair Vick, just one of my hairs…Now I hope you're ready for this?" she tried hard to channel her grief into anger.

"Yes," he whispered.

"Are you ready for this?" she cried out as her adrenalin began to pump.

"Yes," he shouted.

"I want every last drop Vick, every last drop!" this was the spur she needed and she gripped the base of his seat tight.

"I'm gonna give it to you, I'm gonna give it to you ," his voice had reached a crescendo.

"Oh yes,.. oh yes," she rocked backwards and forwards on her haunches and lunged forward with her teeth bared.

Lumaii heard a door crash open somewhere to her left and foot steps approached quickly. The voice she'd heard earlier was now anxious and breathlessly screamed, "She's the girl's sister, the girl's sister......the one from before!"

It was too late Vick let out an ear-piercing scream as Lumaii clenched her teeth hard round his penis. She screamed through clenched teeth in disgust as she tasted his blood gurgling in her mouth, her rage filled every ounce of her body. She shook and tugged at it with all her might like a dog with a rat. She ground her teeth to gnaw though sinew and flesh. She would never let go. She spat blood wildly from the side of her mouth where it ran down her neck and dripped onto the floor. Vick's frantic attempts to pull her head away only increased his agony but Ron came to his aid and drove a large screwdriver down through Lumaii's back with a sickening 'pop smack!' As he tried to retrieve it Lumaii's knees came off the ground and she screamed even louder but wouldn't let go. Vick let out another ear deafening scream and in desperation Ron plunged the screwdriver down into her back again and then hurled it across the room. He grabbed Lumaii's limp body and launched it at the filing cabinet. Lumaii lay there as her life quickly ebbed away, blood and tears ran down her chin. She watched Ron try to help Vick as he cried and shook uncontrollably while his blood made a puddle on the rug. Lumaii swallowed hard and as she felt the lump that had once been Vick's penis make its way down into her stomach she thought of Sumlea's happy face that morning and slipped quietly into oblivion.

Chapter 14

"Good morning sir."

"Morning Brian, got the fencing panel off okay then?"

"Yeah, it's all a bit rusty though. At one point we thought the whole lot was going to come down," grinned PC Brian Makins.

"Whinsper's would just have loved that. Still if they're going to smear blood all over the main entrance they'll have to live with a hole in their fence. We're going to have to find a way to secure that though, for the next couple of days at least." Cosey frowned, would a couple of days be enough to get to the bottom of the case? He made his way between the tapes of the common approach path as it curved round through the back of the Whinspers yard and in across the workshop to the bottom of the metal staircase. Cosey stopped briefly on the landing to survey the workshop. It all looked much the same as it had on his last visit all bar the absence of the big red truck and so he headed on along the short corridor that led to the back door of Vick's office.

"Now then Phil, you finished already?" he asked cheekily. Their partnership went a long way back and Phil looked a lot better now than he had at 7.00am that morning at their initial briefing. Cosey always liked to get him in right at the beginning so that he wouldn't make any mistakes in the way he managed the crime scene.

"I actually finished about ten minutes ago," smiled Phil, "well maybe it was only five."

"Oh yes!" chuckled Cosey, "so what's this you've got for me then?"

"Right, well earlier when we discussed this, we felt that Vick's initial attack happened here," Phil pointed at the blood stained carpet tiles in front of the chair, "and then he was dragged out that way to the front door."

"Right."

"Well there's a splatter pattern on this filing cabinet drawer and I've left it open so you can see here," he pointed. "The pattern continues over those front files there."

"Oh yes," Cosey bent down to take a closer look.

"Somebody's been cleaning up these cabinets, I mean you can smell the bleach even now, but they missed this and they shut the drawer as well."

"Right, I see what you mean."

"I can't be sure exactly how far the drawer was out at the time of the splatter but going by the angle it must have come from somewhere about here, say," Phil pointed at the join between four tiles about two feet in front of Vick's blood stain.

"You think our mystery assailant might have been injured in the attack then?"

"Well I'll know more in a couple of days when the DNA comes back that is unless you want to push it through?"

"No, we'll see how things go," Cosey was thoughtful, somebody was bound to mention the cost.

"I've taken at least thirty samples all the way to the chair outside so I think it's pretty well covered but just in case you're not thinking of........."

"No, I'll keep it closed off for a couple of days at least. I might let them get back in downstairs after that unless you come up with anything."

Phil nodded his head in approval.

"Any sign of Vick's penis then," Cosey couldn't help but smile.

"No, we've been all over this room, not a sausage!" grinned Phil.

"Now, you should have more respect for the dead, even if he was a villain."

"That's nothing to some of the witty banter out here today," smiled Phil as they walked between the tapes back toward the hole in the fence.

"Fine, well I'll catch you later then." With a glint in his eye Phil waved and shook his head.

"Keep in touch."

Now he felt some breakfast was in order. Somehow the balance had been restored but he caught sight of his white outfit. Better get this lot off first, footplates and all he smiled.

Chapter 15

Ron sat in the taxi where Kimberley Street narrowed, on the other side of the viaduct. He just needed to get his head straight before the drive home. He peered round the policeman stood in front of the tapes trailed across the arches and watched Cosey walk up the street in his distinctive parka. Ron finished off the take out coffee, clicked the lid back on and discarded it in the passenger side foot well. It had helped. It wasn't the crap from the Crossroads mind, he'd driven into town and bought a Nero Cappuccino. But things would never be the same, he'd never feel the same. Granted Vick had been reckless and fair do's, he'd paid the price but Ron knew he shouldn't have lost his cool like that. It had never happened before. Ron had always managed to be the one to stay calm in a crisis but last night ... he shook his head. Last night he'd been a headless chicken and then some. If they'd just moved the Thai bitch somewhere out of sight until later and cleaned up, then they could have called the ambulance and maybe Vick would still be alive. It was a terrible choice to have to make, whose need was greater? The time, where did it go? And those medics, they were next to bloody useless, Ron's hands gripped the steering wheel tight, his eyes stared wide with tears. It was Terry's idea to put him on a board and drag him to the ambulance...

"You grab the other side," shouted Terry to the copper.

"What are you thinking?" replied the copper.

"We can roll him off the chair onto the board and between us we can drag him,"

"Good idea, do you think the boards strong enough?" "Don't know, just have to see! Ron, Ron come on, Ron! Help us to get him over," shouted Terry.

"Vick I'm sorry, Vick," cried Ron as he clutched Vick's hand tight.

"Ron! ... Ron, look at me you've got to help!" screamed Terry.

"His pulse is very weak," shouted the paramedic.

"Ron, lift!"

"Come on feller," urged the copper, "big strong feller like you!"

Ron and Terry grabbed a shoulder each and with a hand under each armpit they managed to twist Vick halfway round in the chair.

"Once more Ron," shouted Terry, "one, two, three lift…"

They all fell in a heap but Vick was off the chair and onto his side. The paramedic pushed them to one side, checked Vick's pulse and pulled his eye lid open, "he's deteriorating, we've not much time."

Everybody grabbed a piece of Vick and pulled to get him on the board. As it was his feet hung over the edge. They lifted the end nearest his head and pulled in the direction of the gate as Vick's heels left a trail in the gravel chippings. On the road the board was even harder to move but it wasn't far and they managed to prop it against the back of the ambulance between the open doors. Everybody let out a sigh of relief. Vick suddenly slid down to the ground, his knees bent, head and arms forward. The medic stuffed his fingers between Vicks' shoulder and neck.

"There's no pulse, get him on his back!"

Everybody grabbed something and rolled Vick over onto his back in the road. The female paramedic split Vick's T shirt in an instant and shouted, "Get back!"

Ron closed his eyes, even now he could hear her voice count it down over and over and over again. "Vick I'm so sorry," he rested his head on his hands and cried. The tears ran down his face and dripped off the steering wheel and down onto his black jeans.

Chapter 16

Cosey always felt a bit smug when a villain got their just deserts and what better way to celebrate than with a Crossroads Café All Day Breakfast. To cap it all, it was a nice sunny morning and he strode purposefully across the street, hands in his pockets while his parka billowed out behind him. He wished he still had the Lambretta, could have gone for a blast up the coast.

"Good God, Diane!. Its bin…what are you doing here?" he stopped dead in his tracks on the corner.

"Levi, how nice to see you!" smiled a slim woman with fair hair.

"It's so nice to see you, how long…"

"Oh don't, you'll make me feel old!"

"Old! Don't be daft, you look marvellous," he beamed, but he sensed there was some sadness there. Come to think of it, it had been there the last time he saw her, on the day she left.

"What brings you down here?" asked Diane.

"…Erh," he realised that he'd been staring at her, "I've got an investigation going on over there," he gestured, "and I was going to get a breakfast," damn, he'd probably had his mouth open as well! "Do you want to join me?"

"Well, yes that'll be nice. I don't know about the breakfast exactly, but a coffee'll be…nice,"

"No that's fine thanks."

"Blimey Levi, I hope you're hungry! ... Can I have a bit of your toast?" Diane asked with a finger crooked in under her lip.

"You've got a nerve, after all I've been through to get it! Yes help yourself, do you want some marmalade?"

"Um please, I feel quite... um peckish after all," there were crumbs on her cheek.

"Now then Girl, how you doing?" bellowed a husky, deep voice from behind him. "Is he undercover? It's a good disguise," she laughed and gave Cosey a punch in the shoulder and he nearly punctured the roof of his mouth with the fork.

"That's pretty close to assault," winced Cosey.

"That ain't assault. A salt is what's in the cruet!" she gestured to the middle of the table. "Call yourself a policeman, you don't know shit!" she wheezed a giggle and dismissed him with a wave of her hand. Now he felt like an intruder, he'd missed his opportunity with Diane just like old times! Tina was a flamboyant woman, always larger than life and she would dominate the conversation once she got into the girl talk routine.

"Is this still a good spot?" he gestured with his eyes and a raised eyebrow. It was the best he could do at short notice.

"A good spot?" she mimicked him. "Why, you thinking of changing your career?" she laughed.

Diane smiled more politely.

"Well you've stayed, haven't you, in the area....?" he gestured with the remains of his toast.

"Yes, I like the people round here, it's quite Cosy!" she laughed, Diane laughed, finally, Cosey laughed.

"I guess I asked for that," Cosey bit into his last piece of toast.

"You haven't changed much, you're still a bit too serious for me. You come because of the...?" she nodded in the direction of the Whinsper's place.

"Yeah."

"Serves him bloody right and good riddance!"

"What do you mean by that?" It wasn't quite a rhetorical question, there were a lot of unanswered questions about the Whinspers and everybody had different pieces of the puzzle.

"They're the kind of low life that gives the place a bad name," she spoke in more of a whisper.

"I see." He was about to try and tease a bit more detail when he realised that her flamboyance had vanished.

"They don't have any respect," Tina seemed on the point of tears.

Diane reached over and gripped her hand. "Have you heard anything?" she asked.

"No, I wanted to go and see her but I thought to check with Lumaii and make sure it was okay, but I keep getting her voice mail."

"Maybe she's at the hospital, she'll have her phone switched off. You know what it's like?"

"Yes, I suppose."

"Look, why don't we go to the hospital?" suggested Diane brightly, "we can talk on the way. I've got my car, it won't take long..."

"Yes that's true…Diane, do you mind?" Tina sounded quite relieved.

"No, of course not!"

"I'd feel so much better if I knew. I feel so responsible."

"It'll be just fine!"

"Look, I'll just nip upstairs love and I'll be back in a minute," she stood up and blew her nose on one of the serviettes.

"Okay," Diane gave her a comforting smile but too late, Tina was half way out the door.

"I'm going to have to go, Levi, I'm sorry."

"That's alright, Tina looks a bit shaken up."

"One of the girls got beaten up the other night and I think Tina was supposed to be watching out for her."

"Blimey, no wonder. Where did this happen?"

Diane just raised an eyebrow.

"She wouldn't happen to be a Thai girl would she?"

"I don't know, I've never met her. I don't think she's been around for long."

"Are you going to be around for long?" Cosey knew his time had all but run out.

"Just till next weekend…Oh, there's Tina, I'll have to go," she got to her feet.

"It's been nice seeing you again Diane." Cosey got to his feet and looked into her eyes for anything, just a little glimmer.

"Yes it has," there was a smile in her eyes, yes!

Diane caught sight of Tina and the sadness returned.

"Maybe we could…?" But it was too late, Diane had passed him and the words just faded away. Damn, he never seemed to get it right, there's always something! He surveyed the debris on the table, picked up his bill and dejectedly handed it over at the counter. He'd probably never see her again, not even a bloody phone number!

"That's £8.50," the voice had mellowed. He handed over a tenner. Bloody hell! It had been such a great day up until then. He took the receipt, dropped some of the change absent-mindedly in the tip dish and stepped out onto the pavement. At least the sun was still shining but he felt quite deflated now. One of the forensic vans was still there but the tape cordon across the road had been removed. He headed towards his car parked near the two remaining coppers who'd just finished securing the hole in the fence at the Whinsper's. He glanced down at the receipt still in his hand. 'Sumlea → Terry' was printed on it in biro. It took a lot of self control, not to look back at the waitress because Terry was also in the café having arrived only a couple of minutes after Cosey and Diane had sat down.

"What's the news on the girl?" asked Cosey.

Kalum had answered his mobile almost immediately, "She looks pretty rough, couldn't get much out of her. Face is still very swollen and she's obviously still very frightened."

"Did she have any other visitors?"

"Not since last night, her sister turned up shortly after they admitted her. When Sumlea came round briefly, she said something to her sister that made her run off like a shot."

"What's the sister's name?"

"Lu..m..aii"

"Lumaii?"

"Yes"

"Have you left somebody there?"

"Yes, Scottie's there, she's just come on duty as well, so we'll have some continuity."

"Any news on Fay as yet?"

"No nothing, how about you?"

"I'm not sure, something's just come up. Did you check her mobile data base for appointments?

"No joy, maybe she still preferred an old fashioned diary."

"Maybe she prefers Outlook, do we know where she works?"

"Yes, it's an advertising agency in York. I'll try the flatmate, see if Fay uses a laptop, it may be at home. Failing that I could try and take a peek on her PC at work, maybe I'll come up with something."

"Right, speak to you later."

Cosey came to a halt in front of the bright red tow truck now parked on the road not far from the yard. There were trickles of water on the road below it and traces on the body work to show the truck had recently been washed but not where it stood. There was still heat coming from the radiator and as he walked around to give it the once over there were occasional creaks of cooling metal. It must have been some distance. If Terry drove it, then it would have been there about thirty minutes. Now somebody's been a bit careless, they've scratched the wing, nearside, low down, tiny bit of a different colour in there and that's low enough to have been a car. He wondered if…?

"Now then Mr Cosey."

"Been for a drive today have we?" he had no need to look up, Cosey recognised the unmistakeable wheeze of Terry's voice.

"Yes, bit of a late job. Got a call out to a lorry …ended up towing him back to Liverpool."

"Busy night for you then!"

"Yes, one way and another."

"Bet that will have cost a bit then?"

"I expect so. Ron doesn't do anything for free." Terry's voice was smooth and even but his eyes were alert and followed Cosey's gaze closely.

"Shame about Vick." Cosey watched Terry's eyes for a reaction.

"I didn't realise you were a fan, Mr Cosey!"

"I'm not, but I bet he never expected to go like that."

"No, I guess not."

"What time did you set out?"

"Oh, late about 10.00pm."

"What time did you get back?"

"Well, I stopped off at the jet wash about 9.30am. Then I parked up here and went for a breakfast at the café. You were there anyway."

"You don't sound sure, you just said both?"

"It was .."

"Raining, yes I know!"

"I may have seen a taxi, I can't be sure!"

"Okay, I want you to write your address in my book if you don't mind," he offered him the pen, "and a contact phone number as well please."

He retrieved the pen being careful not to touch where Terry had gripped it and walked over to the last of Phil's forensic team, who'd just packed a case in the back of his van. With his back to Terry, Cosey deposited the pen in a specimen bag he'd lifted from the back of the van and whispered to the officer. He then walked back past Terry who tidied a tow rope and round to the other side of the truck nearest the old Plaza.

"Do you go in the café quite regularly Terry?" he kept his voice fairly quiet purposely in the hope that Terry would be drawn to follow him.

"Not so much these days," wheezed Terry as he stepped around the back of the truck to look at Cosey.

"I was hoping to find Sumlea," there was that tell tale eye movement again, "She's a Thai girl. Don't suppose you've seen her?"

"Well I've seen a couple in there but don't know them by name."

Oh yes he bloody well had. So what is the connection the waitress made? Couldn't say he blamed her being a bit careful, they were an evil bunch of thugs.

"Well if you do happen to see one of them you will give me a bell, won't you?"

"Yes, sure Mr Cosey, I like to do my bit to help the local police," he smiled benignly.

Greasy little git thought Cosy and he stepped round the front of the truck slowly in the hope that Phil's buddy had got the sample of paint he needed testing from the other wing. A raised eyebrow was enough to indicate that the deed was done and Cosey crossed the road to his car.

Chapter 17

One day soon he'd wake up and the sun would cast bright patterns on the floor while the curtains swayed in a warm breeze. Outside a humble bee would noisily inspect his window ledge while a distant small plane completed its monthly circuit routine and then head for the airfield. Mrs Faith's dog would pant heavily as they crunched along the gravel path together at the end of an early morning walk. He'd look at the clock, it would be 9am, the weekend would have begun and he'd just roll onto his back and savour that moment of bliss.

Grant opened his eyes, it hadn't looked very promising but it was very warm and stuffy. He leant out of bed, rested on one arm and with an outstretched hand tried to catch the corner of the curtain and see what was happening outside today. It just tantalisingly eluded his grasp. The skin under his arm began to burn as he stretched it beyond its normal limits but then he lost balance and slid onto the floor with a thump.

"Oh." was the best he could manage, weak though it was, nevertheless it was a response. Maybe he should just stay here...no he was hungry ... and he needed a pee. To untangle himself from the duvet was more difficult than he could possibly have imagined. Finally he stood there triumphantly over it like a gladiator, his boxers swivelled round for all to see that his penis had shrunk to the size of a maggot in the night. Thank God he was alone. That would have been just too…

"Oh it's not a bad day after all," he announced to the empty room as he finally made contact with the curtains. Sun's out, bloody windows shut, no wonder it's so warm in here! He opened the window to an audible puff as the hot air escaped into the open and took a welcome breath of fresh air.

"And it was good!" he announced and stepped over the duvet to swivel his boxers back into position. En-route to the kitchen to put on the kettle at a gallop, he made a hurried pit stop then rushed downstairs to retrieve the mail. The tea and toast were adequate and he opened the mail, but left the large brown envelope and package 'til last. First was the energy bill, second his appointment with Katychmar, that hadn't taken long. He could tell by the size and shape of the package that it was a DVD and sure enough Trudi had finally arrived. Oversized breasts squeezed into an undersized bra and lips that pouted tackily, they all looked the same but the slogan boasted 'Toys, Toys, Toys.' Well that was simple and certainly to the point. The brown paper packet, that would be one of his monthly magazines. A cut above the average top shelf variety at the petrol station! He sighed, flicked through the pages and stopped at a picture of an oriental girl in red suede boots laid on her back. Her legs wide open, she sucked on the tip of her finger. The mood changed and feelings of guilt invaded his thoughts, when he remembered the girl in the lift the day before. He laid the magazine down on the table, scowled at it, then pushed it away and pulled out Katychmar's letter from beneath. The words were familiar and Katychmar's voice echoed in his head, every phrase evoked its own memory against the background patter of the waterfall in the garden.

"You've had an exhausting experience," … sun glistened on the water.

"You've reached a turning point Grant," …wind rustled in the bamboo.

"It's been a very big step for you," … gravel crunched underfoot.

"You're probably going to feel a bit rough for a while," … street busy with traffic.

"Don't worry that's normal."

"Where to mate?" The taxi driver had asked.

"Erm… Erm I can't …. I can't …Karis Court," he hadn't been able to think….

"Is that on Lemont Avenue?"

"Ye…s, yes it is."

He hadn't remembered the ride, just bright sunlight to the sound of the taxi driver's chatter.

"Watch something on TV, nothing too challenging, just moving pictures, try to relax….."

The TV was too loud and frantic, even the wild life DVD was too much effort and he'd just crashed out. He must have slept well because he felt pretty alive a few minutes ago. Now, well now, he still felt rested but calmer, not as hyper, more focused.

Katychmar wasn't a bad bloke after all, he'd been very understanding. Grant felt that probably for the first time in a long, long time he'd actually connected with somebody. He'd found the words, actually been able to describe things, feelings that he knew were there but had never before been in focus long enough to describe.

"Get off me you fucking maniac!" her pretty mouth spat the words at him angrily. The memory made him jump. It had just careered into his consciousness and he grabbed the bar with trembling hands to steady himself.

"Shit! What the hell was I doing?" he whispered. He saw the girl in the magazine and pushed it away. Around the kitchen there were three more similar magazines in a neat pile on top of the tall freezer and he grimaced. He needed some air and steadied himself along the worktops, made his way to the lounge and slid down on the sofa. In neat piles to both sides of the TV were DVD's of Trudi's peers. Opened and carelessly discarded was the 'Big Cats in Africa' DVD that last night had failed to satisfy. Everywhere he looked there seemed to be some hint of his affliction and that is what it was, he never gained any lasting pleasure or relief from any of it, he scowled at the carpet. When he got feelings of guilt about it all, he'd simply change the video or look at a different magazine until the mood passed but the background loneliness never went away. He had pictures of almost every type of girl imaginable and a folder in which he'd collected the best of the lot. Since late teens and despite a number of close calls he'd always managed to talk himself out of the desire to throw it away.

Grant rubbed his face with his hands and pushed the hair back. If you wanted something to change...You have to change something! You're on your own with it, just yourself...and yourself. The thing had just fucked up every bloody thing! And now Fay, shit! What the hell had happened to her? If it wasn't for him, it wouldn't have happened. Well, maybe not so hasty, she had organised it. No she'd done it for him! He grimaced and held up his hands. They may not have gone the distance but now she

"Er yes … Is there any news of Fay?" asked Grant. He backed down the hall and gestured for Cosey to go into the lounge. If it had been Fay he'd have been pleased to see her but once the relief had past he'd have been mad due to the predicament she'd put him in and now more bloody questions!

"No I'm afraid not," Cosey surveyed the room.

"For one moment back then I thought it was Fay … knocking on the door."

"I see. …No I'm afraid it's only me. I've been talking to your friend Leslie."

"Leslie?… ah, Leslie's not my friend."

"No, I didn't think so. Do you think she resented your intrusion?"

"What with Fay you mean?"

"Yeah, they'd been a happy couple and then you come along and spoil it all!"

"Fay isn't gay!"

"And, Leslie?"

"I don't think so. I never gave it a thought, they were more like sisters I'd say."

"Did you ever stay there?"

"At Fay's?"

"At Leslie's?"

"Yes, I….used to stay quite often, Leslie went away a fair bit…That is until recently, we fell out. I'd ….Well I was having second thoughts really, things had been so different since we came back off holiday, we just didn't seem to be able to get it back on a even keel. Then Fay's therapist came up with this idea and well you know the rest."

"Who was her therapist?"

"I don't know actually, I never thought to ask."

"Why was she seeing a therapist anyway?"

"We were … like I said not hitting it off and she thought it might help."

"Didn't she take to all the pornography then?" Cosey nodded towards the over spilling box.

"She didn't mind really I don't think. Maybe I got a little carried away with it lately," he smiled as Cosey lifted a newspaper to reveal another pile of magazines he'd forgotten about. Bloody hell they were everywhere!

"You seem to have more than just a passing interest I'd say. I mean you've got four different mags here and they're all this month's issue, then underneath you've got …well you've got the previous months issues as well and…the month before that and so on, you must have, what twenty mags here not to mention the stack in the box at the door."

"Yes, well…"

"Then there are the DVD's." Grant followed Cosey back through to the front door where he lifted the corner of the box. "There's at least fifteen, twenty even in there, I'm no therapist but I'd say you've got a bit of an obsession. Ever thought of a bit of therapy yourself?"

He began to worry again, things looked about to become serious. He'd asked his girlfriend to …no he'd agreed to go along with his girlfriend's idea. That was one thing but this could make him look …Cosey would think he was some kind of weirdo. If he told him about the clinic it would be all he needed to stitch him up. He'd think that when he'd met Fay things got out of hand and he'd faked a disappearance to cover his tracks. Oh shit! That was exactly what he'd been afraid of all the way through. From the moment those two coppers turned up, he knew that sooner or later something would happen. If he were to tell all he'd... well he'd know ... nothing. Why hadn't he seen it before? Grant began to feel a little easier. Even if Cosey were to stumble across something, Katychmar wouldn't say anything because he was a patient ...but the thing in the lift. Damn, that could look really bad, even Katychmar might think he'd flipped and want to spill the beans in the interest of public safety or something.

"Mr Reid?"

"Yes…..yes I had thought about it, in fact Fay suggested it as well but I decided to do something about it myself, you know a bit of self help!"

"How's it going?"

"Well as you can see I'm removing the temptations," he gestured to the box.

"Did you discuss this rendezvous of yours with anyone else?"

"No, I didn't discuss it with anybody."

"Did you write any of it down, you know, left it on your desk at work and …."

"No I didn't write anything down at all."

"Did Fay discuss it with anybody?"

"No… Well she may have discussed it with Leslie I suppose but she certainly had to discuss it with her therapist once she'd made the arrangements with me."

"Why was that?"

"Not sure really, she mentioned something about the need to approach it in the right frame of mind if it was to work properly or something like that."

"So this was part of her treatment then?"

"Yes I guess so."

Cosey pondered for a while then turned to the door, twisted the handle and asked, "The taxi you saw that night, when did it leave. Before or after you saw Fay?"

"Oh, quite a while before, in fact it left almost as soon as I got there."

"Did you see any other traffic?"

"Apart from the lorry which I've already mentioned, no the road was deserted. Once the lorry had left the only vehicle I saw was the police car."

"Thank you Mr Reid, I'll be in touch." Cosey had almost closed the door behind him when he asked, "I'd like to have one of our forensics chaps take a look at the scrape you had with the lorry. Sooner rather that later will be best, so he'll give you a call to arrange a time … you'll have to be present."

Grant felt the need to ask a last minute question as well, a question that had been rumbling around in the back of his mind for almost a week.

"How does this sort of thing pan out Mr….DCI Cosey?"

"In what respect?"

"A missing person."

"Her details are filed on the system and cross referenced against anybody who turns up, you know …wandering the streets with amnesia or admitted to hospital. They're also

concourse of the shopping centre. The sandwich shop was busy so he looked over the balcony to the level below. Maybe the one by the lights will be better? He couldn't be bothered to queue today.

"So you decided on the blonde girl in the end did you?"

The voice sounded familiar and he turned but there was nobody behind him so he turned back to look over the balcony. Stupid really it was at least twenty feet to the floor below. Then he looked up, well there could have been a balcony above or something, he thought.

"It's no use pretending you haven't heard me!"

As he turned in the direction of the voice the truth dawned on him. He grinned that inept grin, the one used when all around but you could see the obvious.

.

There sat alone at a terrace table over the brass railing to his left was Violet. She sipped a large Cappuccino, glasses perched on her forehead and that insolent, smug little smile of hers beamed from ear to ear.

"The blonde is my sister actually," he replied with dignity.

"Ha…ha," she laughed and promptly caught the coffee drips from her chin with the fingers of her free hand and plonked the cup down. With the other hand she rifled the dispenser on the side of the table for a serviette.

"And you have been a private investigator for how long?" enquired Grant with an air of disdain.

"Years, I'm working under cover!"

"How long have you been here?"

"Long enough!"

"Are you stalking me?"

"Don't you kid yourself. You're not the only one who buys titillating boys magazines."

"Oh really, and what demographic do I represent?"

"The seedy boy racer in faded denim jeans and white trainers, who wears his baseball hat backwards on weekends, demographic!"

"Oh, and where in all this do your preferences lie?"

"I prefer an older man, wearing a raincoat with big inner pockets. He crams them full of girlie mags to save on carriers and everybody thinks he's disabled but in truth it's the weight of all the magazines weighing him down."

"Is the coffee any good?"

"No it's horrible, I feel quite sick!"

"What about the sandwiches?"

"Do you like cheese?"

"Not particularly."

"They're all cheese."

"It's not a Vegi place is it?"

"No they also do a line in dead animal ciabattas!"

"Well I think I'll join you."

"You'll have to wait in the queue," she gestured to the empty space beside her.

"I don't mind, do you want anything else?"

"No, I'm okay thank you," she smiled.

Grant made his way round the railings and down a short flight of stairs to the counter. Blimey, she was a feisty one!

He'd barely spoken to her since she joined the company nearly a year ago but he'd lusted after her since the moment he first clapped eyes on her. The opportunity to strike up a conversation had never presented itself even at the Christmas party when he'd hung around about her a lot. Now, here, in less than three minutes they were firing on all cylinders. He balanced his tea and ciabatta rather awkwardly but reached her table intact as she moved her bag to let him sit down.

"So do you have an eating disorder or are you naturally skinny?" he asked in a bland tone.

"Yes," she laughed, "You really ought to close your mouth when you watch me walk about the office it makes you look vaguely senile when you dribble."

"Are you usually so forthright?"

"Yes, but most people take the hint, you must be a bit dense!"

"You started this conversation."

"Well actually I was just thinking aloud and you gate crashed."

"What time are you due back at the office?"

"That's a mute point given that the 'Pro Food' campaign has had me working all the hours known to man this week."

"Me too!"

"I thought I might go and browse round the shops and then go home, have a bath and pog out in front of the telly as a matter of fact."

"You finished then?"

"Yes, about nine thirty this morning," she said with a smug grin.

"Bloody hell!"

"Well I was in at quarter to seven this morning."

"I didn't know the place was open that early."

"They're open all the time if you know the right person to talk to."

"Yes, and a short skirt makes all the difference."

She smiled. "Have you still got a lot to do?"

"No, not really just some loose ends to tie up, it'll probably only take an hour, if that."

"So you don't have to rush back either then really?"

"No, I don't suppose I have but I'll feel a hell of a lot better when it's all done and dusted."

"You heard anything about your girlfriend yet," she asked with what sounded like genuine concern.

"No nothing," he sighed, "it's so bizarre!"

"Forgive me for saying this in my forthright manner but, I'd have expected you to be combing the streets and in floods of tears if it had been me that was missing!"

"Well, it's not that simple really."

"Not that close anymore?"

"No, in fact our romantic rendezvous as the paper tactfully put it, was a last ditch attempt to salvage our relationship."

"Well it certainly fixed it by the look of things!" she said flatly.

"Yes it's ironic really she was doing it all to help me as well!"

"Why, weren't you intoxicated by her anymore?"

"I was…. no not really. I was when we first went out that's for sure but somewhere along the way it just fizzled out."

"That's the difference between infatuation and love."

"So they say!"

"Have you ever had a platonic relationship with a woman?"

"No, it sounds like the sort of thing you do with a woman who looks like a bus!"

"Don't you think that sex gets in the way?"

"No, I think you have to fancy a person otherwise it's a friendship not a relationship."

"That's not what I meant. You automatically assumed that a woman had to be ugly before she would value your friendship more than your dick!"

"Oh," he felt quite shocked, "No, what I'm saying is, if she's never going to be interested in my, erm… one's …dick," he said in muted tones that made her giggle, "why should one bother getting to know her when she looks like a bus. I mean poor girl's got nothing going for her!"

"So Mr Adonis, all your girlfriends looked like models," she lifted the girlie magazine from its bag, "and they couldn't get over how lucky they were to meet you?"

"I didn't say they had to be glamorous…"

"You said not like a bus!"

"Well that was a figure of speech, they all had something about them that I found attractive but they weren't all really good looking." He gestured with two fingers in the air like quotation marks.

"And so when they fail to measure up," she pointed to the picture of the blonde laid, legs open with her panties pulled back to reveal all, "you loose interest do you?"

Grant just smiled and looked around the terrace. He couldn't compete anymore. In truth he'd always hoped that one of his girlfriends would eventually treat him to a glimpse of what he found exciting in the magazines. Some girls had their moments. Justine had been fantastic in this department. She'd had him directing her as she flaunted her way around his flat. She'd greet him at the door wearing next to nothing, rubbed herself against him and she'd not settle until he'd satisfied her. But she had the most horrendous PMT imaginable. There was only one week in four when she was anything like reasonable. They'd lasted three months and that was enough!

"And what was your girlfriend wearing for this rendezvous?" she pointed to a brunette in a red teddy and hold ups.

"Ha …..No, black leggings and high heels."

"And whose idea was that then?" she smiled.

"Mine!" he raised his eyebrows and laughed, "Yes I know."

"And that turns you on does it?"

"I thought it would … look the part."

"And you were somewhere on North Bay, pretty bleak spot … so nobody could see your grubby little desires?"

"That's not fair!"

"Didn't she dress sexily for you normally?"

"She didn't like the way other people looked at her."

"I don't blame her. Every time a woman wears something a bit sexy, men think she's advertising for a mate."

"Well her top was quite revealing, at least if it's the one I suggested."

"That's not the point, women should be able to dress as they please without the salacious comments and grubby looks."

"Well they send what are quite basic, or should I say, primitive signals and men pick up on them … We're programmed to pick up on things like that!"

"A man thing?"

"Yes, just like …"

"They should exhibit more control!"

"Well if a man were to …."

"Men just like to have it all there own way!"

"Well that's one valid point of view but there are others!"

"And they would be?"

"Its cause and effect the way I see it. Let's just reverse the roles for a minute. Let's say for a moment that I felt the same way as you about the clothes I should be allowed to wear. To make that point I decided to walk into a bar just wearing a very skimpy, tight pair of white boxers and a tight white singlet."

"Right."

"Would I get a reaction or not?"

"Mmm you would!" she giggled.

"That's not fair, I took you seriously and you were winding me up!" he said with more than a hint of irritation.

"No, I'm sorry I couldn't resist the pun. You should be able to dress as you like as well," she said and stoked his arm.

"Bollacks!" he said in a raised voice that echoed round the terrace. They both looked round as if to see where it came from and then ducked down a bit and giggled.

"Look what I'm trying to say is that I think sending a sexual message is something private between the two people involved. I think that if other people become involved because the message is too public then it either causes embarrassment or evokes a more voyeur response and it's like public entertainment. Frankly either way round I think it cheapens things considerably and why would you want to make your partner look cheap in the eyes of other people if they mean something to you."

"Right so let's say this girl, who looks like the back of a bus turns up looking like a million dollars but leans up against you and whispers in your ear that under her clothes she really looks like this" and she held up his magazine and showed him the picture of a tall fair haired naked woman wearing black hold ups and stiletto heels posed casually against a wall in what looked like a Spanish villa.

"What a coincidence!"

"What?"

"That's the photo I was going to put in my collection."

"Ha ... You've got a collection now! I bet you've got a grubby old mackintosh in your wardrobe as well!"

"I've got two, one with extra large pockets!" he grinned.

"So what do you see in these photos then?"

"Some of them are too … overt. There's no hint of affection, well maybe affection isn't the quite right word. They're trying to be rude rather than sexy. Look I'll see if I can find an example." He skimmed through the pages… "Yes here we go look," he turned the magazine round towards Violet. The woman, girl, Grant thought she looked very young, was kneeling, legs wide and resting on her elbows whilst sucking a large vibrator. "That is just plain and simply rude, it turns me off but this," he turned back to the double page of pictures featuring the blonde girl at the villa, "any one of those is sexy in my book."

"Right then I get the picture!"

"Look I'm sorry, I didn't mean to be …"

"Don't get the wrong idea but I know what you mean. I quite like to look at pictures myself sometimes. I'm not a lesbian so you can take the look of horror off your face. I can identify with the situation and imagine myself in their stead and yes, in the right context and with the right person, well they'd be a real turn on."

"Blimey!"

"When I was at Uni I shared a house with two gay blokes and they collected the gay equivalent to your magazine. Well some of the blokes were …"

"Hey, steady on, you'll make me feel inadequate!" he laughed.

"When we all moved on they gave me one of the mags to keep, I've still got it and from time to time I take a trip down memory lane!" she giggled.

Grant looked at his watch it wasn't that he was bored, he'd just realised that it was only lunchtime and he was acting as if it were the weekend and he'd got all the time in the world. If only he'd got into work at quarter to seven!

"Look Violet I've really enjoyed our lunch together and I'd much rather stay here and chat to you than go back to the bloody office but I just have to finish things off!"

"Yes a very plausible excuse."

"No, I mean it," he looked her in the eye and for once she was looking straight back at him with those lovely blue eyes. How was he ever going to be able to concentrate on his work again when she was in the office!

"Okay I'll let you go, but on one condition."

"You don't want me to go over and buy you a magazine do you?" he smiled.

"No," she laughed, "I want you to meet me for dinner later."

He let his breath whistle through his teeth. "Are you serious?"

"Yes, I'm serious," and for the first time she looked just a shade less confident. Grant wondered if she made a habit of picking men up at the coffee bar or was it just one of those things.

"I'd like that Violet, where shall we go?"

"Leave that to me, give me your mobile number and I'll ring you later," she smiled.

It was a warm smile that almost lit up the café and Grant walked back to the office in a bit of a daze.

Chapter 19

"Now then Phil, you any better today?"

"Bloody hell Levi, I'm sorry about the other day. It was Kate's birthday but the restaurant messed up the booking and we had to wait over an hour for a table."

"Don't drink on…"

"An empty stomach, yes, right! Anyway I've got the results of the paint sample from the truck. It's two layers, a touch up paint and a primer. So the car that made the mark will have a specific profile, if you've found it then it'll be quite easy to match."

"Good."

"I don't see the connection with Vick's case I have to admit."

"Well there isn't one really. I'm just trying to verify a young man's story."

"Not another one of your hunches?"

"W..ell."

"Anyway, look I've got to go, catch you later."

"Bye Phil."

Cosey's mobile picked up again straight away. Kalum must have had him on ring back.

"Nice of you to join us, don't like these early starts do we?" smiled Cosey.

Kalum was a little bit tardy at the beginning of the day but he worked hard and put in long hours. Cosey had no problem with that at all but he just couldn't resist the tease and Kalum had always taken it in such good humour after all.

"Yes," chuckled Kalum. "Had a phone call from Manchester police they've found a body that's been identified as Lumaii Bunyasarn, its Sumlea's sister. What's more Sumlea saw Vick's photo in the paper last night and now she's identified him as the man that attacked her."

"This is all very quick, how did they get an ID so fast, there's been nothing on the news over here."

"Well, seems Tina and Lumaii knew this club owner in the Gay Quarter and he recognised her from the local news. Tina did the ID."

"What's their view on the case?"

"The post-mortem's taking place as we speak and it sounds like, if we get a DNA match, they'll be more than happy to pass it over to us."

"I bet they will!" scoffed Cosey.

"How long before we get the results."

"Well the quickest they'll be able to get theirs will be 24hrs and by that time, ours will have come through anyway. Who's running the case?"

"DCI Graham Spencer, do you know him?"

"No, you got his number?"

"Yes I'll text it to you but he said you'd be more than welcome if you went over."

"Right, well I'll ring him anyway. Where are you?"

"Just left the hospital."

"Right, meet me at ….. No pick me up at the station there's nothing in it, I'll be there in five minutes."

"Right."

The Pathologist had pretty well finished Lumaii's post mortem when they arrived and her body lay face down whilst the CSI officer took some additional photos. A tall thin man in a cap, gown and mask broke away from a group of similarly attired people and approached them.

"DCI Graham Spencer."

"Hi, DCI Levi Cosey and this is DI Kalum Benning."

"Hi, thanks for coming, I explained to the pathologist you might be late and he's agreed to give you a brief synopsis but of course you'll get all the usual anyway."

"Well thank you, I much prefer to see things like this first hand."

"Yes, me too."

"You can see the two puncture wounds in her back," began the rather paunchy pathologist. "The one to the right and just below her shoulder blade punctured her left lung and from the bruising around, it was delivered with considerable force. The other lower wound, again a lot of force used here, you can see the bruising from the handle quite clearly there, punctured her heart."

"Murder weapon?" asked Cosey.

"The entry wounds are quite small but the tissue inside is torn so not a knife, I'd say a screwdriver or something similar but long, one wound went right through and into her thigh."

"So she must have been kneeling then?" asked Spencer.

"Yes, that sounds about right to me. There are also dark traces of what we think is old engine oil so maybe she was killed in a garage, but that's conjecture really at this stage. There is some scuffing and bruising to the knees, maybe you could help me turn her over?" he addressed the mortuary assistant.

"Maybe you'd like to help as well," Cosey chided Kalum who was studying the contents of a stainless steel dish.

"Oh my pleasure," smiled Kalum who surprisingly seemed to have quite a stomach for that sort of thing. "I can smell Chinese food," he remarked brightly.

"Bloody hell Kalum!" barked Cosey.

A murmur of polite amusement spread round the assembled group that now numbered ten.

"Well your colleague's right," chuckled the pathologist, "she was found in one of those large wheeled bins in China Town behind a restaurant."

Kalum said nothing but his raised eyebrows said it all.

"Right, judging by the angle of the wounds and as we said, the puncture wound to the thigh, I'd say she was probably kneeling or crouching when the attack occurred."

"There's a lot of blood round her mouth." observed Cosey.

"Yes, but I don't think it's hers."

"Why's that?"

"No, I think your colleague has probably discovered the source of that," he nodded in the direction of the stainless steel dish.

Everybody focused on Kalum who stared into the bowl.

"Kalum!" urged Cosey.

"Oh, er …..Well it looks to me like a chipolata or a very small severed penis," Kalum looked at the pathologist a bit sheepishly.

"Small penis is correct," answered the pathologist and nodded his approval in Kalum's direction, "and we found small shreds of tissue between her teeth which I suspect will match, so I think we can safely say she bit it off and then swallowed it for good measure!" he exclaimed.

"Bloody hell Kalum, let that be a lesson to you."

"Why me?"

"You're still young!" scoffed Cosey to the sound of more polite amusement.

"I thought you meant he had a small penis," chuckled the pathologist.

"Ha …..," frowned Cosey. "Anything else?"

"There are bruises around her neck and to the side of her face. I guess her victim put up a bit of a struggle himself, but the irony of it would have been that every blow or attempt to dislodge her, would have resulted in more agony for him." Another murmur of chuckles broke out but Cosey felt his stomach muscles tighten just at the thought of it all.

"There are additional bruises to the back of her head and shoulders," continued the pathologist, "one of the bruises, well you can't see it now we've turned her over but I have a photo," and he walked over to the work surface and pointed at the last of three photographs lying there. You see the angular edge to that bruise, well look at that filing cabinet over there, the old one in the corner," he pointed at a three drawer metal filing cabinet in dark green.

"Yes," replied Cosey.

"Well just compare that bruise with the label holder. The bruise on her shoulder could easily have come from a handle like that one as well!"

"Right, I see what you mean, so you think she fell?"

"Hard to see how she could have fallen to get the marks like that, no I'd say she was pushed with some force."

"Possibly in a last bid to free himself, he pushed her off and she collided with the cabinet maybe?" mused Cosey.

"Yes I'll go with that," nodded the pathologist.

"Could he have stabbed her as well?"

"No I think that highly unlikely, given the force used, he'd have had to swing his arm and so the entry wound would be angled but these wounds were inflicted from directly above."

"So that means somebody else killed her…maybe trying to save Vick!"

"Yes I think that's a distinct possibility.

"The plot thickens!" murmured Kalum.

As Cosey removed his cap and gown later he felt relieved that Tina had identified Lumaii but now he would have to break the news to Sumlea, as if the poor kid hadn't already gone through enough.

"She's a nice kid is Sumlea, bit naive but that's hardly her fault is it?" remarked Kalum sadly.

Out of the corner of his eye Cosey caught sight of his expression and realised that they must have been thinking along the same lines. There was more than a hint of concern in his voice and Cosey studied him for a moment. Kalum had been dropping in to see how she was getting on quite regularly. Maybe he'd taken a shine to her? Good for him, 'bout time he got out more. Maybe she could help him to remember to take his bloody cycle clips off! Cosey nodded in the direction of Kalum's ankles and with a sheepish smile he removed the offending items. You'd think he'd see them, they are luminous yellow after all! Cosey shook his head.

Chapter 20

It wasn't what he'd imagined. For some reason best known to his subconscious Grant had pictured something more traditional and cosy. Candles certainly and smartly dressed waiters. Well he'd been right about that much anyway. There they stood in a clutch whilst Simon quietly clucked round them like a mother hen. Dressed in black trousers both young men and women alike, black waist coat with a thin black bow tie tied loosely around the neck of an immaculately pressed white shirt with black cufflinks. Their hairstyles were short chic, no long strands to drift across the eyes or trail in your food. One handsome young waiter headed for Grant's table. He sported a thin moustache and tiny beard like an artists sable brush that hung just below his bottom lip.

"Your Campari and grapefruit sir," he smiled politely.

"Thank you," replied Grant genially.

Not being a Dido fan Grant only recognised one of the distinctive tracks that played quietly in the background and now as the last traces of daylight began to fade, the glow of the mood changing coloured ceiling lights cast contrasting shadows down the walls from the pictures and artefacts tastefully arranged above.

The restaurant had filled up and the murmur of polite conversation balanced well with the music to cover the sounds of the waiter's feet as they plied to and fro across the wooden floor. To his right Grant watched the decorative streetlights as they flickered into life down Cross Street and picked out the cobbles. An odd couple of window browsers walked arm in arm past the dimly lit shop windows and shuttered cafes. To his left and at the opposite end of the room a middle aged couple emerged up the stairs from the bar below clutching their drinks. Simon followed ushering them to the seats at the next table and once they were settled with menus and a bright flickering candle he beamed over at Grant.

"Don't take it to heart if she's late," he spoke in a hushed conspiratorial tone and raised his eyebrows to add, "it's just Violet!"

He was so bloody camp, thought Grant. Stood there clutching his hands together, shaking his head from side to side. He smiled like an old woman at a tea dance but, surprisingly, despite it all, Grant found him an endearing individual and he liked him as soon as they'd met. Simon's Arian good looks added a 1940's feel to his white DJ, black bow tie and red carnation. He'd half expected a Bavarian accent and a monocle tucked into the black waistcoat pocket but there was a hint of an accent in his voice Grant still hadn't been able to pinpoint. When Violet had said to be smart he'd immediately discounted the idea of a tie and settled for a dark suit and shirt. He was smart and nicely understated and it had been the right choice. He felt comfortable in his surroundings. He picked an imaginary piece of fluff from his cuff and decided that as now the only vacant seat was at his table, then the next person to arrive had to be Violet. He wasn't disappointed. Right on cue, or rather ten minutes late, he heard the distinctive sound of high heels on the wooden staircase. His heart was in his mouth and blood pounded in his ears, he hardly dare look up.

He first caught Violet's eye just as she reached the top of the stairs and it brought back that insolent but warm smile to her face as she looked him up and down. He rose slowly from his seat and everything seemed to move in slow motion. It was hard to take her in with one glance from her fair hair that hung over the collar of a black bolero jacket to her tight black leggings that stopped short of the ankle and the high heeled sandals with neatly painted toe nails. By the time his gaze had returned to eye level she had stepped round the table and pressed her body close to his with her hand tucked behind his waist. She planted a moist warm kiss over his lips.

"Don't move away," she whispered, pressing herself hard against him, "I need to know how pleased you are to see me!" She looked at his lips, their mouths only a short distance apart and the faintest flicker of a smile flashed across her face as his erection peeked. "Mm…I'm impressed," she added with another short smile and shuffled sideways to plant herself comfortably on the chair that Simon had expertly slid beneath her.

Grant suddenly felt vulnerable stood there with an erection that felt as big as the Eiffel Tower in full view of the whole restaurant and worse, Simon stood there with a big smile on his face and a glint in his eye, as queer as a nine bob note. He dropped to his seat like a stone much to Violet's amusement. He'd have to be careful, one false move and it would snap!

"What do you think Simon?" she said brightly.

"I'm pleased to see you out with somebody at last, I think it was worth the wait," he beamed, waggled his head and reached across to light the candle. "I'll get your menus, would you like a drink Violet?"

"Yes I'll just have tonic water for now, with ice please."

"You're welcome," he minced off in the direction of the bar.

She lent forward with one hand tucked behind her neck and the front of her white top opened enough for him to see down between her naked breasts while her firm nipples made small dark pyramids in the soft folds of her top. He felt unexpectedly embarrassed that she'd noticed him look but when Simon lit the candle the light focused his attention.

"Don't be embarrassed," she said softly as he shifted his gaze abruptly, "I chose this outfit because I wanted you to look, I want this to be a special evening for you, one you'll remember for all kinds of reasons," she gave a warm and disarming smile.

"Look Violet!" he felt overwhelmed by the desire to confess all the wrongdoings of his entire life there and then. "You don't know about me, it's not what you think!"

"Well there's a lot about me, you don't know and that is what this is all about really," she said in a very matter of fact tone. "This is an outfit very much like the one you got Fay to wear, with a few refinements of my own admittedly."

"Yes, but …"

"And you said, correct me if I'm wrong, that sexual messages between people are private and shouldn't be paraded in public, or words to that effect."

"Yes."

"Well I got Simon to save this table and sit you there facing the room so that I could let you see me in a way that nobody else could. Now with my back to the room I'm showing you very discretely something which I think is very personal and I wouldn't share with just anybody."

"Look Violet I think you're getting me all wrong!"

"Let me finish. I know from our conversation earlier that you have an appreciation of this kind of intimacy, one that I share. I wanted you to realise this in my actions and not as some vacuous promise."

"I'm sorry?" said Grant quizzically as he couldn't work out where it was leading.

"I may not look like a bus Grant but if you're going to get to know me first, I wanted you to know that it's going to be worth the wait."

"What?"

"Yes I do want to form a relationship with you and I fancy you a lot but I don't want your infatuation because it doesn't last. I want you to fall in love with me and I want to know that you are my friend and that you'll always be there for me!" she said without a hint of humour in her voice. Her eyes looked straight through him. "If you're prepared to go the distance Grant you know by my actions thus far that I have everything you're looking for in a sexual partner and there's a lot more where that came from believe me!"

"Wow, just slow down!" he pushed the palms of his hands down towards the table.

"I'm not rushing you Grant, just take as long as you want. I can wait for the right person as long as it takes!"

"Your tonic and the menus, but if I might make a suggestion," Simon glanced between them.

Grant felt sure that he must sense that this was not a good time but no...

"I'd go for the Sea Bass or the Duck tonight they are absolutely mouth watering I promise!" chuckled Simon with pride.

"What's Sea Bass like?" asked Grant, with a punch drunk expression, "I'm no expert on fish?"

"Well if that's the case the Sea Bass would be an excellent introduction and maybe the Melon to start," smiled Simon who was obviously enjoying the moment.

"Well it's been quite a surprising evening so I'm going to try it, thank you Simon," smiled Grant as he tried to get his head back into gear after the intellectual battering it had just received. He'd realised that any brief respite would allow time to rally his thoughts.

"And I'll join you," smiled Violet as Simon took the menus and her gaze returned to his eyes. Simon shuffled off to leave Violet's elbows irreverently perched on the table as she rested her head on her hands.

"What do you think, is it worth a try? At least if you don't like me I will have preserved my self respect and that's important to me. I'm not a tart Grant, I don't sleep around. I never have and I don't intend to start now, much as I fancy you," she placed a kiss on her fingers and blew it across to him.

He sat there and looked at her for a while as she stared into the flickering candle, unspeaking just contemplating the events. She was the most exciting woman he'd ever met and she certainly knew what turned him on. He had to agree she wasn't a tart, everything that happened had style.

From what she wore to the way she communicated desire it was fantastic, it was the only word to describe it. Since lunchtime he'd found it difficult to clear his mind of all sorts of things about their meeting that had gelled. Pieces of her personality, sense of humour and outlook on life that fitted so snugly next to his that the joins were imperceptible. It was as if a long time ago fragments of one person had been scattered in the universe and in that short lunch break the energy between them had restored the pieces to their rightful abode. Ever since the other day at the clinic he'd been trying to strengthen the ties with the person he'd found within. A person more at peace with themselves, he felt strangely less isolated from other people, and genuinely more sociable. In his conversation with Violet in the café they had covered a lot of ground but even when they'd discussed the pornography he had been entirely focused on the extent to which he'd connected with her and not tried to chat her up. In fact she had done the chatting up really! Now she was at it again. So what had he to loose. Grant favoured the balance sheet approach to problem solving if the answer hadn't bitten him on the nose first.

On the plus side she was attractive, slim, highly charged sexually, witty, companionable and very easy to get on with, well thus far. He would be proud to be her partner in company, she'd turn a few heads and he savoured the prospect that other guys would be jealous. She'd be faithful without a doubt. On the negative side, could he wait to slate his lust for her? Nothing that happened that evening gave him any hope in that department. Already his groin ached in frustration and that would surely happen every time they met. Would she just tease him on and get her jollies at his expense while he went blind from masturbating? There's also a lot about his obsession that she won't know. He might not be able to conquer it and then everything would go bloody pear shaped as always! So that was it then, they'd both got a lot to learn about each other, he decided. In trying to turn the corner with his addiction she'd probably be the best thing that could happen to him, it would be like having your own 'Page 3' girl come to life but she'd also be your best friend. It all sounded almost too good to be true, maybe she'd turn out to be some kind of bloody psycho! No, there's a warmth about her, he'd expect a psycho to be… different! He had to admit he was curious.

The starters arrived but the waiter, unable to decode the atmosphere between them, almost dropped the plates and ran.

"So you want me to pretend you're a bus." He asked with a dead pan face.

"Yes."

"While you're going to try and ruin it all by devising new and exciting ways to give me a stiffy that I can't use?"

"No! We're going to have a platonic relationship and get to know each other without the complication of sex."

"In all honesty I don't know that I'm up to the challenge!" he smoothed the cloth out along the edge of the table with his hands. "You hardly know me and, well, given that there's a lot about me you don't know … believe me I'd be doing cold turkey."

"So what you're saying is that you have doubts as well and that you think I might not be able to go the distance with you?"

"Yes, that's exactly it. I think what you're after is brilliant if it works and I would be proud to be part of it and truly ecstatic if it succeeds."

"So what have we to lose?"

"Well …nothing I guess."

"I mean hand on heart, are you happy with the ways things were going?"

"Frankly Violet, up until lunchtime, they've never been so crap … sorry I mean so bad."

"Well?"

"I …I've never seen a black bus!"

She leaned back in her chair and looked at him for a while as if savouring the moment then she smiled, sat forward again and said softly, "You'll have to try harder!"

"No I'm sorry I've only ever seen green or red ones. You'll have to go home and change!"

"Everything okay," enquired Simon a little apprehensively.

News obviously travels fast in this establishment thought Grant as he surveyed the room. He picked out the nervous waiter from earlier as he tried to settle a tray of drinks on a table. The sight of Grant's expression distracted him and a customer stood up abruptly from the table and angrily wiped at a very wet patch on his trousers. Serves you right you snitch, thought Grant.

"Yes thank you," replied Violet, "now we've established the rules."

"Fine … Well." Simon stuttered as the waiter cleared the plates and then two waitresses arrived with the Sea Bass lavishly garnished and three smaller bowls that contained broccoli, carrots, roast potatoes and parsnips.

"Simon, you've surpassed yourself!" exclaimed Violet cheerfully.

Grant smiled too, it really did look very appetizing.

"Enjoy," beamed Simon and he waddled away smiling contentedly at the couple at the next table as he went.

"I've got a nice cerise teddy you might like, I could always nip home and get it if you're having trouble with black?" giggled Violet.

"I need to explain, the sex thing, it's not simple...I've been seeing a therapist. Fay went to see one as well and it was her therapist that came up with the idea for the rendezvous but she never knew I was seeing one as well. To be honest I realise now that she probably didn't need to see one at all as it has been my problem all along, it was my fault all this happened.

"Just wait a minute," interrupted Violet with her open hand outstretched, "are you saying that you don't like sex at all!" She looked shocked and put down her cutlery, wiped her mouth with the serviette. Crestfallen and on the point of tears Violet sat back heavily in her chair.

"Not at all, quite the reverse!" he said loudly, then in a much softer tone he added, "Look sit nearer, I can't shout this sort of thing."

He looked around to see if his words had already carried too far and caught the eye of a woman at the next table. She had several double chins, a pointed nose and dark hair streaked with grey combed back in one of those big hairstyles and sported some long dangly earrings. She pecked at her food like a chicken and he smiled at her, nosey old bat!

"Look!" said Violet as she sat forward again, her eyes softening.

He raised an eyebrow in response and found his gaze drifting down the front of her cleavage again.

"So you do desire me then?" asked Violet.

"Yes of course!"

"It wasn't just a fluke then?"

"No but don't interrupt again, this is difficult enough!"

"Okay," she gestured with her knife for him to continue and started in on her Sea Bass.

"I began to wonder if I was different to other men in the sack!"

Violet raised an eyebrow.

"No! I know everybody's different, we all have preferences and so on. What I mean is that when more than one partner makes the same comment …. complains that after the deed they feel rejected or let down, then you begin to wonder don't you?"

"Sure."

"Sure?"

"Yes sure! You said don't interrupt, go on!"

"Well, I wondered if they were right so I went on the internet and found a Sex Therapy site. It was quite interesting. There was lots of advice about all sorts of issues and patients' true life stories. There was a list of different types of problems linked to advice and help lines, you know the sort of thing!"

"Mm," munched Violet.

"Under the heading of 'Sexual Addiction' there was this questionnaire so I thought I'd give it a whirl. Well at the bottom of the sheet it announced that if you'd checked yes to more than three answers you were probably addicted to sex and should at least seek further advice...Well"

"Yes, oh God I can't win!"

"I had six"

"Good!" she giggled, "I'm sorry Grant, just kidding!"

He let the breath hiss between his teeth in exasperation and then continued with a stern expression.

"One of the questions described almost exactly how I felt after sex."

"Hm," nodded Violet.

"It said something along the lines of 'do you feel guilty or ashamed after sex' and erm ... 'do you want to distance yourself from your partner after sex'. I can't tell you how often I've felt just like that, sometimes far worse!"

"So what did you do then?"

"I went to the doctor but to cut to the chase he referred me to this sex therapist called Hector Katychmar."

"He sounds foreign, is he Hungarian?"

"I don't know, but he's helped me a lot. I had a pretty heavy session there the other day and he told me I'd turned the corner. I've felt quite exhausted since what with that and everything else that's happened, it's been quite a week!"

"What does he think the problem is …...was?"

"My mother was a prostitute, I don't know who my father was, I'm not sure if she did really. One night I saw one of her clients beat her up and Katychmar thinks the problems all stem from that and the fact she used to leave me for hours alone in the dark."

"I'm not bloody well surprised! What a way to treat a child. ...I'm sorry Grant I know she's your mother but...."

"It's okay, she put me in a home and frankly I felt better for it. You don't feel so bad when there are other people around who've had similar experiences I think it helps you adjust."

"I'm sorry Grant," she put her cutlery on the plate and slid it sideways across the table, "I am absolutely gob smacked!"

"Apart from Katychmar and of course the kids at the home, I've never told anybody else but you."

"I'm really ....sorry," she gently took hold of his hands as they lay palms down on the table either side of his nearly empty plate.

"And I'm absolutely stuffed!" he smiled with a puff.

"Can you manage a sweet?"

"Phew, no I don't think so!" he replied and sat back in the chair to ease his waistband.

"How about, if we go back to my place for coffee? Actually I've got some nice sweets in the freezer you never know you might fancy one later!"

"Violet that's a great idea but how does this fit with the platonic relationship?"

"Grant, despite everything I trust you, we have a deal."

"We do, I'm just not sure how it works in reality. The drawing board version sounds quite clear but I think we need more structure. Bloody hell, listen to me!"

Simon was visibly disappointed that they hadn't sampled his luxuriant sweet trolley but they left on the understanding that next time they'd have smaller helpings and save space for the sweets.

"What do you think to him then?" Violet nuzzled in under his arm loosely draped over her shoulder as they walked slowly down Cross Street.

"Simon?"

She nodded.

"Actually I quite like him, under all that camp stuff he strikes me as being very professional and he certainly seems to care a lot about you. If he wasn't so obviously gay, I'd be very jealous indeed!" and he gave her shoulder a squeeze.

"He's one of the gay blokes I told you about earlier, you know the ones I shared with as a student."

"Oh right!"

"Well here we are!"

"I didn't realise you lived so near!"

"Yes it's quite convenient. I eat there quite often, I get a special rate."

"Yes, well, I still think you ought to have let me pay!"

"I asked you out remember?"

"Fair enough."

"I own the building, the shop has storage out the back and I live on the remaining two floors above. It's kind of upside down though the lounge and kitchen stroke dinning room are on the top floor because I like the view and the bedrooms are on the first floor."

She closed the door behind them and he followed her beautifully shaped bottom as she slowly climbed the stairs ahead.

"I know what you're doing," she giggled, "I usually run up these stairs two at a time so make the most of it!"

"Two at a time?" he chided and shouldered her in the rump.

"Ah, ooh you…" she squealed and ran up the stairs giggling which turned into a little scream as he caught up with her at the top.

"Bloody hell," he said breathlessly, "two at a time it is!"

"I'm fit," she clicked her fingers in the air and laughed.

Grant couldn't restrain himself and slid his arm round her back and under her jacket. He pulled her close to him and planted a well deserved and loving kiss on her slightly open mouth. She made no attempt to fight him off and curled her arms round his neck and gently ran her fingers through his hair. His erection was swift but he leaned away from her. He had only expressed feelings of affection with the kiss and had no desire to compromise the moment.

"I knew I could trust you," she said warmly and kissed him softly, "but I want you to have some mementos of tonight to remind you of what lies in store should we pull this off. The room at the end is the lounge if you make yourself comfortable I'll make the coffee."

As Grant opened the door she called to him. "Do you have a good camera on your phone?"

"Yes, I do."

"Have you got it with you?"

"Yes," he pulled it from his pocket.

"Yes, that'll do nicely." She disappeared from sight as the door swung to behind her.

Record collections tell you a lot about people thought Grant as he flicked through the wall mounted CD stand. If he didn't find at least one he recognised they had no chance at all! Stereophonics well that was a start, Razorlite … Black Crows, Cheryl Crow …Ah, Sound track from Love Actually. Natalie Imbruglia, yes a touch of Torn would do, nicely turned down low. He slipped the CD into the tray and pressed play. The sound was absolutely deafening and he fumbled with the dials until finally he found the volume control.

"You like your music loud then?" he heard the kitchen door close followed by the sound of feet approach on the carpeted hall.

"I love it and that's one of the advantages of living here…No neighbours!"

"This is a nice big place…they must be paying you a lot more than me!"

"Well, it's actually an interesting story but first have you got your camera ready?"

"Yes it's here."

"Are you ready then? Because I'm only going to give you just two minutes."

"Sorry?"

"Two minutes and your time start's from…" she looked at the clock on the hi-fi, "Now!"

He'd been so busy with the volume control that he hadn't taken much notice of Violet's appearance when she came into the room. She'd placed the coffee on the low table to his right and with one knee on a leather pouffet she was lent forward with her hands close together resting on the table and her elbows turned in. She'd removed her top and now her naked breasts were proudly displayed between the lapels of her jacket and her dark nipples were tantalisingly erect.

"Come on Grant," she said softly but with urgency, "I mean it, you've got two minutes so direct me, the photos are going to have to last you a while so make the most of it!"

"Bloody hell Violet!" he exclaimed as his camera made the shutter noise.

"That's more like it, now be careful, if you shake they'll be blurry!"

"Slip your jacket off…slowly!"

"Ha, that's the boy," she pouted at the camera.

"Run your fingers through your hair! …Play with those strands of your hair with your right hand…yes just the end of the strands…great now put your left hand on your hip, you know like the blonde in the magazine."

"One minute!"

"Oh shit, if you'd told me before I'd have had time to think!"

"Stand up," she commanded and moved to the middle of the room. There she struck her pose, feet about fifteen inches apart. With her fingers splayed she dug her thumbs down the inside of her waistband just either side of her navel. She pouted looking at him through the hair that had fallen across her cheeks. Slowly she forced the waistband down her tummy towards her groin.

"You're going to have to be quick Grant only fifteen seconds left," she reminded him as the waistband slid over her hips.

"Push your elbows together more," directed Grant, his voice croaked, his mouth was now so dry he was hardly able form the words.

"That's as far down as I'm going or I'll have no surprises left for you!"

"Shift your weight over to your right and drop the other hip a little!"

"Quickly Grant seven, six, five, four, three, two, o...ne! That's it, times up!" and with that she stood up straight and pulled the waistband back to its normal position. She slid her jacket back on and fastened the single button on the front.

"Decent again, well more or less ...Oh I almost forgot!" and she picked something shiny from the tray and covered the distance between them with lightening speed. With one hand she clutched his throat with the other she pointed the shiny object at his eye. It was a thin pointed stainless steel kitchen knife the type you would use to bone a joint he recalled from student vacation job at the butchers.

"If you ever and I mean ever, show those photos to anybody, I'll cut your bloody dick off!"

Her eyes were cold and looked right through him. There wasn't a shred of humour in her voice and the knife was barely an inch from his eye. He was off balance, pinned against the wall, downright bloody helpless and completely at her mercy.

"It never entered my head to show them to anybody Violet!" he replied with a distinctly wobbly voice.

"Fine then let's keep it like that shall we," and with that she let him go and took a few steps towards the door. "Oh, yes," she lifted a magazine from the floor beside the sofa, "You might like to take a look at this. It's the one Simon gave me when we shared a flat…remember as students?"

"Oh right," he tried to regain some composure but the relief was still evident in his voice.

Violet smiled warmly and strode confidently out of the room.

"Phew," Grant let out a sigh of relief; maybe she was a bloody psycho after all but he could see her point really, if the guys at work got hold of them, well!…he selected photo album on his mobile.

"I don't want you looking at those now, wait until you're alone!" echoed her voice from somewhere beyond the door.

She must be psychic he thought and reluctantly replied, "Okay."

Grant sat down on the sofa and opened the magazine at the first page and what he saw made his head jolt back in surprise. There in full colour was a full page photo of a naked man in his middle twenties with a Celtic tattoo across one shoulder reclined on a large black leather chair. He had a well toned muscular physique with a pronounced six pack. His forearms rested casually on the arms of the chair and his legs were slightly apart. Rising from his hairy groin to an apex just above the navel stood his enormous erect penis.

"Shit" he'd not been prepared for that. Grant had quickly done the maths. If his own penis were about six inches then that meant that this guy had about nine or ten inches.

"Seeing was believing!" he smiled.

"What do you think?" enquired Violet as she breezed passed him, picked up the TV remote and settled on the sofa beside him. Her black outfit was replaced by a comfortable looking soft dressing gown and as she navigated the Teletex menu with one hand she finished removing the last traces of mascara from her eyes with the other using some kind of moist wipe.

"I feel woefully inadequate!"

"Now you know what it's like for most women when they see pictures of perfectly formed models, air brushed no doubt, which men make such a fuss about. They feel that it's hopeless! Worse still if hubby then comes home with what he thinks is a nice sexy basque!" she laughed and lobbed the grubby wipe across the room into a small metal bin.

"I see your point."

"I think that one's great," observed Violet as she looked over his arm, "I like the fact that he's hairless, well except for his head of course," she giggled, "and I think pulling his foreskin back adds real sexual urgency to the photograph, don't you?"

"Well he certainly looks ready for action,"

"Look, you don't mind, do you? I've got a photo shoot planned for that hair gel thing in the morning and I just need to check the weather forecast."

"No, go ahead."

"Fine and turning to rain later," she read aloud, "brilliant we'll be finished by lunchtime anyway. Do you mind....the tail end of the local news."

"No, not at all," Grant worked his way through the readers question page and shook his head from time to time in amazement.

Violet turned up the sound as the newsreader announced.

"Police today released this picture of a Thai woman whose body was discovered yesterday in the China Town district of Manchester. Police now believe she is the local prostitute who went missing following the bizarre murder of former Moverley taxi owner Mr Vick Whinsper who was found dead outside his office late Monday night.

"Oh shit!... Oh fucking hell!" bellowed Grant, he recognised her, it was the girl in the lift.

"Steady on, they're only pictures, I already know you're big enough for me and that's all that matters," she laughed but as she turned to look at him her expression changed to a mixture of shock and alarm.

Grant was deathly white and his eyes were filled with tears as he touched his brow with trembling fingers.

"I don't believe it, this can't be happening!" his hands shook uncontrollably as Grant struggled to his feet.

"What's wrong?"

"I can't...I can't!"

"What's the matter? Grant look at me!"

"Can't breathe...I can't breathe," he made a dash for the door. "I've got to get some air!" he swung the door to the stairs open wide.

"Wait, I'll come with you!"

"No, let me out!"

"Grant!"

The thunder of his feet on the stairs echoed around the walls. He wrenched the door open and it crashed against the wall. Grant bolted over the cobbles and on through the cool night air. He had to get away before he suffocated.

Chapter 21

She quite liked the tackiness of Moverley, there was a kind of honesty about the candy floss, the bingo on the front and the sea food stands perched near the harbour wall. They were there to take your money plain and simple and in return you got a lung full of fresh air. The fish quay hadn't smelt that fresh this morning. Despite that, in her opinion fish and chips tasted best from the paper at the seaside. She even quite liked the seagulls as they tried emotional blackmail or even levitation to get some little morsel of your meal. The morning was damp with sea mist and the cold air rasped at the back of her throat as she cycled to work the long way round, she had things to consider. Violet liked it best in January wrapped up warm. In her opinion several layers, a ski jacket, good thick gloves and a woolly hat were the best attire for a beach walk on those crisp bright sunshine mornings when the cold north wind cut like a knife. It was the only time in her life that she'd ever wished for a dog. She lent against the bridge railing to get her breath and surveyed the long drop below to the seafront road. No matter which way you took back into town you had to climb a steep hill and Violet felt very unfit.

Things had gone so well last night, in fact everything she'd planned had worked out perfectly. Grant had been great company and taken it all in such good humour. His face had been a picture when he stood up beside the table as she'd arrived …She smiled but it faded fast when she remembered how their cosy, intimate evening had gone so horribly wrong after the news flash about that girl.

"Tickets please!" hailed the guard as he slid the door open.

Violet had been rolling the ticket between her fingers unconsciously since she'd slumped heavily into the window seat and much of the view had slipped by unnoticed as her mind flitted restlessly over recent events. Now the guard picked at his jumper while she tried to unroll it.

"Thank you." With thinly veiled disdain he handed it back but it caught on her fingers and ended up on the floor.

Garforth was the last stop before Leeds and the landscape had changed. The wide open moors and farm land had given way to urban development. Violet caught fleeting glimpses between the buildings of cars queued at traffic lights, streets busy with the lunchtime crowds and day shoppers, each in competition for the favoured window seats. She followed the crowd and joined the queue at the taxi rank near the ticket hall. She never knew with taxi drivers. Had they purposely taken her through the one way system or was that really the quick way round? God knows! Anyway they looked to have made it through the worst of it when the taxi headed down a long winding dual carriageway to some traffic lights. Grant's got quite a long journey everyday really.

The taxi headed uphill again, past the mosque where the road narrowed and became edged with ethnic shops of varied description. Maybe he hadn't gone back there last night … there wouldn't have been a train that late surely? She looked at the large houses to the right set back behind high stone walls and partially shrouded by large trees, as they sped round a slow 'S' bend and wondered what the original owners had done to afford such luxury. Maybe he hadn't gone back at all. If only he'd answer his bloody phone she'd not have to go to all this trouble! She gripped the seat tight in frustration. Finally a sharp turn to the right lead up hill and then down Lemont Avenue, a steep winding road between post war stone built houses with well tended gardens. The taxi came to rest near the bottom of the hill beside a large grass area on the left and just short of the junction where on the right the road headed along the bottom of a woodland valley.

"Karis Court, that'll be £8.50 my love," smiled the driver.

She gave him ten pounds. "It's okay!" she waved a hand at him to keep the change, opened the door and stepped out onto the pavement to take in the view.

As the noise of the taxi faded the sound of a stream could be heard somewhere down the other side of the junction amongst the vegetation. There the trees were all very tall and behind them a steep wooded bank rose to a stone wall. The sound of a car could be heard through the trees, its engine struggled with the gradient. The road must go off up there somewhere. To her left and across the grass three hatchback cars were stood in a small private car park just below the three storey row of flats that rose dramatically above the grassed bank that swept down to the pavement at her feet. She rummaged in her pocket for the piece of paper on which she'd written out the address earlier at work. From there she couldn't identify which would be number fourteen. Violet passed a clutch of sale boards and climbed the steep weathered concrete drive up the left hand side of the flats and wondered how the tenants managed in the snow and ice. The drive levelled off near the top and widened out onto a concrete parking area flanked by two rows of garages face on to each other. To the right a narrow gravel path lead behind the nearest row of garages and around the back of the flats where three short bridges connected to the middle floor entrances. Violet checked the numbers and decided that Grant's flat must be across the middle bridge and on the top floor. She pressed the bell and waited for a response. Back on the path an elderly woman pulled a plastic bag from her quilted anorak pocket and guided an equally elderly dog onto some grass for a toilet stop. That's one good reason not to have a dog! There was no answer and she tried again and scanned the windows above to see if there was any sign of Grant. Just her luck if after all that he hadn't come back, now what was she to do?

A rattle of the door from behind made her jump and she spun round.

"I'm sorry did I startle you?" laughed a young man but it wasn't Grant. He marched across the bridge proudly carrying some full bin liners to the dustbins across the path and Violet had an idea.

"Oh thank God," she laughed, "I came out to put the rubbish in the bin and I got locked out. Now I can't get Grant to answer his door. Bet he's fallen asleep again!"

"Isn't he at work?"

"No, something that he ate last night, at least that's what he says!" She smiled and stepped through the open door while the young man wrestled with the bin lid. She ran quickly up the creaking wooden stairs, knocked hard on the door of number fourteen and bellowed. "I know you're in there, come out with your hands up!"

The young man closed the outer door with a click, "Any luck?" he shouted up between the banisters.

"Not yet, but at least it's not as cold in here thanks to you," she smiled.

"My pleasure," he closed the door to his flat on the floor below.

"Grant, open this bloody door!" she kicked the door frame hard with her toe. Ouch! That hurt, maybe she'd just have to accept the fact he wasn't really in after all. She scowled, turned to lean on the glass door and tried his phone again, the number was still unavailable. Oh how annoying! She cursed to herself, pocketed the phone and turned to give the door one last chance. She swung her knuckles to rap on the glass and Grant's hand grabbed her by the wrist and made her jump.

"If you don't stop I'll call the police!" he turned into his flat dragging her by the wrist behind him.

"Why don't you answer your phone?" she closed the door.

"Because I need time to think and I don't want to be disturbed!"

"I could help you!"

"You can't help me think!"

"I can make tea and be so quiet you'd never even know I was here!"

"So what's the advantage in that?"

"Thinking can be thirsty work! Look at me this morning. I went for a bike ride through town and onto the harbour at 6.00am."

"Why?"

"I needed to think!"

"And?"

"I got thirsty. And I thought wouldn't it be nice if Grant just turned up with a flask of tea." She smiled that impudent, smug little smile.

"I didn't get to bed till late. I've only just got up," he replied sulkily.

"Would you like a cup of tea?"

Grant stood sleepily in the hallway and looked her over. Then he stepped to the side and gestured towards the kitchen with a nod of his head. "Through there."

Violet was impressed there was only one dirty mug in the sink, the drainer was empty and so was the dustbin. She smiled to herself and opened a cupboard. Everything was neatly laid out and so it took her little time to find all the requisite ingredients. Grant sat at the bar watching her but she resisted the temptation to tease him as after all he probably had nothing on under the dressing gown.

"I had hoped we'd be having breakfast at my place this morning. You'd be sitting there drinking my tea and saying you'd slept well when all along your back was killing you from a night on my sofa." She put the mugs down with a smile and lifted one eyebrow.

"I'm sorry it was a fantastic night and I spoilt it, I'm really sorry," he spoke quietly with an apologetic tone in the direction of the mug. He looked her in the eyes, "I'm sorry, you really deserve an explanation."

"I'm all ears, but Grant, be honest." Her face was tense and serious, it was a moment of truth. Whatever the connection with the girl she had to know. It had happened before they'd become an item so he was hardly accountable to her for his actions but there was a line. Sexual addiction, well she'd spent her time that morning reading up on the net, now she was in the picture and a lot clearer about what Grant had been telling her. But was he out of control? Difficult one! Yes, she'd be loyal and support his recovery and if what he'd said was true about how he'd been since the last treatment, well he'd certainly turned the corner. But the case histories she'd read were filled with accounts of broken marriages, relationship and a downward spiral of self indulgence that wrecked the lives of all involved. She had strong feelings for Grant but not at the expense of everything she valued. Would she sacrifice her values and live under a cloud for the rest of her life? No, that's not life, how could you ever be happy. "Whatever it is just say it how it is Grant and we'll have to take our chances. I think these situations are defining moments in relationships and they're very precious so for our sake don't spoil it!"

"You're very good in a crisis Violet, it's very endearing. I just hope you don't think less of me," he smiled and reached across to take her hand.

"Try some tea."

"On Tuesday I had an appointment at the clinic and I got in the lift with a girl wearing a red dress. The lift got stuck between floors and while we were waiting to be rescued ..." He took a big swig of his tea.

"Yes?"

"We ..um."

"No!" They had sex in the lift, was that all it was? There are loads of people who fantasise about that and the idea had crossed her mind at least once…three times.

"Violet it's not funny!"

"No, I'm not laughing," she swallowed a giggle.

"There was something about her I think, to do with the red dress. My mother used to have one she called it her 'uniform'. Well after I had sex with this girl once, I don't know what came over me it was like I was watching somebody else. It was like she was acting out one of my childhood memories. I could hear my mother crying as one of her customers laid into her with his fists." His voice got quieter and tearful.

"Oh Grant, you didn't?" Violet's hand slipped from his. Surely he didn't rape her!

Grant shook his head, "I turned her over, pushed her to her knees and … I didn't rape her, she was up for it but then I just got carried away. Violet I feel so guilty. She kept shouting for me to stop."

"Grant!" Violet gasped and put her hand to her mouth as tears filled her eyes. If it's not rape….Oh God what had he done!

"I was hitting her on the back."

"Oh!" she winced, she daren't listen to it!

"I don't know how long…. But when they came and let us out …I couldn't speak. I wanted to say I was sorry but she ran off swearing."

"Oh bloody hell … Grant!" she jumped up and paced round the kitchen, "I thought you were going to say you'd killed her!" she yelled. The relief made her light headed but she was so mad that he'd put her through the anguish.

"No, she was alive and angry as I don't know what!"

"I'm not surprised she swore at you!" she snapped at him, trying to find some outlet for her frustration.

"No, she was swearing at Katychmar. Well she swore at me in the lift but, no, she was swearing at him when she got out!"

"And?" she was incensed. She'd been in a situation herself when a bloke had got carried away and she'd had to fight him off, and now Grant. Oh Grant not you!

"Just a minute …. He set me up," exclaimed Grant as he stood up gripping his forehead. Then he paced the floor.

"What?"

"Ssh…I'm trying to remember! …yes! She called him a 'fucking idiot' and then she asked him what he was waiting for because he could see I was hurting her."

"Oh Grant!" she put her hand to her mouth, it was so disappointing.

"No, don't you see there's something wrong here. How would he know what was going on in the lift? Why would he wait? Surely she should have said something like 'what took you so long?' if the lift was stuck accidentally. She made it sound like he was aware of what was happening in the lift and still he'd let it go on. She held him responsible for prolonging things unnecessarily."

"She was probably so mad and humiliated she'd have blamed anybody!" Violet could just imagine how she felt.

"Violet look, try and be objective about this!"

"Objective! You rape a girl …"

"I didn't rape her! She was up for it, she made all the moves.

"Right, and what about when she asked you to stop? How's that a right move?"

"It was only towards the end it got out of hand! Up until then she was into it the same as I was!"

Violet was in two minds. Was this over the line? Could she risk that one day the same thing might happen to her? Would she ever feel really safe with him again? She looked at him, angry that he'd tarnished her dream.

"Violet, the girl was wearing a red dress like the one in the photo that I'd always looked at. Katychmar has cameras all over the place and we'd discussed the photo in several sessions. Don't you think it's a bit of a coincidence that she turned up at the clinic with me in a lift that gets stuck. She doesn't panic but instead seduces me. On the TV they said she was a prostitute!"

"Yes they did," agreed Violet pleased to find some ray of hope in all the darkness.

"What if Katychmar paid the prostitute to seduce me in the lift as a way of getting to the bottom of my problem.

"What, and got her to wear a red dress?"

"Yes! I mean afterwards he didn't rant at me about his clinic and the damage something like this could have done to his reputation. He just focused on the progress I'd made as a result of the experience. It was as if he'd given me a dose of medicine."

"Hum," Violet felt it was a long shot but there was some sense in what he said.

"Violet I didn't have to tell you all this and I'm certainly not proud of what happened. I thought you deserved an explanation you wanted me to tell the truth so …" He let the breathe hiss between his teeth.

"Have you spoken to him about it since?"

"Yes I rang him yesterday. He said I shouldn't worry about anything but getting better."

"That's very philosophical of him!" she muttered with contempt.

"There's something else," added Grant thoughtfully.

"Oh, now what!" Violet, threw her hands up in the air and turned to look into the sink.

"Something Katychmar said when he caught up with me at the fountain after the session."

"What?"

"Well it was more of an aside really I don't think he was really taking to me. He said, she's right about your fitness levels."

"Yes, and?"

"Well I thought it was an odd thing to say. I mean, who was the 'she' he was referring to?"

"Fay?"

"Well that's exactly it! She did joke about my appetite … You know for ….sex I mean but she referred to it as my 'fitness level' and if I ever needed a reference etc." He smiled but let it die away quickly having thought better of it.

"You think he knew Fay?"

"Well she was going to a therapist and he is on the top of the list locally!"

"Yes but I thought she lived in York?" puzzled Violet.

"Well I live in Leeds!"

"Why did you choose him? Oh, I guess because you worked in Moverley."

"No, not really, he was on the top of the list for Yorkshire. I'd have gone to Manchester if I'd thought it was worthwhile. It's a bit of a coincidence but I can't think of anybody else that he could have been referring to when he said, she's right about your fitness levels."

"You've never met him before your appointment, you know socially, work?"

"No, nothing. So that makes me wonder."

"What now?" her impatience was a sham. A hint of optimism had crept into her thoughts.

"First Fay. If it was Katychmar that suggested to her about the rendezvous with me at the Bay Café."

"If he did!"

"Yes it was all his idea, the location everything but her dress."

"Yes, like a hooker!" said Violet coldly.

"Well! …." He shook his head with his hands open wide in front of him, "it was supposed to be a fantasy!"

"Go on," she wanted to smile but kept it under control.

"She had to ring him after we'd made the final arrangements for the meeting. Something about getting the tactics right or whatever and then she disappears."

"Right."

"Now, if Katychmar arranged for the Thai girl in the lift… wearing a red dress, she had sex with me and then she turns up dead."

"He was involved…"

"You see…Other than Fay and me, he was the only other person that knew about the details of our rendezvous. The Thai girl knew him. It wasn't the type of rebuke you'd give somebody you hardly knew and the last time I saw her, she was alive and kicking!"

"You think Katychmar killed the girl?"

"Well I think he's somehow involved with both incidents. I was worried, I mean really freaked out last night because I thought the police would suspect me for her murder what with Fay's disappearance looming in the background and to cap it all, Cosey knows about my addiction. If ever he got to know about the lift thing, well he'd have me in straightaway, I would. It's not looking good is it, she's been gone nearly a week!"

"Who, Fay?"

"Yes, I feel guilty there as well. Things between us weren't good our relationship was on the back foot and now… Well now I've met you and I'm glad she's not around to complicate things."

"Grant!"

"Violet I mean, I don't wish her any harm! I was never unfaithful to Fay. I know going on the chat lines and such are not really the way to demonstrate one's loyalty but I never went with anybody else. I didn't even chat you up!"

"You didn't even take an interest!"

"I was interested but I didn't do anything about it!"

"You just lusted after me in silence!"

"Well…yes, I did actually." He looked like a boy who'd confessed his sins for the first time.

"Grant I have to be honest, I feel so disappointed in you. After all that happened last night and you were such a good sport and actually, dare I say it, a perfect gentleman! I feel my trust in you has taken a bit of a hammering."

"Violet I've been dead straight with you right from the start and that's how you wanted it too. I'm trying to get the better of this addiction and I know it can be too much for some relationships but I'm going to give it my best shot with or without you. I'm sorry you feel let down but I can't change the past, I can only make the future better."

"I want to help you Grant but I can't live a lie," she took hold of his hand again.

"Well I'm fed up of being on the receiving end of all this," he slipped his hand free and got up and lent against the bar for a moment. Suddenly he turned and started to pace up and down the floor, "I'm going to get to the bottom of this before it does my bloody head in. I'm going to the clinic tonight just before it shuts and I'm going to have a look round. Who knows I might get lucky and find something that makes some sense."

"Grant, are you sure?" she felt worried about his safety. What if he got caught, wouldn't the police think it suspicious. Wouldn't they be more likely to find out about the girl connection? She pushed the hair back off her face. "Won't that make things worse with the police ....you know if you got caught? What if I come too, least that way I can testify that you're crazy!" She smiled, it seemed quite risky but strangely exciting too.

"You have to be of sound mind to testify at all ...I think," he smiled back, "I'm sorry Violet."

"Don't keep saying you're sorry. It's very irritating and right now that's not a good strategy." Her tone was up beat but with an aggressive edge to it and she crashed the mugs together. "More tea?"

"Yes please."

"You got any food in, I missed my lunch and if we're going to become burglars as well, I for one, need some food!"

"There's some mince in the fridge, although it might be out of date now…"

"No, it's fine," she scanned the label as the kettle reached a crescendo, "onions?"

"Yes over in the cupboard," he pointed below the sink.

"Spaghetti and tinned tomatoes? Does bolognaise sound okay to you?" It was a rhetorical question.

"Sounds just fine, I'll have a shower then."

"Good, you smell!" Happy families, she thought and dragged down the chopping board and cut into an onion. God she hoped she'd done the right thing!

Chapter 22

"I remember you being taller than the other girls and of slightly better stock if that's the right phrase," said Cosey with a very serious expression and it made Diane giggle as she crunched on a celery stick. "I never heard you swear either …and you always called them clients not punters."

"Yes," Diane waved a thin stick of carrot at him. "Tina always teased me about it, said that I was a snob and I spoilt the tone of the place."

"Your hair was longer then and a bit crinkly, with lighter strands running through it."

"It's still got those and they're natural, look!" she smiled, lent forward and held a few strands up for him to see.

"Oh yes and that's odd ….., funny I never noticed any of those before!"

She pulled in her cheeks, twisted her mouth slightly, leant forward again and whispered, "You think you're very funny don't you?"

"Diane I was only kidding, I couldn't see anything of the kind!"

"Are you sure?"

"Well I wasn't really looking, if you'd like me to look again I can…"

"What else do you remember? ….And just you remember, it'll be my turn next!"

"You had dark lipstick and lots of eye makeup and you had those long eyelashes."

"Yes, well those weren't my own, they came out at night!" they both giggled.

"Garlic mushrooms?" enquired the smartly dressed waiter.

Cosey gestured towards Diane.

"The Thai Fish Cakes for you, sir."

"Thank you," replied Cosey, "I'm absolutely starving." He smiled at Diane and they both ate for a while in silence. It's a measure of the comfort you feel in a relationship that periods of silence don't feel uncomfortable. It's pleasurable to share company and she was the most pleasurable of company, he sighed. He wandered what she was thinking? To look at her you'd never guess about her past. Her hair was neatly cut into her neck at the front but longer at the back and her make up was effective but not as pronounced as it was. Her sleeveless top was just low enough at the front to be interesting and the apricot bra strap that had slid down her arm when she clutched her hair earlier, well that looked good against her lovely brown skin. She slid it unhurriedly back into place and Cosey caught her eye. There was a hint of a smile and he felt a reciprocal one break out on his face.

"You're nice and brown Diane, where have you been?"

"I went to Tenerife just over a month ago, for a week"

"It's lasted well."

"Had a couple of sun beds just to keep it going," she raised her eyebrows.

"You're looking really well Diane, it's great to see you again."

"Oh," she grabbed her wine glass and looked across the restaurant.

The same sadness seemed to sweep over Diane from nowhere. It had been such a lovely evening and then he'd made such an innocuous little comment. Had it triggered her memory about some reality that she had been trying hard to forget? Was there life after death? God he hoped so, there were some scores to settle! More importantly right now, he must make the most of the evening. She was easy company and even after all this time ….

"How old were you back then Levi?" Diane's eyes were smiling again.

"I'll take these," said the young waitress and the young man returned with their main courses.

"Roast Duck with Plum Jus for you madam…. and the Steak Diane for you sir."

"Thank you," they replied.

"Your vegetables to share, would madam like some more wine?"

"No, I'm alright for the moment, thank you."

"Well, enjoy your meal," he departed with a polite smile.

"Levi, I…."

"I could hardly have not had the steak Diane when we're … celebrating!"

"Celebrating?"

"Yes, celebrating that we're friends after all this time!"

"I'll drink to that, and yes I will have some more wine!"

"Now as to your rather impertinent question earlier," he looked sternly at her and she giggled, "I was…"

"Do you need to borrow my fingers?" smiled Diane.

"Ha, even with yours I'm going to be a bit short, about twenty three when I last saw you."

"Yes, and very dashing in that uniform."

"Thank you."

"I never liked your sidekick! What was his name?"

"Shaun Hewitt, PC Hewitt to you!"

"Seedy character, he'd always be eyeing you up and down, just like a client but make out you weren't good enough or something. He'd always managed to work some innuendo into the conversation. Not that there's anything wrong with innuendoes, some are very clever and quite amusing in the right context but he was always trying to be…he just seemed to get a kick out of being slimy. I mean you might say something like, 'In that short skirt Diane you're gonna catch more than a cold,' you'd wink and smile and it was okay. But him, well! He once looked Tina up and down, when she was in the habit of wearing those tight leggings…"

"Yes I remember!"

"Well I bet they get nice and juicy! he'd say. Now what kind of …!"

"Now Diane! Yes I see your point."

"Then of course, once he'd found something he knew you didn't like, it became one of his mucky little clichés. Well he even had one for me. It wasn't really mucky actually but it was just over familiar for somebody that was little more than a slug!"

"You didn't like him much them?"

"I didn't like him at all! In those days I didn't wear a bra very often and he'd say, "Good job there aren't any squirrels round here or they'd have both of those.""

"Sorry?"

"He meant that my ..." she said looking down at her chest, "looked like acorns."

"Oh I see," he tried not to look.

"And as we both know, that's not going to be a problem this evening!" she smiled at him.

He pictured the apricot bra strap and could feel his cheeks redden a little.

"Do you remember the time he tried to bust Josey?"

Erm... No, I don't remember a Josey."

"Dark haired girl always wore a head band and big earrings."

"With that description you'd think I would but no I don't."

"Well, anyway she was with a bloke in one of Frank's coaches and Tina was in one of the others settling up with her client when they heard a noise outside. When they looked out they saw Hewitt watching Josey and her bloke at it through the window. He'd obviously been there a while because his breath had steamed up the outside of the window and he'd already wiped the glass at least once. Tina started shouting at him so he barged into the coach and tried to arrest Josey. Well you know Tina! She can be pretty intimidating once she gets going."

"Yes too right!"

"She was shouting and swearing at him, threatened to go down the station and lodge a complaint about him being a peeping tom. So in the end he just cautioned them and walked off."

"Ah, well that explains why I didn't know anything about it!"

"You nearly caught me once Levi," she looked at him through her fringe.

"Yes I do remember that!"

"So do I. You cleared your throat before you opened the bus door and I think you took your time on the stairs."

"Well I could see the windows upstairs above the backseats were steamed up and I'd seen you and that blonde girl …"

"Eleanor, …Oh yes Eleanor," she remembered.

"…on the rounds earlier but on my last round you'd gone so it could have been either of you really."

"Ah you see, that's the difference I meant the other day. You were always there to do your official duty in a crisis. You know, like the incident with Lionel and that poor cat or the accident on the crossing, but you never let your authority or your ego, get in the way."

"That's nice of you Diane. Shaun was actually quite a good copper."

"Hm," grunted Diane.

"He backed me up a number of times in really difficult situations without regard for his own safety. One night I had to try and separate these two guys fighting in the yard at the back of the Lobster pot."

"Oh yes."

"Well one of them pulled a knife and if it wasn't for Shaun's quick thinking, I wouldn't be here now!"

"Um."

"But I know what you mean about him making salacious comments. One of the female officers made a complaint about him once. It didn't lead to any formal disciplinary action. I think he got the message but that will have been after your time I think. Anyway the ego thing, well that was a different matter, it was his downfall really. He got into a car chase with a young joy rider. It turned out that the kid was a better driver, or should I say handled a car better than Shaun because in his attempt to run the kid off the road, he rammed a parked car and wiped himself out!"

"Well I can't say I'm sorry!"

"Blimey Diane, that's a bit harsh."

"Well that doesn't excuse the way he was with us. I know we belonged to the oldest profession but he made out he was so much better than our clients. Well a lot of the clients were okay, just normal blokes really. They weren't all cheating on their wives and you can take that look off your face."

"To be honest Diane, I know it's immoral, and don't get quoting me on this, but it's an arrangement between two consenting adults. There are lots of people who have casual sexual relationships. For that matter there are lots of people who claim to have respectable relationships when in truth the only reason they stay together is for the sex. In fact my mother once said the only reason she married my father was so she could have sex without losing her respectability. So in that context I don't see it's any better or worse but I think it's the payment that's the problem, people find that distasteful."

"Well.."

"Frankly I agree that it does no harm for a man or woman for that matter, to pay for company or sex. The thing I hate is when all the shady characters on the fringes come out of the woodwork and try to turn a profit out of it, you know the pimps and the blackmailers and so on… that's when the law needs to get involved. But I was smiling because you said that your clients weren't playing away!"

"Well the popular view is always that the bloke turns his back on his wife and just wants to indulge himself without regard for the harm it does to the innocent people involved like kids and so on…..but women aren't always the victim. What about the women who decide for their own selfish reasons that they no longer want to have sex in their marriage? You know they've got their 2.5 children, nice house etc and hubby's role is just the breadwinner. Where's the fairness in that?"

"You mean if he'd denied her the children she'd be justified in playing around as well?"

"Well in part," she laughed, "but sex in relationships …when I was younger it always seemed to be about enjoying yourselves together without getting pregnant. Granted one of the reasons for getting married, is to provide a secure environment for children to grow up in, but if the sex was an important ingredient in the relationship before the children arrived, then you can't just switch it off afterwards and not expect there to be consequences."

"You've certainly got a bee in your bonnet about it, Diane. There's a lot of bravado between men about sex, I was surprised to read that quite a few men aren't that bothered about sex either."

"I'm sorry Levi, I hope I haven't gone on too much. There are those selfish individuals who play around and not just with prostitutes, regardless of the harm it does to others and I despise them, I despise them all but to prejudge people without knowing the true circumstances, it makes me see red."

"Yes I guess we should all be a bit more open-minded at times."

"Gender stereotypes! It's amazing that so many couples want to risk settling down at all, finding a counterpart is a minefield!"

"Yes, and even when you find somebody… Well people change, don't they?"

"Did you ever settle down Levi?"

"Yes, I got married if that's what you mean, I don't know I ever settled down exactly," he said with a smile that faded. "She died of Leukaemia about three years ago."

"I'm sorry Levi."

"I'm sorry that she had to go like that but it wasn't a marriage made in heaven exactly. My job isn't conducive to a family life, too many interruptions. I found it hard to shut it out even when I wasn't actually at work. When I look back, we really didn't have much in common. I think circumstances just brought us together and it seemed like the natural thing to do but the troubles pass and you just drift away from each other back to the people you used to be."

"I'm sorry, Tina told me you were on your own but I didn't realise that she'd died ……." Her voice tailed off and the sadness returned to her face.

Cosey fell silent. He studied the serviette on his lap for a while and smoothed it with the palm of his hands as if paying reverence to his wife's memory. He felt guilty. Had he selfishly pursued his job and let the relationship fail? It wasn't that he sought the recognition or promotion he just wasn't prepared to let the villains get away with it!

"I'm glad you never rode a bicycle though!" said Diane brightly.

Cosey pushed his feelings of guilt back into a remote corner of his mind, took a deep breath and replied, "Well, I'm not that old," he smiled. "Eventually they gave me one of those Panda cars. I think it was the last one in the service because it spent more time in the garage than on the road. I applied to become a detective not long after you left and much to my surprise they accepted me."

"Do you enjoy it?"

"I'm not sure I enjoy it exactly but I find it rewarding and you feel you're doing something worthwhile. It's very frustrating when you know you've got a villain but due to their good luck or some quick witted barrister, they go free on a technicality."

"Have you ever been tempted to stitch somebody up like that?"

"Tempted, certainly! But it defeats the purpose of it all if when it suits, you to just go ahead and ignore the law. I can quite understand how it happens, some of the cases, well you just don't want to know. You have to draw the line and keep to the right side of it, so far, touch wood, I've managed to separate the shades of grey. Problem is that as we all become more accountable you know there's always the possibility that somebody following in your footsteps might come to a different conclusion."

"Well, I'm proud of you!"

"Are you?"

"Yes I am, you do it for the right reasons. You always have and it makes all the difference. In this day and age it's important to feel that there are people who stand for what's right. You're not politically motivated, you're not trying to improve your ratings you just care about people getting a fair deal."

"Blimey Diane, if ever I need a reference…"

"I'll give you one, no problem," she giggled.

"How about you then, what's happened to you since you left?"

"Well I saw the error of my ways," she said brightly and with a little giggle that sounded a bit forced, she wiped the corner of her mouth on the napkin. "Mine was absolutely delish' what about yours?"

"First rate, I think I'll have to wait a bit for a sweet."

"That suits me…I left because I wanted to turn over a new leaf. I wanted more out of life but it's very easy in that game to just live from day to day. You know, wake up one morning and you're forty and the clients don't fancy you anymore, then what do you do?"

"Well, true I suppose." he nodded, having never really thought of it in that way before. "I suppose it would be like a forced retirement."

"Yes, well I didn't want it to be like that for me. Anyway there had been this health visitor that used to come round and chat to the girls you know, about regular check ups for

STD's and the like. I got on well with her, I thought she cared about us so, I used to go along with her sometimes and even introduce her to the girls she didn't know. She told me of a similar job to hers going at a different centre and although I didn't have any formal training, she knew they were very keen to recruit from within the industry and would offer all kinds of training incentives and so on. Well, one morning I woke up, it was a lovely sunny day and I just decided that enough was enough and I applied for the job. Two days later I'd had an interview and by the end of the week they'd offered me a place on the scheme."

"Well, that was a turn up for the book!"

"As HIV became more of an issue and safer sex more socially acceptable I found myself more involved with counselling people at risk and also those who regrettably had fallen victim to the disease. I moved away because, well thanks to you, I didn't have a criminal record so I wasn't barred from any social groups. But there were old clients of mine around and I just didn't want one of them turning up in one of my sessions. I still corresponded with Tina, well on and off, but I lost contact with the other girls. As I said, I think they kind of got retired!"

"Are we all finished?" enquired the waiter.

"Yes thanks," Cosey lent back in his chair.

"Yes it was lovely, what have you got in the way of deserts?" Diane smiled at the waiter, but it turned to a devilish twinkle in her eye as she looked at Cosey.

"I think I can manage something now too," added Cosey with a bit of mock bravado.

"I'll bring the sweet trolley over," replied the waiter.

"You're not going to explode on me are you?" enquired Diane with a raised eyebrow.

"I might! But it would be a waste of such a good meal."

"Right then, what …"

"Wow, I think I'll just have coffee," chuckled Cosey.

"You, you're all talk! I'll have some trifle please."

"Certainly, would you like some cream?"

"No thanks, but I will have an Irish coffee when the time comes."

"By all means madam and what sort of coffee would you like sir?"

"Just a normal white coffee for me please."

"Okay," replied the waiter and he rattled the sweet trolley back to its corner.

"This is a good restaurant you've chosen Levi, have you eaten here before?"

He'd have liked to say, Oh, yes all the time! But in truth he rarely went out at all. Fifteen years of married life had raised his awareness about shopping wisely. He had a well stocked freezer but he chose things that on average took no more than about fifteen minutes to prepare and favoured anything that would microwave. He had, however, always tried to have a cooked breakfast and a proper roast on a Sunday, even if it meant a Carvery at a family pub on the ring road.

"No, I consulted the local good food guide."

"Well, it's a fine choice."

"I'm glad you like it. I've always wanted to have a night out with you Diane but circumstances always seem to have conspired against me. Look at the other day even, there we were having a nice chat and Tina turned up in a bit of a flap and then you were gone. I'd enjoyed the moment and missed my chance!"

"Well, you've made up for all those missed opportunities tonight Levi, it's been great!"

He looked into her eyes they looked alive and they were soft and affectionate.

"Are you staying long or are you planning to move back?"

"I'm staying until the weekend and I haven't made any long term plans as yet."

Damn it! She looked away from him across the restaurant. "Will I get chance to see you again before you go?" asked Cosey in a softer, affectionate tone.

Diane looked down at her glass and twisted it in her fingers. She put it down, rested the fingers of both hands on it and looked up at him through a bit of her fringe, "I'd like that Levi, I'm glad you asked me. I'll give you my mobile number," she took a business card from her wallet, "you can give me a call and we'll arrange something."

"I'll look forward to it."

"You're a nice man Levi," she said softly and looked into his eyes.

The coffee arrived with a clunk. The young waitress went through all the palaver with sugar and cream. God, surely they must teach them to choose their moments better than this! The atmosphere was electric and Diane smiled slightly at him across the table but with every nanosecond that passed he could see the sadness return.

"Do you live locally?" Diane broke the silence when the waitress finally fled. The coffee making hadn't gone well but she'd not made a fuss.

"No, we bought a place in the country, it's a bit big for me now but I've just been too busy to think about moving frankly." Now the question he'd waited all night to ask but feared the answer. "D'you ever get married Diane?"

"No, Levi... I never quite found the right person. I did meet somebody after I moved but it didn't come to anything in the end and I kind of stopped looking I suppose!"

"Life kind of takes over sometimes doesn't it?"

"It does. Now if you'll excuse me I'll have to powder my nose," she smiled as she stood and smoothed her skirt.

Cosey watched her leisurely walk through the archway. She still had a slim figure and long legs. He smiled to himself as he wondered what she might look like naked and then motioned to the waiter for the bill. Whatever it was, it was worth it. She seemed to be gone quite a long time and he'd paid the bill by her return.

"I'm going to have to go now Levi, I've an early appointment tomorrow."

"Okay, I'll run you home."

They spoke very little on the journey but exchanged the occasional smile. At one set of lights she put her hand on top of his as it rested on the gear stick waiting for the off. She looked down at his hand, smiled and caressed his fingers. Horns blared behind and prompted him into a bit of a racing start and then fifteen seconds later they arrived at the hotel.

"Thanks for a lovely evening Levi," she leant forwards, and placed a soft warm kiss on his lips. She paused briefly looking in his eyes and before he could say anything she got out of the car and waved.

"Don't forget to call me," she was gone.

Suddenly he felt depressed. It was the longest he'd ever been in her company, it had gone better than he'd dare hope and yet now he felt more alone than ever.

Chapter 23

Without a shadow of a doubt the Lady in Red had lost her appeal although her lovely smooth bronzed skin and eyes, heavy with mascara, still remained a striking image. Grant felt sad that their relationship had come to an end but whatever latent and deep seated desires her eyes had held for him, they burnt no more. Instead he found from time to time that he'd glance round the display area at the clinic to see what point Violet had reached, this being her first visit there was a lot to see. The tall bronze bondage figure got only a cursory glance, the grimace spoke volumes. Her pace quickened at first sight of the Punk Ballerina which she approached with a smile and when their eyes met and she'd giggled quietly raising an eyebrow at him across the clinic reception area. Grant smiled with some satisfaction at the jodhpur wearing Adonis who failed to match up any better than he had to the characters in Simon's magazine. One thing he'd gained from the readers letters was an insight into the extent their problems mirrored those of the heterosexual population. In some ways their predicament to find a suitable partner was far more complex than he'd imagined. One of the letters reminded him of a story on the sexual addiction web site about a young gay man who had attempted suicide three times on his way to recovery due to the overwhelming nature of his addiction. Grant felt relieved that his predilection was only for women. 'Only', what an understatement! Earlier he'd wondered if even Violet's boundless confidence in their relationship had been overstretched. It brought on a cold sweat just the thought of how close it had been. She must have been on quite an emotional rollercoaster. No wonder she looked so shocked. One minute he was saying he'd just stopped short of raping the Thai girl and next minute she thought that he'd killed her instead! Bloody hell, he really should have planned out how to tell her. Anyway, he heaved a sigh of relief, they were hanging in there. It still felt a bit tense but they were in with a chance. Dinner was very nice though, he'll let her cook again.

Somebody was stood next to him and abruptly he awoke from his thoughts. With a smile he turned to greet Violet but his expression changed dramatically. The disappointment must have been obvious to the late middle aged, silvery haired elegant woman in a pale blue two piece.

"Oh, I'm sorry I thought you were somebody else," he said brightly.

"No, it's only me," she replied with a smile. "…She reminds me of my daughter."

"Sorry?"

"The girl in the photo," she pointed.

"Oh yes, she's very…" He wanted to say sexy but would you say that to a proud mother?

"Sexy isn't she?" she said with a naughty smile. "I used to be in Burlesque myself and you'd be surprised just how many of the men I dated eventually got round to it."

"Sorry?"

"They'd want me to take home one of those outfits and parade about in it for them," she said pointing at the brunette squeezed tightly into a lace up basque. "Shallow individuals you men! Anyway, I'm not trying to chat you up. This is my first time and I'm not sure about this bleeper thing," she held it out on the palm of her hand. "The girl at the desk is very nice and all that but she talks too fast. What exactly am I supposed to do with it?"

"Oh right, has it buzzed yet?"

"Oh yes!" she replied proudly.

"Right, well you're on then."

"Oh am I!" she smiled.

"Yes, let me have a look at it," he looked round to see if he could see Violet. He had started with absolutely no plan as to how they would get up to Katychmar's office legitimately and now a plan was beginning to formulate in his head but he needed Violet to be there too. Shit, where was she? "Now if you turn it over there's a small screen and …Yes you've got an appointment see, it's in room 2.9." Thank God he sighed, Violet had just come into sight around a partition nearby.

"And where about is that exactly?"

"Violet darling!" he smiled and opened his eyes as wide as they'd go in the hope that she'd catch on, "our appointment's been called and were in 3.6 but we're going to help this lady get to hers first, I think she's a bit late, is that okay?" he nodded.

"Oh that's very kind of you," she smiled at Violet, "you're so lucky to have such a nice young man, perfect manners."

"Right," replied Violet. She looked a bit stunned but at least she went with the flow.

"The lift's are over there," he gestured and the three of them filed off towards the lift lobby. As the lady got out on the second floor Grant pointed out how the room numbers jutted out at right angles above the doors.

"It looks like yours is the last one on the right up there," he pointed, "can you see the number is illuminated?"

"Oh yes thank you, such a gentleman," she beamed.

"Such a gentleman!" mocked Violet as the doors shut, "Bet she was only after your dick, the grubby little parasite!"

"What, you're not jealous of a middle aged retired Burlesque dancer are you?"

"Yes, they're the worst kind!"

"This couldn't have worked out better Violet, we're the last people in the building. We need to find somewhere to hide for a while until she's had her appointment, then, when she's left and it's all quiet, we can get out and nosey about."

"Is that official detective jargon? Get out and nosey about! It sounds like a Rap song."

"Ssh! We're here," whispered Grant.

The lift chime announced their arrival at the third floor.

"Why are we whispering, that thing's told everybody that isn't deaf that we're here anyway?" she whispered.

"Lifts sometimes do that don't they, you know open and the person that called them has already gone in an earlier one!"

"Got yer!" she giggled.

Grant stuck his head out of the lift and checked out the corridor. Room number four was in use but otherwise the coast was clear.

"Right come on," he grabbed her hand and pulled her along gently behind him. After a few steps he stopped. "Just a minute." They retraced their steps back to a single door close to the lift. "This might be just what we're looking for."

The door opened easily and they stood still inside once the door had closed and listened for the sound of approaching feet or anything that might suggest they'd been spotted. All was silent but for the sound of their breathing.

"Hello tough guy," she smiled, draped her arms round his neck and leant her chest on him.

"I'm no ruffian," he replied in mock disdain, glad that there was genuine warmth back in her voice again. "I don't go in for all that spitting and fighting lager lout stuff," he pushed back the few strands of hair that obscured her eyes.

"You're not afraid to stand up for yourself though Grant, I mean look at us now?"

"No, this is different. I feel I owe it to Fay. I know I wasn't right for her but if Katychmar's involved… Maybe something I said triggered the whole thing off and then there's the Thai girl, look what happened to her. If this comes out okay maybe I'll feel a bit better about that too!"

"So what are we going to do while we wait then?"

"That's not fair! I still feel awkward Violet, you know …about everything and …"

"Look I was disappointed Grant but you have to live with that. If doing this helps you atone for your sins then maybe by helping you, I'll feel better as well."

"You're pretty damn special you know that Violet?"

"Anyway as I was saying …if we survive the test …" she smiled, "you'll be surprised just how enthusiastically I make good on my innuendoes."

"Well I hope you've got plenty of stamina because I'm an addict and I can do innuendoes morning, noon and night," his smile faded fast. "I don't like to think of myself in those terms Violet, in fact since my last session with Katychmar I've not been anywhere near as frantic about the whole thing. I've not been on a chat room. I just haven't felt the need and that is a first, so I can thank you for that I think," he smiled and kissed her tenderly.

"We're good together Grant," she said softly.

"You bet."

"Hm," she hugged him tighter.

"Actually, while we're here, you can tell me the story about your house."

"Oh yes, well …shall we move away from the door, don't want to be overheard," she nodded.

"Yes it looks like it goes round at the end."

Violet followed him round and they settled themselves next to each other on the table.

"Right, I took a fancy to the shop quite a long while ago but it had stood empty for several years because somewhere along the line there'd been a poor structural report and you know how it is, word gets round."

"Yeah."

"Well Simon thought it would be a good investment if it came up for auction and about two years ago it did, come up for auction that is. He discussed it with his partner Brain, he was my other flat mate."

"Oh yes."

"Well he's an architect, does all these waterside development projects and there can be refurbishment involved with some of them, you know old warehouses and the like.

"Right,"

"To cut a long story short, Brian came round the property with me and he felt sure the survey had exaggerated the problem but to be sure he got the guy who does all his structural work to give it a once over as well. Later we all had dinner and came up with a plan."

"Bet that cost a packet!"

"It's not what you know, it's who!" she smiled.

"Yeah!"

"So on the day of the auction it came down to me and this snooty little woman and her yappy little dog. The auctioneer didn't like it at all, the damn thing wouldn't shut up. At one point Simon thought that the dog was actually doing the bidding."

"What?" they both giggled.

"Yes, anyway eventually I got it at just less than half the market price."

"Well done you!"

"The mortgage was a bit steep at first until I leased out the shop. It's better now I've even managed to start buying a few things for it at last. I didn't have any proper curtains in the lounge until about three weeks ago."

"Well it looks pretty homely to me, you've done really well. I'm impressed."

"What about you. Do you own your flat?"

"Yes," he replied with a note of distain, "I'd never buy a flat again."

"Why?"

"Well you must have noticed all the signs up outside?"

"Yes, there must be … about ten of them."

"Exactly, and I've only had two people to look round in the last six months."

"You need to change your agent!"

"Well he gave me the best valuation!"

"It's only worth what people will pay for it. He'll have given you an inflated price just to get your business."

"To be honest I've not really pushed it. I've been letting all sorts of things slide recently Violet because of this damned obsession."

"Look if you like I could ask Simon if he's got any ideas."

"Well I don't…"

"He's really well connected and just maybe he knows somebody who specialises in flats. You don't know till you ask?"

"Hum."

"Look it's only like selling protein drinks or hair products, we both work in advertising, Grant if we can't sell it, who can?"

"Yes you're right. It's bloody stupid really. I've just not had the right attitude from the start, I've got side tracked. I need to get my shit together man!"

"Yo baby!" she laughed.

"What do you reckon then?" he nodded towards the door.

"I think it's worth a peek."

"Yes me too," and with that they slid off the table and walked to the door. They listened intently at it for a moment or two, then Grant turned the handle quietly and they slipped into the corridor. The light was still on over room four but Grant guided Violet towards Katychmar's office.

"If the light's on for room four he's not going to be in here," he whispered.

"Right."

Grant leant on the door and gradually increased the pressure until it started to open, the only sound came from the draft excluder bristles as they caressed the edge of the door. Through the small gap he'd made, Grant could clearly see Katychmar's desk but there was no sign of life. He edged the gap still wider and was eventually able to get his head in to take a look round. He felt Violet's hands on his waist.

"Okay there's nobody here," he whispered and stepped into the room, Violet close on his heels. The door gave a soft click as it closed behind them. It was almost dark outside and the desk light gave the only illumination in the room. The distant sounds of voices could be heard and Violet walked carefully round the room and paused at each of the doors to listen. Grant moved towards the desk, oddly he felt that the sounds came from that direction. Stood by the desk he caught Violet's eye and nodded.

"No nothing," she replied in a loud whisper and set off carefully across the room to join him at Katychmar's chair.

"Take a look at this," he said with a hint of amazement.

On the bottom right monitor the picture showed Katychmar in one of the consulting rooms engaged in an obviously heated conversation with a stocky bald man in a black T shirt and black leather jacket.

"Can you turn it up?"

"Not so far, I've tried pretty much everything, wait a minute," and as he pushed up the large fader on the extreme left, Katychmar's voice became quite clear.

"It's the master fader. I've been trying all the individual channels …"

"Shsss!…Listen!"

"I do understand it was a difficult choice you had to make Ron, but let's face it Vick died anyway!" said Katychmar.

"I couldn't just stand there, flesh and blood runs deep at times like that!"

"Well if it's any consolation I thought Terry's choice of final resting place was strangely apt. Thai girl in a Chinese Skip, it's almost politically correct," smirked Katychmar, "but we're getting off the point. Did anybody see you coming in here?"

"What do you take me for?"

"You should have waited for me to let you in through the fire escape as usual. You've taken a ridiculous chance coming in the front way just at the moment." Katychmar's voice had developed quite an edge.

"Look nobody saw me, I waited till the old woman left, the foyer was clear, I even waited till the receptionist went in the back before I sneaked in. Believe me nobody but you knows I'm here!" said Ron who was obviously getting to the end of his tether.

"Oh yes they do!" giggled Violet.

"Sh," hissed Grant.

"So what was so important that you needed to see me here?" asked Ron, his was voice tinged with impatience.

"You said the police were digging into your phone records and I didn't think you'd want them to have a record of our conversation right now!" explained Katychmar.

"I think they're trying to build a case linking us to Fay's disappearance. I've taken the precaution of moving the truck into storage but I can't be sure if it's not too late. Terry seemed to think that one of those crime scene blokes might have been looking at the truck whilst he was talking to Cosey."

"Well you'd better find a way to deflect their interest back onto Grant."

"That's being taken care of as we…."

"Did you hear that!" said Violet excitedly.

"Sh," hissed Grant.

"You'd be well advised to mothball your operation and get rid of anything that could be risky. If you have to save anything, do it a long way from here. Can you get down there as yet?"

"Vick's office is still out of bounds and there's a bobby there during the day, but as long as we keep to the right side of the tape, we can get into the workshop and so on. Night time, well that's different, there's no bobby. Anyway, even if there was, we grew up in that yard. We can get in and out of there anytime and they'd be none the wiser."

"Over the years Ron, our relationship has been mutually beneficial but events of late have led me to realise that its usefulness has run its course."

"Yes well just remember that all this clever CCTV stuff doesn't last for ever and without me you'd not have had anything quite as sophisticated."

"Granted."

"You'd also not get anymore of these," Ron pulled out a plain black DVD case and laid it on the table.

"What's that?"

"Edited highlights of Lumaii's little experience in the lift, just as you like it, courtesy of Lionel."

"Oh …yes I see," and he took the case and slipped it into his jacket pocket.

"If you ask me, some of this stuff," he pointed at the DVD in Katychmar's pocket, "could cost you your licence if it got out."

"Don't you threaten me Ron Whinsper I've got my own insurance as far as you're concerned. Granted the materials you've prepared for me would be very embarrassing in the wrong hands but just remember that you're the egotistical one who wants to immortalise yourself on film, whilst indulging your sadistic pleasure."

"You're in this right up to your neck the same as the rest of us," growled Ron.

"No I don't think so," snapped Katychmar, "voyeur I maybe but I've never laid a finger on any of your victims. That brother of yours, even in clinical terms, is an animal. I should never have let him out!"

"Ah but you did and that's my insurance because it's well documented too isn't it?"

Katychnar hissed through his teeth. "There isn't a day goes by when I don't picture that poor child."

"It would have been difficult for you to recover from that so early in your career."

"Yes, well I made my choices," said Katychmar with resolve, "and you made yours and now you'd better get your house in order or you'll bring us both down!"

"So you brought me here to try and dissolve our partnership did you?" said Ron threateningly as he stepped towards Katychmar.

"Partnership!"

"Yes, well you'd better play your part right when they come back to talk to you, and they will," Ron pointed his finger at Katycmar and he backed towards the door. Then he turned, paused with his hand on the handle and looked at his feet. "It'll take Lionel another two days tops to finish editing the last film and then I'll do what you suggest." He looked over his shoulder at Katychmar, "I'll shut it down," and with that he let himself out.

"Quick," said Grant, "we need to follow him. I don't know what this is all about but I'm sure this is exactly the lead we're looking for."

The chime announced the lift and he knew that in a few seconds Ron would be on his way down in what must be the slowest lift in the world. Katychmar was settling down with some paperwork so this was their chance.

Grant found Violet's tomboy approach on the stairs endearing. He took two at a time and she was right behind him. Not that his emotions needed any coaxing. He had fallen head over heels in love with her. Each new facet of her that emerged drew him more under her spell and he had no desire to apply the brakes.

The occasional squeaks from their trainers on the pale green stair covering that strangely twinkled in the halogen lights were accompanied by the drone of their hands as they clutched onto the metal banister and careered down the stairs. Near the bottom there was a thump from the floor below followed by the clunk of a mechanical door closer. Grant pinned Violet to the wall out of sight. The sound of a crash bar followed and the brief wave of street noise convinced Grant that there was a fire exit below. After a few seconds they followed suit and emerged into a dark alley leading to the street. They were just in time to see the shapely figure of the receptionist turn right in the direction of the car park.

"If she's leaving this way," said Violet, "it probably means that the front doors are locked."

"Yes, but where's Ron?" Stood in the shadows of the alleyway they checked out the street to the left but then to the right an engine started up and a Triple 'A' taxi moved sedately from the curb.

"That's it! That's it!" declared Grant excitedly.

"What?"

"I'll explain later! Wait here while I'll get the car and watch where that taxi goes," he pointed. Grant then ran like a madman, tore through the car park, vaulted the railings and dropped into the street below where he had parked the car earlier. As luck would have it the car was facing the right way and it started first time. He brought it up the short incline careful not to squeal the tyres as he stopped to pick up Violet.

"He's just turned left onto the main road," she waved her hand excitedly as she zipped herself in with the seatbelt. "I was right about the boy racer though wasn't I," she giggled and looked around at the immaculately kept interior, "It's very clean and tidy."

"Don't knock it, there aren't many of them about anymore and this car and I have got history together."

"It's a Capri isn't it?"

"Yes 1.6LS."

"Down there, he's just turned right," she pointed.

"It wasn't as neat when I bought it and to be honest I chose it because the price was right… Well I like black cars as well so that was also a consideration."

"So what was all that excitement about back there in the alley?"

"Right, the night Fay disappeared there was a Triple 'A' taxi leaving when I got there!"

"So you've jumped to the conclusion that Ron is in the taxi because of that?"

"Why doesn't that make sense?" he replied assertively but his voice tailed off.

"Well it's a bit of a long shot don't you think?"

"Oh God, I just thought!"

"Look out he's turning left just opposite the café."

Grant slowed down a bit but didn't indicate. Violet's conclusion made sense and now he had to face the possibility that the best, no the only lead that he'd got to unravelling all the events of the past few days, may have gone off in a completely different direction. He slapped the wheel hard with his hand in frustration. As they neared the junction Grant slowed right down and tried to see round Violet's head what had happened to the taxi.

"He's parking up, just past the viaduct," said Violet at a whisper.

Grant just caught sight of the reversing lights before they passed the end of the road.

"I'll pull in here." He violently steered the car behind the launderette into a narrow entrance next to a high stone wall and came to an equally violent stop in front of some dilapidated wooden gates. Before Grant switched off the lights Violet just had time to pick out the name in faded gold letters on the flaking and discoloured wooden gate.

"The Whinsper Empire," she read out quizzically, "It doesn't look very grand to me!"

They got out of the car as quickly as they could. Grant caught up with Violet as she peered round the corner of the launderette in the direction of the viaduct. Beyond the corrugated iron fence she'd made out the shape of a man in a black leather jacket with a bald head making his way behind the railings and pointed excitedly.

"It's him!" she whispered," it's him."

"Shsss!"

"But it's…"

"Yes its Ron, thank God, I really thought I'd blown it all back there!" he whispered.

Now that Ron had moved out of sight they ran along beside the corrugated fence and came to a stop just short of the railings. The police tape flicked against the fence but otherwise it was silent. This time Grant took a peek and was just in time to see Ron disappear through a hole he'd made between the sheets of metal cladding on a large hanger like building to their right.

Violet had already started making her way through the undergrowth behind the railings to follow Ron's lead.

"Oh shit, bloody shit!" she whispered loudly.

"Shss, you're supposed to be a lady, oh shit!"

"Nettles!" she remarked sarcastically. She pulled her sleeves down and grasped the cuffs from inside to form makeshift gloves and led the way fending off the weeds. At the metal panels she stepped aside to let Grant go through first. It seemed very dark in there at first and he felt his way along what he concluded to be a large metal transport container. Violet tucked her fingers into the back of his waistband and followed close behind. It was all a bit scary and he had to admit to himself that he was grateful of the company and found the physical contact reassuring. On reaching the end of the container he had to duck down even further to get behind a large red tool chest with the lid up. He crouched right down to get a look round it into the darkness beyond. To the right a car stood with its bonnet up and a small inspection light lay on the rocker box. It was the only source of light in the place. He heard the sounds of somebody moving about and the distinctive noise of a ratchet spanner but it seemed a way off further round to the right. Ahead he just made out a metal staircase that lead up to what looked like portable office units. There was a movement below the stairs and although he wasn't able to make out what it was, he didn't have to wait long for the answer. The sound of a heavy catch or lever was followed by a shaft of light that swung out from the doorway across the floor to cast black shadows from an assortment of equipment, tyres and vehicles that stood in its path. Grant screwed up his eyes. The light was far too bright, and he crouched back behind the tool box. He allowed himself the use of only one eye to watch what happened next. A large figure with hair that dangled in rat tails shuffled from within towards the doorway accompanied by the distant sound of rock music and as he reached the threshold Ron stepped into the light and spoke.

"You okay Lionel?"

"Yeah"

"You've got two days max."

"Hm," nodded Lionel as he continuously shifted his enormous weight between feet.

"Do your best because after that I'm shutting it all down."

"Oh Ron!"

"I'm sorry Lionel it's all getting a bit dodgy round here, so keep the door shut and don't let your music get too loud okay!" The tone was firm but with a note of warm understanding that seemed out of character with the man that Grant had seen in Katychmar's consulting room less than an hour ago.

"Okay Ron," Lionel shuffled round and went back inside.

"CLANG...CLUNK...CLING!

Fuck! That made him jump, his heart was pounding. Grant felt Violet's hand grab his waistband really tight. The noise was from the tool box just above his head but it echoed all around, somebody had just thrown some heavy metal object into it.

"Fucking hell, Terry!" called Ron in an angry shouted whisper as he looked in the direction of the tool box.

"I'm sorry Ron," said a wheezy voice from somewhere very close by on the other side of the toolbox.

"What's the point us creeping around and working in the bloody dark, if you're gonna make that kind a fucking noise!" snapped Ron as he strode up towards the large individual who'd now moved to stand so close in front of Grant that he could smell his sweaty body. Grant and Violet shuffled back behind the container just in time to see Ron's shadow on the floor as he swiped the woolly hat from Terry's head and slung it across the workshop.

"I know it's not easy working nights like this but it's all we can do until things quieten down a bit. How much longer are you gonna be?"

"Probably half an hour on this one and I'm not sure about the Ford yet, could be a couple of hours or so," replied Terry.

"Right I'm gonna get off..."

Granted nodded urgently to Violet in the direction of their entrance, it was time to leave and fast. If Ron came their way they needed to make tracks. Violet was just about to squeeze herself between the metal sheets and out into the open when Grant grabbed her and he squeezed them both into the small gap between the end of the container and the metal panels with only seconds to spare. Ron hurried by and slid effortlessly through the hole. They waited what seemed like an age. The sound of him rustling through the undergrowth died away and then the distant sound of a car started up. As it drove away they felt convinced that it was safe to shuffle out of their tiny hiding place and ease their aching muscles. Grant slid through the hole first, checked the coast was clear and motioned to Violet to follow. Neither of them spoke as they hurried back to the car.

"Will you watch me out on to the road?" asked Grant.

Violet nodded as she wrapped her arms round herself, she looked cold thought Grant.

They made good time on the way back into town but Violet looked weary. She'd looked quite worried when he'd explained how he intended to return the next night and get a look at what Lionel was up to.

"You've been great tonight Violet," he said warmly after he'd caught brief glimpses of her while driving, "it's been quite an interesting date really!" he smiled.

"Yes I'm bushed and it's late. Do you want to stay over?" she said softly as the car came to a stop at the back of the shop, "house rules apply of course," she added sleepily.

"House rules sound just fine to me," he replied.

"You're doing really well with all of this Grant. You're turning out to be quite a man. Who'd have thought, hey!" she smiled and rubbed the back of his hand as it lay on the gear stick.

"Oh Shit! What day is it?" cursed Grant.

"What?"

"What day is it?"

"Thursday," they said in unison.

"Damn!" he cursed and thumped the steering wheel with both hands, "I've got the bloody forensic bloke coming to look at the car tomorrow."

"Well ring him and put him off."

"He's coming at 8.00am and I don't know where he'll be coming from. Frankly I don't want to put him off! I want them to prove that there was somebody else there on Friday night. There were big tyre tracks on that back road, I saw them. I mean, what if the truck ran into me on purpose as a distraction, a delaying tactic, while somebody else snatched Fay and later they bundled her into the lorry up on that back road."

"It sounds a bit far fetched Grant."

"Well, the longer this thing goes on the… It's just doing my head in …What if she really has been abducted? I feel I should be doing something but I just don't know what!"

"I'm sorry Grant it must be awful, not knowing."

"Maybe this'll give the police something to go on. I best go," he said dejectedly. "Thanks Violet you've been a real mate you know!" he added with a weary smile.

Violet kissed him on the lips cupped his face in her warm hands. "Will you be in at work tomorrow?"

"Yes I've only just taken the morning off. I'll ring you, let you know."

"Okay, bye now," she smiled and shut the car door. Grant watched her disappear inside, gave a little wave and set off for Leeds deep in thought. The events of the night and the last few days swarmed about in his head, so much so, that he failed to notice the car that followed him.

Chapter 24

Next to visiting a grieving relative this was the part of the job Cosey disliked most. Dead bodies could be horribly mutilated and smelly enough to turn even the strongest stomach but you were often able to brace yourself behind a false detachment because they were people no more. No matter the suffering they'd endured it was now over and you felt a bond with them, a duty to them, that in their memory you'd find and bring to justice those responsible. It was more difficult with a missing person because over the days you'd been searching, you'd also have got to know them a little. Sometimes you felt an affinity with them, even found parallels in your own life. Cosey had liked what he'd gleaned about Fay and Leslie was right to be protective about her friend. She certainly seemed to have stronger feelings for her than Grant displayed and now if the body on the beach turned out to be who he thought it was well, there was more heartache to come!

Earlier Sumlea, still traumatised from her own experience, had taken the news of Lumaii's death badly. Cosey had felt hopelessly inadequate. Sat on the bed at the hospital waiting to be taken home to Lumaii's flat, Cosey had seen her smile brightly for the first time. The worry Vick was still lurking out there somewhere had been removed, she obviously felt more secure. He'd looked into her wide eyes that had been full of hope and seen her smile fade as she'd begun to read his expression.

"Sumlea, I've got some really tragic news …"

She'd cried her heart out the poor little mite. Thank God he'd taken Joyce with him. As Family Liasion Officers go, she was easily the best he'd known. He felt he wanted to stay longer but news of the body on the beach reached him just as he'd arrived and the time had come for him to get down there and manage the scene ASAP. In less than four hours the tide would turn and any evidence they hadn't retrieved would be lost.

The mist of yesterday had gone completely and it had developed into a lovely sunny morning. When his car pulled up he'd seen, some way from the promenade this side of the distant waterline, a prone figure laid on the sand. A line of tape secured on spikes cordoned off the beach in both directions and was guarded by what looked to be PC John Till and a rather short bobby with blonde hair he'd instantly recognised as PC Marcie Scott. Known to the boys as Scottie, she may not have looked much older than a school girl but she was the sweetheart of the station. The gathering of curious people and of course the ubiquitous reporters stood quietly just in front of the tape erupted with a new interest. They sensed things were finally about to happen as Cosey stepped out of his car and walked a short distance to where Phil stood scanning the beach with a pair of binoculars.

"We're going to have to wrap this up quickly, the tide will soon turn," observed Phil.

"What do you think?" asked Cosey as Phil passed over the binoculars.

"Somebody's been up quite close and there looks to be paw marks,"

"If we take the common approach path up to the right of those tracks, round to left and the body."

"Yes, fine."

"Doctor's on his way, once he's pronounced life extinct you can get started."

"What about pathology?" asked Phil, as they made there way down across the sand.

"New guy, Rick Cantor, sounds more like a jockey. He's not coming down, going to meet him at the mortuary."

"Is this the girl that went missing on Friday?" asked a female reporter.

Phil raised an eyebrow and side stepped the remark and made off to get started directing his team.

"I really don't know who it is frankly, but I hope not, it would be rather tragic don't you think?" he stepped to one side as PC Till intervened and then made his way across to PC Scott.

"Good morning sir," Scottie spoke quietly, her eyes full of tears. Cosey said nothing but put his hand on her shoulder. There was nothing you could say at this moment that could offset the mixed feelings you felt. On the one hand, a pure dismay at the inhumanity of man and on the other a strong sense as to the frailty of ones own mortality.

"What have we got in the log so far then?" Cosey stared out to sea.

"The body was found at 6.45am by Mr Graham Turner while walking his dog. He's the feller over there in the pale blue tracksuit."

"Right."

"He hadn't got any closer than about ten feet of the body but the dog was a bit of a problem."

"Yes I saw."

"Once he got it on a lead I made him walk back over my tracks to here."

"Why didn't you let John go?"

"From Grant's description I realised that it was quite likely going to be Fay" she said quietly.

"You were at the Bay Café on the night when she went missing weren't you?"

"Yes sir," she nodded.

"Anything else?"

"The water was just beyond her when we arrived, since then the sand's dried out around her body. The crabs ….. I had to turn away because I couldn't stand to watch them."

Cosey took out the photo of Fay he'd copied and wished he hadn't. She was so full of life in the picture and as he looked through the binoculars again, he could tell this corpse was so far from that! Even at this distance there was a strong resemblance. This was going to be difficult for Leslie, he thought as he lifted the mobile to his ear.

"Kalum are you up?"

"Yes! I've been here since 7.30am."

"Well you'd best contact Leslie, I think we've found Fay and she'll have to do the ID as we've still no news on the mother. Arrange for a car to pick her up and get yourself over to the mortuary to meet her will you. I suspect Joyce may still be with Sumlea so see what you can do about an alternative FLO."

"Right, see yeah," Kalum hung up.

"Cosey nodded in recognition to the doctor making his way out to the deposition site between the tapes. Cosey felt cold, it may be sunny but it's not summer yet, these spring mornings were deceptive and the slight breeze now felt like a gale. As there was little else he could do there for a while Cosey marched off briskly to get the circulation going in his legs and made for a café he'd spotted on the front. As yet there was sod all to go on. All he'd got was Grant's story. Well he'd verified one piece of that. Terry had been near the scene at the time for sure. Cosey took a seat at a small table, looked out to sea and stirred his tea thoughtfully. Terry obviously knew that Ron was around there in the taxi but had tried not to give too much away. It still seemed too much of a coincidence. Girl goes missing and two known villains were cagey about where they were lurking. It was all happening for the Whinspers, served them right! There have always been little snippets of things about them but nothing big enough to get your teeth into, now for the first time, maybe he was going to get somewhere. He got two take-outs for the PC's. They'd be in need. He set out across the road back to the beach and his parka flapped around him.

Diane looked pretty damn good last night he thought casting an eye down the beach. Phil had got his little tent up okay but he'd have to get a shift on. The tide had definitely come in quicker than they'd thought, it must be flatter out there and pools had already formed inside the perimeter tapes. Last night it had taken him a while to get to sleep as the memories of his early days in the force had invaded his thoughts. Vivid glimpses of Diane in her youth had appeared and made him even more restless. Finally he'd got up to make a brew and paced about. It had all been very sudden the way she'd left. He remembered being sat in the café, he'd looked up and there she was, just stood in front of him looking a bit apprehensive.

"Hi, I've just dropped in to say goodbye and…thank you for keeping an eye out for all us girls, you know," she looked a bit embarrassed. Tina stood outside and talked loudly to one of the other girls.

"Oh, I didn't know you were planning to leave?"

"Yes it's all been a bit rushed really," she looked a bit sad and cast an occasional glance out the window to smile faintly at Tina.

"I hope everything goes well for you Cosey," she held out her hand.

"And you too Diane," he'd smiled and stood up to shake her hand. It had all seemed so very formal. "I don't think it's going to be quite the same around here without you."

She'd smiled again. It wasn't a happy smile, more one of somebody resigned to make the best of things. As she'd closed the door behind her he felt a big chunk of him had just walked out the door with her.

"Now then Kalum what can I do for you?" His mobile was a rude intrusion. For a moment he felt things were very nearly out of control as he tried hard to clear his mind of Diane and focus on Kalum's voice. With the mobile jammed between his shoulder and cheek he struggled to balance the take-out cups precariously on the railings.

"They've picked up Leslie, she'll probably be here in about an hour and a half. How's things with you?"

"Phil's going to get his feet wet soon so I guess we'll have to get the body off within the hour. Did you get anywhere with Fay's diary, sorry …Outlook?"

"Yes and no. I had a look and I got a list of her appointments with Katychmar but otherwise this month she'd very little listed. One hair appointment next week, that's it."

"No mention of this weekend meeting with Grant?"

"No, no mention at all. I also checked her 'Sent Items', it went back weeks but nothing that relates to Friday's rendezvous."

"When was her last appointment with Katychmar?"

"Twenty-third of March."

"Three weeks ago. Right, if I can squeeze it in, I'll get over and meet this Mr Katychmar later. Thanks Kalum, keep in touch."

Phil had emerged from the tent and was waving to his colleagues.

"Looks like he's finished and just in time," Cosey handed the take out to Scottie who nestled the hot cup in both hands. "By the way that was a good bit of policing you did the other night, sending Grant to the fish shop in the patrol car so he didn't get spooked and do a runner. Nice touch," he smiled at her and set off down the beach.

Chapter 25

Ron was grumpy. He'd dumped Fay's body in the sea last night but it had proved more difficult than he'd imagined and on three hours sleep he was worse for wear.

He'd shoved the body over the sea wall without any difficulty during a lull in the traffic and it had landed on the end of the pontoon landing stage at the least popular end of the small marina. Unfortunately for him it had been bad timing. Almost as if on cue and to the sound of the Killers, a group of revellers had spilled out from a large motor launch onto the other end of the pontoon nearer the quay. They'd sat there, rolled a joint and talked animatedly about Keith's Jet Ski exploits of the day in loud voices. Shortly, more people joined them and Ron expected that someone would surely catch sight of the body where it had fallen, wrapped in black plastic bin liners and gaffer taped together. All he'd needed was three minutes and he could have dropped Fay's body in the dinghy and he'd have been able slip out of the harbour unnoticed. His frustration had grown fuelled by the fact that it had reached chucking out time and the number of people about seemed to grow by the second. There had been nothing for it, Ron had acted quickly. He'd shimmied down a mooring rope onto the pontoon like a pirate just in time to avoid being spotted by some drunks who'd stopped to have a pee on the way home. He'd made it to the pontoon undetected but got wet up to his waist with only a few feet to go. He slid her body into the shadows alongside a large wooden boat and waited there until the sounds had died down. The rest had been straight forward. With an hour to high tide he'd rowed the dinghy up behind a small red and white motor launch that had just become afloat. He kept it between him and the beach and slit the bin liners carefully with a Stanley knife. Fay's body had slipped quietly into the water.

Chapter 26

Terry's mobile was ringing but could he find it in that bleary eyed state? Could he hell! Sleeping in the car wasn't his favourite occupation but Ron had been so insistent that he should follow Grant back to Leeds, there seemed no other way. The windows were all steamed up but the sun was out now and he wound the window down to get some air and clear his head. "Where's that bastard phone," he cursed angrily and pulled at the door catch? He eased his big hairy belly into the open, placed two oily rigger boots on the tarmac and stood up awkwardly to shut the rear passenger door. Once he'd opened the driver's door the phone was clearly visible on the floor where it vibrated impatiently. Terry snapped it up.

"Yeah!" he croaked.

"What kept you?" Ron's sounded irritable and tired.

"I couldn't find the phone!"

"What's the crack at your end …Have you done it yet?"

"No, it's not going to be that easy. There's a security code and an intercom."

"You'll have to think of something. When you've done, give me a call and I'll decide best how to tip off the police."

"I'm not sure I can do it Ron …."

"Just do it okay!" Ron snapped and hung up.

That was alright for him to say, thought Terry but how the fuck was he supposed to plant the bloody screwdriver in Grant's flat and not get caught? From his position on Lemont Avenue, Terry could see Grant's curtains were still drawn at the front at least. Better check the back and he lifted a small rucksack onto his back. Terry found the climb was hard work and had to stop for his third rest to catch breath near the gravel path. From there he was able to see Grant's bedroom curtains were also closed. Well it was alright for some and he glanced at his phone ….7.55am. Terry decided to check out the garage maybe he could force the lock and plant the screwdriver in Grant's car. Yes, why hadn't he thought of that last night? Well he was so bloody tired he hadn't been able to think straight, that was why! He'd had enough of all the working in the dark and sneaking about. He had begun to feel like an old man. If it hadn't been for the perks he'd have jacked in the job years ago but it had now become a way of life and Ron, well Ron had always paid well. Terry trudged along close to the garages on the right just in case somebody looked out of the flat windows. He put on a pair of the pale plastic gloves from the work shops. He'd driven up the drive last night not realising it was a dead end but before he'd swung his own car round and back down to the road, he'd caught sight of Grant's taillights disappear into the last garage on the left. He looked over his shoulder to check the coast was clear, bent down with difficulty and tried the handle. He's either got so much money it doesn't matter to him or he's bloody stupid, grinned Terry as first he turned the handle and then he lifted the door slightly. The up and over door groaned but Terry pulled it to the left, yes the wire was loose and the lazy bugger hadn't fixed it! Nevertheless Terry had the measure of it and lifted it quietly just as he heard the sound of hurried footsteps on the gravel path. Terry stepped inside the garage and pulled the door down slightly so he couldn't be seen. There was no time to lose. First he tried the tailgate and then the driver's door. No luck! The car was too close to the garage wall on the other side so he'd no chance to try that door. Now what?

From outside and somewhere near the flats beyond the garages he heard a man's voice.

"Good morning, Eric Headley, forensics, I've come to look at your car Mr Reid."

He must have been using the door intercom thought Terry as he scanned the interior of the garage for an idea.

The response was something like 'Oh right ….I'll come down' in that distorted metallic intercom voice. Had he said forensics? Yes he had and Terry suddenly knew just who Grant had been talking to. It was that nosey little bastard who was snooping round the truck. Cosey's got him to look at Grant's car. He'll want to match the paint in the scratch on the tow truck.

He heard the sound of a distant door open and a younger male voice. That would have been Grant's voice. Any minute now the pair of them would turn up at the garage. Terry was galvanised into action, he'd better get a move on or he'd be caught in the act and he shuffled sideways down the side of the car towards the back of the garage. There a small work bench stood in front of the rear wall on which was mounted one of those DIY tool racks boasting a display of cheap screw drivers and spanners. Terry smiled as he slipped a freezer bag out of his rucksack sealed with duck tape. He peeled back the tape and let the blood stained screwdriver slide out onto the bench. Then he reached across and pulled the largest screwdriver from its place. Well they were the same design but Grant's was smaller …needs must!

Chapter 27

"Hi, the car's over there in the garage," Grant pointed beyond the pebble dashed wall along the far side of the gravel path. He stamped his feet in the doorway in a vain attempt to get his trainers on without undoing the laces, "more haste less speed," he added.

"Okay, I'll follow you shall I?" said the wiry little man brightly as he shifted the black case to his other hand.

"It's no good," Grant bent down and dug the tongue of his trainers out from under the instep, "ah, that's better."

"It's quite a nice spot Mr Reid."

"It's quite a nice day too," they crunched along the path, "I think I'll go for a walk when you've finished up." Grant felt quite invigorated by the sun on the trees and the mild breeze, "it's quite spring like."

"Yes, very pleasant," mumbled Headley.

The garages were in short supply and much in demand but surprisingly their condition was generally poor. The concrete forecourt was in no better condition than the drive but it was particularly weathered in front of his garage where a puddle had formed from the overnight rain.

"It's drying out quite well," observed Hedley cheerfully, "I might even be able to cut my lawn later."

Grant remembered running from the car in the dark when he'd got home the previous night, his trainers still felt damp at the toes. He grabbed the chrome 'T' shaped handle and twisted it with a clang. Odd bits of pale blue flaking paint floated to the ground as he lifted the up and over door. It groaned and settled at a rather jaunty angle with the right hand side only just high enough to clear the car.

"Don't you lock it then?"

"I tried it once and broke the only key so, no I don't," Grant stepped inside along the driver's side of the car.

"Never had anything taken?"

"No, least not that I know of anyway."

Grant started the engine first time and eased the car out sedately.

"Sounds okay have you had it from new?"

"No, a new car's beyond my budget, in fact it wasn't in this condition when I bought it. The engine was okay but the body work at the front needed attention."

"Looks like it needs a bit of attention again."

"Yes, bloody hooligan!"

"Did you see who did it?"

"Well it was big and red but it was dark and raining stair rods. I'd recognise his horn again, it nearly deafened me! What I don't understand is how he managed to get so close without me seeing him. There were no vehicles about as far as I could see and then suddenly there he was lights blazing, horn going. You'd have expected some warning, you know, see his lights at least, well before, wouldn't you?"

"You would," Headley scraped at the collision mark and collected fragments of paint in a little plastic dish. "I'm going to have to scrape right through to the metal I'm afraid just to be sure that this red paint isn't something showing through from underneath."

"Help yourself … That's quite a compact little case you've got there."

"Well it wouldn't do to arrive without something important," chuckled Headley.

"Yes I don't like working in a mess myself. I mean just because I work in an office all day doesn't mean I'm afraid to get my hands dirty. I just don't like untidiness and mess.

"Do you mind just signing this form to say you were present when I took the sample and so on?" asked Headley.

"Oh right I'll ….." Grant looked round for somewhere to rest.

"Ah, over there," Headley gestured to the work bench and laid the pad down next to a large screw driver.

"Have you cut yourself Mr Reid?" enquired Headley in a strangely serious tone.

"No I don't think so." Grant flicked his hands over quickly to examine them, "no why?"

Headley tilted his head on one side and looked more closely at the screwdriver on the bench. He put out his hand out, "Could you just step away from the bench a little Mr Reid, there's a good chap," and pulled a self sealing plastic bag from his case. Even though he was wearing pale plastic gloves he pushed one hand up through the base of the bag and adeptly grabbed the handle of the screwdriver and then pulled it back into the bag sealing it one polished move.

"Why are you doing that?"

"Is this your screwdriver?"

"Yes I suppose so," Grant looked at it absentmindedly and then at the tool rack. "No, hang on a minute!"

"What?"

"Well I've got a screwdriver missing from the rack true, but that's too big! Look they were a set and that's not the next size it wouldn't even fit in the slot. How did that get there?"

"Yes I see what you mean. I'm afraid I'm going to have to take this away for analysis, Mr Reid and so you're going to have to sign another one of these as well."

"Why?"

"You said you'd not cut yourself."

"Yes!"

"Well there's blood on this screwdriver. If it's not yours then whose is it? For that matter if it's not your screw driver as well, whose screwdriver is it?"

"I don't like the sound of this," Grant sighed. Suddenly another set of innocent circumstances had taken a decidedly unexpected turn for the worse. "Oh bloody hell what a week! ….What happens now?"

"I'll take it for analysis, then I'll write a report and CID will take it from there. If I were you Mr Reid, I'd not touch a thing in there until you get the all clear from them." With that Mr Headley had scurried away across the forecourt.

Grant watched him disappear out of sight down the drive. He felt it had clouded over in more ways than one and debated for a while whether to put the car back in the garage or not. He felt unsettled by the fact that unbeknown to him, somebody had been in his garage. All this time he'd never bothered because there'd never been even a hint of an intruder but now he'd wanted to lock it and lock it tight! Left like it was, somebody would complain about the car, they always did. So reluctantly he moved it down to the road and comforted himself with the knowledge that he'd be able to keep a better eye on it from the kitchen window.

Chapter 28

Joyce was still writing and so Leslie drifted back into her swirling, twisting memories of Fay and she sipped the coffee. She remembered their first Christmas tree had stood crookedly in the corner of the room. Sat amidst debris of coloured paper and glitter that had spilled off the newspaper and onto the bare boards, they'd tried to finish making decorations in a drunken stupor. They had laughed themselves silly when she'd mimicked Fay's tongue as it waggled between her lips while she concentrated on cutting out a paper Santa.

"I like the smell of fresh coffee," Joyce, tried to make Leslie feel more at ease.

"Yes this isn't bad at all!" Leslie rejoined her thoughts as she turned to look out the window.

The countryside had been glorious in the warm spring sunshine on the drive over from Leeds and under any other circumstances Leslie would have been babbling poetically about country life and her romantic notions of marrying a farmer, having ten kids and so on. Had she not been able to find a farmer then she'd have quite happily settled for a woman's commune in the Scottish Highlands. There was more than enough space up there! She'd been brought up in Camden and rich though the life and culture may have been, she found it claustrophobic and yearned for open spaces, free from cars and people. She liked peace and quiet, time to let her mind mull over all the ideas and information she'd hurriedly stored for such a moment. She had found in Fay a soul mate, one who understood her and respected her privacy. She was in many ways her counterpart and if she had any lesbian tendencies then Fay would have been her ideal partner. As it was, Leslie only wanted her to be happy and felt Grant had undermined her confidence at a time when Fay seemed to have finally recovered from her previous catastrophic relationship. She thought Grant was sleazy, what with his internet porn sites and his demeaning attitude to sex. Leslie had no desire to discover twenty–five different ways to make love. One was quite enough as long as you could get pregnant. In fact the absence of children in her life was a real heartache and as a suitable mate continued to elude her, she'd discussed with Fay the idea of adopting a child on more than one occasion. Fay had no real desire to have children and saw sex as something of a leisure activity but she found it hard to come to terms with the fact that Grant was possibly the first man she'd failed to satisfy. Now the twisted letch had been instrumental in her death. What a waste, poor Fay! The unmarked police car pulled up sedately just passed a blue and white hospital sign labelled Mortuary.

"Hello Miss Turner," smiled Kalum, "DI Benning."

"Yes I remember," she gave a short polite smile.

"I'm sorry we have to meet again in such circumstances but thank you for coming," continued Kalum.

"What's that smell?" Leslie covered her nose with a hand as they passed through the second set of doors into a wide lobby area. It was a strong acrid chemical smell, like bleach only ten times stronger.

"Its formaldehyde, you'll get used to it in a while, this way," Kalum pointed between two metal cabinets and they walked down a short corridor towards a dark wooden door.

"Right," said Kalum softly, "This isn't going to be easy Leslie so we'll do it when you're ready okay."

"Yes," Leslie whispered nodding her head.

"So when you're ready I'll open this door and let us in. The body will be covered over and positioned somewhere in the middle of the room. We mustn't get too near, maybe no closer than this, he stepped away from her. When you're ready just nod to the mortuary assistant and he'll pull back the cover far enough for you to see her face and then I will ask you the question, 'Can you identify this body' and I'm afraid you're going to have to respond."

"Okay let's just do it, I've been awake half the night as it is," she whispered and dried her eyes with a sniffle. She shook her head from side to side, took a deep breath and straightened her shoulders. Kalum opened the door quietly, touched Leslie gently on the elbow and guided her through the doorway in front of him. The room had something of the appearance of a chapel of rest but there were no flowers, just a young man stood at a short distance from the body which lay under a white cloth on a trolley with shiny metal legs supported on black rubber wheels. Kalum brought Leslie to a halt near the head. The young man took up a position level with them on the other side and stood still with his hands loosely clasped in front of him. They stood reverently for a moment in silence. Leslie nodded and the assistant pulled back the cover. She hadn't known what to expect but it was unmistakably Fay. With sand and small bits of flotsam in her hair it no longer looked like the Fay she'd known and she turned away quickly as Kalum asked his question but she jumped in with her answer before he'd finished, "Yes, Yes it's Fay. Oh God!" she ran for the door, she had to get away from that smell. She rushed down the corridors, out into the open and tried desperately to rid herself of the image she'd just seen. She concentrated hard to replace it with one she preferred from happier days when they'd just moved into her flat. It made her cry, it was just so damned unfair!

"I'm sorry, I'm not very brave am I?"

"You've done just fine," smiled Kalum sympathetically as he stood a few feet behind her.

"God, I hope I never have to do that again," she sniffled and turned to look at him.

"That's the hard bit over with Leslie, but we will have to go to the station now and Joyce, one of our Family Liaison Officers, will need your help to complete a formal written statement. Throughout the journey waves of bottomless sadness had broken over her and she sobbed quietly the whole way.

The sadness was still there but for the moment although exhausted from worry, she was holding it at bay. There was closure of sorts but now there were different questions about how she'd died.

"When will I be able to arrange a funeral?" she asked.

"That depends on the Coroner, he'll have to release the body and a Post Mortem will have to be carried out before that," replied Joyce.

"How long will that take?"

"I'm sorry it really depends on the findings of the Post Mortem, surely her mother would arrange that anyway?"

"Bit of a mute point really, they fell out, it's been eight years!"

"Yes, so I gather. We have tried to find her but she's not at home, neighbours think she's on holiday."

Chapter 29

One day soon Grant hoped to sell the flat and move to Moverley but even on automatic pilot the journey seemed to take for ever. In part that was due to the hour and thank God he'd not gone for a walk, at least he might still make it before lunch. Mid morning the traffic had a different pace and he couldn't ignore the fact that the emotional battering he'd taken over the last few days had made him really quite impatient. Just when he thought things were slowing down, he'd hit another unexpected pit fall. The screwdriver thing …what was all that about? He just had to get there this morning …afternoon at this rate, touch base with normality for a while and chat over the events of last night with Violet.

He felt as though they'd made progress by visiting the clinic. Ron and his brother Lionel were thick as thieves with Katychmar. He hadn't understood what hold Katychmar had over Ron but the business over Lionel, well that sounded like Ron had helped him cover up something pretty serious that Lionel had done. They'd struck up a deal, it had saved Katychmar's career and Lionel had got back his freedom. Lionel must have been editing DVD's for Katychmar of events that took place at the clinic? A wave of embarrassment made his cheeks glow. He suddenly remembered that one of the monitors in Katychmar's office had shown a view inside the lift. What if he had footage of him with the Thai girl? Should he expect a blackmail letter? Would that be the next unexpected twist to the week? And then there was Ron, what sadistic pleasures had he immortalized on film? He felt that surely there had to be a sexual aspect to all this given Katychmar's specialty. So if Ron supplied CCTV equipment, maybe he made dodgy DVD's. Lionel edited them but what was Katychmar's role? Had he supplied the actors? There must be plenty of people going to the clinic who would have jumped at the opportunity to indulge themselves. He had. Oh what a bloody fool he'd been! Only they wouldn't be actors would they, they'd have done it for real while Ron looked on with his little camera! It made him feel sick in the stomach to think he'd been hoodwinked into some kind of freak show.

Bloody caravans on this road make you sick! Look at them three in a row, how the hell were you supposed to get round them. It wasn't the Wild West!

"Expecting an Indian attack are you?" he bellowed as he finally overtook a balding man in a four wheel drive, "you and your posh looking tin box." If they just left space between them then you could at least get round them one at a time!

Surely it wasn't just all about making videos, Katychmar had a good reputation and you wouldn't get one of those unless he really cured people. Grant still genuinely felt that he had turned the corner so maybe Katychmar was screwed up too. He tried to help people but all the time he was fighting a loosing battle with his own voyeuristic addiction. Lionel was going to finish editing the video then they were going to mothball the whole thing. So whatever Lionel was editing, was going on in that container and was obviously dodgy or there wouldn't be all the secrecy. Grant realized that the only way he could get to the bottom of it all was to get inside that container. He'd only got until tomorrow evening, assuming things didn't go quicker than Ron had expected.

Thank God that's over, Grant pulled into the office car park, what a bloody journey!

The thought of seeing Violet soon took the heat out of his frustration and no doubt she'd make some witty little quip about sleeping in when everybody else had been slaving away. So he stepped from the lift with a more positive attitude, through the doors, turned past the water station and made for his office as usual. His heart jumped when he caught sight of Violet at her desk and smiled. Her reaction wasn't that welcoming and he felt crestfallen. In fact as he opened his office door and strode round to face the monitor on his desk, he thought her expression difficult to interpret. He dropped his bag on the desk and logged in quickly. When he looked up there were two men stood in the doorway.

The one on the left was DI Benning, Grant recognized him from the Saturday morning fiasco. The other was a complete stranger to him but Grant knew this was bad news by the serious look on their faces. Through the window to the left, he could see Violet, her eyes wide as saucers and her hand held up to her mouth.

"Mr Grant Reid?" asked DI Benning.

"Yes, hello again," he felt sick, now what?

"My name's DI Benning and I'm arresting you on suspicion of being involved in the murder of Lumaii Bunyasarn at The Whinspers Empire on Monday 10 April. You're not obliged to say anything but if you do it may be taken down and used against you…."

Grant stared through the partition window at Violet. It was all just like a nightmare. When would it end, how much more of this could he take. As directed he crossed his wrists in front of him and the detective fastened the cuffs. He felt helpless, unable to influence the events that controlled him and as he ducked into the waiting police car, he felt completely alone. Sat behind the passenger seat with the unknown detective beside him, Grant stared out the window and nobody spoke, no banter or polite chit chat, just silence punctuated by the sound of the indicators and the upholstery as it creaked on the driver's seat. The car sped through the town bathed in bright sun light but it all seemed to be moving too fast and Grant closed his eyes, trying to clear his mind. He stared into the blackness. With the sudden change of direction and a muttered curse from the driver, Grant was brought back to reality as they breezed past a group of clamouring reporters and cameramen at the gate to the compound adjacent to the Police Station. He was helped from the car and led in the side entrance along a brightly lit corridor. The detective addressed the sergeant almost before they'd reached the desk and it seemed strange that having arrested him once already the detective was asking for permission that he be detained. Grant was still pondering this when the sergeant asked, "Do you understand the reasons for your arrest?"

"Yes," replied Grant.

He hadn't had time to discuss his brainwave for the new hair gel campaign with Violet. What would she be thinking? Nothing seemed important now. He just wanted to get to the truth and get out of there. By stark contrast to the events earlier things suddenly seemed to be moving painfully slowly. He felt frustration well up inside. Grant shuffled his feet and tried to find something of interest on the walls to focus upon.

"Are these your flat keys?" the sergeant held up the bunch by a large mortise lock key.

"Yes that's the outside door, the Yale is the front door," replied Grant vaguely. God they would soon be all over his flat. A mental picture crossed his mind's eye of silent men in white suits and face masks who walked in slow motion amid his belongings with blue plastic covers over their shoes. What would they make of his DVD and magazine collection neatly stacked in boxes by the front door? If only he'd gone to the tip this morning! Would they think he was trying to turn over a new leaf? Was he destroying evidence? Maybe they'd think he was just a very tidy pervert? Shit!

The track suit was quite comfortable although not a colour he'd have chosen but he guessed they were trying to match fibres and look for blood stains. They're not going to find anything incriminating on these, he thought and placed his clothes in the plastic bags. As they were spirited away along with all his other belongings Grant felt a hot flush of anxiety flood over him. What about his jacket and trousers from the afternoon in the lift. They were bound to find at least one hair on them from the Thai girl, maybe even traces of fabric from her dress. Oh shit what about DNA traces of her vaginal fluids on his flies? As they walked him down to the cells he longed to be alone and to have a few moments of privacy to collect his thoughts and prepare himself for what was to come. The echo of the door as it was slammed shut brought relief. Far from feeling trapped, he felt protected from the forces outside that seemed determined to take control his life. He sat heavily on the chair, rested his head back against the wall and tried to clear his mind from the random recollections that darted into his consciousness.

"Do you have a solicitor Mr Reid?"

"No, I don't have one."

"We can get one for you if you like."

"Yes please that will be great thanks."

"Interview of Grant Reid commenced at 2.45pm on Friday 14 April. Those present; DCI Benning, DS Varley and Mr Reid's council Mr Roderick Plessey."

With no watch Grant had lost track of time down in the cell but it had seemed far longer than two hours since he'd arrived. Varley was an expressionless and fastidious individual who laid out his folder and pen precisely on the desk in front of him. Roderick Plessey was a disappointment but his aftershave freshened up the room that had smelt stale when they arrived. Varley stared at his hands laid palms down on the table for some time before he spoke again.

Mr Reid do you know this woman," Varley placed a photo of Lumaii on the desk in front of him.

"I met her at the Katychmar Clinic but we were never introduced. I don't know her by name."

"Her name was Lumaii Bunyasarn."

"Right."

"Could you describe the circumstances of your meeting?"

"Yes. I had an appointment at the clinic with Katychmar at 2.00pm and I waited in the foyer looking at the displays until the bleeper summoned me to my appointment."

"How did you meet Lumaii?"

"We got in the same lift."

"And?"

"And the lift got stuck between floors and so we had to wait for them to get us out."

"And how did you pass the time."

"We chatted for a bit you know and......."

"Mr Reid …"

"Its' embarrassing really and I'm not that sure how it got started really but we…." Grant looked at his hands, rubbed palms together. This was easily the most embarrassing thing he'd ever had to do.

"Mr Reid?"

"Had……sex."

"You passed the time while you waited having sex."

"Did Miss Bunyasarn agree to have sex with you?"

"Well she really instigated it to be honest!"

"Then what happened?"

"They managed to recover the lift and let us out."

"Is that it?"

"Well then I had my consultation with Katychmar."

"Is that it?"

"Yes, pretty well the bare bones of it, yes," Grant was hoping they wouldn't need anymore detail.

"Was that the last time you saw Lumaii?"

"Yes, she went off to the ladies room to tidy herself up."

"Okay Mr Reid that as you say is, the bare bones. What about the detail? Did you know she was a prostitute?"

"Not then."

"When did you find out?"

"It was on the news, I saw the broadcast on Wednesday evening."

"So you didn't pay her?"

"No I didn't know her…She…she said she was a patient and I just assumed she was …well a bit over sexed…and that was her problem…. you know the reason she was at the clinic."

"She was willing to have sex with you and she never asked you to stop …or anything?"

Oh shit he knew that was the big one, and now he'd be the monster whatever he said and they'd try and pin everything on him!

"Mr Reid?"

"Erm …Katychmar set me up with her to get to the bottom of my problem, he said it was to do with a childhood experience. My mother was a prostitute and she wore a red dress like the one that …Lumaii wore." Grant was speed talking. He'd not planned what to say, it just came out all garbled. "After we'd had sex the first time I just got carried away and I think towards the end it must have been hurting her, but that was when they came in."

"Who came in?"

"Katychmar and the male nurses."

"Then what happened?"

"Lumaii started shouting at Katychmar, she asked him why he'd waited so long."

"You're saying it was planned then, you didn't rape her and you didn't use her as a prostitute. It was some sort of role play supposedly contrived by Katychmar to trigger a deep seated suppressed memory that caused your excessive sexual behavior?"

"Well…," Grant was overwhelmed.

"I don't think my client can answer that question," interrupted the solicitor.

"Just a minute, I've remembered something Katychmar said to Ron," said Grant excitedly. "He mentioned somebody by name but I can't remember who it was now, but he said, 'the final choice of resting place was strangely apt. Thai girl in a Chinese skip, it was almost politically correct.' He thought it was quiet funny."

Varley sat motionlessly for a moment and looked at Grant straight in the eyes.

"Ron who?" he said quietly.

"Ron Whinsper. We went to the Katychmar clinic on Thursday evening and…"

"We?"

"Yes Violet and I, she's a friend from work."

"Okay," Varley gestured to continue.

"We overheard a conversation between Katychmar and Ron. They talked about all sorts of things we didn't really understand. Ron also said that you were trying to make a case linking them to Fay's disappearance and Katychmar told him to do something to deflect the attention back on me. Ron …. Ron said it was in hand……." Grant's voice tailed off. What if the screwdriver had been used to kill her? "I need to consult with my solicitor. Mr Varley, I really think I ought."

"Yes….okay, but one thing first though. "Did Violet witness all this as well?"

"Yes, she's been a great support ever since this all started," answered Grant with an affectionate tone.

"Hm," grimaced Varley, "you don't waste much time Mr Reid. Interview terminated at 3.15pm." He popped the tape from the machine and sealed it in a bag.

The door closed behind Varley. Grant waited a few seconds for him to clear the other side of the door.

"Look, Mr Plessey," Grant turned to face the silver haired pin strip suited spiv to his left. They'd had their chat before the interrogation began but it had been so difficult to remember every detail when so much had happened, "I'd forgotten about Ron's reference to deflecting attention on to me. Do you think he planted the screwdriver in my garage?"

"Well Mr Reid," he sat back in the chair and opened his hands out in front of him, "it's not what I think that matters, it's what we can prove. It's good news that you had a witness to the conversation though, because if either of you can recall some detail that hasn't been made public knowledge it may help your case."

"What sort of case do you think I've got?"

"As I said earlier, they have to link you to that screwdriver and just finding it in your garage isn't enough. They also have to link you to the scene of the murder and my guess is that, as they haven't mentioned it thus far, they may not have been able to do either of those things as yet. In addition they also have to prove the screwdriver on your work bench was the murder weapon. So they may have some way to go, in which case time may be in your favor."

"Well it makes a change that something is in my favor!" frowned Grant.

"Is that everything?"

"No. I hadn't realized until the other night that Katychmar was also Fay's therapist."

"I'm sorry you've lost me."

"One of the reasons we went to the clinic is that I felt it was a bit of a coincidence that Katychmar also knew the two women that had gone missing. Up until then I'd thought I was the common denominator."

"Ah, yes I see what you mean. If they... or even if just Ron was involved in Lumaii's murder, then were they involved with Fay's disappearance?"

"Exactly!"

"With the exception of Fay, me and possibly her flatmate Leslie, Katychmar was the only other person who knew the arrangements for Friday night. Also and this is something else I forgot to mention, Ron drove a Triple 'A' taxi back to the Empire after he left the clinic."

"You've lost me again!"

"There was a Triple 'A' taxi near the spot where Fay disappeared ...well it left as I got there but it's a bit of a coincidence nevertheless. I mean Ron could also have been at the Café that night."

"The plot thickens!"

"Because I'd got all this whirring round in my head I needed to speak to you. I didn't want to just blurt it out."

"Quite. I think for the moment we'll just leave this conspiracy theory of yours in abeyance and deal with clearing your name in respect of Lumaii's murder. Once we've done that, you may find they have a more listening ear for your theories involving Fay's disappearance. Have you heard anymore?"

"No nothing as yet! It's nearly a week now I can't believe it, so much has happened in a week!"

Chapter 30

"Beep!"

"Good afternoon Felicity and how are things in reception today?"

"Under control as usual Mr Katychmar," she replied.

Yes and she'll have done that irritating wide smile, shake of the head and a giggle routine as usual thought Katychmar. He focused one of the foyer cameras in on the receptionist. He'd never been able to pinpoint why he found her so irritating. She was a handsome girl and the clients always held her with such regard so there she remained, a vacuous blond Muppet, figurehead to his entire operation, such irony!

"There's a DCI Cosey here in reception, he's wanting to have a word with you," giggled Felicity.

"What's it about?" Katychmar had a fair idea.

"He said it was police business."

"Where is he now?"

"Em…"

He saw her stand on tiptoe, look around the foyer as her blond hair swished from shoulder to shoulder.

"He's over by the display looking at the picture of the blonde in the little white cardigan."

Katychmar navigated through the menus to bring up the closest camera. With the joystick, he turned the camera and zoomed in on the mousey haired, rather unkempt looking man in a parka who studied the picture.

"I see him. Leave him to wander for five minutes okay, then ask him to come up. Let me know when he's on the way."

"Okay Mr Katychmar," she giggled.

Ron was right. Katychmar always knew that one day the police would come to interview him but his fear had been that by some means they'd discovered that he'd covered up Zoe's murder. This visit, well it could only be Fay or Lumaii. If only Ron and his merry little band of psychopaths had just a little more self discipline …well they wouldn't be …oh!" He stood up in frustration and walked round the desk. He glanced at the monitor and watched Cosey at the picture of the woman in the red dress. There must be a way he could rid himself of The Whinspers once and for all that wouldn't implicate him. If only he'd arranged Grant's experience for later in the week. Ron would have been up to his neck in it and there'd be no way he could be drawn in but now… Now he was as much a common denominator as Grant. There was of course one bonus to Grant's excess in the lift and Lionel had done an excellent job in the editing suite. Lumaii had developed the most erotic way of displaying her feigned sexual pleasure and excitement with a client. It was her best video yet. Interestingly, although she knew about the filming, she was never curious to see the end result. Probably just as well, he savoured a mental picture of her taught thrusting buttocks. Yes, the three other camera angles she hadn't known about had provided some stunningly intimate detail.

"Bleep…bleep."

Maybe tonight he would just savour some more, a smile broke out on his face.

"Bleep…bleep."

"Oh …yes," he cleared his throat, "Felicity."

DCI Cosey's on his way up Mr Katychmar," she giggled.

"Thank you," he clicked off the switch irritably. What's was so funny about that?

The door opened softly to the muffled graze of the draught excluder. Cosey walked in smoothing his hair down and shook Katychmar by the hand.

"DCI Cosey, thank you for seeing me Mr Katychmar," said Cosey in a flat tone, "you get a nice view from up her don't you?"

"Yes, in truth I think it was the view that sold me the building, the rest developed ad lib."

"Well that's quite an unusual display for a medical practice down stairs."

"Many of my patients have difficulty coming to terms with their sexual desires or the desires of their partners. Others are confused about their own sexuality and then there are those whose sexual cravings are in control of their lives."

"Is that it in a nutshell?"

"No," smiled Katychmar, "just a taster to put my little display in context."

"You showed an interest in the blond in the white woollen top yourself Mr Cosey."

"Did I? Do you have this place wired?"

"I've a very sophisticated monitoring system, yes. Surely you saw the signs?"

"Hm," grunted Cosey.

"It allows me to observe my patient's uninhibited reactions and interests and thus when we meet I can discuss things in more detail. In some cases it helps cut to the chase and so speeds up the recovery."

"So you can cure somebody of sexual addiction then?"

"Some yes, in fact quite a high proportion but not all. So how can I help you this afternoon?"

"Mr Grant Reid, he's a patient of yours I understand?"

"Yes, that's correct. He's been coming to see me for about six months."

"Making progress is he?"

"I'm not prepared to answer that question, in fact how did you know he was my patient?"

"He told me. In fact he told me that you arranged for him to have sex in the lift with a Thai prostitute called Lumaii on Monday afternoon."

Katychmar hadn't expected such a direct approach it tipped him completely off balance.

"Er ... I can't believe he could say such a thing after all the help I've given him." He was playing for time. Could he rebut the accusation? There were serious implications and he had to be convincing. Sometimes his treatments sailed very close to the law and this was just one of those. Damned Whinspers they were so undisciplined!

"Mr Katychmar?"

"I'm just shocked and I have to say, stunned by the cheek of the man. He attempted to rape one of my clients in the lift which had got stuck between floors. It was only by the swift intervention of my nursing staff that we managed to rescue Lumaii."

"Did you know she was a prostitute?"

"She was a patient. I treat people from all walks of life, status is not an issue here!" snapped Katychmar.

"So what happened in the lift was not of your design?"

"No, it was an unprovoked assault and he's very lucky she didn't press charges."

"Well a lot of good that would have done her now, she's been murdered!"

"Yes, yes it's tragic I saw it on the news. She was found in Manchester."

"Yes, dumped in a skip in the China Town Area. Taking political correctness a bit far don't you think?"

"Yes," smiled Katychmar, oh why had he done that? "I must say your sense of humour does you no credit DCI Cosey!"

"Really, I thought you enjoyed the joke!"

"Ssss…" Katychmar let the breath hiss between his teeth. That was careless, he was a clever little policeman this one.

"Fay Crosswell, she a patient of yours?"

"Yes, that's a mystery isn't it, her disappearing like that, it was on the news," Katychmar tried to sound concerned.

"As I understand, it was on your advice that they had their meeting at the Bay Café in the first place?"

"I'm not prepared to discuss the case history or any treatments with you DCI Cosey, I'm sorry," replied Katychmar firmly.

"Well I respect your professionalism but I'd like you to consider the following. Lumaii was a patient of yours who you claim was assaulted by another one of your patients, Grant Reid who is at the police station as we speak, helping us with our enquiries. The former girlfriend of Mr Reid was a patient of yours, who disappeared last Friday under suspicious circumstances and washed up on the beach this morning. Now Mr Katychmar, Mr Reid may be known to both women but so are you and it's only by the skin of your teeth that I haven't arrested you on a charge of conspiring with Mr Reid in the abduction of Fay Crosswell."

"Oh…Yes I see. Yes, I do see what you mean. Well… Well under those circumstances and to help you to proceed with your enquiries I'll try to be as helpful as I can," he said thoughtfully. Now that was a turn up for the book. It had been interesting treating both partners. He'd never attempted such a thing before, it had always been too risky but he hadn't been able to resist the temptation. Then Ron had become infatuated with her and that's where it had all gone wrong. Those damn Whinspers!

"Do you know Ron Whinsper?"

"Er…" He couldn't speak. It was as though a giant hand had gripped him by the throat and despite his best efforts the words wouldn't form in his mouth.

Cosey's eyes twinkled and Katychmar knew that he had him, no sense in denying it. Sooner or later it would come out.

"Erm …yes I do remember the name, his brother was a patient some years ago I recall," Katychmar had recovered from the initial shock.

"Which one was that, Victor or Lionel?" asked Cosey.

"Lionel. After the mother died Ron looked after them both."

"When was the last time you saw Ron?"

"Well, way back, years ago, when I discharged Lionel I guess."

"Fay Crosswell rang you before she went on her rendezvous with Grant. What did she say, can you remember?"

"Well, she just rang to tell me about what Grant had asked her to wear and just to ask advice about the best way to play it."

"Why did she do that then?"

"I asked her to. Often in these cases, when there's an imbalance in sexual interest or appetite one would try to help the couple bridge the gap as it were, tackling the problem from both ends."

"Find a mutual compromise?" offered Cosy.

"Yes exactly, but of course self doubt creeps in and I've found it works well to offer a listening ear and bolster any flagging confidence."

"But in Grant's case he doesn't lack confidence. He's addicted, cold and unresponsive after the deed."

"You've been doing your homework. As a result of Grant's seeming rejection, Fay was losing her self confidence. I knew that Grant was reaching a crucial stage in his treatment. I didn't know of course that he was going to behave so badly in the lift but since then he has made significant progress. It was something to do with a suppressed memory and of course, the red dress was a significant trigger factor. If Fay hadn't disappeared and the rendezvous had gone as planned Grant's recovery would have been perfectly timed for him to, as you said, find a compromise."

"Yes it couldn't have worked out better if you'd planned it that way!" said Cosey with a raised eyebrow. "Tell me why didn't you call the police after Grant assaulted Lumaii?"

"Oh…" he was such a tricky one … "I managed to convince her that Grant was under a lot of stress after his girl friend went missing and she said that it was an occupational hazard for her and that it would serve no purpose if he was ill anyway."

"That was very understanding of her!"

"Yes I thought so too!" Katychmar smiled.

"Do you keep video records on file as it were?"

"Yes, sometimes if I'm still unsure about interpretation."

"Any record of the incident in the lift?"

"No, Grant told me everything I needed to know." replied Katychmar blandly but he felt the hair stand up on the back of his neck.

"Right, well thank you for your help Mr Katychmar," Cosey got up and admired the view once more, "yes, very nice," and he let himself out.

Katychmar had mixed feelings about it all. Would Cosey rush off and dig out Lionel's file? Had he covered his tracks well enough? Only time would tell, he'd just have to wait it out. All these years he'd feared the police might delve into his affairs because of Zoe's death but now the prospect no longer seemed as intimidating. How much of his conversation with Ron had Grant overheard? If that new girlfriend of his was there as well it could be really serious. Ron would have to do one last favour. It was a big one but he'd better get it right. He can have Violet as payment for his sick bloody film but he wanted Grant's head on a stick for all of the girls; Fay, Lumaii and Violet. What about all the others before, God how many were there now? His hands trembled as they rested on the edge of the desk. Ron and his sick buddies, was it worth the price? To live in fear all those years, not just for Zoe. If it had stopped there it would have been bad enough but to have paid for Ron's help in their blood, it was the slippery slope. He opened his desk drawer and pulled out the brandy bottle, poured himself a large one and gulped it down greedily. It had to end, "this had to be the last," he coughed to the sound of the glass as it rumbled on the desk as he placed it there uncertainly with a shaking hand. The Whinsper's cooperation had stabilised his practice and he'd been able to help lots of people who otherwise would have suffered, but Christ what a cost! He reached for the bottle again, poured a small one and struggled to calm himself. He took deep breaths and tried to picture the faces of patients whom he had successfully treated. Slowly, slowly his panic subsided and his breathing became easier again. He lifted the glass to the light and tasted it, savouring the blend on his tongue and allowed the warmth to spread down his throat. He breathed out gently, a long sigh of relief and lifted the new 'Pay as You Go' mobile to his ear and called Ron.

"Can you talk? ...Right, I think the young man is going to talk his way out of his predicament. When he does, he'll try to clear his name again, so use the girl. I'm sure she'll entertain you. And Ron, make sure you stitch him up properly this time. No amateur dramatics, make sure it sticks…Fine, don't call me again, I only want to read about it in the papers, understand!"

Chapter 31

Stood in the entrance to Lumaii's apartment block Kalum waited for the lift as the luxurious surroundings wrapped round him like a warm blanket. It was dark outside now and through the glass entrance knee high lights picked out the path amongst the herb planters to where he'd parked his bike. Small halogen down lights in the timber clad ceiling created soft pools of light on the warm coloured thick entrance carpet. The walls were covered in a suede texture and tasteful close up autographed prints of flowers and woodland where picked out at intervals under the lights. As he travelled the four levels to Lumaii's floor on the top of the building, his thoughts drifted back to earlier that evening in Leeds when he'd stood at Grant's window, high up above the trees and watched the breeze stroke across the new leaves. Every now and then, when the sun came out, it had been like watching waves on the sea. If he'd a view like that Kalum would put a chair just there where he stood and settle down after work each night and chill out. It was quite a peaceful little oasis that spread out in front of him, down the grass banking across the road and up the other side under the huge trees. Earlier the traffic had been quite busy along the valley road but then around tea time it had become almost deserted. The body language of the couple who strolled down the valley in the lovely spring twilight was leisurely, they'd enjoyed the respite from the hustle and bustle of a large city. The only noise was the breeze in the trees and a distant voice of a woman calling her dog.

Kalum had grown up in a back street terrace and the only trees around were short stumpy things that the council decapitated every five years or so and they grew to look more like giant dandelion heads turned to seed. As kids they'd pull off the new shoots that sprung at the base and use them to whip at weeds along the high backed alley walls as they waited out the long hot summers before returning to school. The bicycle he'd got for his twelfth birthday had been a real liberation and with his best mate Pete they'd found a new lease of life. Even on an evening after school you could make the nearest village on a bike and in about half an hour you could savour those sweat smelling fields after harvest. Later they took up fishing and with a rod tied to the crossbar they'd set out early on a Saturday morning full of expectations and the maggot container would bump along happily beside the sandwiches in a large black saddle bag on Pete's bike.

Grant was a lucky chap to have such a great place to live. Yes that was just what he needed, it would have been so easy to just drift off into your thoughts and let all the pieces just comfortably fall back into place in their own time. Kalum checked his pocket as the lift door opened for the paper on which he'd written the names of the estate agents from the boards he'd seen down by the road.

Outside Lumaii's door he paused and reflected on the progress the white suited officers had made on Grant's flat.

"All done?" enquired Kalum hopefully.

"Yes, just these bags and it's all yours," replied the last of the two officers. He held up one of the bags as if in proof and they filed out the door. "I think they may still be working over at the garage though."

"Right I'll just take a peek then."

As he crunched along the gravel path and round to the garages Kalum had taken in the air. It wasn't as good as those country fields but then he hadn't suffered from hay fever in those days, he grimaced. "How's it going?" he called over the tape to the white suited officer who'd just appeared from around the side of Grant's garage carrying a footprint cast.

"That's it really," he replied and slipped the cast into a plastic bag, "it got a bit warm down there when the sun came out earlier." he pulled the mask down his face.

"Hello Headley I didn't recognise you in your Telly Tubby outfit!" joked Kalum, "what have you got there?"

"Somebody was standing here," he pointed, "earlier today too, the mud's not quite dry."

Kalum slipped under the redundant tape and walked over to take a closer look.

"Maybe when I checked the paintwork we weren't alone, Mr Reid and I!" speculated Headley.

"Well I have to say it does seem a bit coincidental. I mean... can I? Kalum gestured towards the bench."

"Yeah," nodded Headley and fastened up his case.

"Pretty well all his possessions are neat," Kalum nodded towards Headley.

"Yes even the porn's in chronological order!" chuckled Headley.

"Right and now the tools, they're cheap and tacky DIY stuff and admittedly the big one you found is of a similar design but it won't fit in that rack. What's more it's more robust, the sort of thing a proper mechanic would own."

"Yes I'd agree but it's the murder weapon alright."

"You reckon?"

"No doubt. Right that's me for the day," Headley stepped clear of his white outfit.

"Don't suppose there's any chance of a lift to the railway station is there?" Kalum, tried not to sound helpless, "Need to get back to Moverley by 6pm."

"No problem, go right past it. I'll just get the tape down then…"

"Hello DCI Benning," smiled Sumlea from the doorway.

"Oh…Hello Sumlea. Sorry," he shook his head, "been a busy day. How are you then, now you're out?" asked Kalum brightly. He was really pleased to see her looking so well. Her lips had healed quite well in three days and the bruising round her eyes looked less vivid but the dressing still made her nose look quite raw. She still seemed to have a bit of trouble walking.

"I am doing okay…" she said brightly but looked away and the smile disappeared as she settled gingerly on the sofa, "you like the view?"

"Well yes I do. You know I was looking out of another apartment window today, over woodland and I was strongly tempted to look into buying it but this, well what a view!"

Through the trees to the left the lights twinkled on the harbour and floodlights picked out the crumbling battlements of the castle above, whilst across the wide expanse of sea to the right the very last vestiges of daylight glistened on the waves. Here and there in the far distance small lights barely moved across the horizon as ships plied the main shipping lane.

"It's very decadent isn't it?" she smiled.

"Well," he shook his head, "It's that too!" In her company he always had a smile on his face. From the time he first met Sumlea he'd felt a strange affinity toward her and they always chatted comfortably, well he did most of it at the beginning. Her background had intrigued him. It seemed quite magical by comparison to the terrace streets of his childhood and the distance she'd travelled. He found it hard to comprehend as he'd never been further than Great Yarmouth.

"Are you hungry then?" she asked with a slightly apprehensive look. There was a distant smell of cooking on the air as he came in but Kalum had just assumed she'd already eaten.

"Well, I'm going to get something on the way home I just called to…"

"I know, ever since I was in hospital you have just been calling in on the way home, and this time I thought you might like to relax a bit. I've cooked you something special. A thank you for being so kind to me," she smiled but a tear broke through which she scooped up quickly and beckoned him to go through the glass doors.

The dinning table was laid out for two with chop sticks to the side of split bamboo placemats. The lighting was turned down low and a small light flickered gently at each end of the table. Sumlea appeared from the kitchen via another sliding door to the left carrying bowls of food which she placed gently on an array of empty place mats on the right of the table. While she returned to collect the last batch Kalum peered through his own reflection in the sliding doors to the balcony where an illuminated fountain was set against small stones and bamboo grass with a seated Buddha who meditated upon the view across the bay.

"Would you like to sit down," she laughed and pointed at his ankles, "Do you feel more comfortable with those? You've always got them on."

"Oh," he said as his cheeks coloured up, "Cycle clips, I just forget...I just do!" he shook his head, slipped the offending items in his pocket and sat down.

"They're a nice colour maybe you could buy a different colour to match each outfit and start a trend and everybody would join in," she giggled and took her seat across the table.

"I've not used these before," he held up the chop sticks.

"By the end of the meal you'll be an expert. Hunger and the taste of my cooking will force you to learn quickly!"

"You're a bit of a tough customer, aren't you?"

"I have a bicycle in Bangkok," she added brightly, "but I was thinking of trading it in for a scooter."

"My Dad wouldn't let me have a scooter or a motor bike, said they were too dangerous. Which of course they are but kids like to have fun."

"Do you like children?"

"Yes love them. I was an only child and it was horrible. Spent most of my time round at Pete's house. He had three brothers and two sisters, it was great."

"I'd like to have children one day," she looked sad.

"I know it's still difficult Sumlea but it does get better."

"I knew something had happened, Lumaii was always hot headed but it's so sad," the tears rolled down her cheeks, "this place is so lovely and…now she won't be able to enjoy it after all …she went through."

"Have you told them in Bangkok?"

"Yes, not the detail, I just said she been in a motor accident. There's no need to tell them, what good will it do?"

"Yes, I see your point."

"I discussed it with Joyce, she's very nice you know."

"Yes she's very genuine I think that's what makes the difference."

"Yes."

"Sumlea, you won't forget, but you will come to terms with it I promise!"

"I do hope so Kalum," she replied tearfully and stared at the flickering light as Kalum looked out of the window. He'd become very fond of her over the last week but she would need time to recover. Her own assault was hard enough but losing her only sister like this must have been absolutely devastating. Kalum was conscious he had to get back to the station this was neither the time nor place to express his feelings for her. The time would come, he felt sure of it.

Chapter 32

Ron was excited by the prospect of a new prey and with trembling fingers he assembled the camera equipment. If Grant was still at the police station then his girlfriend wouldn't be far behind. He could follow her from there, failing that he'd catch up with little Violet at her home. This whole damn thing wouldn't have happened at all if only Vick had kept his cool. He'd have kept his dick a little longer too! Now Katychmar had the upper hand again just when it was looking like he'd regained the edge. One day he'd fix the slimy little bastard and fix him so good… Ron clenched his teeth in frustration but shook his head to clear the thoughts of revenge from his mind. There would be time enough to plan that when this was all over, while he lay on a beach somewhere. Now he needed to let Terry know the score, might as well get the whole team together for one last bash! He smiled to himself as memories of previous insane exploits flooded his mind. It felt good to shed the tension of current events like an old skin, it was like being reborn.

The smile was short lived, his reincarnation incomplete, the fire that burnt in his eye, barely a glimmer and then it was gone. Ron had just caught sight of something he knew was going to be trouble. Through the window into the workshop he'd expected to see Terry finishing off the 'Beamer' and sure enough there he was but stood next to him with his head under the bonnet, well he'd recognise that bloody parka anywhere. Who else would wear one anyway? The fucking little weasel was all over them like a bloody rash. Ron grabbed a piece of paper and scribbled, GO COP SHOP PHONE ME WHEN GRANT LEAVES. He pushed the camera gear angrily into his desk drawer and made his way out into the workshop, down the metal staircase.

"Terry!" shouted Ron as he walked towards the dark blue BMW.

"Yeah," replied Terry as his head appeared over the raised bonnet.

"Need some spare parts. Go down to Collier's and get them ASAP will you feller?"

Cosey stuck his head round the side of the bonnet.

"Mr Cosey, fancy seeing you here again, at this rate you'll be wanting a retirement package. Have you finished with Terry? I do have a business to run!"

"As a matter of fact I have, thank you but I'd like a word with you if I may?" it wasn't really a question and Cosey walked past him towards the stairs. Ron knew he would have to follow.

"Terry!" shouted Ron waving the piece of paper, "Your list. If there's anything on here you don't understand, give me a ring on the mobile, okay?" he opened his eyes wide. Would Terry pick up on them? No, the bloody idiot hadn't even looked at him properly, just grabbed the paper.

"Terry! … Check the list!"

"Oh right boss…Right," he wheezed irritably… "No, that's okay, I've seen these before," and this time he had looked at Ron.

"And after, I want you to come straight back here, you've got some overtime tonight."

"Right," Terry scuffed along, his boots squeaked noisily on the floor.

"Do you want to sit or stand?" Ron followed Cosey into his office, spun the large executive leather chair round, plonked himself down heavily and leant forward attentively with his elbows perched on the desk.

"I'll sit this time I think, it's been a busy week," replied Cosey wearily as he took the soft fabric chair opposite.

Ron watched him take in the room as he shuffled on the seat to get comfortable. First the far end which doubled as a gymnasium with a shiny steel multi-gym to the right and large racks of free weights stacked on frames against the back wall. The windows along one side of the room were shaded with slim aluminium Venetian blinds and he'd painted the walls dark to make his display of champion weight lifters stand out. Bet he doesn't recognise any of them. Ron wasn't that impressed with names anyway it was the trademark copper tan and sinewy taught muscular bodies that spoke volumes to him about commitment and perseverance. Cosey showed little interest in his row of neatly labelled black filing cabinets but his eyes came to rest on the black plastic flooring that glisten under the halogen recessed ceiling lights.

"What is this," Cosey pointed at the floor.

"What the floor?"

"No, the sparkly stuff."

"Its graphite makes it non slip."

"It's been a busy week for you too hasn't it Ron. You'll not be able to go in next door for a while by the way," gestured Cosey in the direction of Vick's office, "not until we iron out the inconsistencies. First your brother loses his manhood in the most undignified circumstances and then under the cover of darkness you have to go grovelling to Katychmar!"

"You …What the bloody hell are you talking about!" Ron blustered but it had completely taken the wind out of his sails. He'd been expecting questions about Vick's murder. How the hell had he found out about his visit to Katychmar? Maybe Katychmar had incriminated him? No, he'd too much to loose but Cosey was a tricky little bastard and Katychmar was used to asking the questions, he might not have been so bloody clever when the boot was on the other foot! "I haven't seen him for, well quite a while. Now Kactychmar, there's a name that doesn't exactly slip off the tongue!"

"You had a meeting on Thursday night at the clinic did you not?"

"No, on Thursday, I was out in the taxi earning a living."

"Does he still see Lionel?"

"Well you have done your homework. No, I don't think he's seen him since Lionel was released."

"Why did you move Vick, why not leave him in the office?"

"What …," Ron croaked. It was still all so vivid. Would he ever be able to think of Vick without the image of him sat in that chair clutching between his legs as the dark red patch of blood grew on the rug. The memory of Vick's eyes haunted him, fixed wide open as tears ran through clammy sweat on his face while he spoke in short stuttering bursts between the shakes that had gripped his whole body.

"I can't ffff ....find it Rrr..on!" Vick cried.

"What can't you..?"

"Mii...co...ock. It's not th.....ere!" he spat. "What's sh.....e doi......g. ?"

"She's dead. That bastard....bitch has just gone and fucked everything up!" screamed Ron as he swung his foot well back and kicked at her as hard as he could. His aim had been wide and it barely glanced the side of her head, still it was enough to knock her sideways, over onto her face.

"Oh God I've no co...ck!" screamed Vick as he plunged his hands down between his legs to feel under his seat but the effort induced a bout of fearful coughing and he tore at the neck of his shirt with blood stained hands to ease his breathing.

Ron remembered how everything seemed impossible. Vick would bleed to death without medical attention, he couldn't imagine where his dick had gone and then Terry arrived and started to panic. He could barely hear himself think with them both whining and cursing and panicking! Suddenly he became aware that Cosey had spoken to him and he tried to shut out the memories.

"Ron?" repeated Cosey "Why did you move Vick, why not leave him in the office?"

"We knew they'd have trouble getting him in the ambulance." Ron looked pale faced and his eyes glaze over again, "so Terry helped me to get him to the chair outside."

"D'you drag him out on the rug then?"

"No, we used an engine lift. It's portable but we had to drag him the last bit over the gravel because the wheels had got stuck," said Ron vacantly. The words came out on automatic pilot but his mind's eye had returned to the vivid memories of what had really transpired. Vick's eyes bulged through another coughing spasm as he lay on the rug while they dragged him down the corridor towards reception leaving a red trail behind them. He tumbled off the rug by the door in reception and it was then that Ron noticed the patch of Lumaii's blood over the bottom corner with other marks where she'd spat blood whilst she leant against the cupboard.

"Ron," said Vick, his voice horse and strained, "you got ttttt..o ..sort the girl, medics will see her."

Ron knew even then, he had seen it in Vick's face, heard it in his voice, Vick was getting weaker by the second. If he didn't get medical attention right away Vick would be on the way out. He'd seen his attacks before but back then, Vick hadn't been so big, he used to get some exercise and he ate better. These days he ate crap and just sat in front of his computer and watched mostly porn. It was as much as Ron could do to get him to his feet …answer the question …answer the question!

"He was very heavy and we were going to try and get him in a car…" continued Ron vaguely.

"Why ring the ambulance?" asked Cosey.

"We realised he was in bad way when we got him stuck near the front door. By the time we got him out on the gravel he was just a dead weight. It was all we could do to get him onto Lionel's chair …."

Ron pictured himself scrabbling round on all fours as he looked for Vick's dick while Terry tried to stuff Lumaii into a large plastic bag from a replacement windscreen. There were just too many things to do and so little time. With buckets of water and bleach they'd wiped down the cupboards and floor for the second time that night. Fortunately Vick's blood had been contained to a large extent on the rug and had only started seeping through badly as they'd reached the corridor and so the vinyl surface was easier to clean. Ron bagged the rug and helped Terry load Lumaii into the tool vault of the truck and then they'd stuffed the rug on top before slamming the lid tight. It was a struggle but they made it in twenty minutes. Then Ron had sat with his arm round Vick and waited for the ambulance to arrive while Terry hid the truck in the lock-up under the arches next to Frank's old place.

"You've done good for us all Ron, you've always looked after us, even before Dad died, you were there for me and Lionel."

"Vick I've fucked up this time though, big time," he'd wept like baby at the sight of Vick's helplessness and he felt that at the end he'd abandoned his brother to save his own skin.

"I'm grateful that you tried to save me Ron but she had the upper hand don't beat yourself up about it. It's okay…."

"Ron!" shouted Cosey. "You said you found Vick at around 7.30pm …Ron?"

"Yeah …yes there about's." Ron had to make a huge effort. He was on the point of losing it again….

"You didn't make the call until 7.55pm. What were you doing for twenty-five minutes?"

Ron took a deep breath. "Like I said we were trying to get him to the car and we hadn't realised he'd lost his dick! For Christ sake I was looking all over for it!"

"How did you come to find him again?"

"What?...Like I told the officer that night Cosey, I heard him shouting and screaming and I ran up from the workshop and there he was clutching himself and blood everywhere!"

"Vick didn't give any hint as to the identity of his attacker?"

"No!"

"You didn't see anybody leaving. You didn't hear ..you know…the sound of a car starting up…?" Cosey gestured with his hands. Ron sensed that his frustration was getting the better of him.

"Like I said before to the copper, DI Benning and every one of your bloody lackies…"

"Yes, you didn't see anything or anybody. Yes but he didn't rip it off himself did he?" snapped Cosey.

"You ever seen this girl before?" Cosey quietly slipped Lumaii's photo across the desk.

Ron braced himself and tossed the picture back across towards Cosey, "Yeah I've seen her from time to time at the café but not in a while. Why, you looking for her?"

"No, Ron I know exactly where she is, she's down at the mortuary. What's more I know where and who she's been with. I even know what she had for lunch and I'm pretty clear how and why she died." Ron felt his jaw begin to twitch slightly and he tightened his grip on the arm of the chair.

"She was a prostitute, a bit above Vick's taste I would have thought."

Ron looked hard at Cosey.

"Did Vick know Lumaii?"

"He may have done but I don't know. It's a busy day for me DCI Cosey, are you nearly finished? We seem to be covering all the same ground again," he added wearily.

"Well I have to say it's not exactly my taste Ron," replied Cosey as he stood up and glanced round the room again, "but it's a darn sight tidier than next door. I bet there was stuff in there had never been moved since ... I was beat copper. Like that clippings rug under Vick's desk, now what happened to that then Ron?"

"Oh," he was like a bloody pit bull... "The police officer asked about that and at the time, I couldn't remember but I think Terry burnt it."

"That's destroying evidence!"

"Evidence of what? Nobody was hiding the fact he'd been bleeding, it was there for all to see. I never liked the rug so I wasn't going to try and clean it!"

"Nevertheless you destroyed what I call vital evidence!" snapped Cosey.

"I'm sorry," replied Ron blandly.

Cosey's eyes had come to rest on something over Ron's left shoulder and he turned in his chair to see what it was.

"Do you still get out to the boat Ron?"

The old family boat photo hung next to a large gilt frame containing red boxing gloves and a white robe signed by Muhammed Ali.

"No… It doesn't look quite so pretty now though, nobody bothers with it much. It was moored up on one of the high spring tides years back. There's probably only a handful of times in the year when you could get it afloat again."

"And where's that?"

Ron stood up to read the label, 'Bolt Hole.' Yes and at 7.00am on Saturday morning he was going to sail out to sea in it, to a spot not too deep, and sink the bloody lot. Terry had already shipped most of the films to the boat in watertight containers the night he dumped Lumaii. When things quietened down again Ron looked forward to the opportunity to indulge one of his other hobbies, deep sea diving. Yes one day he'd salvage the lot and make a bloody fortune! "Is that it then DCI Cosey?" smiled Ron as he sat back down in his chair.

"That's it for now Ron," Cosey made for the door. "What's happened to the truck by the way?"

"Terry was on a recovery job near Woolley Edge on Thursday lunch time, and somebody stole it in broad daylight from the lorry park while he was getting some food."

"Did you report it?"

"Yes I did." Cosey shut the door.

Ron gave him the bird.

Chapter 33

Cosey swung his car round and pointed it in the direction of the police station. At this time it wouldn't take him long to get back and he was curious to know how much progress the new interrogation team had made with Grant.

He knew that his instinct wouldn't let him down but Ron was a slimy little git and he'd known Katychmar better than he'd let on. Cosey had seen it in his eyes but to prove it was another matter. At times like this there was no room for self doubt, you had to stay focussed. Vick's death had knocked Ron well off his perch that was clearly evident and it made him vulnerable. He'd had his work cut out to keep Ron focused in fact there had been times when even with the tan, Ron had looked pretty shaky and on the point of collapse. Then there was his lack of reaction to Lumaii's photo. Yes he was very self-disciplined alright!

Cosey had been tempted to hint about the other blood stains and see if he got a reaction but it seemed too risky and he kept it for another time. As for the rug ... Ron's eyes gave him away. He was definitely thinking creatively for that answer. The same could be said about the truck hijack, pure fiction. Ron probably had the truck squatted somewhere to use it for parts and who knows what. Least he'd got forensics over it beforehand and there was plenty to go at when the time came round.

Yes … time, that was a luxury he was short of and now he would have to make time for a trip to the pathologist. He's very keen this new bloke, Walter wouldn't have agreed to go back in for an 8pm meeting. Let's hope it's worth it. The police station came into view. What he really needed was a Tardis.

Chapter 34

"And you're quite sure of that?" DS Reg Varley asked with a fixed and serious expression, as he lent across the table towards Violet.

"Yes!" Violet replied confidently nodding her head, "he said that 'the final choice of resting place for the Thai girl was a Chinese Skip,' he thought it was 'almost politically correct.' Seemed to think it was funny. If you ask me, I think he's in need of a bit of therapy himself."

Cosey smiled at her candidness as he watched it all on CCTV. He enjoyed watching a trained interrogator at work.

"Anything else you remember?"

"Well it's all a bit of a jumble really, such a lot happened that night, it's difficult to keep it all in focus at the same time. Well …Ron seemed to think 'you were trying to build a case' about their involvement in Fay's disappearance. Then there was something about the truck in storage because I think he said someone called Terry had seen people snooping about. Katychmar wanted Ron to get the attention back onto Grant and I'm pretty sure Ron said that it was in hand …I'm sorry! I can't remember just how he put it" she smiled apologetically, "that's not a lot of help really is it?"

"Quite the contrary really…." replied Varley thoughtfully.

"Oh yes," Violet interrupted excitedly, "Ron gave a DVD to Katychmar, said the stuff on it could loose him his licence if it got out. Then they started a kind of cat and mouse game trading threats, it didn't make any sense to me."

"Did either of them mention Lumaii by name?"

"I think she might have been on the DVD, 'edited highlights' I think Ron said."

Cosey looked at Kalum. "What do you think?"

"I think she's genuine!" replied Kalum.

"I'm going to have to ask you to wait here a little while longer I'm afraid," said Reg, "but I'm sure we can organise a nice cup of coffee to keep you going," and with that he smiled politely and disappeared from the screen only to emerge from a door just to the right of Kalum.

"Thanks Reg, what do you think?" asked Cosey.

"There are parallels in their responses and they've got individual recollection about the facts but it all ties up. I think they're telling the truth," Reg nodded his head.

"Well that mean's that Katychmar and Ron have intimate knowledge of Lumaii's death, doesn't it?" smiled Kalum, "we never released the details about the skip."

Cosey gestured with a nod of his head and they both followed him along the corridors to his office, pausing briefly at the kitchenette where he asked a young policewoman to add Violet's coffee to the tray of drinks she was preparing.

"I think we need to take stock," Cosey slumped wearily into a chair.

"It's getting very messy," answered Kalum and wiped his hand across his mouth.

The drinks arrived, "Thanks," they said in unison.

"Will you just pull the door to…" asked Cosey but the deed was done before he'd finished the sentence.

"We're not getting very far with Fay's case at the moment. I can't help feeling there's a link but as yet, it's no more than a hunch," Kalum was keen to get the discussion going.

"Yes, well I'm happy to hear your hunches Kalum. You've had some good calls in the past but we've had Grant here what," he consulted his watch, "four hours and we're fast running out of reasons to keep him here."

"Do you believe him, about the screwdriver I mean?"

"Forensics can match the blood and the small fragment of tissue caught in a burr on the shaft to Lumaii's DNA, that makes it the murder weapon. But!....Phil's team could only find one trace of blood anywhere and as for the tissue in his car. Scottie said in her report that Grant was dabbing his knuckles on Friday night with a tissue, he'd caught his hand on the café door. We won't get DNA on that until tomorrow. Frankly there's not enough of it. The wound in Lumaii's thigh punctured the femoral artery, there'd be a lot of blood."

"I hear what you're saying," said Reg, "but I'm not that happy about trying to prove a positive using negatives,"

"How do you mean?" asked Kalum.

"You've no forensic evidence to link Grant to the murder weapon and we can't put him at the scene. Doesn't mean he didn't do it…could just mean we haven't found the evidence yet."

"As for it being in his garage, well" added Kalum, "that's just too much of a coincidence. He's very tidy, tools all in their right place and there on the bench plain to see, the murder weapon the very morning the forensic feller turns up! No I don't buy it," Kalum shook his head. "And there's also those footprints in the mud, down the side of the garage."

"Hm, no news on matching those I suppose?"

"No, not yet. You're convinced she died in Vick's office then?"

"Yes, I don't believe Ron's explanation. I think he caught her at it and in an attempt to rescue his brother he, or Terry for that matter, stabbed her with the screwdriver… but we've no prints on it."

"Well you see that's another thing," interrupted Kalum, "you'd expect the murderer to have wiped the blood off it if they were going to wipe the prints."

"Even if they wore gloves say, there would probably be a print from earlier usage, even a smudged unusable one!"

"Yeah. What was Ron's explanation for the delay in calling the ambulance?"

"Bullshit!...they obviously realised that with Lumaii's body lying there, all those blood stains and so on, they'd be in trouble if anybody else turned up. I think they panicked, I think they believed they'd get away with it if they dumped Vick in Lionel's chair. They could make out that that's where it all happened and then there'd be no reason for anybody to go into his office. In any event they would have had a bit longer to clean the place up. As it was, I think they realised too late that Vick was in a serious condition and when Ron rang the emergency services he knew then that they'd botched things up even more. The irony is that if they'd not panicked and just disposed of Lumaii's body, Vick might well have survived and now Ron or Terry wouldn't be facing a murder charge, if we ever get close to proving it that is!"

"Well Vick's one less villain and either Ron or Terry will make another so, I don't think you need to get too downhearted Sir," Kalum beamed with smug satisfaction.

"If Ron was involved in Fay's abduction and certainly the paint from the truck matches the paint on Grant's car, then I think Katychmar is involved too."

"Yes I've been toying with that one," murmured Kalum thoughtfully. "Other than Fay and Grant, he was the only other person who knew about the rendezvous. He chose the location as well!"

"Yes, this abduction was well planned, Lumaii's murder was not premeditated, and I don't think the Whinspers are exactly sophisticated crooks are they? So Katychmar chooses the location, victim confirms date and time, villains lie in wait. Grant had to arrive early to keep watch so they had plenty of time to spot him and organise a distraction. It fits!"

"There had to be two villains, one to cause a distraction, the other to snatch the girl!"

"Right, Terry took out the truck, he says to check it out and Ron drops off a fare nearby."

"Grant says the taxi left pretty well as he arrived though!"

"Well he said that it set off towards the castle but it didn't have to go all the way there. Grant wouldn't have been able to see anyway. Let's say Ron was the taxi driver and he drove down the front but only as far as the link road, turned back along the top near the gardens and up onto the road behind the cafe. Terry was in the truck and distracted Grant while Ron snatched Fay."

"Yes it works, then what?" Reg asked.

"Then they took the poor girl and…..What makes people do things like that?" Cosey shook his head.

"She drowned then?"

"Yes but it would have been a close run thing. The pathologist said her other injuries were severe enough for her to have died from shock, severe blood loss…." Cosey shook his head in disbelief. "I'll know better later, I've got an eight o'clock with our new young Home Office Pathologist, Rick!" He raised his eyebrows in mock disdain.

"What about Grant then?" Kalum asked.

"The Whinspers obviously want us to focus on Grant," said Cosey thoughtfully.

"Do you think he's stumbled across something, you know about the Whinspers that's important to them and they just want him out the way?" asked Reg.

"If we let him go, it might force them into something a bit desperate," suggested Kalum.

"Hm," Cosey murmured. What would he lose if he kept Grant that he might gain if he let him go? This was a bit close to call! If things went well then nobody would bat an eyelid but if …Yes, then the knives would come out! Better get the Crown Prosecution Service involved spread the burden of responsibility.

"My instinct is to let him go," Cosey broke the pregnant silence. "He's got a problem alright, there was enough porn in his flat to keep even you busy for a lifetime!" Cosey nodded at Kalum.

"Oh yes?" Kalum replied in good humour. "He seems to have dropped on his feet with his new girlfriend though, she's a live wire. If anybody can keep him on the straight and narrow, she can, and good luck to them."

"Right I'm going to run it past CPS."

Kalum and Reg nodded in approval.

"Kalum, you'd better draft me something for the press," Cosey spoke in a positive and upbeat tone, "and in the event that CPS go for it, you'd best be ready to inform Violet. We can let him out the side door, you know the routine. Thanks Reg, you did a good job in there today."

Chapter 35

"Let's get something to eat," Violet took Grant by the arm as he emerged from the side entrance of the police station. The press out front were focused on Cosey as he read a short statement. "You certainly know how to show a girl a good time," she smiled squeezing his arm close to her.

"How did you know where to find me?"

"You mean apart from the TV coverage and the fact I was there when you were arrested?" she frowned, "call it feminine intuition."

"No really, how did you know I was coming out there," he gestured over his shoulder as they passed the crowd of reporters listening intently to Cosey and hurried down the street, keeping close to three of the tall media vans. They sneaked across the road and down an alley onto the main road, doing their best not to break into a run in case somebody spotted them.

"Thank God that's over," said Grant, "Bloody Hell what a nightmare!" he stopped to take a deep breath of air. "Phew…No I mean it, how did you know I'd be coming out at that moment from the side entrance?"

"I have my sources…DI Benning told me where to wait. He said you'd be out in a minute and you were," she placed a warm kiss on his lips. "I was worried about you when I saw them take you away. They'd been waiting for you about ten minutes. I wanted to warn you but there was no time!"

"So he …you were at the station?" he asked as they began walking again.

"Yes, they came and collected me in the middle of the afternoon, it was all very dramatic. The detective that arrested you, right, he just appeared at my desk. They must have special silent shoes or something, it's really spooky man!" she giggled.

"It's nice to be out in the open," smiled Grant. He found Violet's high spirits infectious and he felt the clamp across his temple start to loosen. "How about a pizza?"

"Sounds great to me!" she beamed.

They scurried across the road and up a cobbled alley, through the narrow entrance and into the Parmesan Restaurant. The interior was decked out like a small village square. Tiny white lights twinkled like stars from the deep blue ceiling above the terracotta coloured tiled eaves that jutted out from the corners of the room. Small tables were arranged around the perimeter of the square under the eaves and the stone flags radiated from the central fountain to create quite a plausibly authentic feel.

"It's just as I remember Tuscany," observed Violet.

Small lights flickered inside coloured glasses on the tables and opera music played quietly in the background.

"Well, what a great atmosphere!" she slid into one of the two corner booths opposite Grant who sat with his back to the window, lest a stray reporter spotted him. "Do you want to share a deep pan with me?"

"I'd love to share lots of things with you Violet but for the moment the pizza will suffice!" he smiled.

"You can be very romantic," she looked a little bit dewy eyed.

"Really, I didn't mean to be I was just …."

"That's what makes it romantic," she brushed his hand with her finger tips.

"What topping then?"

"I'll have the vegetable feast."

"I'll have chicken and mushroom, you're not a vegetarian are you?"

"No, it's just what took my fancy, we can share if you can spare some of your chicken that is?"

"I don't know, I've been in prison most of the day!"

"That's why I picked you up, I like the danger, it turns me on!" She giggled, "Anyway I don't know why I'm being so friendly, you stood me up the other night!"

"What?"

"Yes! You took me out on an exciting adventure date and when I was all ready to spend the night with you, cuddled up on my sofa, you have the nerve to say that you'd had a better offer!"

"What?"

"Yes, a better offer, from a midget policeman with a big black bag!"

"Yes that's true. God, it seems like a lifetime has passed but it was only this morning!"

"Well life in the fast lane, hey!"

"What did they want you for anyway…this afternoon…."

Violet looked blankly at him.

"The police came to the office."

"Right, they took me in for questioning," she said in a mock American accent, "bright lights and rubber hoses." They both giggled and sipped their drinks.

"Are you going to tell me or what?"

"I'll take the what!"

Grant shook his head. It felt good to let off steam.

"Okay, first they kept me hanging round for while and then I had an interview with a police woman. Then I had to wait in a smelly little room for over an hour. Then when I'd almost lost the will to live they took me to see this funny little man called Varley and he asked me a load more questions about the clinic and what I remembered of Ron and Katychmar's conversation. I obviously must have said all the right things. Well, I don't know, I just told them the truth and that's that. He went off for about half an hour and then DI Benning arrived, said you were to be released and well you know the rest."

"I had a chat to the...."

"Your pizza sir, the bowl for your salad madam and another orange juice for you sir. Bon Appetito!" interrupted the cheery waiter.

"Thanks...I had a chat to the solicitor," continued Grant, "he said they'd be more interested in my theories about Fay's ...Oh God it's awful."

"I'm sorry Grant. It was on the news. You must feel terrible."

"I wish I'd done more but I just...at first I thought she'd just turn up like before, but as time went on ...there was nothing I could do!"

"No, that's true Grant, there really wasn't any more you could have done! In fact you found all the clues and they didn't follow them up quickly enough if you ask me!"

"The solicitor said that once I was in the clear over the Lumaii thing, they'd be more receptive to my suggestions about Fay. Well, Cosey listened okay, but I don't think he took it on board really. I feel like a weight's been lifted over the Lumaii thing but I feel worse than ever about Fay."

"There's nothing more you can do Grant!"

"Well there is actually!" said Grant with conviction. He'd had plenty of time to think it through. "I'm going down to the Whinsper's tonight and I'm going to get in that container, the one Lionel came out of..."

"Grant, haven't you been in enough trouble for one day?" she exclaimed with more than a hint of exasperation.

"Lionel's trying to finish something and it's so important that Ron won't wind things up. I reckon if I can get a peep, it might just unravel the whole thing." His voice was thickly laced with optimism.

"Leave it to the police!"

"They're too busy with Lumaii, they're not going to do anything about Fay's murder are they?"

"There's more than one of them you know and I'm sure they always have lots of cases going on simultaneously."

"There isn't time, I can't possibly sneak up in broad daylight. You heard Ron yourself, 'two days,' well by this time tomorrow it'll be too late, so it's got to be tonight!"

"I'll come with you!"

"No, you've done a lot for me today already. You've been a great ally, but this is something I need to do for

314

Fay. There's something about these guys. They're not like Katychmar. He called Ron's brother an animal and I don't want you anywhere near that place!"

"Grant I'm frightened. You're not an SAS… person, you work for an advertising agency, you're out of our depth!"

"I'm going to do this for Fay, no heroics, I'm just going to look that's all. I've lost one girlfriend to this lot already I reckon and I'm not going to loose another!"

"So I'm your girlfriend now am I?" she tilted her head to one side.

"Yes, wanna make something of it?" he leant forward on his chair and brought his lips to within an inch of hers.

"I wanted to make something of it the other night but you stood me up!"

"Well I'm going to give you the opportunity to make up for that…"

"I don't need to make up for anything mister!.."

"You can let me use your shower."

"I haven't got a shower curtain and people will be able to see your naked body,"

"Well, people had better keep their bloody eyes shut!"

"The shower's next to the window and it's above a busy street!" she laughed, "Ha, you thought I was going to peep…"

"I'm tough I don't care, let them stare!"

"But what about my reputation?"

"Are you a woman of ill repute?"

"That's my business! Put your money away, this is my treat!" she smacked his hand as he tried to pay the bill at the till.

"I feel like a tart. You buy me nice meals and then try to get me back to your pad, all cosy like."

"Save your money, there's not much point having a shower if you're going to put that shirt back on Mr Smelly!" she chided as they walked up the cobbled alley towards the shops.

"I don't smell….do I?" he asked in surprise.

"No, but I just thought secret agents always put on clean clothes before they went on a mission."

"True."

The first shop only had cheap T shirts with gaudy logos on them but the 'open all hours' one just down the street from Violet's house had a good sale rail. He could have bought several but the black shirt seemed the most appropriate for a night time operation. Grant showered in the dark, well more in the glow of the streetlight opposite to be more accurate. Now they stood in the narrow kitchen and enjoyed a quiet moment together. From near the open window, the sounds of the early evening bustle floated in on the twilight and they both enjoyed the warm proximity of each other as they cuddled.

"I was thinking about what you said regarding my flat," said Grant softly and Violet looked up at him. The orange streetlight behind the shop shone dimly in through the window providing the only illumination and his face looked pale. "I rang another agent. Thought I might rent it out for a while and maybe look for somewhere to buy here in Moverley. They seemed to think I could get some buy to let deal."

"What a good idea!…Grant you will be careful. Promise me!…Look at me…Promise!"

"I promise, once I've seen what's going on I'm out of there. Promise."

They hugged each other for some minutes, just enjoying the moment, not wanting to let go.

"I've got to go. The sooner I get started…."

"The sooner you'll get back," she smiled nervously. "Here and look after my car!" she added offering him the keys.

"Thanks Violet, you'd better get some milk. I can drink both tea and coffee without milk but I'll struggle with the cereal," he smiled. "Will you wait up?"

"I won't be able to sleep until you get back. Here, I got you a spare key, you can put it on your key ring next to the police midget's!"

"Ouch," he'd bang his head, "Get some light bulbs, this energy saving business is dangerous."

"I thought you were a romantic?"

"I am, forget the light bulbs, buy chocolate…"

The words faded as he reached the bottom of the stairs and she listened to him lock the door. She decided that it was better to be active and do a bit of shopping at the late store, come back, have a bath. Then set up a little cosy nest with the duvet in front of the TV and wait for Grant. Yes there were house rules but they could still cuddle on the sofa that was allowed.

Chapter 36

"Right I've got quite a lot to discuss with you since we first examined the body, it's a very interesting case this, lots of different dimensions," smiled Rick Cantor the new and relatively young looking Home Office Pathologist. "And I've even been able to use some of my West Indies experience on this one ..."

Cosey found him irritating on their first meeting and now he was well up his nose in the first ...or was it six short glib sentences?

"...I like the seasons here in England daft as it may sound."

Yes I remember thought Cosey as he tried to focus on the task at hand and bottle his impatience. "She's a bit of a mess isn't she?" he said sharply. Stood by the long work surface, browsing the pictures, he got frequent flash backs to Fay's holiday photo and now the thing that lay on the steel table ....God, it bore little resemblance to her.

"Right let's begin," chirped Rick. "Marks around both wrists and ankles indicate she was cuffed, manacled really, for a prolonged period, may have been days. During this time she was beaten and sexually assaulted. From the bruising and damage inside her vagina the attacker was either well endowed or used something quite large, either way she was treated savagely. Right?

"Yes," nodded Cosey.

"So no change there. The traces of lubricant weren't exotic so not a lot of help I'm afraid. However, the traces under her toe nails were of human blood, three different ones, not hers."

"Three?"

"Yes, I'm afraid so. I think who ever did this, has done it before. I'm guessing but you see these bruises on her back," he pointed at three photos laid on the table, "I'd say she was cuffed to some type of rack, there do you see and on this one as well."

"Hm," murmured Cosey, it seemed a bit far fetched.

"I think these traces were from the previous victims and got under her nails during the ordeal. Now to the really interesting bits," Rick caught sight of Cosey's disdain, "I'm not without heart DCI Cosey. I mean interesting because I can't help feeling that what I'm about to tell you will go a long way to helping catch the fucking bastard that did this!"

Cosey was speechless. He'd never heard a pathologist swear. In fact he'd never seen a pathologist display any strong emotion at all. He'd assumed it was one of the basic criteria used in the selection process. Maybe he should have been a little less hasty in judging Rick!

"Right what have you got then?" Cosey replied apologetically.

"First of all the tissue damage to her upper body is extensive and we discussed my shark attack theory."

"I thought we'd discounted that….I mean off the coast of Moverley?"

"Well it's not beyond the realm of possibility, that is, unless you know your sharks. Look just bear with me on this and I'll explain."

"Your West Indies experience?" Cosey muttered.

"Yes, this is the bite of a Tiger Shark and to my knowledge they don't inhabit the waters around the UK."

"Right," said Cosey.

"What's more, whilst I have no doubt about the shark, largely because I found a tooth to be honest, the bite pattern well…it's just not right. The bite should be more ragged and torn but this, it's too clean cut, more like a Bull Shark or even a Great White.

"Is it possible?"

"Not unless the Bull Shark was wearing the wrong dentures!"

They both chuckled.

"Yes, that's very good!" smiled Cosey.

"Now moving onto these lacerations…I found another tooth. Actually if you look over here in the dish you'll see. There on the left, that's the tiger shark tooth, see its hook shaped."

"Right."

"The one on the right," he pointed, "that's from the diagonal laceration across her torso, that's a Mako Shark tooth."

"What!"

"And that's…"

"Straight and pointed," murmured Cosey, "Well!"

"Exactly. Admittedly their natural habitat does cover a wide band stretching roughly from the tip of Africa to well, as far north as Scotland say, but this shark prefers deep water and so our victim is highly unlikely to have actually come in contact with one in the wild."

"So where does that leave us then?" Cosey thought he knew where it was all heading and now suddenly, the trail had petered out in front of his eyes.

"I'm still a bit unsure about the amputation bite but…" he added with a glint in his eye, "shark teeth can be bought easily and are used even today for ceremonial weaponry across the world. The Maori for instance, have a ceremonial knife called, now my Maori's not that good but that's how it's spelt," he pointed to a print out on the metal table.

"Mira Tuatini," chuckled Cosey.

"Yes that's what I thought," laughed Rick. "If you turn it over there's a photo of one."

The flat wooden tool looked to have been carved from a tree branch about twelve inches long and the base of the handle was still rough as if just snapped off the tree. Above the smooth handle it widened out where a creature had been carved. Shark teeth were attached at regular intervals along the tail as it continued the line of the handle until it touched the creature's nose. Two feathers were attached by a short leather thong to the base of the handle.

"It doesn't look much like a knife to me!"

"Nor me but I thought it might be a start!"

"And these are for sale on the internet?"

"Yes, that and lots of other types too, that one…"

"Yes, that looks more like a knife …The Gilbert Islands," Cosey studied the photo.

"I mean, it's just a theory but I'd say that whoever did this expected the injuries would be identified mistakenly as inflicted post mortem, while she was floating in the water, but in fact I think it more likely, they were inflicted by the assailant," said Rick with an air of triumph. "It's not uncommon for a shark to loose teeth like this. They've got several rows of them and a new one just moves forward to fill the gap but I think the teeth were planted in the wounds."

"Why's that?"

"You see on the picture you've got there, the teeth are attached to the wood by some kind of thread or braid that goes through a hole in the tooth."

"Yeah."

"Well the Tiger shark tooth doesn't have a hole, I think they planted that one …"

"Bloody hell," exclaimed Cosey, "the Mako tooth's got a hole in it!"

"I think it broke off the knife they used and they didn't notice."

"That would explain the two different teeth alright."

"Well that's a real turn up for the book, you're right it is interesting, poor girl," he added suddenly feeling guilty of being disrespectful but if this were to lead him to the killer then that was something to get excited about.

"That's not all," added Rick with a glint in his eye.

"The victim drowned in sea water, but I don't think she died in the sea. No, I'm jumping the gun. I don't think she died in the sea at Moverley."

"Oh!" Cosey was intrigued.

"In the victim's lung I found this," Rick offered Cosey a stainless steel dish with something brownie red in colour lying on it.

"Yes, I remember. What is it?"

"Seaweed. Normally I'd not be able to pinpoint the area in which a person drowned in a sample of water from the lungs, the traces would be far too small and the tide and current along the East Coast, well it would be out of the question really. But this," he said pointing at the sample, "this seaweed, like other things that live in the sea, absorbs traces of things in the water."

"Like pollution you mean."

"Exactly, pollution!"

"Right."

"You wouldn't expect to find traces in seaweed on the East Coast with higher than normal levels of radio nuclides like ceasium."

"Why?"

"You'd need to have a Nuclear Power Station somewhere in the proximity."

"Where then?"

"I've checked the CEFAS data and the most likely, bearing in mind I've not had that much time to do this…" He said apologetically.

"No go on!" urged Cosey, desperate to get closure on something.

"I'd say Cumbria, somewhere north of Sellafield."

"What! You think she drowned off the cost of Sellafield?"

"No, I said the seaweed came from somewhere north of Sellafield. You see, and now you may think I'm treading on your toes here but …"

"Fire away," said Cosey encouragingly, he'd never been one to get touchy about areas of responsibility as long as the baddy got what they deserved and he liked people who thought outside of the box.

"Why would you go to the trouble of drowning somebody in the Solway Firth, for example, drag the body out, transport it all the way over to Moverley only to dump it back in the sea again?"

"You seem to know a lot about sea water, for a pathologist?" observed Cosey.

"Well let's just say, I have an interest in preserving marine life around our shores and I just indulged my interest a bit too far on this occasion!" he smiled.

"Lucky you did," Cosey shook his head, "but I see what you mean. Yes, they wanted the body to be found in Moverley."

"Well they might not have wanted it to be found…"

"Yes, off the Cumbrian coast," they smiled at each other in mutual recognition. "Normally I don't relish this aspect of the job Mr Cantor," added Cosey, "but today it's turned out to be just that little ray of hope I needed, really it has," he felt quite moved as he cast an eye once more over the photos of Fay's body, "thank you. Is that all?"

"Yes that's it, and when people say Mr Cantor it sounds to me like they're talking to my Dad, so Rick will do just fine in future."

Chapter 37

Terry stood against the wall next to the restaurant, watching Violet's reflection in the shop window opposite. He recognised Grant from the clothes he'd worn earlier at the flat but now Terry only got glimpses of the back of his head. Ten minutes had elapsed since he'd phoned Ron as the two love birds slipped past the reporters at the station. Now he was feeling ready for a meal himself as it had been a long day and the evening was looming ahead. Italian food was not his taste, all that tomato, he hated it even as a kid. No, he'd be quite happy with a curry, fish and chips or even a Chinese. Didn't matter, first shop he came to would do!

He'd never been allowed to do this part before, it had always been Ron's job to stalk the victim. She was a bonny looking lass though, bit on the skinny side for him. He preferred them with a 'bit of meat on' but she was right up Ron's street. He was going to be disappointed this is such a rush job. Last time he got a girl like her …only her hair was jet black hair, he'd tied her up in one of the old containers for a week. He'd just nip in every couple of hours or so and give her one. She was Welsh, big bright lips. He smiled when he remembered that she had a real gob on her and Ron had slapped some gaffer tape over her mouth, no messing. Terry was so caught up in nostalgia that he didn't notice Ron until he stood just next to him and said.

"That bloody Cosey, I never thought he was going to go! Are they on the puddings yet?"

"They call them sweets in here Ron, it's not the Crossroads Café!" he said dryly with a wheezy chuckle, "and no, they've finished the main course. Been talking a lot so you've not missed much I guess."

"Right. Tonight I'm going to take the last of the stuff to the boat and with any luck she should float on this tide. So, is there much left still to pack?" Ron took his camera from its case and removed the lens cap.

"No, I'm going to get a bite to eat and then I'll clear the studio, just leave what Lionel needs. I'll put anything even a little bit dodgy, into a water tight container."

"Right, how long will that take?" Ron pointed the camera at the reflection and zoomed in slowly.

"An hour tops, like I said it's all pretty well done. Amazing what you can store in such small spaces these days!"

"Too right!"

"If you can take the last one with you Ron and load it on the truck yourself, it'll give me time to sort our lass out for the weekend. Then I'll come back early Saturday afternoon for some fun and games hey," he chuckled and coughed. "What you gonna do with all the editing gear?"

"We've had our money's worth out of it, I'll trash it, start again, state of the art, why not!"

"Every cloud…"

"Has a silver lining. Okay off you go I'll take it from here, and Terry," Ron took Terry's hand in a firm hand shake. "Thanks for helping me out with Vick and the girl. I think you should get a good bonus this year feller."

"It was a real shame Ron. I was pleased I could do something to help but …anyway, see you later," and with that he shuffled off onto the main road and out of sight.

Chapter 38

Ron crossed the narrow street and squashed himself right back into the shadows of the recessed shop entrance and focused the camera on Violet through the side window pane. That's nice thought Ron, much better than a reflection. He found it really interesting studying people's faces while they were talking when you couldn't hear the words. Some people were really animated and employed frequent arm and hand movements whilst their face remained almost expressionless. Others and this girl was one of them, used subtle facial expressions and yes…she did have particularly expressive eyes. They spoke volumes. She was in love with this prick. When she spoke her gaze shifted frequently from eye to eye. She was checking that she still had his attention and interest. From time to time she just touched his hand, nothing fussy just kept contact. Now she slipped off her jacket and Ron got his first glimpse of her tits as she slid out of the bench and made her way…to the toilet, he surmised. He caught her full frontal as she returned and zoomed in slowly on her torso so he could gauge the size and firmness of her breasts as she stepped under the light. Hm, they hadn't bounced or swung so they must be quite firm. She had a slim figure but not boyish, there was a nice rounded bum, plenty to get your hands round. Ron held his breath. She'd suddenly looked straight at the camera. For one tense moment he thought she'd spotted him but then she gestured to other things on the window and he realised that she'd merely noticed the menu stuck there.

Ron was getting bored with the view, he wanted some better shots of her and so he began to try and anticipate which way they'd walk to get to her house. It wasn't that far. They'd almost certainly go up the street so he could stand in the bus shelter and film from there no problem. But from there they could take either Lever Row or Mendil, they both led to Cross Street. Best thing to do, he decided, was to take whichever street they didn't use, run to the other end and then film her as she walked towards him. He looked back at them. Shit they'd gone! No, there they were paying the bill, no time to lose. Ron came out of the shadows and made double quick time up to the bus shelter. He sat on the bench just behind the advert, elbows braced tight against his ribs and pointed the camera round the metal roof support. The sound of a woman's voice and footsteps grew much louder as Grant and Violet turned the corner and headed diagonally across in front of the shelter in the direction of Lever Row.

"Look they're still open. I'll try in here!" exclaimed Grant.

Ron came out the shelter quietly and watched from across the road. Grant was sorting through a rail of shirts and he focused in on Violet pointing and offering advice. He guessed it was about, 'was it a suitable colour or maybe design?' Either way she wasn't very approving. Ron turned round quickly to appear as though he were looking in the decorating shop window as Violet and Grant burst out onto the pavement again.

"If you'd bought it, you'd have had to walk along in front of me! Why didn't you buy one of those T shirts anyway," she giggled, "all the best dressed Chav's wear them!"

"Don't show me up, they'll think I'm your carer!"

Ron let them go about ten yards then set off back towards the shelter. Over his shoulder he checked on their progress. He could see they were far too busy chattering to have noticed him, so he ran full pelt round and up Mendil. About half way up he waited in the shadows of a small alley that connected both streets. Grant and Violet paused at the far end for a snog. Oh shit, hissed Ron but then Grant moved on leaving Violet stood there alone.

"We can go down here, its quicker, Grant …" She shouted pointing. Then she looked down the alley into the dark and Ron focused up close on her eyes. They looked very appealing, pupils wide and the whites appeared to shine in the dark. "Oh Grant!" she moaned disappointedly and trudged off out of sight. Ron ran the rest of the way to Cross Street and secreted himself behind the stacked boxes and crates outside the Vegi Bazaar.

Violet walked arm in arm alongside Grant but checked her look in the large shop windows. Ron focused up close again as she turned her head from side to side and pouted from time to time.

"My lippy doesn't show up very well in this light!" observed Violet with a hint of frustration.

"That's because it's probably plastered all round my mouth instead!" protested Grant as he wiped his mouth with the palm of his hand and held it out for Violet to inspect.

"No, it doesn't show up any better on your hand!"

"They make lipstick out of monkey's naughty bits you know!"

"You have got to be kidding!"

"No, I read it in a magazine!"

"Get away, you can't read, you just look at the mucky pictures!" she giggled.

"Violet!" he railed in mock disdain. "Do they sell clothes in the Late Shop?"

"Sometimes," Violet scuffed her feet in the doorway.

"What about this then?" asked Grant with panache, "and this...how about this?" he stood in the shop with a quizzical expression on his face. Violet weighed up the choices as he held up each shirt by the hanger in turn.

"Secret agents always wear black!" she laughed.

"Black it is then!"

Ron focused in on Violet as she paced slowly up and down outside with her arms folded, She looked down at her feet for a few moments, cast a glance up or down the street, looked at her watch and then over towards the first floor window of her house. Grant emerged with his purchase clutched in a rustling white plastic bag and Violet dug the keys from her bag and let them in the front door. Ron had some good footage.

On previous occasions Katychmar had arranged the abductions in consultation with Ron. They'd discussed carefully the timing and type of distraction and sometimes they'd even rehearsed the whole thing when it was to happen in a public place. The more people about, the more chance there was that something could go amiss. Ron spent time choosing camera angles and on several occasions he'd also set up remote CCTV cameras so the victim never caught on. They'd snatched women from trains, bus shelters, taxis and once even from a public toilet. He grimaced, it had been very smelly in there. Now he was going to have to improvise. Time was short and he'd no way of knowing what these two were up to. Let's hope they weren't going to shag all night. We wouldn't want you to wear her out Grant! He slipped quietly down the dark passage between two shops and emerged in a narrow alley lined with high brick walls broken occasionally by a high wooden gate. Behind Violet's shop a nearby streetlight buzzed and cast a pale orangey tint to the stone sets. Ron had decided to wait his moment and then scale the wall up onto the extension roof. The first floor window was open and Violet was making hot drinks whilst along further to the right he could just make out the figure of somebody behind a steamed up window drying their hair with a light coloured towel. Later he could just see the top of Grant's head as he stood in the kitchen to the indistinct sounds of their voices that came and went on the cool evening breeze. Ron gripped both hands round the lamp post and bracing his feet against the wall, lent back and walked his way up the wall towards the roof. After a tricky little manoeuvre near the top he managed to get one foot jammed between the lamppost and the wall and then swung his body onto the flat roof. The rest was child's play and now, crouched just below the kitchen window, he listened to Grant and Violet say their goodbyes.

"Ouch!" Grant collided with something hard in the gloom, "get light bulbs!"

"I thought you were romantic?" laughed Violet.

"I am, forget light bulbs, buy chocol......" Grant's voice faded to the distant sound of feet on the stairs and then a door slammed shut and Ron guessed Violet was now alone. He heard the sounds of the kettle boiling and a spoon in a cup. Then cupboard doors were opened and closed.

"Bread, milk, light bulbs…hm, I wonder what cereal he likes…"

She was making a shopping list. Good, when she went out he would nip in through the window. He heard Violet scoop up her keys from the work surface, the sound of feet on the stairs again and the door slammed shut. That was his cue. Ron stood up, reached above his head and gripped the open window frame. With a foot on the bend in the sink waste pipe he scuffed up the brick work and eased himself onto the sill, pausing briefly to lift the window a little wider with his shoulders. He rolled in through the window and dropped softly to the floor. Ron took out his camera and shot footage as he moved from room to room to catch the eerie high contrast effect of the streetlight as it stabbed through the darkened interior. The sound of keys in the door made him stop in his tracks, that hadn't taken long. Ron just had time to step to the side of the door to the stairs as it opened pinning him against the wall. Violet walked quickly into the kitchen and dropped the shopping onto the work surface. He moved quickly and stood behind the open lounge door. He was just in time. Violet passed by clutching a large lavender coloured towel, shut the door to the stairs and walked into the bathroom to turn on the shower. He heard distinctive sounds as she took off her clothes, walked over bare foot on the tiled floor and pushed the door too. The splatter of her feet could just be heard over the noise of the shower as it cascaded into the creaky shower tray. Ron came out from hiding. The bathroom door was ajar and standing deep in shadow, he was able to push it just a touch wider. Like Grant, she hadn't turned on the light and as she stepped out onto the shower mat, her naked body became silhouetted against the orange glow of the streetlight on the steamed up window. With her back towards him, Ron filmed her tall slim body with her arms raised as she dried her hair. Ron's jaw dropped open as she turned slightly and brought her firm breasts quivering into view. His lips felt dry. This was fantastic footage. He became erect but shook his head to regain focus on the task at hand. If he got sidetracked now he'd make mistakes and that was when things went wrong. Sensing Violet's next move Ron quietly slipped into the kitchen and hid behind the open door. No more than fifteen seconds elapsed before Violet, wrapped in a towel, walked into the kitchen. She emptied the shopping on the work surface and selected a slim cardboard package, stripped the cellophane and removed a short white light tube. Violet fiddled about under the wall unit cursing softly for as few seconds before the light came on and spread a soft glow along the work surface and across the floor. Ron slid quietly still further behind the door out of sight as Violet dispatched the remaining items quickly to their new homes and tasted her drink.

"Er.." she exclaimed, "milk!" she popped the seal and added some to her drink and walked out the room. The distant sound of a hairdryer was followed by the noise of drawers and wardrobe doors being opened and closed. Ron knew this was the moment. Shortly Violet would return, dressed by the sound of things and collect her drink. He reached into his pocket and pulled out a small plastic bottle. He unscrewed the lid, tipped a small amount of the colourless liquid into the lid. He poured it into the hot drink and stirred it in silently with the spoon that lay nearby on the work surface. Cupboard doors slammed shut, the hair dryer was unplugged. They were warnings enough for Ron and he returned to his hiding place behind the door. Seconds later Violet returned, wearing a snug fitting pair of jeans and a blue grey long sleeved top and there was that smell again. A soft fresh slightly fruity smell, it must be something she put on her hair. But for that he'd have never known she was at the garage the other night. He'd caught the fragrance on the night air as he left through the hole in the wall at the yard.

"Ooh, sugar," she grimaced and added a spoonful, "that's better, now what's on the telly," she absentmindedly, scooped up an armful of magazines. Ron listened to her footsteps fade into a distant room and then stood patiently for ten minutes. That's all GHB takes, he thought and then, well four hours, maybe longer, of fun depending on her stamina!

Stood in the doorway Ron surveyed the scene. No need for stealth now. Violet lay slumped on the edge of the sofa and Ron lifted the empty mug from her hand, walked back into the kitchen and carefully washed it. At the second attempt he found the cupboard with the mugs and secreted it well to the back. He returned to the lounge, turned off the TV and lights, then picked Violet up effortlessly and swung her over his shoulder. At the bottom of the stairs he paused and opened the door slowly, trying not to make a sound. The Late Shop young lads were chatting loudly to each other about the football. Ron stepped into the street, locked the door quickly and made the short distance to where he'd found sanctuary earlier, behind the pile of boxes and crates. He pushed Violet well in behind one of the biggest crates, made his way back down the alley and a short distance onto the road where he'd parked the car earlier. That much he had planned, now all that remained was to get her in the car. Ron drove round onto the main road and then reversed down Cross Street to the stack of boxes and opened the boot. He moved a few boxes towards the car as he scanned the street and doorways for any unexpected witnesses. There was never a copper around when you needed one! He smiled and lifted Violet quickly into the boot, curled her legs up carefully, then slammed the lid shut. One had to be careful not to spoil the goods! He sent the boxes skidding back into a pile, started the car and sedately eased it out of Cross Street undetected. Mission accomplished, he felt quite smug. It had all been very last minute but this time Grant was in for a big surprise and so was Violet. It was going to be hard not to have a little nibble of her before he set out but then Lionel would only start. Better to play it calm after all, he was going to have to leave her with Lionel for a while. Still he had the film to finish and that would keep him occupied until the early hours at least. Every cloud has a silver lining, yes maybe Terry's right, this was going to be some weekend!

Chapter 39

From above, the sound of a train rumbled rhythmically over the viaduct and the squeal of its wheels and brakes cut through the night as it negotiated the bend. Grant remained motionless in the darkness between the arches and tried to conceal his warm breath in the cool night air. It had been more than half an hour since Terry left but Grant wanted to be sure this time that the coast was quite clear. He stepped gingerly between the nettles that hugged the shadows along the rough stone wall. The moonlight cut striped shadows across his path from the metal railings to his right. Everything was quiet but for the blood that pumped in his ears so loud that surely somebody would hear. He passed through the hole in the galvanised panel, crept along behind the large container and slowed down as he neared the far end to peer round. The workshop was silent and dark but for the small red and green lights that flickered randomly on a large metal control panel standing next to the hydraulic ramp. From the window on the first floor of the units a dim pale green light glowed. It cast a shaft of eerie light barely strong enough for Grant to pick out a route across the workshop floor that was free from obstacles. He ran softly on the balls of his feet to cover the twenty feet in less than four seconds and crouched down below the metal staircase. He remained motionless for a few seconds listening for the sound of any movement. Nothing stirred and the air was thick with the smell of oil and dust. He could just make out the distant sound of rock music that came from behind him and so he moved towards the door he'd seen Ron use last night and turned the heavily oiled lever. He opened the metal door and went inside. Now the music was much louder and he closed the door quickly in case the sound should travel too far. Bright shafts of light struck through the dusty interior from gaps around a door at the far end and Grant moved towards them carefully in a crouched position and groped the darkness for obstacles as now his night vision had gone completely. He peered through the gaps at the room beyond and tried to detect any movement within. Several feet beyond the door was an empty high back leather executive chair turned slightly towards him and behind this stood a mixing console and a row of monitors, speakers and rack mounted processing equipment mounted on shelves. Screen savers bounced randomly across the monitors as pale green, yellow and red lights dance rhythmically to the music across two compressors on the instrument panels. Otherwise there was no movement at all. After a pause of about a minute Grant put his weight against the door which moved easily. He peered round, saw nobody was there and went in. To the right was a door and another on the same wall as his entrance. The music seemed so much quieter now but, even so, it was quite a contrast to the silence outside. Grant stepped forward to the mixing console and touched the mouse to see if any programmes were running. The monitors clicked and fizzed into life. Two contained fuzzy stills of what Grant decided where close up sections of the smaller wider image on the middle screen. He clicked the time line and the images advanced so he checked over his shoulder. Then he returned to the screen and clicked the play button.

The picture of a tall, slim, dark haired young woman was displayed on the centre screen. She strode confidently across a busy street of clothing shops and entered the glass fronted shop on the right of the picture. A short black section of about three seconds was followed by a close-up sequence of the same woman filmed from behind. She bought a pair of high heeled patent leather black shoes, picked up the brightly designed carrier, turned towards the camera to leave the shop and Grant's mouth fell open in surprise as he let out a short gasp, "Oh my God, it's Fay!" Another short black section was followed by similar footage only this time Fay bought black leggings and a further sequence completed the outfit with the purchase of a short black raincoat. Grant paused the film. This was scary stuff. Someone had been stalking her. Even before that fateful Friday night, somebody had designs on her. He began to get a really creepy feeling about the whole set up. Maybe Violet was right after all, he was way out of his depth. He sat and listened beyond the music for any sound that might indicate danger. No…there was nothing but all the same he now felt very uneasy. How much of this was there? He'd promised to get a peek and leave but now he needed to know where this led, without that he had nothing. Shit! He clicked the mouse and the film came to life again. From the panning in the last section they must have been positioned across the road. It was clear that without a hint of camera shake they must have used a tripod or some kind of rest. Grant recognised it was not amateur footage and based on his recent 'Promo' video experience at the agency, this was quite a professional looking setup too and he paused the film. He looked around the room again. Yes he'd seen a lot of this type of equipment before. One thing was for sure, somebody else knew about their rendezvous and also about the text he'd sent to Fay. Katychmar! It could only be him, so that's why he wanted to know the final details before the event! He shook his head in disbelief, checked over his shoulder again for good measure and clicked the play button once more. The next section showed a wide angle view of the Bay Café as the rain lashed down and it zoomed in on a dark figure that emerged from the shadows to stand on the edge of the pavement in the buffeting wind. "It's Fay," he whispered and watched her look anxiously up and down the front whilst she tried to keep the strands of wet hair from getting in her eyes and mouth. He paused the film, rested one elbow on the edge of the console, ran his finger tips over his bottom lip and studied the still.

This must have been taken from across the road but there was nobody there once the taxi left and that was ages before anyway. It must have been taken from higher up really to get that angle. There was another road higher up! Now he remembered he'd seen the streetlights when he was having a pee! The taxi was one of Vick's, he was the one in the paper that got murdered. Ron was driving one of his taxis the other night and now he'd got footage not only of Fay at the shops but also at the Café. What if Ron was in the taxi and realised that when he arrived things were about to begin. Then Ron made out to be driving down the front but instead, took the slip road or something and doubled back, parked on the top road with his camera? He'd never have been able to see him in the dark, even without the rain. It fits and that would have given him the right sort of angle as well. He nodded, "yes that's it," he whispered to himself with a little smile and clicked play.

There was new movement in the shadows behind Fay and another figure emerged, big and muscular with a strange type of ski mask. It had white rings around the eyes and mouth. He wore a tight black vest that gaped at the front to reveal a hairy belly above matching black tights and boots like those a boxer would wear. He grabbed her around the waist from behind with a hairy arm and lifted her off her feet whilst his free hand, clasped tight over her mouth. Fay's arms and legs flayed about frantically but he carried her off in the direction of the archway with apparent ease and disappeared from sight, all in a space of less than six seconds. Grant wiped his eyes partly in disbelief and partly to rid himself of the tears that had welled up unexpectedly from very deep inside. Another black section followed and so Grant clicked the fast forward button impatiently. As the figures emerged between the gap in a stone wall beneath some trees, he slowed it done to the normal speed. Grant recognised the road instantly, he'd found it on Friday night behind the café and there at the roadside stood the red recovery lorry. "So that's what it was!" he whispered. Fay was obviously tiring because she struggled less and the man dropped her awkwardly to the ground on one foot. He grabbed the collar of her coat and he hit her hard in the stomach.

"Oh God!" Grant's eyes filled with tears, "Oh Fay!"

On all fours she gasped for breath, her hands sunk into the muddy silt as she struggled to get her breath. Meanwhile her assailant climbed onto the back of the truck and unlocked the tool vault behind the driver's cabin. He jumped down to the ground and roughly manhandled Fay up onto the back of the truck where he punched her so hard in the face that it propelled her backwards into the vault. He slammed the lid shut and fastened the padlock. After an athletic jump to the ground, the assailant reached out and shook the hand of the cameraman. After a brief black section, there followed a distance shot of the lorry indicating as it made a right turn before it drove off out of shot.

Grant paused the film. He was torn between a desire to bare witness for her in these dark moments and his fear of the bottomless pit in his own emotions that opened wide every time he considered the desperate fear and loneliness of her plight. He remembered the extract Fay had once read to him about a woman who'd been abducted on holiday and lived to tell the tale. How he'd had little time for it and been chastised for his lack of humanity. Now what was he to do? There was a real danger that the very large Lionel creature was probably lurking about somewhere and could come back any moment and catch him but he felt duty bound for her sake, to see it through. The prospect opened up the overwhelming hole of sickening doom that he had felt after sex and he struggled to stem the flow of tears as he fast forwarded the film some more.

The camera panned what looked like a medieval dungeon and came to rest on Fay where she hung by her wrists. Her body fastened in a star position with hands and legs tightly fastened in metal cuffs. A very large individual with his back to the camera had greasy strands of hair that dangled down his shoulders below that familiar style of ski mask. He was tugging at the hem of Fay's black top with one very large hand whilst the other hand daintily held a very long pointed knife. Despite his size he wielded the blade with surprising skill, pulled the hem towards himself and ran the blade from beneath right up to the neck band to slice it clean. Then with equal skill he lifted the top at each shoulder and sliced it through in like fashion and allowed the garment to fall to the floor. He ran his large hand over her left breast but Fay remained motionless with her head hung forward limply. Wherever this was filmed it must have been cold because her breath was clearly visible in the air. Was there no end to her humiliation, she looked so helpless, poor Fay, Grant wiped his eyes. Another slimmer but still heavily built man came into frame and crashed a bucket of water over her head. The two took it in turns to shake her head and slap her face as Fay began to revive. "Leave her alone you bastards!" he whispered in a horse low voice. Now steam began to rise from her skin and she began to tremble uncontrollably. Grant searched the console for a fader or a switch that would bring up the sounds of the film but stopped short of implementing his plan when he realised it might alert Lionel to his presence.

That's who it is! Grant thought there had been something strangely familiar about the shuffling movement of the biggest man, it was Lionel. He remembered him stood in the doorway the other night with Ron and he was the one Katychmar referred to as an animal.

Now Fay's leggings received the same treatment as did the top and she stood there naked, shivering and pleading with them. Her pale skin had a strange iridescent hue in the eerie light and he noticed her small triangle of pubic hair was trimmed in just the style he'd requested.

"Oh Fay!" he cupped his hand over his mouth to stifle his reaction. With eyes closed tight he felt that the darkness would consume him, drag him down and down into the abyss. His shoulders heaved in grief and his tears pattered onto the console and the floor.

Dare he open his eyes again, what horror would Fay suffer next? After a lapse of several minutes he rested his head sideways on one hand and watched the screen again. As his sight cleared he realised that the focus of the film had shifted to a bizarre contraption being demonstrated by a smaller similarly attired muscular man. He used a series of levers to control a hydraulic mechanism that operated a set of shark jaws fastened to the metal frame. Lionel's accomplice was in attendance and held a large marrow between the shark jaws. Now that he faced the camera Grant realised he was the one who'd snatched Fay at the café. The first two levers were operated and the jaws snapped tight on the marrow. Then the third lever was pulled and slowly the jaws closed and finally the end of the severed marrow fell from sight. The assistant redeemed it from below and proudly presented it for the camera.

Grant's stomach tightened as he speculated as to the relevance of the demonstration and the purpose of the contraption. The camera panned to the left and settled on Fay's limp figure as it hung heavily on the cuffs that bound her wrists. In the time he'd been too overcome to watch, she'd obviously suffered a severe beating and Grant grabbed his temple with both hands. "Oh no Fay!" and he slid his fingers into his hair. Her one eye was badly swollen, almost shut and her nose was bleeding. Her lips split and swollen as blood dripped over her chin and down her chest. There were numerous lacerations to her torso and the one so large that it spread from her right clavicle almost to her navel was very jagged at the margins and wept trickles of blood down her tummy from little breaks in the wound.

"Oh Fay, I can't…I just can't. I wanted to be there for you but I just can't do it anymore."

A large strong hand gripped him round the throat and lifted him onto his toes. A deep wheezy and sickening voice whispered in his ear, "You gonna miss the best bit…. you gonna miss Jawsy. Yes Jaws, he's the best bit!"

Gasping for breath Grant tried desperately to free himself and pulled at the podgy fingers with all his strength.

"It ain't no use buddy, it ain't no use struggling," said the calm wheezy voice of his assailant who brought him up and round, face to face and Grant got his first close up introduction to Lionel. For what seemed like a long time Lionel just looked at Grant expressionlessly, rolled his lips together and made little grunting noises. Then Lionel slowly let Grant down off his toes and forced his face round to rest on the console a short distance from the middle screen. With the other hand he deftly used the mouse to fast forward the film.

"Now then here we go!" said Lionel with pride, "…open your eyes!" Lionel tightened his grip and not only was Grant unable to breathe but the pain in his neck made him open his eyes and mouth wide.

"No!" Spat Grant, "Argh!" Lionel tightened his grip still further.

"Open your eyes or I'll snap your scrawny little neck!"

"Ohy!" Grant spluttered, he couldn't stand the pain any longer and he opened his eyes.

"Yes, that's better," said Lionel as though speaking to his pet rabbit. He released the pressure and restarted the film at its normal pace.

In the film, Lionel, it was definitely Lionel, had his arm over the top of the Jaws mechanism and his hand held Fay's right breast tightly between his thumb and forefinger. He then gripped it tighter and pulled it through between the open jaws. Desperately weakened, Fay cried out pitifully as the tension told on her restraints. The first two levers were pulled and the Jaws snapped shut. Fay's head jerked back suddenly her teeth bared as she screamed, shaking her head and writhing in a futile attempt to free herself. Blood bubbled between the teeth and ran little rivers down her tummy and out of sight. Lionel was grinning manically and the operator cheered the success of his invention. Grant opened his mouth to scream but no matter how hard he tried, no sound came out. The third lever was pulled and the Jaws juddered and began to close even tighter as Fay shook her head. She screamed, she spat blood at her attackers, it was all she had left to do. Suddenly the top front jaw broke free and the operator slapped Lionel on the back. Lionel responded by grabbing the jaws in his hand and with his teeth clenched, squeezed them together and Fay passed out just as the severed end of her breast fell from view. Whilst Lionel supported the mechanism the operator picked up the breast and paraded it in front of the camera. He dangled it from the nipple and danced it across the screen like a floating jelly fish.

Grant lay across the console exhausted from the gory spectacle. He took in short shallow breaths now that Lionel had released the grip a little more. Unconsciousness was only a short step away. The camera panned back to the two men as they grabbed the bottom of the frame that held Fay captive. As they lifted the frame it pivoted in the middle and the camera followed Fay's head as she turned gradually upside down. Fixed to the floor at the base of the frame support was a large glass tank full of what looked like sea water with seaweed and flotsam on the surface. When the frame reached only a few degrees past the horizontal position, the back of Fay's head touched the water and within two to three seconds her head was totally submerged. Fay struggled briefly but the whole ordeal had taken its toll and she stopped moving after about twenty seconds. All the time her torturers bared their teeth in frenzied and ghoulish expressions. Then when it was over, they swaggered about slapping her dead body and one of them grabbed her by the scruff of the neck and planted a grotesque kiss on her lifeless lips.

"What kind of animals are you?" croaked Grant at just above a whisper, "I hope you rot in hell…"

Grant let out a sigh of relief and despair. It was all over but now what fate awaited him. He was utterly exhausted both mentally and physically, he'd not been able to free himself even a millimetre, Lionel was immensely strong.

"Now I think it's your turn maybe," wheezed Lionel as he lifted Grant off the console and into the air. Grant spluttered protests. His arms and legs flailed about till he felt a glancing blow with the chair. He tried desperately to grab at it with his feet. If only he was able to just take some of his weight off, he might just snatch a little air. Suddenly, inexplicably, he was falling and groped the air for anything to break the fall. Inexplicably his leg became entangled in the arm of the chair. He fell backwards, bounced off the console, slid to the floor and pulled the chair over on top of him. Above and to his right he heard Ron's voice shout above the sound of fists connecting with flesh.

"What are you doing you fucking idiot," yelled Ron, "you'll get your chance. Didn't I promise? Didn't I?"

"Yes Ron," replied Lionel apologetically, "I'm sorry Ron!"

"I promised but not now, not like this! If you do it my way he'll take the rap for Fay, the Thai bitch and this one here and we're all home and dry. Do you understand Lionel, all home and dry!"

"Yes Ron…I'm sorry Ron!"

Grant rolled over on his side, struggled for air and gasped in despair. There laid still, slumped and discarded against the wall with her head back, eyes closed and mouth open, was Violet.

Chapter 40

"You take him," gestured Ron in Grant's direction, "and make sure you fasten him tight. It's not ideal but we'll have to make do."

"Needs must," replied Lionel.

"That's right Lionel, needs must!"

"Needs must," wheezed Lionel quietly as he half lifted and half dragged Grant towards the door.

"We haven't used this in a while have we?" Ron smiled and unlocked the door which groaned with neglect as he pulled it wide open.

"Needs must," Lionel dragged Grant roughly through the doorway and caught his ankle on the metal threshold.

"Aargh!" cried Grant as a sharp pain shot up his leg and seemed to find its way right to his temple. It made him feel sick.

Ron switched on the light just as Lionel caught the bare light bulb with his head and crazy drunken shadows spun around the room. To the left and just inside the entrance was a second door that stood proud of the wall. It had two locking levers to its right-hand side like the bulk head doors on a ship. Next to it and fixed to the wall with long brackets was a frame similar to the one Grant had seen on the video that had held Fay captive. Lionel now propelled him into a chair on a large circular metal base. From the brief glimpse

Grant caught of it before he crash-landed in the seat, it reminded him of a barber's chair but this one was entirely made of wood. From nowhere Lionel seemed to produce a zip tie. He lashed Grant's left wrist to the arm of the chair and then reached above and beyond his head to pick another and fastened Grant's free arm to the other armrest. Lionel's huge mass pretty well obscured Grants view of the room but for the floor which was made of rusty metal sheeting fastened together with metal straps. Only the areas at the perimeter still retained a chipped and flaking gunmetal grey paint. Ron discarded something with a thump on the floor just behind Lionel and between his legs Grant caught sight of Violet as her hair fell softly from her shoulders to the floor. Lionel began to shuffle around again and now Grant could see Violet more clearly. She lay on her side with arms limply crossed in front of her. He looked hard at her, was she still breathing?

As if he'd read his mind Ron said, "She's out cold," and he placed a chair in front of the frame. "I hate using drugs even GHB, you never know just how long it's going to take." He lifted Violet under the arms and plonked her on the chair. He clutched her collar with his left hand and held her in an upright position against the frame while he reached down a zip tie from the dispenser above. With his knee against Violet's chest he raised both her arms above her head and fastened them to the frame with another zip tie. Ron lifted her head back by the chin, smoothed away her hair and pulled at her right eye lid.

"No, she's gonna be out for a while," and with that he let her head drop back down again.

Lionel had shuffled to the doorway by the time Ron had finished.

"I've got things to do before I can set off tonight for the boat," Ron stood up, stretched a bit and yawned. "It doesn't leave me much time but I have to go tonight, we need a good high tide to get the old tub afloat again and I can't afford to miss this one." Lionel stepped over the threshold. Ron followed him adding, "I can sink the lot and we can salvage it later." He scooped up his black leather jacket from the floor and slipped it back on as he turned to face Lionel in front of the doorway. "Now you've got to get it finished Lionel, I'm counting on you. There'll be plenty of time to have your fun later," he nodded in Violet's direction with a leer. "If we play this right, Grant here," he gave him a slimy smile, "will take the rap for everything, do you hear ....Lionel!"

"Yes, needs must," groaned Lionel.

"Yes, needs must!" He turned to Grant and sneered, "Well I hope you'll be comfortable till I get back!" Ron slammed the door shut with a tremendous 'CLANG!!!' that reverberated around the container and made Grant's eardrums rattle. Through the dying rumble he heard Ron turn the lever on the outer door to let himself out. Now Lionel restarted his rock music but thankfully it too sounded distant. Grant had overdosed on Lionel's taste earlier and it evoked strong horrific memories of the video that he was desperately trying to suppress. How could anybody who thought themselves to be human, have gained so much pleasure from such inhumanity? Could any sane person have done such things? But that's it, they were insane! They had to be. He wasn't able to get his head round it and the questions and the disbelief swirled round and round. He gripped the arms of the chair and braced himself against the peaks of anger and troughs of helplessness on his roller coaster of emotions. The horrific images of Fay's mutilated body and her pitiful plight crashed over him in waves of nausea. He looked around the room, desperate to find something on which to focus, something that might combat the images. But there were menacing parallels between the medieval dungeon of the film and his present surroundings and he knew deep down it wasn't over yet. He needed to brace himself, focus on the future. If he was to avenge Fay's murder, he wouldn't be able to do it in his current frame of mind. How long would he have to come up with a plan? Ron said that Violet would be out for hours and he looked in her direction but couldn't detect if there'd been any change.

He'd never noticed before just how many different colours were in Violet's hair. Some strands were light as if bleached by the sun and they caught the bright light from the naked bulb. Whilst others were much darker and there must have been hundreds of shades in between, some were quite gingery. He remembered how soft her hair had felt in the storeroom at the clinic and it had a slight fruity smell. Now it hung loosely onto her chest and even in this stark lighting, it had a lovely soft sheen. He'd noticed at work how she generally dressed down but somehow she managed to do it with style. Her pale blue grey top had a wide round open neck. It had been pushed off her shoulder earlier to reveal nice brown skin and a thin cerise bra strap, whilst the long sleeves were pushed up her forearms. Her jeans were a good fit and stylishly faded and bare ankles showed below with cerise trainer socks just visible inside some unusual white split toe trainers with Velcro straps. She had no jewellery which was untypical of Violet. The girls had often congregated near her desk to admire the most recent purchases on one of her lunchtime shopping sprees. He felt a calm wash over him at long last. It was a welcome respite to all that had gone before. He put his head back, closed his eyes and tried hard to relax. If he were to figure a way out of their seemingly hopeless situation, he was going to do a better job if he cleared his mind and looked at it objectively. After a short rest when mercifully all he'd seen was blackness, he found memories flood in of beach holidays with the kids from the home. He'd seen 'Nico' and 'Sprig' pull that giant jelly fish along the beach on a big lump of seaweed while Richard and another boy whose name he couldn't remember, had grabbed every big stone they could scavenge from the sand and pummelled the corpse to shouts of 'Yeah' and 'Whorr.' Later Nico dropped his ice cream cornet, soft end down but caught it on his foot and everybody applauded and giggled as he tried to salvage as much as he could, before he doused his foot below the ice cold shower next to the beach toilets. Needs must shouted Nico and Grant felt himself smile.

"Needs must," but it was the wrong voice, it was wheezy and deep. The happy beach memories faded fast and Grant opened his eyes but the bare light bulb was straight in them. He shut them again quickly, shook his head and tried once more. Lionel shuffled past him. He opened a large wooden cupboard stood on the floor with two metal brackets that fixed to the far wall. The contents made Grant gasp and suddenly he felt cold and sick to his stomach. Neatly arranged below the lid stood maybe twenty black wooden handles and as Lionel browsed the neatly arranged rows he pulled a few up to reveal sharp steel blades and some rather misshapen tools like cork screws. Everything was in its place and Lionel seemed to be stock taking. He pointed to an item and then recalled how many there should be followed by a count down to check; Six ….hum, one, two, three, four, five, six. His fingers wandered to another group; Three, yes, one, two, three and so on. Grant turned in Violet's direction, nothing had changed and better for her that it hadn't with this latest revelation. How long had he been asleep? Lionel had finished his counting and left the lid up and he shuffled past again. He paused momentarily to check Violet and then that deafening CLANG!! And he was gone.

Violet's head moved, "has he gone?" She whispered.

"Violet!" Grant whispered loudly with a mixture of astonishment and relief, "are you okay?"

"I've been better…bit woolly in the head," she was trying to focus on him. "You bin fighting?"

"Not exactly, why?"

"You've got a bloody nose," she smiled, "it suits you."

"I'll remember that!" he smiled back.

Suddenly he no longer felt so all alone, it was so nice to have some normal conversation but what should he tell her about everything? The smile faded from his face, Violet's head had dropped again.

He tried to rock his chair but although he got some movement along the floor he'd need a lot more to tip it over. Maybe he could shuffle it over to the cupboard. If he could, then with his teeth, he might just be able to lift something out. It was a long shot but as no better idea came forward, it was worth a try and the sooner he started the better.

"Where are we?" asked Violet in sleepy vacant tone.

"We're in a container at The Whinsper's Empire. Do you remember that big bloke that came out and spoke to Ron?"

"No not really," she smiled wearily.

"Lionel's his name, he had long rat tail hair, he stood in the doorway, shuffled about a lot," Grant was losing the battle but if he could get her to think about things maybe it would help her to come round. Her head slumped down again…maybe not!

"He's very smelly," she muttered from beneath her hair.

"He is that," smiled Grant.

"What are you doing?" she asked as her head waved about as she tried to focus through the strands of hair fallen across her face.

"I'm trying to get this chair over to that cupboard."

"Why?"

"To see if there's anything in it that I can use to get us free," he left out the bit about the knives as their mere presence might provoke questions he'd rather not answer.

"That's a good idea, I would never have thought of that," said Violet from beneath her hair, as her head lolled about.

"I was worried about you when Ron first brought you in."

"That's really nice, to know you care. I feel okay really, I just don't seem to be able to move my arms and legs."

"He gave you some GHB, said you'd be out for hours, so you're doing quite well really."

"What's gh…."

"It's a date rape drug."

"Trust you to know that!" she giggled weakly.

"It's a long story."

Grant rocked the chair again. There were only another few more feet to go. It was difficult to gauge how much of a swing he needed. If he thrust his body forward and then swung his legs it worked best but if he misjudged the balance between the two, the chair simply spun round and left him facing the wrong way. Only a couple of feet left. But his movement seemed to be parallel to the cupboard and he looked over the armrest to discover that the base was running along one of the metal straps. He swung his legs up onto the cupboard and managed to push backwards and raise the edge of the base just enough to clear the strap.

"Oh shit!" he gasped as the chair rocked further backwards than he'd intended. It began to wobble. As he pirouetted round Grant tried to steady himself with his heels on the cupboard. For a moment the chair just seemed to balance not sure which way to go and then thankfully it settled down forwards and settled unevenly. With great care he inched his head to the left and took a look at the floor. The base was well over the strap. If he was just able to use his legs and heels to pull himself towards the cupboard, without the chair twisting round on the base, he'd be there. One careless move now and all was lost, he'd topple over on his face and that would be disastrous. He tensed his body, pulled on his heels and the chair began to right itself. He felt his stomach muscles begin to flutter and then the shakes began to radiate to his chest and thighs. With a sudden scrape the chair slid forward and collided with the cupboard.

"Yes!" It couldn't have worked out better. He'd come to rest with his head hung over the knife handles and he slipped his lips over the nearest one and got a grip with his teeth. The knife was too long he wasn't able to lift his head any higher, so he let it go. The next was shorter but still, just that little bit too long. When he tried to move the chair, it twisted slightly and he realised that there was still a grave danger that he might end up on the floor. Suddenly the music stopped. Had he made too much noise or had Lionel just had enough of the bloody racket? Was Lionel about to appear at the door before he could fulfil his mission? He looked over towards Violet she was watching him wide eyed. She nodded towards the door. He shrugged his shoulders carefully and whispered, "Who knows?" If Lionel came in now he was too close to the knives for comfort, it was now or never! The longer he hesitated, the more chance there was that Lionel would return. He pulled hard on his knees and stretched his neck as far as it would go. He just managed with his lips to coax the handle of the third knife into his mouth and gripped it with his teeth. The short knife came out of its home quite easily. Had he lost concentration or just overstretched? The question was academic now the chair was wobbling again and Grant had no idea where he was going, as his legs slipped off the cupboard. With a painful thump his heels hit the metal decking and the chair came to an abrupt stop. For a moment Grant just sat there in silence, the handle of the knife barely held in his teeth and the short pointed blade glinted in the harsh light of the naked bulb. He could see Violet's eyes stare at him wildly and her teeth were clenched tight. He raised his eyebrows as a question.

"You need to be careful with knives," said Lionel with a grin and his big hand daintily pulled the knife from Grant's mouth.

"Please don't," cried Violet.

Grant's mouth was open but he couldn't speak, the mechanism somehow wouldn't work, his mouth was too dry. He felt himself begin to tremble, he was frightened and more vulnerable than he'd ever been. Now Lionel took another short step towards him.

"No, please!" cried Violet.

Lionel's eyes flicked in Violet's direction but he had hold of Grant's hair and pulled his head over onto his shoulder. From the corner of his eye Grant caught sight of the blade glinting in the light as it headed towards his neck.

"Oh shit!" spat Grant.

"Don't! Please don't," pleaded Violet.

Lionel's eyes flicked in Violet's direction again as Grant felt the point of the knife prick the skin on his neck, somewhere between his jaw and his ear.

Grant braced himself, his whole body trembled uncontrollably, he clenched his fists and gritted his teeth. This was what Lionel wanted. The sick animal set him up. He'd left the cupboard open on purpose and was just waiting to see how long it would take before Grant took the bait. He looked out the corner of his eye at Lionel's face and that was confirmation enough. Then Lionel's expression changed. Was he having second thoughts? He released Grant's hair and swapped the knife to his other hand. What sick alternative was this crazed animal considering now? Lionel shuffled round in Violet's direction and Grant's relief turned to anxiety.

"Lionel, lost your bottle have you?" chided Grant, but it had no impact. Lionel continued to shuffle toward Violet and he got a view of his back with Violet tied to the frame that held horrific memories of Fay's torture. His stomach tightened still further when he saw the knife held daintily in Lionel's right hand as his arm hung loosely by his side.

"Lionel!" shouted Grant authoritatively.

Lionel ignored him and just reached down and grabbed the tie that held Violet's hands from where Ron had hooked it. He lifted Violet slowly to her feet and hooked the tie over the top of the frame. Violet's expression was becoming fearful as she looked between Lionel's cold eyes and Grant's mixed expression of hate and fear. She kicked out at him with all her might but her trainers were soft and except for the groin kick that noticeably stalled Lionel, he proceeded unimpeded. Despite her greater speed, he grabbed one leg just above the knee with one hand which made her wince and cry out. With the other hand he reached down a zip tie. Having secured her one foot to the base of the frame Lionel followed the same tactic to secure the other. The bending was very difficult for him and his breathing was strained. Lionel paused, rested his hands on his knees between rasping bouts of coughing that reverberated round the room and shook his huge frame. Grant prayed that Lionel would have a heart attach and die like the rabid dog that he was, but no such luck. After another minute or two, Lionel began to get his breathing under control again. He stood up from the crouched position he'd adopted throughout. Lionel stepped close to Violet again.

"Lionel, remember Ron said you had to wait!" bellowed Grant.

"Needs must," croaked Lionel.

"Yes, needs must, you've got to finish it!"

"I have finished," smiled Lionel.

"Yes Lionel, later is better!" Violet even managed a glimmer of a smile.

But Lionel was having none of it. He grabbed the hem of her top and pulled it tight and sliced through it to the neck band in one well rehearsed action.

"Needs must," smiled Lionel and he gave the sleeves and shoulder seams the same treatment.

"You didn't have to do that Lionel," barked Violet indignantly. But behind the bravado Grant detected the tremble of fear in her voice for the first time. Lionel lent back slightly as if to admire her bosom neatly packaged in a soft cerise lace bra.

"Ha," grunted Lionel as he hooked the point of the knife under the middle of the bra, where the cups meet. With a short upward movement the bra split in two revealing Violet's perfectly formed breasts. But without a pause Lionel proceeded to the shoulder straps and then pulled her clothing away and discarded it on the floor. Violet looked enquiringly at Grant with her eyes full of fear. Would that be it or was this only the beginning. Grant feared the worst.

"Is that Ron," enquired Grant in loud firm tone, "I'm sure I heard him!"

Lionel seemed captivated by her and ran his large hand over Violet's right breast.

"Yeah, needs must," he leered.

"Lionel!" shouted Grant.

Violet shuddered, "No …ugh N…" her voice tailed off as she seemed to recognise the impact her rejection had on his face, now contorted with anger, he began to snort. For a second or two it wasn't clear what was happening, was Lionel getting angry or was he getting excited. Violet's expression changed.

"Don't be so rough. Oow! Don't nip Lionel, it's not sexy." Her voice was calm and hinted at a growing affection as he responded to her. He shifted his attention to her other breast, cupped it in the palm of his hand and squeezed it between his thumb and forefinger.

"Lionel, that's enough!" Grant had seen that move before.

"Oh God Lionel, that fucking hurts!" screamed Violet.

"All girls like me in the end," smiled Lionel and with that he touched the tip of the knife high up on her breast.

"Lionel! Be careful," Violet voice trembled, "I'm sorry, I didn't mean to upset you. It just takes a girl time to get used to a new man. Lionel I'm sorry, let me make it up to you. Her voice became much more intimate and flirtatious.

"See I told you, I told you," said Lionel triumphantly as he twisted the point of the knife, pivoting it on Violet's skin.

"Ow, Lionel that hurts, Ow!" and a small trickle of blood ran down her breast, "Argh..Lionel!" Violet turned slightly to see what he'd done. Lionel stop, stop you're hurting me!"

"Lionel!" Grant pulled on his ties and tried to move the chair closer. "Ron'll be here in…he's going to be so mad with you!"

"Argh!" screamed Violet, "Argh!… Argh! ..Aaaaargh!"

Lionel pushed the knife slowly down into her breast which he lifted slightly, he was trying to see whether it had come through below.

"God Lionel what kind of fucking animal are you!" screamed Grant at the top of his voice as he rocked his chair frantically toward him.

Violet was crying and screaming in pain and anger, "You animal," she spat at him through the tears as blood ran in little rivers down her tummy and made a large dark stain on her jeans.

Grant swung his legs out and hit Lionel in the thigh. He thought he might get lucky and knock him off balance.

"Oh God Ron, what's keeping you!" yelled Grant.

"Ha…Hm" giggled Lionel pleased with his work. The knife was in up to the hilt and the point of the blade was just visible below her breast. He stepped back slightly as if to admire his work but in a swift flick of his fist, he sent Grant spinning round on his chair and it rocked about drunkenly. Lionel stepped forward again and took Violet's right breast in his hand.

"Oh no Lionel, no!" she pleaded as her voice broke between the tears.

"Lionel for God sake, enough," yelled Grant, "enough! For God sake that's enough!" Grant managed to rock his chair back close behind Lionel again and was ready to have another go but the room spun round in his head.

"No, Lionel be gentle, it's much better when it's gentle," said Violet in a soft and seductive tone. Put your lips to my nipple Lionel, it's very nice for me if you do that Lionel. I'd like you to do that to me Lionel, I really would," she smiled warmly.

For a moment Lionel paused, he just stood there and wheezed. Then slowly he bent his knees, ducked his head and cupped his lips round her nipple.

"Oh Lionel!" she sighed, "such a gentleman! That's ….oh, so lovely." She looked at Grant with a forlorn expression and mouthed the word 'I Love You' silently.

Grant smiled back and mouthed a silent reply 'I Love You" and Violet smiled. She's such a brave girl, oh the bastard, but he dared not distract him, despite the volcano of rage that welled up inside him. Lionel was for the moment distracted from his violent binge. Damn it, where the hell was Ron!

"Oh Lionel, that's a real treat!"

Suddenly Lionel swung out at Grant again, only this time with much greater force. He'd either caught sight of their silent exchange or he just hadn't liked Grant being witness to his pleasure. Grant and his chair careered across the floor like a spinning top and when the base caught a metal strap it cart wheeled into the corner with a tremendous boom and crack.

Chapter 41

"You're making fun of Lionel!" he barked angrily.

"No, no it's really good," Violet replied warmly, "don't stop, you're a good lover," she smiled, "see you don't have to hurt me to enjoy yourself and you're turning me on as well." She raised her eyebrows and looked hard into his eyes.

"No, you're lying! Girls always lie to me and then they feel the pain and they always change their mind. Then I know they're telling the truth!"

"No, Lionel you are turning me on really," her voice was warm and soothing.

"You're lying, just like the rest!"

"I'm not and I can prove it!" she gestured with her eyes down to her groin, "touch me down there Lionel," she smiled encouragingly and added, "she won't lie to you."

Lionel ran his large fingers between her legs.

"Now can you feel Lionel?"

Lionel massaged her roughly.

"Gently, Lionel gently," she whispered as she looked in Grant's direction and tears flooded her eyes. At least he was breathing but laid motionless with his head in the corner of the room he was too far away to help her.

"No, you're just lying to me!" He stepped away from her, turned and stomped to the cupboard selecting another knife only bigger.

"No, Lionel you have to be gentle, it won't work as well if you're rough!"

He was almost back to her, his eyes fixed on her right breast. She tried to turn away from him but the sharp pain in her left breast took her breath away and she could see the bleeding had started again.

"No Lionel, no … just stroke me, stroke me, you know, you liked it remember?" Her voice was getting higher and higher and the words were rattling off her tongue, "Lionel, don't."

He took her breast in his hand and pulled at it between his thumb and finger.

"Lionel wait, there's still time to enjoy it," she screamed, "Lionel," the point of the knife touched her skin, "Lionel!!" she screamed at the top of her voice and braced herself.

"Lionel!" shouted Ron as he yanked hard on Lionel's hair.

Lionel swung the knife over his shoulder in a stabbing movement and narrowly missed Ron's eye. Twice more he lunged. Ron eluded the razor sharp blade and shifted his grip to Lionel's throat and they careered forward into the container wall with a thud that resounded and boomed round the walls. Ron grabbed Lionel's knife wrist and hammered it against the bulk head door lever which turned with a groan. Lionel had almost turned to face Ron when with one last effort Ron slammed his wrist down hard again. The knife came loose and flew over their heads and clanged and clattered its way across the container as it ricocheted off objects in its path. Lionel tried to lift him off the floor but

Ron broke his grip and slid down Lionel's arm to the floor, between Violet and the bulk head door. Ron grabbed the bottom lever to help himself up but it turned and the door came ajar and Ron slipped and landed on his back. Lionel tried to stamp down on Ron as he wasn't able to reach down far enough to take hold. Ron was agile enough to wriggle past him like a crab and get to his feet. He charged at Lionel and ducked under his outstretched hand, grabbed the bulk head door and swung it wide open. Lionel turned clumsily towards Ron and lurched at him. Ron comfortably ducked out the way and as Lionel rocked off balance, he summoned all his strength and tackled Lionel from behind with his shoulder lodged just below the buttocks. Lionel went straight through the doorway, bounced painfully off the jamb and landed on his back just over the threshold of a dark room beyond. Ron stooped down to grab one of Lionel's flailing feet that hung over the threshold but thought better of it, waited his opportunity between kicks and slammed the door tight. He just managed to get one lever fastened when Lionel's feet crashed against the door with a deafening boom. Ron got the second lever in place and slid to the floor to get his breath back.

"Lionel!" shouted Ron, "save your energy. I'm not letting you out till I get back and that's that!"

Lionel's feet thudded on the door and the sound echoed around the walls.

"Save your energy and oxygen Lionel it's going to get very stuffy in there!"

Two more thumps and then it stopped.

"That's better!" said Ron in a more sympathetic tone, "you carry on like that and you'll just hurt yourself and then you'll miss out on all the fun later!"

Ron got to his feet wearily and dusted himself down.

Violet whimpered softly at the sight of her breast impaled on the blade. It made her feel sick and the wound throbbed painfully but the blood, thankfully, now only oozed slightly. Ron looked at her pleading eyes and then at the knife.

"It's better for everybody if we leave that where it is," he said authoritatively, "It'll stop infection getting in and as you can see its pretty well stopped the bleeding as well." He stroked her other breast, "he doesn't know how to treat a woman really but I've got a nice big snake and you'll get to meet him later," he sneered.

Ron walked over to Grant, watched him for a moment and then kicked him hard in the legs.

"Looks like your boy friend's been pretty damn useless!" he picked up the stray knife and dropped into its slot in the cupboard. As he walked back towards the door, he stopped once more in front of her, "Does he normally sleep on the job?" and slid his hand between her legs. "Hey?" he sneered, sticking his tongue out at her in a licking motion. "Bloody tide! I'd like to oblige, I really would, but I have to go!" With that he kissed her on the forehead, stepped over the threshold and paused briefly to say, "I'll leave the door open, I don't want you to suffocate before I get back."

Violet hung there as she listened to his sickly sneering laughter fade and then he was gone. "Grant, help me!" she felt so alone, so utterly alone. "Oh Grant please wake up!" her voice echoed emptily around the container. A crash on the door reminded her that she wasn't alone. Lionel was just behind the door. "Grant, help me!" she cried softly, "Oh Grant, wake up please!"

Chapter 42

Grant lay in the corner of the room and drifted into consciousness reluctantly. He left behind happy vivid memories of his childhood and the black Ford car they'd found one holiday. It had been like something out of those old American gangster movies, it even had indicators that flicked out like ears from the frame next to the door. Sprig was driving as the car hurtled free wheel down the steep field whilst Grant and Nico bounced about on the back seat. They had completely drained the battery using the starter motor to inch the car forward while in gear from its resting place behind the food trough. They'd only just managed to jump in through the window as it gathered momentum and tumbled into the back howling with laughter.

"Oh shit!" bellowed Sprig as the car picked up speed.

"Don't be a wussie!" shouted Nico.

"What about the fence," Grant shouted but his voice was so quiet he couldn't make them hear. The fence was getting nearer and nearer... "What about the fence at the bottom, pull up, pull..."

Grant's eyes opened and he could hear a man's voice somewhere behind him and then something hit him hard in the leg. The voice sounded metallic and boomed in his ears. Now it sounded much nearer but it made no sense.

He could hear something else now the footsteps had faded. It was somebody crying softly over his shoulder.

"Grant, help me….Oh Grant wake up please!"

He tried to turn over but there was something behind him that wouldn't move properly, it seemed to rock. He was lying on his left shoulder but his right arm seemed trapped somehow. He rolled over as far as he could and slid his left hand out to wipe the cobwebs and dust from his face. Something was attached to his arm by a zip tie, he began to remember. He looked down to his feet to see they were also tied but he pushed them against the wall and managed to spin himself round. He remembered the cupboard with the knives but now he was able use his left hand, the broken arm of the chair hung loose from his wrist. Lionel had hit him, yes and everything had spun round but now he would get free if he was just able to get to his feet.

"Grant, help me!" cried Violet softly.

"It's okay," he whispered, "my arms free, if I can stand up and hop over to the cupboard I can cut us free.

"Hurry Grant, it hurts!"

"Just hang on in there girl, I'll have you out in a jiffy!" All the practice earlier now paid off. Even with the one hand free, it was so much easier. He lifted a knife from the middle of the rack and carefully cut through his remaining ties. Immediately he felt at least a tonne lighter and sprang over to Violet. He released her ties and carefully helped her to avoid the knife that still pierced her breast.

"Shall we try and get it out or what?"

"No!" Violet seemed to turn white even at thought of it.

"Shss!" whispered Grant.

"You don't need to whisper, Lionel's locked up in there and Ron's gone off to some boat. No! Leave it," she insisted brushing his hands away. "Ron said it was stopping the bleeding and no infection can get in," she tried to manage a smile now that there seemed to be some hope. Her cheeks were tear tracked with mascara and she looked exhausted.

Grant reached into his pocket for his mobile.

"Grant, whatever it is that Ron is doing, I think he's covering his tracks…" Violet suddenly wincing from the pain. "Remember what Katychmar said 'if you have to hide anything, do it a long way from here' I think that's exactly what he's doing …Grant, you need to get after him."

"I can't leave you Violet, look at you!" Grant felt very emotional.

"Give me your phone," she snatched it from his hand. "I'll ring the ambulance and the police. I can easily manage that," she snapped and keyed in the numbers. "If you don't go quickly, you've no chance of catching him… Grant, go I'll be alright, Argh…. Grant!... for God's sake….go!" she cursed through clenched teeth.

"Violet how will you…"

"Hello I need the police and an ambulance…"

Ron was buying some pink and white marshmallows in a crackly plastic bag and a bottle of water at the motorway services. Grant was just able to see him with one eye as he dare not come further round the display stand in case Ron caught sight of him. He took a terrific risk even being in the shop but when Ron had pulled up in the lorry park on the A1 ten minutes ago, there was no way of knowing what he had planned. Grant just had to take the risk. Violet had been right, he knew that now but she'd looked so helpless. It hadn't seemed the chivalrous thing to do when she'd been so brave and composed while all the time that bloody evil bastard had been trying to stick a knife in her and touch her up like that, God!… He knew that he'd never loved anybody before but he certainly loved her. Grant was so angry and upset by it all he shook from head to toe with pent up emotion. Now he had to get a grip otherwise it had all been in vain and while he waited for Ron his thoughts drifted back to his last glimpse of Violet sat on the floor talking to the emergency services as he stepped gingerly out of the container and headed for the workshop.

He'd slid between the corrugated sheets of the garage and run out onto the road past the railings and ducked down immediately into the shadows. The large headlights of the truck had struck out through the dark towards him, as it crept forward out of the lock up under the viaduct, near the Crossroads Café at the other end of Kimberley Street. Fortunately, Grant had parked Violet's car behind him in a side street and so he scurried back, past his earlier hiding place and fumbled with the keys in the lock. The engine started first time but it sounded tinny, not like his beloved Capri and the breaks were very keen. He reversed, lights out, into the road and came to a bumpy halt, in the shadows, where he'd waited for Ron to load the last two containers. Grant wondered how far they had to go, where was the boat moored? A long way away could have meant pretty much anywhere and he checked the fuel gauge, it was full. There you go, he smiled, she was so organised. Had it been his car, it would have been nearly empty. If it were on a river, well that wouldn't have to be that far, twenty miles if that but it hadn't sounded likely. The large engine of the truck roared as it turned left down the main road and Grant rolled the car forward to the crossroads and peered round the launderette. The breakdown truck wasn't going to be difficult to follow, even at that distance, some three hundred yards at least, you wouldn't mistake the bright row of little lights high up across the back of the cab. Grant turned to follow at this safe distance but hadn't remembered to switch on his lights until he'd travelled nearly a mile. He caught sight of the dashboard clock. That can't be right! He glanced at his watch, bloody hell it was just turned 1.00am!

He hadn't felt tired, in fact quite the reverse. Ron was taking it easy. Even on the dual carriageway, as the streetlights came to an end and all around became dark, he still kept a steady 60mph. It was a clear night and Grant turned every now and then to look over the dark hedgerows to rest his eyes. He'd caught a brief glimpse of halogen lit farm buildings and on another occasion, cosy warm bedroom lights that reached out into the darkness. Above, the starry sky the moon turned the passing landscape into silhouette. They reached the A1 just north of Dishforth and continued heading north. For most of the time Grant had been able to keep at least one car between Ron and himself but when he indicated for the Services at Scotch Corner, Grant was forced to slow right down so as to have plenty of time to slip into the car park and watch where Ron was going.

"How much for the drinks love? There's no price…"

The unexpected sound of Ron's voice brought Grant back up to speed with a jolt as the indifferent assistant swiped the bottle under the scanner.

"£1.20 and are you having those as well?" she nodded.

"Yes love."

"£3.52 then," she held out one hand and brushed her fringe out of her eyes with her other.

Ron counted out the correct change, gathered up his purchases and headed out across the walkway towards the toilets. Grant slipped out from his hiding place and grabbed a bottle of water, slammed the correct money down on the counter and made quickly for the exit. It wasn't his normal practice to urinate in public but his car was at the far end of the car park, well away from anybody else and now with the car between himself and any possible onlooker, he took a long overdue toilet break. Thankfully Ron must have been equally in need because Grant comfortably made himself decent again and got in the car by the time Ron appeared and trotted athletically across to the truck. The big engine roared into life without delay and to a hiss of air brakes, Ron was on the move again.

Maybe Ron felt refreshed by the stop or was he just running late, who was to know but now the big red truck topped 70mph at every opportunity. Gradually the hedge rows gave way to dry stone walls and Grant sensed the A66 was gradually taking him high over Bowes Moor. Well that was the East Coast out the window, maybe it wasn't a river or the sea after all, it could just as easily have been a lake and Cumbria was full of them. Grant was so sure they were heading for Windermere that at Penrith he had to swerve violently when, out of the corner of his eye, he saw the truck heading down a different slip road and onto the M6.

"Phew that was close!" Had it been 2.30pm and not 2.30am he'd have been the cause of an accident. As it was, now he had 400 yards between himself and the truck but they were the only vehicles for about half a mile in either direction. Grant's spirits began to wane, he'd been okay about the Lakes but if Ron was heading to Scotland then …Shit! He tried and failed to slide the seat back further. The Capri was good for long journeys, you could just ease yourself down in the seat, put on one of those great classic rock driving CD's and breeze along on automatic pilot. He ran a hand through his hair, rubbed his eyes, broke the seal on the water and took a long swig. He rummaged in the glove compartment and cast a hasty glance across the back seat but no sign of a CD anywhere. Bloody hell, Violet girl! He was going to have to educate her. He had a good collection of CD's in his car, music for all occasions, even several comedy CD's he used for traffic jams and a French language course. If Ron stopped again that's what he'd buy, a small thank you for the loan of her car, yes what a good idea! Way up ahead, Grant now saw Ron indicate for the Carlisle exit and he slowed down a little so Ron would have time to reach the top of the slip road before he joined it. Ron continued to indicate and turned left at the roundabout.

This was going to be more difficult because now on the urban dual carriageway, they were the only three vehicles on the road. Suddenly the car in front made a left turn no indicators just heave-ho which left Grant as the only vehicle in sight following Ron into the suburbs. Up ahead the traffic lights changed. Shit! Why do they do that when there's nobody about? He slapped the wheel in frustration and slowed to a halt behind the truck. The car interior glowed red in the taillights. This was too bloody close for comfort! What would he do if Ron were to appear suddenly round the back of the truck like he did at Moverley last

Friday night? One thing was for sure, King Kong was a bloody good nickname for him. Maybe he should suggest it when they met next time. Would he have to confront Ron, man to man? He was no match. No, he'd have to be careful not to leave himself open to that possibility. The very thought brought on a sudden cold sharp stabbing pain that gripped his intestines. It was always the same when he'd got nervous or really wound up. Even when the lights finally changed and he began moving again, the pain took a while to ease. In the meantime Grant tried hard to focus on the road now edged on both sides with railings and bathed in that unnatural orange streetlight. Beyond, the warehouses and factory units gradually gave way to houses where rows of wheelie bins stood like sentries awaiting the next day collection. A shopping precinct struck off to the left at the roundabout but Ron headed on towards Bowness on Cliffe. The road became quite narrow once they'd left the streetlights behind and the dry stone walls that had been a constant companion on most of the journey, now gave way to hedgerows. Gradually even those petered out to be replaced by flimsy low wire fences that edged the road between the occasional tree. They passed a deserted camping site and later his headlights picked out a 'Caravans Welcome' sign nailed to a gatepost. Here and there small bungalows were bathed in moonlight but traces of mist now lingered in the dips. The truck, some three hundred yards ahead, bounced and rocked noisily along the road. Over the brow of what round here must have been referred to as a hill, streetlights came into view illuminating the road again and soon he passed cottages to both sides that bounded narrow pavements. Up ahead a squeal of air brakes echoed eerily as the truck made a tight right hand bend by a clump of trees. Grant slowed down, made the bend and came to a halt. For the first time in nearly three hours the truck was nowhere to be seen. All around was darkness but for the road that in his headlights, seemed to narrow still further as it disappeared into the low mist ahead but not a sign of the familiar row of lights he'd followed all night.

"Shit! Where the hell's he gone?" croaked Grant and took a quick swig of water. To his right stood a pub and restaurant and he rolled the car to a halt just level with the car park entrance. He wound down the window, switched off the engine and listened. At first all he heard was the rustle of some small creature in the hedgerow but then to his right suddenly a clang rang out, metallic like the bolt on a farm gate. There, in between the trees, he saw brake lights accompanied by the unmistakable hiss of air brakes. Grant smiled, "Yes!" He started the engine, slipped it into reverse and drove slowly the twenty yards back to a narrow single track road between the side of the pub and the trees. The small white sign he'd missed earlier pointed to Bolt Hole. Right, nice and easy and he turned to side lights. The road must have been a tight fit for the truck and the visibility was now made worse by the settling cloud of dust it had thrown up. A scattering of twigs that had been wrenched from the overhanging trees littered the broken tarmac. Maybe only twenty yards on Grant reached the metal farm gate on the left, brought the car to a halt beneath the large willow tree just beyond it and switched off the engine. He opened the car door. The sound of the big diesel engine ticking over came from just the other side of a large bush to the left and he crept along the hedgerow until he saw a large wooden barn. Ron was fixing back the last of two large wooden doors, before he climbed up into the cab and eased the truck into the barn. A short burst of air brakes followed, then all was silent but for Ron's feet on the gravel as he unloaded three or four large plastic containers from the back of the truck and lashed them to a red four wheeled trolley. He bolted the doors shut and set off to the right, pulling the trolley behind at a good pace, down between two small boats covered with tarpaulins and under the large trees. Grant followed at a distance but kept to the road which Ron joined ahead of him after a short while. Grant kept one eye on his shiny bald head as it caught the moonlight and glanced down frequently to peer through the mist that swirled around his legs, in an attempt to avoid stepping on anything that would crackle. In the nick of time he just avoided a discarded lager can. Up ahead he could just make out another slip road to the left with a large sign painted with the words 'Cliffe & Solway Yacht Club'.

Ron headed onward unperturbed by the mist. He crossed a wide open area that sloped to the right where small masts stood at jaunty angles in the mist and Grant took this to be a concrete slipway. It pleased Grant no end to hear Ron curse as his shins collided painfully with a short wooden post only just visible above the mist.

Now the path meandered along beneath the trees and along a hedge where the mist was less prevalent. The ground was more uneven and the trolley rumbled and bucked its way along behind Ron. Grant felt a little more confident that his presence would go undetected. To the right, wooden plank walkways supported on stilts stood just proud of the mist and snaked away from the track into the dark. Some led quite a long way, others only fifteen yards. Some ended abruptly between tall piles that stood drunkenly in the mist with a yacht moored up tight. Others boasted strange make shift structures built haphazardly from reclaimed timber, old doors and packing cases. There seemed no logic, it was so random and to grace it all there were rough hand painted warning signs like KEEP OUT and BERTH HOLDERS ONLY, nailed to a convenient stump or crooked post. Next to some of the shanty huts were moored quite large white yachts of varying designs but the further they walked the older and more neglected the boats appeared. A large hulk loomed out of the mist. It was clearly worse for wear after a fire. The bare carcase jutted out of the mist like the ribcage of a giant fallen animal. As Ron passed by an owl screeched and took off from a tree, flying low across the mist and made them both jump. It reminded Grant abruptly that this was far from a sightseeing trip. It was truly a bizarre place but Ron looked strangely at home in it. Quite unexpectedly he stopped in his tracks. Luckily Grant was hidden from view by a low branch. Ron looked round and then when he seemed sure he was alone, he turned to look out along the last wooden walkway to a large wooden boat that listed heavily to one side. With the exception of the boat that had caught fire, it was the most dilapidated vessel of the entire trip. What little paint remained on the hull was flaked and faded but in stark contrast, the wheel house and cabin behind appeared to have been restored. The mist spread out like a blanket as far as he could see just below the level of the walkway. Ron stooped and picked up two of the containers from the trolley and hesitantly stepped out onto the walkway. It looked and sounded rickety as Ron placed his feet carefully on the wet boards and picked his way between the broken planks. Above the sound of Ron's creaking journeys up and down the walkway Grant heard the sound of waves lapping gently and to the left made out small dots of light over on the horizon. Ron carried the last container and Grant realised that on the back of the truck there had been at least twice that number. Ron would surely have to return to the truck. In which case he'd better find another hiding place somewhere off the track and 'sharpish' while Ron was at the boat. Grant slipped round the tree, over a short fence into an adjoining field and made his way quietly behind the bushes to a point beyond where Ron had left the trolley.

He waited for a good while until the distant sound of the trolley could be heard as it rumbled over the slipway back near the yacht club, climbed the fence and regained the track. Grant was far from enthusiastic about the walkway but his curiosity had taken control. He'd come too far to bottle out now and absentmindedly recited the eight times table as he gingerly stepped from one creaking slippery plank to another. After what seemed like an eternity Grant reached the boat. It looked even more neglected close up and a fusty dank smell hung in the air. He stepped over the rail, stood awkwardly on the deck and tried to maintain his balance. The deck sloped quite steeply away from him and swayed slightly as the boat began to right itself on the rising tide. In the distance he heard the sound of Ron approaching with his rumbling trolley as it bumped round the bend in the track and he ducked down quickly out of sight behind the row of containers on deck. Even in the dark the whole thing looked like a wreck, surely it would never float. A pile of large plastic buoys were the only recognisable shapes amongst the mass of splintered timber, tangled ropes and tarpaulins that littered most of the deck.

The sound of the trolley stopped abruptly and after a short pause Ron started creaking his way towards the boat. Shit! Now what? Where could he hide? Grant quietly tried the door handle but it wouldn't budge. The walkway creaked, Ron had got a lot closer. There was nothing for it he'd have to hide amongst the crap! He crept quickly to the opposite side of the deck and managed to slide in under one of the tarpaulins. Phew, it was far from fresh under there. The creaking stopped and a crash that reverberated across the deck signified that Ron had arrived with the first batch of new containers. Two more similar trips followed before Ron clambered aboard just as Grant felt the boat move more noticeably. So this was it, the boat and all those containers where destined for the bottom of the sea. Grant was overwhelmed with curiosity. What was in the containers that could be so incriminating that Ron would only feel safe when they were at the bottom of the sea? Grant froze and tried desperately to control his breathing as Ron plonked one of the containers down right next to where he was hidden and sat down heavily on it. Ron's breath was laboured. Those last containers must have been heavy. The boat swayed again as it lifted to a more upright position. Grant had read once on holiday that on some tidal estuaries the water came in very quickly and it felt like this could be one of them. Ron grunted and he heard the sound of keys and then the sound of a door groan on its hinges. Sounds of a generator being cranked followed from somewhere down below, then a light grew brighter as it crept under Grant's tarpaulin. Ron lifted several of the heavy containers through the door and down some metal stairs. He returned and stepped quickly back onto the walkway. It sounded like he was in a hurry to get back to the truck. As the sound of the trolley faded again Grant emerged from his hiding place and just caught sight of Ron before he disappeared under the trees beyond the slipway.

This was his chance. This is what he'd been waiting for. Grant stepped cautiously past a string of bare light bulbs trailed across the deck and followed them down the stairs. Grant turned the corner at the bottom and stopped dead in his tracks. He felt suddenly cold and sick, then sad and angry and then all those things, all at the same time.

"Urgh ...Urgh..." he grunted in disgust and anger. He struggled to breathe, the stench was grim. Before him on the rusty slimy floor stood the four containers Ron had carried down earlier but there to one side stood a tall metal frame and behind it a large glass tank full of sea water. The walls were grimy, hung with chains and manacles. It was the medieval dungeon of Fay's video and nausea swept over him in waves. "Oh fuck!" he sat heavily on the nearest container. Tears rolled down his face as the memories of Fay's last minutes of agony revisited him vividly, the pitiful sight of her upturned and struggling body in its death throe. "What kind of animals are they?" muttered Grant as he pulled off the lid of the container next to him to reveal neatly stacked DVD covers all labelled with girls names and dates.

"The kind you shouldn't turn your back on, you meddling little shit!" Ron kicked him savagely in the back. The blow sent him careering across the floor, where he landed painfully against the glass tank. Down on the floor the smell was even more putrid and the slimy surface stuck to his fingers. Grant could no longer contain his nausea and wretched violently.

"Your like a bloody cockroach, everywhere I turn there you are!"

Suddenly the boat moved under their feet and came to an abrupt halt that tipped them both off balance. Ron grabbed one of the chains to steady himself as Grant vomited once more. The string of lights swayed to send long shadows across the floor as the chains scraped along the walls.

"Yes," said Ron with a tone of pride in his voice, "a lifetimes work, some of the best Snuff and S&M video masters money can buy. Some of these are worth a fortune and some, I'd never sell whatever the price. Copies of these," he grabbed several from the container and held them out for Grant to see, "have street value of over two hundred pounds each. And now you and that nosey little bird of yours have fucked up a very profitable business. But don't worry I'm not going to kill you. No, I'm going to take you back to star alongside your pretty assistant who unfortunately will die miserably at your hands. At least, that's what it'll look like on the film. Then I'll send a copy to that bloody Cosey dickhead detective and dump you where they'll find you easily. He'll be tripping over the evidence. There'll be so much of it, they'll send you down for ever!" Ron eyes were wild with anger. "Meanwhile I think Cuba or Fiji might be a good resting place until things cool down enough for me to reclaim my little nest egg here," he tried to push the lid tight again.

There was nothing left he could do and in sheer desperation and anger, Grant sprang to his feet and charged at Ron. They collided and fell against the wall as the boat swung more violently this time and sent them both sprawling to the floor amidst the containers. One of them pitched over and spilled its contents over the floor with a clatter. Grant struggled to his feet as the boat lurched once more this time he careered across the slimy deck. He clutched out at anything that might delay his fall as his feet slid on the DVD's. He caught hold of the string of lights and pulled them off the ceiling to the sound of splintering and popping glass. Ron struggled against the momentum of the boat to get his balance and sprawled on his hands and knees amidst a wash of shiny discs. The next lurch sent a wave of stagnant water crashing down on Ron as it broke over the edge of the glass tank. Grant was sent skidding sideways towards the stairs.

"Argh…Shit!" His left foot slipped and hit the bottom rung painfully but it was all the chance he needed. Ron was on his back amongst fallen containers as Grant climbed the stairs two at a time. He limped to the door, crashed out onto the deck and drew in a giant gasp of fresh air as he hung over the rail. He shook from head to foot with fear, exhaustion and anger. The broken stern line lay frayed on the jetty to his left as the boat, still not quite afloat at the bow, swung round hard against the piles again.

Chapter 43

Grant ran drunkenly as his feet skidded on the slippery walkway. It was as fast as he dare but still he overbalanced, clipped one of the short piles and fell headlong into the mist. His head, already buzzed from the hammering it had taken but the sounds in his ear reached a crescendo. The cold air rasped at his throat as he ran for his life through knee high vegetation that swished at his legs and sapped his strength. A loud crash and the sound of splintering wood meant that Ron was back in the chase and then, after a few heavy footsteps on wooden planks, he too landed in the grass and swished his way through the undergrowth behind Grant at an alarming rate. How far was he able to run like this? Not far, not nearly far enough. God, Ron was gaining on him fast!

With numb legs, he felt the impact of his feet hitting a path as shock waves that with every step reverberated through his body, to all but loosen his teeth. Over a lump and back into some grass he heard the distinctive swell of the sea break over a bank but where? It was out there somewhere, God only knows where. The ground suddenly seamed smoother and he scuffed against tufts of swamp grass that whipped his hands. It seemed sticky underfoot, was he nearing the shoreline? He daren't slow his pace for a second. Ron was nearly on him, his strained breathing now alarmingly distinct over Grant's shoulder. A few steps more and then the mist cleared a bit as he ran up a small sand dune where his legs all but gave out. Before he really knew what was happening, Grant collided headlong with a wooden danger sign just as Ron's toe clicked his heel. He tumbled through the air. The entangled remnants of a rusty barbed wire fence that rattled and zinged wrapped round him as he scuttled down onto the mud. Ron jumped high in an attempt to clear the devastation but the wire caught his ankle, turned him over in mid flight and he landed with a wet slap on his back in the sticky, foul smelling mud. Grant's left arm and shoulder were painfully enmeshed in the barbed wire and every time he breathed the wire cut deeper into his back and waist. The wire disappeared up over the dune and held him fast. Grant looked down his body quickly and was momentarily glad to see his legs were free. Only a few feet ahead though, Ron was already getting up but his right leg had sunk to the knee in the mud. He tried to shift his weight but this only pushed his other leg deeper. His eyes blazed at Grant and he spat the sand from his mouth.

"I'm going to rip your stomach open!.....you're gonna wish we'd never met!" He pointed a finger and then clenched his fist in rage. But Ron's expression changed dramatically, he'd seen something just over Grant's shoulder.

Grant rolled over slightly, raised his eyes back, the way they'd come to see the sign that twitched in the barbed wire. 'Danger, Quick Sand'.

" Eee...argh!"

Grant whipped his head round. Ron had just made a dive for his legs and was now up to his waist in the mud. He'd managed to get a finger into Grant's laces and was trying to work the rest of his fingers up to the ankle. Grant kicked out with his other foot and gasped as for one frightening moment, Ron's muddy free hand caught his shoe but then slithered over out of harms way. As Ron got a better grip on his other foot Grant felt the barbed wire tighten around his neck and chest. He tried to take the strain off but there were too may wires. Which one to hold, which one?

Grant's leg began to disappear into the mud as well. Ron was pulling him in. He felt the ground slip under him and all the time the wire got tighter and tighter around his chest. With his free arm he just grabbed at everything now.

"Oh God!" he whispered . "Oh God!" panic seized him and he flailed about.

"You slippery little bastard! …If I'm going, I'll take you with me!"

Ron's eyes bulged as his ears slipped into the mud.

"No,no…..Oh God….NO!"

Ron's nose blew a small bubble in the mud and then he disappeared but Grant was still being dragged down, Ron still had hold of him.

"Oh, oh no," he began to cry like a child. "Oh no," Ron's fingers slid off his ankle but he still continued to sink. Again he tried to pull himself out using the barbed wire. His whole body shook with the exertion. He let out a gurgling grunt and spittle dribbled from his clenched teeth as he tried to blank out the pain. It was no use, he'd nothing left it was all gone. He lay there and gasped for breath. Above the sky was just turning blue and the mist had all but disappeared. The dawn chorus had started. It was a new beginning but not for him.

"Oh God …Oh God, not like this …oh not like this …Violet!" he wept pitifully as slowly he sank further into the quicksand.

Something struck him on the chest with a dull thud.

"You're not gonna die Grant, grab hold of the rope! Get it under your arms if you can. Come on feller, get a shift on!"

He wasn't able to see anybody, but the voice came from above him somewhere. He did exactly as he was told, despite the pain and with fingers that trembled from fatigue. He was nearly up to his waist. "Ready!" he shouted at the top of his voice.

"Right, come on pull Kalum, pull!"

"He's not moving" said Kalum anxiously.

"Get your bloody back into it and save your energy for pu….lling!"

The wire tightened round him, the barbs dug deep.

"Aargh…Aargh…Aargh..oh!" Grant felt a small movement in the right direction. Yes, there it was again! Yes…Yes

"Yes! Yes it's working, it's working!"

Grant clutched to his lifeline and progress increased with every pull. Finally his head nestled into a tuft of swamp grass and he lay there gasping for breath as a sand flea emerged and scurried away. Through the rustling grass above him he heard the approach of swishing feet.

"And I thought I'd had a bad day. You look a bloody mess feller, but you're alive!" gasped Cosey with a broad smile. "Violet's gone to hospital, she's quite a girl that one!"

"Is she going to be alright?"

"I think so. She's been through a lot, poor girl."

"Yes, she has…how did you know …how…where I was?"

"Well that's all down to a little bit of seaweed feller," smiled Cosey as he and Kalum collapsed in a heap next to Grant. They lay there for a while, exhausted, stared at the sky in silence and smiled.

"I think it's going to be a nice day," croaked Kalum

"I think it's going to be a beautiful day. Kalum, you'd better see if you can get the wire off him before he chokes."

Chapter 44

"Can I help you?" enquired an immaculately dressed Asian receptionist, as his slender, busy fingers rattled a keyboard.

Through the glass to his right Cosey watched some elderly people having afternoon tea in the restaurant but the only sound in the reception was the air conditioning and then a ping as the lift announced itself.

"I've come to see Miss Diane Swift," he spoke in a whisper not to spoil the atmosphere.

"Just one moment please." The receptionist answered brightly and dialled the room number on the desk phone.

Behind him dark wooden pigeon holes stood empty and the digital clock advanced to 15.00hrs. Cosey ran his eyes round the room and focused on a little cleaning lady as she gathered up her materials and stacked them in a pale grey wheeled container.

There's no reply at the moment, is she expecting you?"

"Yes, she invited me," replied Cosey. Shit! As if he wasn't nervous enough.

"Maybe if you'd like to take a seat, I'll try it again in a minute or two."

It was very unnerving, he hadn't expected it and as for 'taking a seat' well, no chance. He paced the floor. She'd been fine when they spoke on the telephone earlier. She'd been very pleased that Ron had got his 'just deserts' and was well impressed with his heroics on the estuary as well! It was so frustrating, he kicked a bit of fluff on the carpet, but there is just not enough evidence to link Katychmar and get a successful conviction. Diane had been quite incensed that the real villain, as she put it, was going to get away with it Scott free. "What about Fay? What about her life? Where was the fairness in that?" Blimey she'd really got upset. In fact, on reflection, he now thought she might have been in tears. He hoped she was alright. Maybe he ought to go up...

The phone rang at reception and cut through his thoughts.

"Miss Swift says, you can go up, I think she was in the shower or something. She's in room 407. If you take the lift to the fourth floor, turn right, you'll find it, fourth door on the left." And he pointed towards the open lift.

"Thank you."

Cosey caught sight of himself in the brushed stainless steel cladding as he stepped into the lift. It certainly smoothed out the wrinkles but his first impression was of a drab looking individual with his hair stood up.

"Damn," he smoothed it down and checked that the collar of his shirt wasn't caught underneath the collar of his leather jacket.

Ping, announced the lift and he stepped out into a wide, oval lobby in the middle of which stood a dark wood table, burdened by a display of large dried flowers. To his right, the brass plate above the corridor showed Rooms 401-420. Fourth door on the left then! His palms were definitely damp, he wiped them down his trousers then flexed his fingers in the hope they'd stop trembling. He stood outside the door for a moment. There was not a sound but for his own breathing and he tried to compose his thoughts. He'd decided on the exact words he would use the other night but he'd spent odd moments of the day, when he could be alone what with all the excitement, to practice them out loud. It was important that they sounded natural and spontaneous. He knocked on the door.

Visions of Diane had invaded his thoughts increasingly over the last few days. It was like he'd made contact with something safe and durable and the disappointment and heartache that had weighed him down so much after Rachel died, had been replaced with something hopeful. It was as though he'd woken from a dream.

"Hello Levi," said Diane in a warm and welcoming voice, "come on in."

"I'm actually on time for once!"

"Yes, I'm impressed," she smiled and led the way along a short corridor into a small lounge.

"This is very nice, Diane, your own lounge and the view's pretty impressive too. You can see the tower from here."

"Yes, I decided to spoil myself. I can recommend it!"

"I think you might have a point."

"I hope you don't mind meeting me up here, I thought it was a bit more private and I wanted us to be relaxed." She smiled, but there was a far away look in her eye that Cosey hadn't expected.

"Diane…I've got something I want to tell you."

"Have you?" she replied softly and now he realised that she'd been crying. "I've got something I want to tell you as well…" Her voice tailed off and she took hold of his hand as they stood and looked out the window together. "Oh, I'm so sorry Levi, I really didn't want to spoil this moment." They stood there in silence but like this it was uncomplicated, just being there was enough to warm the heart and put things in perspective. They exchanged smiles in their reflection. She cupped her hand round his bicep and nestled her forehead on his shoulder.

Cosey knew he'd feel such a fool if she rejected him for allowing his ambition to blindly misread the situation. What if she'd only been glad to see him for old time's sake and that their meetings were a mere coincidence and nothing more? Fate hadn't lent a hand at all, he'd just read it like that because deep down, it was what he always really wanted. But now he couldn't believe that was true. Her head was on his shoulder, there was something between them he could feel it. He kissed her forehead and she squeezed his arm a little, lifted her face towards him, she pursed her lips and he kissed her. It was all so natural, no last minute nerves, no doubt now, she'd definitely kissed him back. They were stood so close they could feel each others warm breath on their cheeks.

"How long have I wanted to do that," whispered Cosey.

"Me too," and she tucked her head in under his chin and he put his arms around her. And there they stood happy to be alive and enjoying the physical contact that fate had denied them for so many years.

"Was it worth the wait?"

"Yes," she pecked him on the neck.

"We need to talk."

"I want to Levi, but please not yet, not yet."

There was something childlike and pleading in her tone, and he sensed a distant sadness was heading his way. Was it something to divide them or was it something that together they could beat?

"Ok my love."

"Thank you," she answered softly and squeezed him round the waist.

With her, like that, he felt strong and unassailable and he had enough resilience for both of them. When it came to stamina in a crisis he had an excellent track record. He'd done it before and for Diane he could and would do it all again! Finally he felt that her grip on him had relaxed. She stepped away a little, kept hold of the zipper on his jacket and looked at him with tears in her eyes.

"We need to talk Levi…would you like a drink? I know I need one."

"Yes, I'll pour us both something" he looked around the room. On a corner table, was a bottle of Napoleon Brandy and two glasses. "You remembered."

"Yes," she tried a small laugh.

They sat together on the sofa and Cosey raised his glass.

"To you Diane, and the moment."

"And you Levi, and you."

"Diane, I've had all sorts running through my head since you've been back. Regrets about the way we were back then, the missed opportunities and so on… and I think finally the only way I can make any sense of it is ... Well if I could turn the clock back just a week even, would I do anything different? And the answer is no, I wouldn't. I feel more alive now than at any time in years. If you do turn me down Diane, if you don't feel anything for me, I will be disappointed and I will regret asking. But if I didn't ask, then I'd always regret that as well."

"Levi I love you, I always have," smiled Diane though her eyes were still tearful. She took hold of his hand again and stroked it with her fingers. "It's complicated, and like you, I've had anxieties about the way you might react. The future for me is ...is very uncertain and I think it would be very selfish and wrong of me to take advantage of your feelings and burden you with something ..."

"Diane the reason we're sitting here now is because I didn't share my feelings with you earlier, because we didn't take our opportunities then. Life's too short, we won't get another chance, and we've got to live for the moment!"

"Oh Levi, you don't know just how many times I've said that recently, it's the only thing that's kept me going." She drew hard on her drink. "It's not that I'm unclear about my feelings for you," she put her hand to his cheek, "and I don't have any doubts about you," she looked him straight in the eye, "but there are things, things about me and my past you don't know, things you should know," the tears flowed down her cheeks, "things I have to tell you," her voice began to croak and the words broke up, "things that are finally going to ruin every... every ...thing," she sobbed uncontrollably.

He put his hand on her shoulder and she heaved a gulp for air.

"Diane, you've got my full attention and I've got all the time it takes, so just take your time girl."

It was minutes before she was composed enough to speak and Cosey just sat there with his arm round her shoulder, nestled her head in his neck and rocked slightly.

"Levi, the other night when I said I'd moved away because I was being bothered by old clients and I was trying to go straight."

"Yes"

"It wasn't quite like that."

"It doesn't matter Diane, really!"

"Yes it does," She leant away and fixed him with a look that made the hair stand up on his neck. "You don't know how hard this is for me, but if I'm going to do it then I'm going do it right."

"Bloody hell Diane, I didn't ….."

"Nobody knows around here, although maybe Tina suspects something, it was the way she looked at me when she asked me how I was."

"It's not making much sense Diane.."

"I left because I got pregnant and I didn't want my child to grow up round here, and more particularly I didn't want her father to know. I was fairly sure I knew who it was so I went to see him before I left and asked him for a lock of hair. He even gave me his mother's locket to keep it in. When my daughter was born I had the DNA checked against hers, it matched."

"That must have cost a bit!"

"I had to know. Anyway the bit about counselling on the HIV programme, that was true. About three years later I met Colin, he was a medical student who also worked on the project. It was my first proper relationship and so before anything happened, I went to the clinic to have myself checked over for every possible STD know to man, and I got a clean bill of health. We'd been going out just over a year when I saw an advertisement about donating blood and I decided to go along with one of Colin's nursing friends. A few days later I got a letter asking me to attend the blood clinic at the hospital. They said that they were concerned about the sample of blood I'd given and they wanted to do more tests. A few weeks later a very nice Asian doctor told me I'd contracted HIV. They'd checked all the other samples that day and ruled out the possibility that I'd been infected by any of the equipment at their centre. 'Was I in a sexual relationship? Had I had more partners? Did I inject drugs?' God!.. I know they have to ask but it was all too much for me, I just had to get out of there. All that time I'd been on the game and nothing, it's so bloody ironic!" She got up and paced up and down, waved her arms to push a point home and all the time the tears ran down her cheeks and she snatched tissues from a box on the unit.

"The bloody little bastard had been knocking off one of the girls, one of our clients… on the scheme"

"Oh shit!"

"Levi, I broke his bloody nose right in front of a seminar at the drop-in centre."

"Good for you!"

She was smiling, he laughed, they both laughed. Now Levi had tears in his eyes too.

The smile on Diane's face faded quickly, she sank to her knees in front of him and took hold of his hands. She was shaking and her hands felt cold.

"Levi, I'm frightened… I'm really frightened."

"It doesn't automatically mean…."

"No, I'm frightened."

"Diane look at me … look at me," he stroked her hair, her eyes were frightened and glazed with tears.

"Three weeks ago…they told me …they told me Levi …it's already happened."

"Oh my God Diane, I'm so sorry," he pulled her tight to him. They sat there and rocked from side to side in each others arms and wept for several minutes.

"Oh, it's getting dark!" Diane sat up suddenly. "What time is it?"

"Twenty past five."

"Levi, you'll have to go …I've got an appointment, I'll have to get ready," she said firmly, picked up the glasses and put them back on the tray.

Cosey felt dazed. "Diane do you have to go, can't it wait?"

"No I'm afraid this one can't," she replied pointedly drying her eyes and opened the door.

"We've still a lot to discuss…."

She looked at him pulling at his coat, "are you sure you want to…?"

"Yes, quite sure thank you!"

She leant forward and kissed him on the lips, "I love you."

"I love you too, Diane."

"Ring me tomorrow, Levi I must……."

"You can count on it."

Chapter 45

Hector preferred a shirt and tie any day and particularly for a special occasion when he would often sport one of his special bow ties. He trimmed his nose hair in the mirror wondering if Diane had aged much. She always had such wonderful skin and he paused for a moment to reminisce. He pictured her fair hair cut into the nape of her neck and down her long smooth naked back. Her slim waist and rounded buttocks revealed her naked fanny as she leant forward over the desk in front of him and he felt his penis come to life. He examined his reflection and wondered how he'd changed. Grey hair on his temples certainly and a few flecks here and there but he decided they gave him a distinguished look and after all, he still had all his hair.

He wandered through to the bedroom and surveyed the two suits laid out on the bed. Yes, the dinner jacket would have been a bit too much. Maybe if he were to choose the tie first. Nothing that was too flamboyant or business like. Perhaps the grey silk was best, the one with the blue sheen and a small geometric pattern …yes, grey shirt and the black suit. That would do nicely as they say! He smiled to himself.

It was like old times, it hadn't made him feel young again exactly but the events of the last few weeks had put him under a lot of pressure and he now felt the tension above his eyes begin to lift. He checked the time and began to dress. Finally he turned off the Ray Charles, donned his jacket with a flourish and came to a halt in front of the mirror. Downstairs he picked up the car keys from the table, turned to lock the front door and remembered about the awkward lock at his flat above the old premises on Feltergate. Then he used to have a regular monthly date with Diane, always dinner and the best wine followed by a taxi back to his flat. He turned the key and his Jaguar came to life, sedately crunched its way down the drive and out onto the main road. As he headed for town he soon slipped into automatic pilot and memories of Diane came flooding back. Once inside the door she would become the seductress, slowly climb the stairs in front of him so he could admire her fine rump and stop occasionally to look over her shoulder. At the top of the stairs she would pause, long enough to unzip her dress and allow it to fall slowly as she walked along the corridor and step out of it when it reached the floor. He noticed the twilight settle as the streetlights came on and watched people hurrying to get somewhere they wanted to be. He loved that air of expectancy, such a contrast to the expressionless trail to work. She'd open the door to the lounge and turn on the small table lights from the switch on the wall, walk slowly and casually around the perimeter of the room while he made himself comfortable in the middle of the sofa. She'd then make her way in front of him to the rug in the middle of the room and slip off her remaining underwear except her panties. After a brief pause while he took in the beauty of the moment, she would step up close to him and submit to his every desire.

He parked the car and scanned the restaurant from across the street but there was no sign of Diane amid the atmospheric lighting and table settings within.

"Good evening, do you have a reservation?" enquired the receptionist as the door closed behind him.

"Tonight, I am the guest of Miss Diane Swift," he replied with a smile.

"Oh yes," she pointed at the book. "I'm afraid she's not come down yet but maybe you'd like to wait for her in the bar"

"By all means," he walked confidently to the bar where he was plied with a Jack Daniels and soda with well practiced flare. The room was quite crowded, the low murmur of polite conversation broken only occasionally by a brief outburst of laughter and Hector settled on a vacant stool at the corner of the bar to savour his drink. Before there was time to return to his reminiscences a familiar voice cut though his thoughts.

"Hello Hector, still as suave as ever," Diane's voice was silky smooth and welcoming.

"Well," he turned and his smile broke into a grin as he caught sight of her. "My, time has stood still for you Diane, you do look well," he beamed.

"Those flashes of grey look good on you too Hector," she gave him the once over, "you look like you've become successful."

"I like to think so!" he smiled, "but first, what would you like to drink, Martini and lemonade?"

"Yes, why not, let's do it for old time's sake!"

Fortuitously a sofa became free as the menus arrived but they'd not chosen anything when the waitress returned twenty minutes later. Her next return visit forced them both to make a hasty selection, Hector choosing Roasted Camembert followed by Beef Wellington and Diane selected the Stuffed Aubergine followed by Monk Fish Kiev.

Their conversation buzzed along with Hector's witty anecdotes and Diane's reminiscences of life on the game. It was only at the coffee stage that it returned to the moment.

"And so what brings you back to Moverley after all these years Diane?"

"Well, I guess a bit of nostalgia and I wanted to try…"

For the first time ever Hector saw tears in her eyes.

"Whatever is the matter Diane?"

"Oh," she tried to dry her eyes with her fingers and then produced a tissue from her bag. "My daughter and I fell out while she was here at University, so I decided to look her up and try to make amends."

"I guess by your reaction, it didn't work out?"

"No, things just got a whole lot worse!"

"I'm sorry Diane"

"I shouldn't have left it so long but time moves on, things happen and then one day you wake up, look in the mirror, realise how foolish and stubborn you are and you feel ashamed."

"Is there no chance?"

"No, I'm afraid not Hector, I'm afraid not… but this isn't how I pictured the evening going. I wanted you to help me blot it out. It's been great so far. So tell me about your plans now. Are you still at Feltergate?" she dried her eyes and attempted a smile.

"No, I moved from there about five years ago. My work has become much more specialised in the area of sexual addiction and I get referrals from as far away as Mexico and New Zealand. It's very profitable thanks to the internet and the under funding of the National Health Service. People just don't want to hang around on waiting lists while their relationship goes to pieces."

"Well you must be pretty successful Hector!"

"I've had a few ups and downs but since I moved, things have been very good."

"Hector," she said softly reaching across the table to hold his hand, "Would you like a nightcap …in my room …for old time's sake?"

Hector paused, he had been on the verge of describing the concept of the building and the displays in the foyer and how his approach involved role play and so on …

"But of course." He'd tried to read Diane's body language all night for any hint that they might rekindle their intimacy. And there it was, like a bolt from the blue. "What a marvellous idea," he added with a twinkle in his eye.

Diane led the way to her room on the fourth floor and as they reached the door she handed Hector the keys. He unlocked the door and held it open as she stepped inside. As the door clicked shut behind them Diane placed a soft warm kiss on his lips and turned her back on him.

"Will you unzip my dress?"

He fumbled for the zipper, the emergency lights were very dim but as his eyes grew accustomed to the light he could pick out her bare back and the curve of her buttocks as she stepped from her dress. A small shaft of light picked out her breasts and erect nipples as she turned towards him and paused briefly so that he could take it all in. Two small steps brought her close enough that she could rest her body against him. The warmth and firmness of her breasts penetrated his shirt. She put her arms up round his neck, closed her moist lips over his and then leant back a little so as to loosen his collar and tie. Then she took a step back, turned on her high heel and walked slowly to the door. Hector admired her beautifully balanced movement and the way the seams on her black hold-ups completed the iconic pose. As he reached the door Diane lit the last of many candles that sent flickering shadows of her figure onto the walls.

"I want you to take off your clothes Hector, you're not paying for me tonight. When I come, it's going to be the real thing, not an act, so lie on the bed and enjoy it."

"Diane I'd always hoped that one day…" his voice was soft but croaked with emotion as it tailed off. Diane drew a chair in front of the bed and draped herself erotically over it while he removed his clothes. Her eyes were dark and stayed focused on his groin even while she changed her pose. "Hector you've grown," she whispered.

He slid down his boxers, climbed on the bed and settled himself in a semi-reclined pose against the head board.

Chapter 46

For a minute they just stared at each other and then Hector picked up the condom packet from the covers.

"Would you like me to do that for you?" asked Diane.

He nodded and Diane straddled his legs and slid up the bed towards him. She took hold of his erect penis and massaged him for a short while but was careful to only partially unroll the condom and hide her actions as she took him in her mouth. She drew hard on his erection and Hector took in a mighty breath of air and spread his hands out on the bed as if to stop himself becoming airborne. She repeated this several times and Hector became increasingly animated. She sat back on her haunches, paused to get her breath and then peeled off the flailing condom with her long fingers. She leant across him, reached into the bedside drawer, pulled out a small packet and tore off the edge. Hector gazed at the ceiling and tried to catch his breath.

Diane's mind was in turmoil her plan was underway but her demons returned. Was it so unspeakably immoral to punish somebody like Hector when the law seemed so impotent? What of the victims of crime they had lives too! She'd met people from all walks of life at the clinic, HIV hadn't discriminated. Some had known they'd been careless, others had fallen innocent victim to another person's indifference. Diane was resigned to her fate but of all those people she'd met none had deserved to die. It was always a tragedy. But now she'd planned to turn the disease into a weapon and prayed that God would forgive her for there would be many on earth who wouldn't. Hector had to pay the price. He just wasn't going to get away with it, her mind was made up.

This was one she'd prepared earlier for him, the bastard! The words rang around in her head, now she had to focus and took the severed end of the condom, held it tight between her fingers and unrolled it over his erect penis. She changed her grip and took hold of his penis near the base so her wrist blocked his view of her handy work.

"I hope you approve of these Hector, they're new, supposed to be closest you can get to feel the real thing."

She looked him straight in the eye, slid right up close to him and gently let herself down onto his erection.

"Ooh, Diane it's just unbelievable," he whispered and closed his eyes.

This was her trademark position; years of Pilates exercises had given her a well developed pelvic floor and she concentrated on pulling his penis up inside her without the need to bounce so much on the bed. She watched his reaction carefully as she wanted this to last and last….

"Ooh," he moaned.

That's a good boy Hector soak it up, she was going to give him a damn good dose! The bastard, how could he have done it, how? She hoped he'd rot in Hell, along with his sick evil friends."

"Ooh Diane, that's…"

He prayed on the weakness of other people to satisfy his own sick cravings.

Hector eyes were wide with fright, "Diane what's wrong... stop what's got into you?" He tried to fend off her blows with his hands and arms.

Tears ran like a river down her face as she hammered her fists into his chest and stomach. "How could you do it? You bastard!" She lunged across the bed to the drawer again and pulled out a photograph. "Do you recognise her, do you?"

"What is this, who is this? She's..."

"Yes you recognise her now, don't you, yes!"

"She's Fay," he answered in astonishment.

"She was my daughter!"

"Oh Diane!"

"She was your daughter too, you evil sick fuck!"

"My..?"

"That was why I left, to give her a chance... away from all this... I came back to say my goodbyes but you stole that from me. I never saw Fay again. Your sick little buddies murdered her.

Hector was speechless, his mouth moved silently but words failed him. With eyes wide he lay still and stared at her. His face looked drawn, he'd aged ten years.

"Well I've got a nice present for you Hector, something you truly deserve," she slid herself back as his softening slimy penis flopped into view with the remnants of the condom forming a ragged rim at its base. "I've got Aids and now you're going to get it too!" she screamed.

"Ugh...No ...no, get off!" he gasped and wriggled but to no avail, Diane had him well pinned down.

"I wanted you to see her. I wanted you to see this, and I want it to be the last thing you ever see, you fucking bastard!" she yelled and gripped his head tight in both hands, pulled herself above him and with all her body weight behind her, she let out a terrifying scream and plunged her thumbs deep into his eyes.

Printed in the United Kingdom
by Lightning Source UK Ltd.
136306UK00001B/37-108/P

9 781438 939803

Bolt
Hole

by
Adam Gontarek

authorHOUSE®

AuthorHouse™ UK Ltd.
500 Avebury Boulevard
Central Milton Keynes, MK9 2BE
www.authorhouse.co.uk
Phone: 08001974150

First published by AuthorHouse 1/6/2009

ISBN: 978-1-4389-3980-3 (sc)

Printed in the United States of America
Bloomington, Indiana

This book is printed on acid-free paper.

Acknowledgements

Throughout the writing of this book I have been bowled over by the interest people have shown and the amount of time they were prepared to set aside to help me with the project.

In particular I would like to thank Dr Charlie Shaw and Dr Martin Lucas of the School of Biological and Biomedical Sciences at Durham University and Linda Hughes of CEFAS Lowestoft for their invaluable help regarding marine biology and environmental monitoring. I would also like to express my gratitude to Detective Superintendent Patrick Twiggs, Ex. Detective Chief Inspector Geoffrey Cash and Ex. Detective Inspector Nigel King for their insight, patience, and understanding.

To Darin Jewell my Literary Agent a sincere thank you for having faith in my ability and all the work he has done to get this book published.

Finally I would like to thank my wife Lynda who has been so very supportive throughout.